BLOCKBUSTER
Gerald Green

Blockbusting: it goes on today in every major American city. The unscrupulous real estate developers who use intimidation to manipulate the lives of others have made headlines from coast to coast. And in this tense and suspenseful novel—based on an actual case—Gerald Green portrays the human drama, and the human cost of their callous greed.

BLOCKBUSTER is the story of seven families who find a luxury high-rise planned for the site of their rent-controlled walk-ups on Manhattan's Upper West Side. Overnight the peace and quiet of their homes are shattered by obscene phone calls, unexplained fires, and increasingly terrifying forms of harrassment. One by one, the tenants learn the meaning of fear and helplessness, until only two couples remain . . . who find not only their apartments are threatened, but their lives as well.

BLOCKBUSTER

BLOCK

BUSTER

GERALD GREEN

DOUBLEDAY & COMPANY, INC., GARDEN CITY, NEW YORK

1972

All of the characters in this book are fictitious
and any resemblance to actual persons, living or
dead, is purely coincidental.

Library of Congress Catalog Card Number 73–171294
Copyright © 1972 by Gerald Green
All rights reserved. Printed in the United States of America
First edition

FOR NANCY, TED, AND DAVID

These vast urban masses are comparable to a routed and disorganized army, which has lost its leaders, scattered its battalions and companies, torn off its insignia, and is fleeing in every direction.

—LEWIS MUMFORD

1

The first loud thudding noise from the adjoining house shivered the kitchen. The second—or so it seemed to David Loomis—made the tea he was pouring leap from the china cup. *Thonk. Thonk. Thonk.* The blows continued in heavy cadence. Whoever was hammering at the old walls next door was a professional.

"What is it, honey?" Carry Loomis called from the bedroom. Her voice was weighted with morning drowsiness and the burden of a long, difficult pregnancy. "A Puerto Rican blood feud?"

"Sledge hammer." Loomis had to shout to make his voice heard over the invasive pounding. "Someone's knocking a wall down right opposite our kitchen. Never a dull morning on West 84th Street."

He buttered a slice of whole wheat toast and set it next to the tea. No lemon, no milk, no sugar. His wife was slowly emerging from a long siege of vomiting, weeping, and exhaustion, seven months of misery.

"Hmmm," Carrie said, as her husband entered with the tray.

"Maybe this will bring me on early. Dr. Hershkowitz said it might be a good idea if I delivered before schedule."

There was morning sunlight in the bedroom. The bright walls, splattered in Jackson Pollock style, the day-glo spreads and curtains, had a healthy, reviving look. Carrie had done the decorating herself before the angry fetus had ravaged her system.

David set the tray on her knees. The living mound nudged it. "What will bring you on early?" He kissed her temple.

"That racket." What can they be doing?"

"An old West Side custom. On Mondays they knock walls down. Old Puttering may be renovating. Then he can be decontrolled. Raise rents."

A reverberating explosion from the adjacent house drowned their ears. A huge chunk of wall seemed to have fallen.

"Oh, David, I swear Junior jumped."

Loomis touched the precious load. "Steady there, kid." He worried about her a great deal. In the fifth month, she had been so overwhelmed with projectile vomiting that Dr. Hershkowitz had sent her to bed and fed her intravenously for two weeks. It had worked: the cycle of retching had been broken. Since then, she had slowly regained strength.

"I mean it," Carrie said. "Maybe I should deliver early—"

"Nope. Lightfingers Hershkowitz can keep his hands to himself. Our child will get a full nine months like any American child. It's in the Constitution."

Carrie Loomis sipped the tea. She was forced to eat and drink slowly. "Whatever you say, David. But I feel real good, as the astronauts say."

The clamor next door was diminished now, as if the wielder of the sledge had moved to another apartment. Carrie and David heard shouts from the street—a curse in Spanish, a woman yelling. Nothing unusual about such noise on West 84th Street. But 8:30 A.M. seemed a bit early. These were nighttime sounds.

2

"Listen," David said. "I'll stay home and work at the big table today."

Loomis was an architect, the youngest member of a small firm on lower Park Avenue. During his wife's prolonged illness they had let him work at home a great deal. In one corner of the bedroom, against a high window, was a cluttered drafting table. Alongside it rolls of blueprints and renderings were stacked.

"No, no. Why do you have to listen to me burp all day? Really, David, I'm pretty disgusting. I'm still spitting a lot, also."

"I don't know. That racket—"

"Your staying home won't make it quieter."

Loomis stroked her tiny hand. She was a small-boned, elusive woman. "You sure?"

"Of course. I'm going out for a walk later. The sun's out. A matter for a May morning. That's from Shakespeare. But I forget what play."

Loomis got up. "Come to think of it, Tony Paz said something about Puttering planning to renovate next door. It might get us a better class of neighbors. Less bongo parties."

He walked through the apartment, into the white-walled living room, with the marvelous old oak furniture Carrie had brought from her mother's Victorian house in upstate New York. He looked down at the street.

During the night, an enormous green metal bin had been deposited in front of 500 West 84th Street, the house next door, where the destruction was taking place. One saw them all over the West Side: huge receptacles for the innards of old brownstones and apartment houses. This one was being filled. An unhinged door sailed from an upper-story window and landed with an ear-splitting *craaack!* Several chunks of plaster followed, exploding in puffs of white dust. A Negro workman in blue coveralls emerged from the house, carrying part of a bannister.

"They mean business," David said, returning to the bedroom.

"All those poor people. God, there must be forty of them in that rattrap."

"Maybe they'll be better off. Maybe they'll be sent to a nice housing project."

Loomis put on his jacket. "That isn't the way I hear it." He kissed her again. "Don't let it get to you. And don't walk too much."

She clung to him. "I'm beautiful, baby," Carrie said. "That's what Claude Brown said to Senator Ribicoff. Senator, you're beautiful, baby."

"In every way I can think of."

"Go design your mod supermarkets and your cool high-rises, David. As soon as my vital juices work over the tea and toast, I'm off for a walk. I met the nicest pusher the other day. Only fourteen, but full of ideas. *Hey, lady, you wan' good feex?*"

Carrie had been an off-Broadway actress. Loomis, a square stranger in that world, was always delighted by her accents, her intonations.

"Okay," he said at the door. "But if you poop out, come home."

She blew him a kiss. From the street raucous shouts, wild curses roiled the morning air.

"Maricón! Moyeto!"

"Basta! Oi, oi, que pasa?"

"Hands off, spic."

Walking down the narrow stairs of the brownstone, Loomis felt the need to talk to someone about the violent events next door. After all, the two buildings shared a landlord. And how long would the racket go on? But the truth was, Loomis barely knew his fellow tenants. Archie and Liz Allister, their fourth-floor neighbors (WASP lords of the manor, Carrie called the two young couples), were passing acquaintances. They were probably off to work by now—Allister to his office in Wall Street, Liz to one of her lucrative modeling jobs. As for the other tenants, they observed the customs of the country: they

4

remained behind double-bolted, double-locked doors as much as possible.

Thus far that arrangement had suited him. Loomis was a shy and insular man, not unfriendly, but wary of strangers, content to go his own way. Nothing had been easy for him, and he expected nothing from the world—no bonuses, no free rides, no gifts. He had suffered through an impoverished boyhood in central Ohio, the son of an impecunious high school teacher, and only a last-minute scholarship to the school of architecture at Cornell had afforded him a chance. Cornell had been difficult for him, very difficult. He had waited on tables and worked as a janitor, and had made do with four hours of sleep. The course was rugged, demanding, the class filled with brilliant New York City boys, and he had barely passed. But the fact of graduating in itself had buoyed and encouraged him—a miracle he had brought about with his own hard work and brain.

"Open up, David," Carrie would tease him, "you're here, you're in the big time. Career, wife, home, baby on the way."

Loomis—who nurtured a sly, self-deprecating humor, in contrast to his wife's theatricality—would shake his neat blond head in mock sorrow. "Can't help it, honey. It was all those low-protein meals I had to eat as a kid. All those mashed potatoes and canned spaghetti. Underdeveloped central nervous system. No big laughs and no hearty handshakes with strangers."

Strangers. They were all strangers to him (less so to the ebullient Carrie) in 502 West 84th Street. Loomis did exchange greetings with Tony Paz, the tiny man in 1A, or with the Schlossmanns—father and daughter—in 2B. But the others, the two gay boys in 3A, the nice-looking black family in 2A, the blond woman, Mrs. Gilligan in 3B, the mob of Puerto Ricans in 1B, were unknown to him.

Tony Paz was standing on the first step outside the brownstone. His arms were folded· and his face was intense.

"Good morning, Tony," Loomis said. "Lots of action."

Paz was a miniature. He could not have been more than four feet, eleven inches, and it was unlikely that he weighed over a hundred pounds. Moreover, he was always slightly stooped, as if in pain.

"Yeah, they throwin' people out," Paz said darkly. "Landlord gonna fix up the place, so he's evictin' everyone."

A pile of soiled furniture was growing at the curb: a toxic green velvet couch, bleeding kapok from wounds, a dismembered double bed, some scarred kitchen chairs. On an ancient dresser, an oleograph of Jesus in garish colors stared at the misery.

"Can they do this?" Loomis asked Tony Paz. "Can they just throw people out?"

Little Tony shrugged. "They do what they want. They got eviction papers."

There was a scream, loud weeping. The Negro workman emerged, carrying a lamp and a plastic-covered chair. A Puerto Rican woman, a stout, black-haired housewife in a pink bathrobe and fluffy pink scuffs was clinging to him. *"Por favor! Por favor!* Please! We got no place! No place to go!"

"Beat it, lady," the black man said. "I got a job. You tell your old man to get one. You won't get thrown out on your ass."

"My husban' got job!" she howled.

The husband, a wiry man with skin the color of an English Market cigar, came running out of the house. "A curse on your mother!" he shouted at the black man. "You t'row poor people out one day, you sell your mother the next."

Latin taunts were lost on the implacable wrecker. A second Negro came out of the house. This one bore a mattress on his back. Inside, sledges pounded at the old walls. More plaster shattered and fell.

"Jesus Chris'," the dispossessed man shouted. It was less an appeal than a cry of outrage. He turned to Tony Paz on the neighboring stoop. The man was still in his pajamas, his small feet in elegant pointed pumps. "Hey, Tony. Tell them. I no bum. I work. I am dishwasher for ten years. I got job—"

"Non importa, Carlos," Tony Paz called to him. *"Quando* you get eviction, you go."

6

Loomis's face was uncomprehending. For almost a year he and Carrie had lived on the West Side, but it was still a wild and alien place to them. The interminable crises of blacks, Puerto Ricans, the poor, were like events in a foreign country. "But . . . but . . . if the man has a job," he said to Tony Paz, "why is he getting thrown out?"

"Is an old trick," Paz said. His doll-like face frowned, full of street wisdom. "Puttering no send him rent bill for two, three months. So the guy is a sucker. He don' pay. Then Puttering hit him with three months' rent. By now he spend it all—beer, soda, movies, toys. So he got no three months' rent, he get dispossess."

On the curb, the evicted couple, Carlos Rios and his wife, sat on the sagging green sofa. The woman sobbed. Rios put a protective arm around her. "Lousy *maricones*," he called at the black men. "Pickin' on us because we poor. You no good."

His voiced suffocated in noise. What must have been an entire wall floated, sailing crazily, from an upper window and struck the metal bin in a deafening explosion. Loomis dusted bits of plaster from his jacket. He saw the Rioses dimly through a gesso haze.

"What the devil is going on down there?" Leora Sims, the black woman on the second floor, thrust her head out of the window.

David looked up. "Evictions. Puttering is throwing families out."

"Good God a-mighty, what a racket," Mrs. Sims said. The mahogany head with the bushy Afro bob vanished.

A second Puerto Rican couple stumbled out of the house, older people in sedate clothing. They huddled together on the stoop, as one of the workmen carted out a cardboard box filled with kitchen utensils. He tossed it to the curb—a coffee pot clattered to the sidewalk, a ladle leaped.

"Watch what you do!" Rios cried. "Those are mine, *moyeto!*"

"Then haul it out yourself, spic."

"Don' call me spic, you hear?" The slender man rose, and his wife dragged him back to the sofa. The poor, Loomis decided, made their own defenses. For Rios and his wife, it was the temporary safety of the green sofa.

Tony Paz shook his head. "He askin' for trouble, Rios. You can't fight back once they got papers."

"Well . . ." Loomis said. The drama fascinated him, held him. Secure, well-paid, educated, he was momentarily intrigued with those who lived on the edge of disaster. "He didn't have to call him a spic. That wasn't necessary."

Another terrifying crash came from the house, as if another wall had tumbled.

When one of the Negroes emerged, tossing a sink into the bin, the Rios woman leaped from the sofa and began to claw at his back. "*Puto! Maricón!* Why you do this to us?"

The black man shook his massive shoulders and swatted the woman away. Challenged, Carlos Rios leaped from the sofa and onto the Negro's back, grabbing at his throat. His wife now had a change of heart; they might both get killed. She clutched her husband's pajama legs and yanked at them. The flimsy trousers fell, and his buttocks were exposed. The black man tossed him off.

"Tony . . . shouldn't we call the police?" Loomis asked.

"What for? They got to get out. They end up in welfare hotel. Junkies, muggers, nice company. Rios got four kids."

Loomis could think of nothing to say. Disturbed, he walked toward West End Avenue. So far he and Carrie had been able to ignore or sidestep the violence of the city. It was close to home now.

In Father Hasslinger's office, Danny Hart sat like a penitent schoolboy, his arms folded. He was a pale young man with delicate features, except for a long, off-center nose. His lank brown hair (too feminine, Father Hasslinger thought) reached his collarbone.

"You know we can't pay you a cent," Father Hasslinger said.

"I don't want money," Hart said. "Just a place to sleep. I'll manage."

8

The priest—he was an Episcopalian, director of the West Side Parish House, a community betterment group—frowned. "I'm not so sure, Danny. You spent a week in Bellevue last time you tried to manage on your own. Malnutrition, chronic bronchitis."

"It was winter, Father."

"It always seems to be winter for some of us. Danny, I have to be frank with you. Working with the poor isn't a hobby, or a calling, or a dilettante's game. It's dirty, lousy work, and you have to be tough and patient and practical."

"And I am none of these?" the young man asked.

"I'm afraid not. Danny, your heart is full of sympathy for the poor, maybe too much. We're long past feeling sorry for them. They want action, results, someone to fight alongside them. God knows they're hard to deal with. I lost my misty idealism years ago. I don't want to kiss their lead-eating children, or embrace the junkies. I just want to organize them, give them the idea that they can put pressure on the powers, give them a little more confidence."

"You have a wrong picture of me," Danny Hart said. He smiled —a vague boyish smile. "I agree with what you've said. Everything."

"Sorry, Dan. We sent you over to help them fix up the day-care center in the abandoned ice house, and what happened? You tried to organize an orchestra, and the place remained as filthy as it was before I sent you. I asked you to take the Red Emperors out to clean up the lots on West 92nd Street and what did I find? They were reading Romeo and Juliet in Spanish."

Hart brushed his hair away. "I wanted them to find out the truth about *West Side Story*. How they had been used."

"Oh, no," the priest said. "Priorities, Dan. And while I'm at it, these Latins, and the blacks, and certainly the old Jewish ladies, don't appreciate your hair, or your bell-bottom denims, or your Indian sandals. The poor are conservative, Dan. They'd like you better in a crew cut and a military uniform."

"So. . . ." Hart leaned back.

Gaunt, bloodless. The minister wished he would find another line of work, eat better food.

"I've got an obligation to you, I suppose." Father Hasslinger tugged at his white collar. He was an overweight, ruddy man in his late forties, bald, soft-eyed, deceptively clumsy in his moves. "When the boys at Union Theological Seminary sent you here, I felt I had to take you in."

"A charity case?"

"Not quite. They said you were probably the best student they ever had to flunk out. It wasn't a case of your having lost faith, but having too much of it. No room for a St. Francis these days, especially one who never finishes anything he starts."

Hart laced his bony fingers around his knees. The flesh all but peeked through the worn denims. "I admit I cut classes too much. Never wrote my term papers. I almost finished one once— on the actual location of the Crucifixion. But after I got through reading the Israeli archeologists I concluded there wasn't any Crucifixion at all."

"Some of those birds at Union would agree with you." The phone on Hasslinger's desk buzzed. "But that isn't your problem, Dan. You simply never—" He picked it up and stared at the green plasterboard walls of his office. A poster stared back at him:

RENT TRIAL AND TENANTS RALLY
CHURCH OF THE ASCENSION
Tuesday, May 12
ALL WELCOME

Hart turned his fragile head and tried to catch the voice at the other end of the line: *Spanish, excited, a man.* He wanted to stay at the Parish House. It didn't matter what they wanted him to do; he'd do it. And he wasn't so sure his hair and his sandals offended the Puerto Ricans. Across the huge barren room, Sarah Liggins, the black woman with the A.B. from Smith and the doctorate in urban affairs from NYU, was interviewing a couple. A lost cause. Sarah was too upper-crust, too dignified, too professorial. They didn't dig her, nor she them. How could he convince Hasslinger that he had the touch?

"Evictions?" Hasslinger was asking. "Four families?"

Wisps of an excited voice came through the speaker: one of Hasslinger's army of poor. Hasslinger was scribbling on a pad. Hart read the upside-down writing: *502 West 84th Street*.

"Okay, okay, Tony. I'll send someone over." He hung up. For a moment the clergyman frowned, rubbed his bald pate, looked around the barnlike room. In the waiting area, on camp chairs, a half dozen petitioners awaited him already—Mrs. Federspiel, one of the ancient Jewish ladies, powdered, rouged, leaning on a silver-headed cane; a beautiful Puerto Rican girl with skin like ivory, pregnant, two children with faces like the heavenly host clutching her skirt, a drunken black man in grease-stained work clothes. Sarah Liggins beckoned to the grande dame and Mrs. Federspiel tottered over to the desk.

"Landlord is dispossessing tenants in one of those brownstones on West 84th Street," Hasslinger said. "That was Tony Paz who called. You remember him."

"The little man. With the littler wife."

"He says the landlord has certified the evictions. One of the tenants is an old man in a wheelchair and won't go. The other families are all over the sidewalk."

Hart got up. "I'll go."

The minister was gazing at Sarah Liggins: a fearsome, handsome woman, with a hard gaze and a patrician accent. *"Now, Mrs. Federspiel, we cannot be worrying about every fahncied insult you claim the superintendent directs at you . . ."*

Evictions were a sticky business. There was little the Parish House could do. The city would take over, send the homeless to some nightmarish hotel, one of the decaying dumps where they would become SRO's—single-room occupants.

"All right, Danny. Run over there. Paz can be helpful. He's a tough little guy. But . . ."

Hart waited. Sometimes it seemed that Father Hasslinger had flipped. His eyes grew vague, he found trouble articulating his thoughts. Twelve years at the Parish House had worn the man down. After a few scotches, he would admit that his frustrations stemmed as much from the resistance of the people he sought to help as it did from the powers—city, police, landlords, real estate operators. It was this abrasive knowledge, Hart felt, that upset Hasslinger, that made him forgetful, careless.

". . . if it looks sticky, if you can't do any good, turn the whole mess over to the District Rent Office."

Danny Hart nodded. Lightly on leather sandals, a free soul in a gray sweatshirt and worn denims, he left the West Side Parish House, hearing Sarah Liggins voice rise: *"Mrs. Federspiel, you are not listening. . . ."*

When the wreckers had gone to work that morning, sledges and picks flailing at the adjacent house, Werner Schlossmann was at his rattling Adler typewriter. It made such a fearful clatter that it was some moments before he reacted to the destruction next door.

"An outrage," his daughter Hilda said. "Such noise at eight-thirty in the morning. I shall complain." She tugged at a mannish beret, tossed a dark-blue scarf around her neck. It was a mild May morning, but the Schlossmanns always dressed as if living in some cold north German city, awaiting bleak winds and killing frosts.

"No, no," Schlossmann said. "We must not impede the natural course of disaster."

"I appreciate your cynicism less every day, Papa."

"It is not cynicism, Hilda. Armageddon, the Apocalypse, the Last Judgment, all these come to us on the installment plan. A wall knocked down here. An old lady murdered there. This girl raped. That boy a hopeless addict. A man goes insane inside a hotel room on Broadway and no one hears him. A policeman is corrupted by bribes from a bookmaker, a baby eats plaster from a wall and succumbs to lead poisoning."

"Bah. Since when are these disgusting incidents apocalyptic?" Checking the books in her massive leather briefcase (it had been Schlossmann's when he was teaching in Berlin), she seemed eager to pursue debate, but wary of encouraging him to think she was.

"But they are, *teuere Tochter.* No more earth-consuming holocausts. We have had all we needed. Now the final solution comes with a crowbar and a hypodermic needle, *nicht wahr?*"

"Ah, you make me sick sometimes. You don't believe that nonsense." At the door of the bleak, high-ceilinged apartment —the walls were a mottled dark brown, and every available horizontal surface, desks, tables, chairs, couch, battered trunks, exhausted valises, was covered with books, magazines, papers —she paused. Her father's back was to her, stooped in the faded maroon bathrobe. The twin cones of his iron-gray hair rose like pointed ears. A wasting, unbearable pity welled up in her. Useless, useless.

Schlossmann spun about in his swivel chair: *Herr Professor, eyes merry, fingers forming a tent.* "Of course I do not. But it helps me survive." Something creaked, ripped away from its moorings, fell with a terrible echo. "Survive . . . but how . . . ?"

"You may philosophize, Papa, but I shall complain. Mr. Puttering is also the landlord next door. I shall call him and let him know what I think."

Schlossmann swiveled around again. "By all means. Absolutely. How dare they disturb us?" Then he squinted at the white sheet in the typewriter.

CHAPTER III

*National Socialism: Wish Fulfillment for
the Lumpen Masses and the Bourgeoisie*

Wrong, wrong, he told himself. Not just the *lumpen* masses, not just the middle class. Except for the leaders, the working

class in Germany also. Loved the brown shirts and the slogans
—blood, death, war. What a joke on Marx! How little he knew!

"*Auf wiedersehen, Papa.*"

He waved at her. They never kissed any more. When she had
gone, Schlossmann brewed a fourth cup of tea, and sipping it,
stood in the center of the dark brown room, addressing the
incessant pounding.

"Strike ax! Hit hammer!"

In a military parody, he clicked the heels of his felt slippers
and gave the Nazi salute. "*Sieg heil!* You are defeated before
you begin! I am Werner Schlossmann, honor graduate of Terezin,
Auschwitz, and Buchenwald! Knock, bang, slam. You cannot
frighten Schlossmann."

He returned to his typewriter.

*The enthusiasm with which Germans on all levels of life,
the most refined, the most educated, as well as the grossest and
most brutalized, responded to Hitler, should be a warning to all
technological societies. These societies are as yet imperfectly
understood. . . .*

On the street, a settlement of cheap furnishings and ruined
lives had grown. In addition to the Rios family, four others
had been evicted. Some had left, seeking help from the various
"poverty" agencies in the neighborhood, from the district rent
offices. One tenant, a black prostitute, had shown singular
courage. She had spit in the wrecker's eye, showed him her
Gem razor when he tried to strike her, and then walked off—
defiant, high-rumped, a gold-toothed queen of the night—with
her four children in tow—to find lodgings with a relative on
Amsterdam Avenue. Only the Rioses rested amid the ruins of
their home. They seemed reconciled, numbed, refusing to leave
the green couch.

"What about the old Polack?" one of the Negro workmen
asked the other.

Tony Paz had not left his post on the stoop of the adjacent

house. "Hey. Hey, lay off him. Nordetzki is cripple. Let him stay. I call for someone to help."

They paid no attention to him. "He say he got a special dispensation. Ain't no papers to git him out. He disable." The two black men looked at one another. Then, the bigger man, captain of the crew, picked up a sledge and went into the building.

"Hey," Tony shouted. "What you gon' do?"

The other workman giggled. "Knock the damn wall down on top of him, tha's all."

Two men shared apartment 3A, the third-floor front, in the brownstone adjoining the one that was being evacuated. Their names were Barri Dane and Ronald Lobello, and both were asleep when the clamor erupted.

"Oh, Mother," Barri moaned. "What is that racket? Ronnie, is that you making all that noise?"

Lobello jerked upright. The men slept in adjoining double beds, great divans with polished brass steads and lavish satin quilts. Above the beds hung a reproduction of Correggio's *Leda and the Swan,* framed in antique gold-leafed wood.

"Darling, I couldn't hit anything that hard if I *tried.* I'm spaced out. Cut it out next door there, whoever you are."

Ron Lobello staggered from the bed. He was a dark beauty of a man, sinuous, lean as a hurdler. He stumbled to the wall from which the thudding noises emanated and pounded at it. "Hey, in there. Cut that out, or I swear I'll off you. I'll waste you."

Barri Dane laughed, rose from the rumple of lavender sheets and rose quilts, and put on a black silk happi coat, emblazoned with a Japanese pictograph. "Darling, no one would ever believe you. Not with that sweet Italian face of yours."

"Oh, is that so? Since when are *you* so tough?"

"I'm an actor, lover," Barri Dane simpered. "Haven't you heard? The West Side is full of us. There are so many actors moving in, it isn't safe for the Puerto Ricans." He clutched his forehead. "Jesus, I'm hung over. No more wine tasting, at least not when I'm working. Where is that *dread*ful script?"

15

Dane was a small man, fatless, his hair a frizzy red, his eyes porcelain blue, his skin lightly freckled. Had he worn a ragged straw hat and cut-off overalls, and carried a bamboo pole, he might have played Huckleberry Finn.

Ron Lobello put on his own happi coat—it was styled the same as his roommate's, but the color scheme was reversed, a black character on gold—and walked into the kitchen. He always felt better in the kitchen. Lobello was an interior decorator and had done the apartment himself. But the kitchen was his pride: bricked walls, a Dutch oven, an antique refectory table from a Carthusian monastery, a set of Shaker implements, and a dazzling array of pots, pans and bottles—Danish, French, Belgian —dangling from the soundproofed ceiling.

"Who are they killing next door?" Lobello called, as he ground fresh coffee beans. "And why so loud?"

Barri Dane called back to him: "It's called rehabilitation, sweetie. Renovation. Renewal. All that dreary crap. They intend to make modular *automatons* out of us."

Lobello smacked his hand against his dark forehead. "They'll send me up the wall with that racket."

Poking his red, freckled face into the kitchen, Barri Dane stuck his tongue out at Ron. "You've been there before, lover."

Shortly after 10 A.M., Tony Paz saw the Lincoln Continental cruising down West 84th Street and he knew Rudy Dukes had come back. With the first reverberating blow of the sledge hammer in the house next door, he had smelled Dukes, and now he saw the car, and even before he could read the license plate: RD 147, he knew it was Rudy.

The Negro workmen had stopped their demolition of the building's interior and were smoking at the curb. Every now and then Rios and his wife, still on their sofa, would appeal to them in gentle Spanish.

"Don't bug us," the chief wrecker pleaded. "We got a job. You didn't pay rent, you got to get out."

Barri Dane, looking out the window, also saw the white

Continental. "We're getting a better grade of pusher in the neighborhood, Ron," he said. "Get a load of that heap. *God, it's as big as the Andrea Doria.*"

Windows tinted, moving silently on giant wheels, the car came to a halt in back of the green bin. It was a car that appeared to breathe, to live. Tony Paz squinted at the interior. That was Rudy, all right, his curly head lolling against the white leather in back. He rode like a king. Alongside him, vaguely outlined through the darkened glass was a strange shrouded figure, sloping shoulders, a blunt face. It dawned on Paz: it was a giant dog.

"He comin' up," Tony said to himself. "Big car. Big dog. Chauffeur."

The man at the wheel of the Continental opened the door and walked toward the Negroes. He was a stocky, elderly fellow, with a mop of stiff gray-white hair, thick mangling eyeglasses, and a mobile face. Halfway up the stoop he saw Little Tony staring at him.

"Hey, *paisan!*" the chauffeur cried. "Remember me? Your old buddy Shlep? *Com' esta?*"

"Oh, I remember you, Shlep. Mr. Sharmak. You drive for Rudy now, like I used to, hah?"

"That, and other things, *paisan.*" The gray-haired man glared at the Negroes. The joviality he had used with Tony was patently false. When he spoke now his face was cold, baleful. "What the hell is this with that Polack, hah? Throw him out, like the rest."

"He tied hisself to the radiator and he got a bread knife a foot long, Mist' Shlep."

"What? You want I should throw the bum out?" Sharmak's eyes were invisible behind the torturing lenses. "An old gimp with a knife?"

"I ain' gonna argue with him," the black man said.

"Me neither. I paid to knock down walls, not get cut."

"Chrissake," Shlep Sharmak said. "Come on in wit' me." He turned to face the automobile. "Rudy? I'm gonna get him." Then he grinned at Tony on the opposite stoop. "Like old times, hey, Tony? Remember when we cleaned out the St. Charles Hotel?"

"Yeah, old times, Shlep."

There was a sharp tapping from the car. Inside, in its air-conditioned, leathery nest, Rudy Dukes was tapping at the window, beckoning to Littly Tony. Paz descended two steps, and with great emphasis, a violent toss of his head, spit in the direction of the Continental.

The wreckers also awakened Mary Gilligan, the tenant in apartment 3B. Groaning, she turned from prone to supine in the disheveled bed, and as she did, the pain of hangover moved from her right temple to her left, crossing her head with iron steps. "Oh, God, stop," Mary said, "stop the racket."

One eye opened, she peered into the hallway. "Markie? Stevie? You kids get off okay?"

There was no response. They were reassuringly self-sufficient boys. For a moment she experienced a twinge of guilt. For over six months, ever since her husband Frank had gone off to Vietnam—a volunteer, no less!—she had found it increasingly difficult to hold her job at the Butternut Bakery and be a complete mother. Luckily, the boys were resilient and intelligent. She cooked for them, shopped, did their laundry, and took them to her parents' farm in New Jersey every other weekend. But rising early—particularly after a night of too many beers with a boy friend—was more than she could handle. She was a night person; early morning was a bad time.

"Cut it out in there," Mary said hoarsely. "Boy, you greasers never let up. Watcha doin', killin' each other with Indian clubs?"

She slipped off her nightgown: black lace and chiffon. Frank had bought it guiltily before he left for Saigon, his cushy job running an officers' bar, and his gook mistress. It had all come out. She had gotten an anonymous letter from a man in Frank's outfit. Mary had an idea who it was—a man named Louro, who had propositioned her once in Seattle, where Frank was running a recruiting office. But she never challenged her husband. Mary was a fatalist. If that was what the rat wanted, let him have it. He'd come back, or he wouldn't: either way she'd manage.

Her body pleased her—hairless, pale pink, lithe, leggy. The hips and thighs were a little too full under the hard narrow waist, but everything was unblemished, uncreased. Not bad for a married woman, aged thirty-two, with two kids, a no-good husband, and a job in a bakery.

"Cover the face and I could be a model," Mary Gilligan said approvingly. She thought: *it's the Ukrainian in me, indestructible, unyielding, healthy flesh.* At seventy-one, her mother still planted cabbages and Swiss chard and spinach at the farm in Hopewell Junction. The old lady cooked, and baked, and pickled, and smoked, and bottled, and canned anything that was edible. And her father, only a week ago, had beaten the tar out of a drunken farmhand who had come at him with a knife.

"Us Ukerainians," she said deliberately mispronouncing the word by adding a syllable. "Can't get the best of a Ukerainian." She made a wry face to the mirror, running a hand through her matted yellow hair. "We'll go first-class today, Gilligan. Wash and set."

In the gloomy corridor she found Markie's hockey stick and began to clout the wall with it. "Cut it out, you bums. Stop that hammering." They couldn't hear her. It seemed to be on the floor above, in the adjoining brownstone.

In the kitchen she made coffee, lit a cigarette, and shuddered as a deafening crash echoed through the room. Morose, she looked at the remains of the boys' breakfasts—a few floating cornflakes and a quarter inch of milk in Markie's bowl, the crusts of the tunafish sandwich that was Stevie's morning meal, year in, year out. "It gives me energy, Ma," he explained. "I can't eat none of that crappy cereal."

Good boys, she reflected, as she inhaled deeply, too good for us. She wondered about the kids. What would they become? Where would they end up? Markie was almost twelve, Stevie ten. What if Frank decided he wouldn't come back at all, that the slant-eyed broad in the slit dress was what he wanted? Mary yawned: to hell with him.

Some hours later, bathed, powdered, her thick yellow hair tied with a white ribbon, Mary Gilligan was buttoning up her starched white bakery dress when the phone rang.

"Mary?" a hoarse voice asked. She knew it at once.

"Yes."

"Mary Gilligan? Who was once Mary Waslyk?"

"Yes, yes."

"This is Rudy. I'm back in business."

"Business? What kinda business? The laundry room at Dannemora?"

He laughed—a short humorless noise. "Tough Polack, hey, Marushka?"

"Ukerianian. Don't mix us up. How'd you get out?"

"It was easy. Good behavior. They knew a class guy when they saw one. It was a lousy rap, that thing at the St. Charles Hotel. I wanna see you."

"Nope. Not a chance."

"Your old man run out on you. I heard. Jerk went off to Vietnam and left you with the kids. I'll be around later."

"Forget it, Rudy. That's over. I'm working, anyway. Late."

"Where? I'll meet you there."

"No. No."

He laughed again. "Ah, Mary, you kill me. As if I can't find out. Look, kid, I can find out anything on the West Side. I'm in charge. I'm running everything. And legitimate too. Let's have dinner tonight."

She hesitated. Rudy Dukes had always been able to force his will on her. He was untiring, relentless. After he had been tried, sentenced, and sent off for a two-year prison term, she had felt curiously mixed emotions—relief that he was gone, a sense of loss.

"We're through, Rudy, finished."

"Got another guy, huh? Some young spic stud with Vitalis hair and pointy shoes?"

"No. I'm a good girl. I got the boys to take care of."

"Wasn't I good to them? And to you?"

Mary paused. "Yeah. Except when you were belting me around. I been hit by men before, but I don't like getting it from professional welterweights."

"I'm comin' over—"

"Don't bother." She hung up.

As she walked toward Broadway, enjoying the bright spring weather, she felt excited, freshened. She knew Rudy Dukes would not be discouraged. The brief shudder of terror she had felt when she heard his voice now vanished. Against her will, she began to anticipate their reunion.

Shortly after the white Continental had parked alongside the house on West 84th Street, Danny Hart turned the corner and walked toward his new assignment. Father Hasslinger had sent him on the mission with less than enthusiasm. Hart was no fool; he read the resignation in Hasslinger's voice. A brownstone being renovated, a few families being tossed out—sad stuff to be sure, but low priority, with teen-age kids dying of heroin, grown men turning to crime because they had no work and no future.

Tony Paz recognized the long-haired kid. He had hoped that the minister would come himself. Hasslinger was tough, intelligent. He knew the angles. Danny Hart was one of those under-fed college kid losers. The storefront agencies were full of them. Tony regarded them as more of a pain in the *fundillo* than a help.

A curious sight greeted Danny Hart as he approached. The old tenant in the wheelchair, Ignatz Nordetzki, was being borne down the steps by two men—a Negro workman in blue coveralls, and a gray-haired bespectacled man, whom Hart had seen around the neighborhood before, often walking an enormous yellow dog. He noted the metal bin full of debris, the piles of scarred, cheap furniture, the Puerto Rican couple.

"Excuse me," Hart said. "Excuse me." He planted his frail

21

figure in front of the two men bearing the wheelchair. "I'm Daniel Hart, from the West Side Protestant Parish House—"

"Never heard of ya," Shlep Sharmak said.

Vaguely, Danny recalled a photograph in a history of the New Deal era—the executive of a corporation being carried out of his office on his swivel chair by two soldiers after a losing battle with Roosevelt.

"Well, I work with Father Hasslinger, and he, ah—"

"Outa our way, kid," Shlep said.

Old Nordetzki looked at Danny Hart. "Listen, boy. Tell it them I pay rent. I no bum. I work it all life. But got no family. No kids take care. I got to stay here."

"You can't throw this man out," Danny Hart protested.

"Who's throwing?" Shlep asked. But he paused. He and the Negro set the wheelchair down.

Tony Paz leaned across the balustrade. "Hey, Danny, Mr. Nordetzki got papers from the city because he disable. They got no right throw him out. You tell Father Hasslinger call Welfare, they get him back in."

"Hey, squirt," Shlep Sharmak shouted. "How'd you like a fat lip, hah? Can't you keep your spic mouth shut?"

"You don' scare me, Shlep," Tony Paz cried. "You still just prat boy for Rudy Dukes." He pointed to the white car. "Hey, kid. Hey, Danny. The guy in the car. He's the one. He is givin' the orders."

Danny Hart looked at the automobile. The windows were darkly tinted, a strange amberish color. There was a man seated in back, and next to him the rounded head of a dog.

"Oh? Him . . . ?" Hart halted. "Is he the landlord?"

"Nah, nah," Tony said, laughing. "You find out what he is. We all find out."

"Outa our way, mister," Shlep Sharmak said. "Look, we don't want no religion. Go get a haircut and a pair of shoes, if you're from the minister. I know Hasslinger. He'll understand everything." He nodded at the Negro. "Pick up the Polack."

22

"No, no, *shakref*," Nordetzki protested. "If I have it knife now, by God, you no throw me in street."

"Look, I'm asking you to stop," Hart said weakly.

"Beat it, kid," Sharmak said. "Don't futz with us. Don't futz with Rudy Dukes." He grinned at Hart. "What's a matter, sonny? You new on the West Side? Ain't you heard of Rudy Dukes and his goon squads?"

There was a sharp rapping. The man in the back of the Lincoln was tapping on the window. Shlep Sharmak looked at his boss. Unmistakably, Dukes was gesturing with his hand—*back, back.*

"Whah?" Sharmak called. "You want to put the old guy back? Okay, Rudy, whatever you say." They hefted the man in the wheelchair around and carried him into the brownstone. Danny Hart, puzzled, walked up the steps of 502 West 84th Street and stood next to Tony Paz. "Is that Dukes in the car?"

"Sure. You see the plates? RD 147. Welterweight champ, Parris Islan' Marines. Tha's what he tell you, anyway."

"But what does he do?"

"Management. He took over the building. I once work for him."

Danny Hart was encouraged. He had had his confrontation and had won—easily, it seemed. With only the slightest mention of the Parish House and Father Hasslinger, he had gotten Nordetzki back in his apartment.

"It was nice of him to put the old man back in," Hart said.

"Hah. You find out. He don' want no trouble right off. Wait, wait, you see what happen. Don' you know what is Rudy Dukes?"

"No. I've never heard of him."

"Man, he's the blockbuster. He is back in business to clean these houses out. Out. Empty. That's his job."

"But there are regulations, the city, the rent office. . . ." Hart looked innocently at the small man. Paz was coiled, tense, a mechanical toy of a man, a windup Puerto Rican.

23

"You got plenty to learn, Hart. You better go back to Parish House and take care of the little kids in day-care center." Paz studied the young man's pale face, the long unkempt hair. Rudy Dukes would break someone like Danny Hart in half, crack him over his knee as if he were a dry stick. "I know him. He put Nordetzki back so you don't squeal to anyone, and when you not around—*pah!*—throw him out on his *fundillo*."

Hart said nothing. Shlep Sharmak came out, dusting plaster chips from his trousers. "No hard feelings, sonny boy. Tell the minister what nice people we are." He laughed insolently and hurried down to the waiting Lincoln.

As David Loomis took his seat on the downtown Broadway bus, he saw Liz Allister stepping into a taxi. Odd: they must have not noticed each other waiting on the corner. Loomis would certainly have offered to share the cab with his neighbor's wife. He mused a moment. It was quite possible Liz had seen *him* and had decided to ride alone. She was a model, a tall, spectral, white-faced woman, expressionless, silent. When Carrie had tried to become friendly—an offer to share a gift basket of Florida fruit from David's mother—the woman had been chillingly unresponsive. "It's not unfriendliness," Carrie said after a fourth snub, "it's just that she doesn't relate. That gorgeous head is somewhere else."

Loomis was a tolerant, reasonable man. "You can't tell with very beautiful women, or very handsome men," he told Carrie. "What you think is conceit or remoteness is often plain shyness."

"Or stupidity," Carrie said.

He would have enjoyed riding downtown with Liz Allister. Not only was she a unique-looking woman, one whose face (as an architect, Loomis appreciated good lines) was worth study, but he wanted to talk to someone about the crashing of the walls in the adjoining brownstone. Tony Paz had bothered him with his dark hints of trouble. And sharing the same landlord as the miserable Puerto Ricans in 400, he sensed a vague unease.

The bus halted opposite a dark dirt-layered hotel in the West

24

Eighties. Indolent, sodden blacks lounged on its steps. The lower windows were covered with tin sheeting. The miserable Rioses, dispossessed that morning, would end up in one of those dumps. Loomis had read about them—nightmarish dungeons where muggers and rapists roamed the hallways. People like himself, and Carrie, and the Allisters, were like settlers in a strange savage land. The West Side belonged to the Rioses, to the Negro wreckers smashing the building next door, to tough little customers like Tony Paz. He would have to get to know Paz better. If there was to be some kind of crisis with Puttering, the mysterious landlord, Paz would be a good ally. He was gutter-bred, multilingual, and had done volunteer work with the minister at the West Side Parish House. Hassmiller? Hackenbush?

In morning sunlight, Broadway was bearable. The bursting food shops, the erotic corsetoriums, the decaying movie theaters, the efficient-looking banks, offered a vigorous impression of busy life, productive activity. It buoyed Loomis for a moment and eased his apprehensions. They were safe. They were secure. Others were mugged, knifed, destroyed. In February an elderly Jewish lady walking her poodle in Riverside Park had been murdered for the twelve dollars in her purse. Horton Sims, the schoolteacher in 2A, had been mugged by two of his soul brothers a few weeks ago and relieved of his money, his watch, and his Phi Beta Kappa key. The blond woman in 3B, the one with the two wild towheaded kids, had complained that her apartment was regularly ransacked. "There's nothin' left to steal," Loomis had heard her say to McIsaac, the reliable superintendent. "I might as well leave the door open, so they can get in. Except I hate the kids not having the television."

Yet it was often hard to believe that these violent events, these assaults on life and property, ever really took place. The neighborhood was such a hot, spicy stew that the ingredients were often unrecognizable. The mumbling junkies and the dangerous losers existed there, of course. But so did thousands of eminently respectable people—professionals, business types, working girls, not to mention hundreds of decent, wage-earning blacks and Puerto Ricans. It was as if the West Side were a Jekyll-and-Hyde locality, uncertain of its true nature, given to bursts of blood and death, but at the same time sober, creative, comfortable, interestingly varied.

Moreover, Loomis reflected, unless you were directly assaulted (he and Carrie had never been) you began to feel immune. They, like the Allisters, secure in their upper-middle-class success, appeared to be untouchables. Grace under pressure, he concluded, an ability to be cool and aloof amid the terrors. That and double-bolted doors, a night light, a schedule for walking the streets—and always in pairs, since the local knowledge had it that muggers attacked only solitary strollers.

But people like Rios and his wife, despite all the cozy theories about a "culture of poverty" that presumably armored them, were born victims. The iron ball struck; they were demolished. For a moment Loomis wondered if he should have done something to help them. But Tony Paz—who knew the rules of the street, who was wise in the tricks of landlords, the resources of tenants—had done nothing. In fact, he had been the one who had explained to Loomis why they would be so unceremoniously thrown out.

The Theater of the Real, Carrie had called the drama of the side streets. As an actress (an intelligent one) she saw the West Side as a great arena stage. The performers were the poor, the black, the Latins, the lost souls. Those who could afford the best apartments, the higher rents, who had the luxury of steady work and good pay, were the audience. Actors, David told her, outnumbered the public. But the spectator (like the old lady murdered for twelve dollars) was sometimes forced to get up on the stage, as in some off-Broadway theater, where undressing actors tormented middle-class playgoers into shivering participation.

Loomis was grateful that he and Carrie were not only in

26

the audience, but were hicks, out-of-towners, who barely related to Carlos Rios, or Tony Paz, or even their black super. The architect was from Ohio, she was an upstate New York girl. They were still innocent enough to be thrilled by the city, and, in their small-town simplicity, unafraid of it.

Suddenly he recalled something that Epstein, one of the senior architects, had told him at lunch one day. "We're grateful to the blacks," Epstein had said, after two scotches. "Better *they* get it, than *us*." Now after seeing the Rioses weeping on the sidewalk, he understood Epstein, even though the knowledge was not inspiring. He would make a modest effort to know Tony Paz better, as well as the various Latins—Fuentes? Escobar?—who lived, in proliferating numbers it seemed, in apartment 1B. He and Carrie might even brush up on their Spanish.

By late morning the pounding and crashing had stopped. Carrie Loomis sighed with relief. Sipping her third cup of tea—Dr. Hershkowitz had advised her to keep something in her mouth at all times, to stop salivation—she decided to go shopping, perhaps buy some things for the baby's room. She felt the need for bright colors, now that she was coming out of the long dark passage of her illness. The nausea, the vertigo, the convulsions were over, the hours of watching the colorless nourishment drip into her vein from a suspended flask, the dread of losing the child. Hershkowitz's good sense and David's patience had brought her through. It would be like coasting downhill from now on. The child would redeem the months of pain.

At the window, she inhaled the spring air. New York smelled clean and fresh. A breeze from the Hudson was sweeping the filth and grime from the city. Below, the forlorn furnishings rested on the pavement. The evicted tenants and the workmen were gone. The great metal bin, with its load of dead doors, wrecked moldings, jagged chunks of rubbish, squatted at the curb. When it was full, it would be loaded on a tractor and towed off. New apartments would be built next door. The world was renewing itself, Carrie felt.

"I'm over the bad times," she said, dabbing pale lipstick to her small mouth. "Everything gets better from now on." She put on the beige maternity suit on which David had splurged at Saks Fifth Avenue, after receiving a bonus for work on apartments in Staten Island. Up to now, depressed by her constant illness, she had been unwilling to wear it. As she started toward the door, her mouth flooded with saliva, and she raced to the kitchen sink to unload. *Ptyalism*, Dr. H. called it: excessive salivation, a complication in hard pregnancies. David had found an old terra-cotta jug in a Third Avenue antique shop. It had been his gag present to her, her portable spittoon. She would insert it in the middle of her large canvas tote, and covertly expectorate. It was a disgusting ailment, but it caused her no pain, no loss of energy. "I'm a spitting wonder," she said to David. "When this is over I can audition for Westerns and play Gabby Hayes parts."

Buoyant, exhilarated, she felt the need to be neighborly. It was a pity that she and David barely knew the other tenants. Even the Allisters, who shared the fourth floor with them, were nodding acquaintances. (Archie seemed friendly enough, but Liz, with that icy mask of the high-priced model, was hard to approach.) On the third-floor landing she remembered that one of the young men in 3A, was a decorator, and evidently a good one. She had seen his picture in a home magazine a few weeks ago—a lean young *condottiere*—demonstrating some weird ideas with nautical ropes. On impulse she decided to ask his advice about drapes and fabrics. An actress, she did not fear or dislike homosexuals, and she recalled that Barri Dane, the other tenant, was in the theater.

It was Dane who came to the door. "Oh. Mrs. Loomis. Good morning. Hmmmm. Any day now, I guess."

"Another seven weeks. Is Mr. Lobello in?"

"You bet. Come in. Gosh, what a pleasure. I think we have

some mutual friends in the theater. Weren't you with the Journeymen?"

They chatted briefly. Dane was an engaging little man; with his American Boy face, all freckles and snubbed features, and his tough little body. They were standing in a foyer that obviously had benefited from his roommate's high taste. The floor was tiled in a checkerboard pattern. Against one wall was a curious bower-shaped affair, combination full-length mirror, clothes rack, phone table. Carrie found herself staring at it.

"What a lovely piece," she said.

"Tell Ron. He'll fall down. It's a sixteenth-century baldachino that he found in his grandmother's village in Sicily."

Lobello walked into the foyer. He was shaving with a straight razor, in long expert strokes, and his happi coat was folded and knotted above his waist to reveal his muscled chest and corded arms.

"It's Mrs. Loomis, Ron, from upstairs. Is that a way to appear before a guest?" Barri Dane simulated shock.

"Hi," Lobello said. "Golly, you're about ready." He studied her abdomen with innocent eyes. "A new baby for the house, isn't that lovely? Oh, don't smile like that. I'm not putting you on. I mean it. It's the Italian in me."

"I'm not laughing." Carrie was delighted with them—harmless, funny, making the best of their status as outsiders. "And I think your apartment is fabulous." Beyond she could see a mélange of wild colors, cleverly transformed antiques, campy lamps, and mad statuary. Yet it was attractive, done with humor and style.

"Well, aren't you a doll." Lobello looked at Dane. "You see, there are nice people on West 84th Street."

There were some shouts from the street; something to do with the wrecking of the brownstone.

"I hate breaking in on you like this," Carrie said, "but I was thinking of fixing up the nursery. I've been so ill up to now I couldn't face it, but I'm fine now. I remembered once, when we first moved in, my husband and I dropped in here and I admired some nubby drapes you had. I was wondering—"

"No problem, dear," Lobello said. "I'd love to help you. Look, I'll bring some swatches back tonight. Maybe you and your husband can come by for a drinkie—"

"I didn't want to make it a project for you—"

Barri Dane's pale blue eyes opened wide. "You'll *pay*, you'll *pay!*" he cried. "Ron doesn't do favors. He's a Sicilian, Mrs. Loom—"

"Carrie."

"Well, Carrie or Mrs. Loomis, he'll get his lira's worth."

Lobello flicked a towel at the small man. "Don't mind him, Carrie. You'll get my discount for pregnant ladies."

The phone on the baldachino rang. Dane picked it up. "This is Barri Dane. It's your dime. Yes, this is apartment 3A." Then, as the caller responded, his face turned scarlet in a blush that began at his neck and rose, painting his ears, his cheeks. He turned his back on Lobello and Carrie, cradling the phone. Suddenly he exploded.

"What? Oh, is *that* so? Oh, is *that* right?" He spluttered, spun around. "Well, shove it up yours, you big fink, whoever you are! You dirty mother! Tell that to your wife if you have one!"

There was a mashed voice on the other end. Dane cursed violently and slammed the phone down.

Carrie felt her salivary glands working. She raised the tote to her flooding mouth, and as Lobello and Dane looked at one another, she let fly.

"What the devil was that?" Lobello asked. "Another of those damned cranks?"

"Oh, this was a new one, a beauty. Not the heavy breather, but a mumbler. He said we'd better move out because he didn't like faggots, and that if we didn't he'd"—he looked at Carrie—"I won't repeat it in front of a lady. Oh, the pig."

Lobello laughed. "He sounds adorable. Thank God he's *your* friend. You get the mumbler, I'll take the heavy breather from now on."

As she left, she felt heartened by their courage. There was something to be said for them. If they listened to different drummers, they at least kept some kind of step. Withal, they were productive, noncriminal, and well-mannered.

It was odd, she mused, the hidden qualities in so many people on the West Side. But they were doomed to be alien to one another. One had friends, but one rarely knew one's neighbors. Proximity bred caution in the old houses.

As she heard the clacking of Werner Schlossmann's typewriter, she realized how much she and David might have benefited from knowing the old man and his daughter. But the Schlossmanns were the ultimate hermits in a building of loners—he at his typewriter, or wandering the streets, his eyes vague and moist, she in her braided hair, mouse-colored sweaters, and low-heeled shoes, lugging an overloaded briefcase to Columbia. Carrie could guess their history—Germany, concentration camps, family deaths, tragedies borne like wounds or speech defects. And yet, and yet . . . Schlossmann and his Hilda had quality, an unyielding and unbreakable strength. When the old man tipped his battered black fedora—it had a hole in it—or when Hilda nodded a short spastic greeting with her head, Carrie sensed a certain fineness, an aristocratic courtesy in them.

When she reached the stoop, the spring sun roused and invigorated her. It was amazing what the first good day in May could do. Dirt, bad odors, and depression were obliterated in the warm clean sunlight. A good day to get things done, she thought.

She remembered the wall outlet under David's drafting table. It had been sparking wickedly, and had already blown a set of fluorescent bulbs in his gooseneck lamp, requiring him to use an extension cord. She decided to see McIsaac, the huge, polite black man, their superintendent, who lived in the basement. As she descended the narrow stone steps to the freshly painted door—McIsaac was a compulsively neat man—she thought again about the hidden qualities in so many people.

There were sounds of conversation behind the door. She

knocked twice and McIsaac, his vast bony face solemn behind steel-rimmed glasses, opened it.

"Good morning, Mrs. Loomis," he said.

Behind him Carrie saw a scuffed cardboard suitcase, bound with clothesline, two cardboard boxes, similarly tied, and McIsaac's old ironing board, folded. "Well . . . I . . . I thought I'd ask you to take a look at the electrical outlet under Mr. Loomis's drafting—"

Someone was wandering around in McIsaac's apartment.

"I'm sorry, Mrs. Loomis. Can't help you. I been fired."

"What? When did this happen?" It was like hearing that one's favorite teacher, the reliable teacher one went to for advice, had left school.

"Today. Mr. Dukes fire me."

"Who is Mr. Dukes? And why? I mean, don't the tenants have a say . . . ?"

From the dark interior of the basement room, a figure appeared—a slender man in a fringed suede jacket and soiled tan chino pants. She could not see his face, but she noted that he was egg-bald, his head shaven like a Marine recruit's. He turned away, and began unpacking a duffel bag.

"Mr. Dukes in charge now," McIsaac said.

"But the tenants like you," Carrie protested. "You're the best building superintendent anywhere. Do you have a job?"

"Oh, that no problem. I got me jobs. But it was convenient here, bein' near my church and all." He picked up his valise, the cardboard boxes, the small ironing board. "That fellow there, Mr. Dukes send him to take the job. You talk to him about it."

There were the small crises of life that could produce panic. Life with McIsaac had been easy, easier than any of them knew. He was an electrician, a carpenter, a plumber, a kind and resourceful man. In all the city they would never find another like him.

"Say goodbye to Mr. Loomis," McIsaac said. "Sorry I can't

fix the plug for you. That new fellow, he supposed to do all the things I do."

McIsaac walked by her, laboring under the weight of his goods. Then he was gone. The door had remained open, and for some reason, Carrie was thankful that it was—light, air, an exit.

"Oh, excuse me," she called. "I don't like bothering you when you're just moving in—"

The new super turned—he had been stacking cans on a shelf—and walked out of the murk. He was taller than he had first appeared, and older. The shaving of his head emphasized the supraorbital ridges over his eyes, and the hollows below them. The eyes themselves were almost colorless, a dead gray.

"Hi. I'm Mrs. Loomis in 4A. I was telling Mr. McIsaac about the—"

She stopped. He was grinning at her. It was not the playful sort of smile that she had gotten from Barri Dane. There was something impudent and threatening in it.

"By the way," she said firmly. "What's your name?"

"Captain Speed." His voice was thin.

"There's no need to be insolent. Whoever Mr. Dukes is, he's working for our landlord, and I can report you. I merely came by to ask someone to fix the outlet."

"Okay, okay. Dang, if you got to get sore at me." There was a suggestion of a southern accent; it accorded with the fake Western jacket, the narrow chinos.

"All right. But please try to come by today. It's quite an inconvenience to have to run extension cords all over the apartment."

She turned, and at the door he materialized, having darted around her on sneakered feet. In the daylight, she saw that his face was lined, smudged. "Lady—"

"What is it?" A twinge of fear shivered her.

"Gimme ten dollars."

"Absolutely not."

"Gimme five."

"I'll give you not a damn thing. You do your job, and we'll tip you when we feel you should be tipped. Don't think you can come on this job and begin to intimidate tenants. I've heard about supers like you."

"Listen." His arm blocked the doorway. "Ah need the dough. Just for some groceries. Dukes won't advance me no money. Gimme five now, Ah swear Ah'll pay you." There was a whine in his voice. It offended Carrie more than his attempt at menace.

She slammed his arm down. "Get out of my way."

The super moved back. "Okay, lady. Damn cheap thing when you won't help a man get his grits."

She walked outside and started up the basement steps.

"Hey, lady. Hey."

Carrie turned on the steps. The man had stepped outside the door. His fly was open and he was exposing himself to her. He looked like an obscene gargoyle, an illustration from a medieval text on deadly sins. Carrie said nothing. Acting had endowed her with a talent for simulating calm. But her heart beat mercilessly as she walked up the steps.

That evening, Loomis met Archie Allister on Broadway. The men were returning from work, and Allister was struggling with his attaché case, bakery boxes, bags loaded with fruit and vegetables. David relieved him of some of the burden.

"Thanks, man," Allister said. "Liz has one of those damned late jobs. Some fruity photographer who can't get inspired until the sun goes down. I get to be the woman of the house."

Allister was a startlingly handsome young man—lean, prematurely gray at the temples, with firm, hard features. He had the kind of physical excellence that engendered confidence rather than envy in other men, and a sense of security in women. Loomis was not certain what he did. It was something in Wall Street.

"How's the frau?" Allister asked.

"Big and bouncy this morning," David said. "I think it'll be a piece of cake from now on. Even the racket next door didn't upset her."

Allister snorted. "Wasn't that a bummer. Man, they really were pounding the walls."

"Those old brownstones were built to last. Solid. Heavy studding. Thick plaster." Loomis laughed. "I sort of felt sorry for the old place going down like that. Buildings should be respected. Good ones, anyway."

Allister—what was he? broker? investment counselor?—looked appreciatively at him. David sensed his attitude: respect for a technical man's hard, professional knowledge. Loomis was grateful. He was the kind of low-keyed, self-questioning man who wondered about his own abilities. Admiration from someone as surefooted, as good-looking as Archie Allister was a help. Loomis could not put his finger on it, but there was something about Allister—his handsome face, the brazen mod olive suit and wide green tie, surely a bit too brash for a Wall Street office, the dazzling wife, the glib speech—that aroused envy in him. Loomis had trouble making a decent knot in his tie, and his suits ran to rumpled seersuckers with outmoded narrow lapels. And his face was distressingly vague (a kind, honest face, Carrie said) with its blunted nose, wide forehead and long upper lip. Somehow the arts of physical excellence had eluded him. Canadian Air Force exercises had not helped, and if Carrie bought him a dashing gold shirt, he would find it out of sorts with his open, plain face.

"Those poor people next door," Loomis said. "No one went to bat for them. Paz said Puttering simply didn't collect rents, then hit them with a huge bill."

"Tough. I don't know how those people live anyway. Puttering might do worse than pull the same stunt on that noisy mob on the first floor."

David said nothing. The Puerto Ricans in 1B were unknown to him—a swarm of dark-skinned itinerants. But they did not bother him. They seemed a rather sober bunch. True, they

35

played their radios too loud, and the odor of frying oil from their cramped quarters was sometimes overwhelming. But for the most part they seemed a cheerful, inoffensive lot.

"They just about filled the damn thing," Allister said.

The great metal bin was loaded with the rude innards of number 400, great chunks of plaster and wood and glass ripped from the house, a castle of rubbish. A lone Negro workman was sweeping plaster dust into the gutter.

"Paz said he was going to renovate the place," David said. "Up the rents. I suppose it'll make our building more desirable. But how long will it take?"

"Beats me," Allister said.

Loomis studied the façades across the street. Three buildings, his own, 502, the adjacent 500, which had been ripped apart that morning, and a third, 498, which had for the past three months been vacant, the high windows blinded with tin sheets, were obviously a trio, the work of one architect. They were identical four-story affairs, built of a lovely dark-brown limestone, a hard, unyielding rock that had not chipped or cracked since the buildings were erected in the latter part of the nineteenth century.

Loomis doffed his hat to the unknown designer. The three buildings made a marvelous unit. The lines were noble, original, severe. Whoever the architect was, he had come under the influence of Renaissance orders, and he knew how to use the flowing lines with great effect. With a professional's eye, David had admired the handsome dormer windows, two to each house, a total of six harmoniously arranged peaks. Curiosity had led him to his books and he had discovered that the dormers were exact copies of the Château of Blois. No less elegant were the high mullioned windows, and the massive carved cornice with its egg-and-dart motif. Where in heaven's name, David wondered, did they find craftsmen to create such marvels? There was more of the sixteenth century and of French-Italian styling in the graceful pilasters that rose from stoop level to the cornice. And somehow it all seemed *right,* combinations of lines, arrangements that pleased the eye. (The high stoop with its clumsy balustrade, the supports shaped like Greek vases, was the only jarring note in the grand design; but Loomis forgave his departed colleague.)

"Well, I suppose the guy is ready to fix up 498 and 500," Allister said. "I often wondered why he left 498 vacant so long."

"Money's tight," David said. They crossed the street.

"Not the way I heard it. It's true none of us have ever seen Puttering, or even know where his office is. But I'm told he's rich, rich, rich."

A faded yellow and red sign nailed to the boarded-up door of 498 West 84th Street read:

PROPERTY OF

HAMAN, LORD & FAWCETT

118 LAW ST.

NEW YORK, N.Y.

NO TRESPASSING

"Now there's something I've never figured out," Loomis said. "If Puttering is the landlord, who are *they?*"

"Probably brokers, agents. Puttering is a phantom, we know that. The guy operates through third parties. Never sees daylight."

"Does he exist? I don't think anyone in the house has ever seen him, or spoken to him."

David walked over to the Negro sweeper. "Are they going to start renovating here? How long will it take?"

"No idea, man. I just here to clean up."

As they climbed the stairs, Allister asked him: "Dave, are you getting some uneasy notions. Like maybe we're going to be renovated also?"

Loomis frowned. "I doubt it. Heck, this building is sound,

37

and filled with people who pay their rent. I can't see them knocking the walls down around our ears."

"Let's hope so, buddy."

Before dinner, Ron Lobello and Barri Dane dropped by. The young decorator brought a booklet of fabric swatches. Carrie was delighted. She paged through them, made some selections for the nursery and for the living room, and exchanged theater talk with Barri Dane. The latter had, that day, auditioned and gotten a good part in a television play at CBS.

"I'm playing a teen-age killer," Dane said. Suddenly, his airy, delicate manner changed, and he spoke in Brando-adenoidal style. "Like, ah, man, I could waste you right now, you dig?"

Carrie and David laughed. He was a likable little squirt with an engaging sense of humor.

"Isn't he too much?" Lobello asked. "You should have seen him scare the pants off some creep hanging around the house today."

"What happened?" Carrie asked.

"You tell it, Barri," Lobello said.

"Typical West 84th Street lunacy. God knows we should be used to it by now, living in this bat's nest. When I came down to go to the studio, there was this bald-headed nut sitting on the stoop. You could smell that he was a junkie."

"In a suede jacket? A thin man?" Carrie asked. She tried to keep her voice from rising.

"Yes," Barri said. "That's the fellow. He wanted ten dollars from me. In exchange for . . . no need to specify, but it wasn't very nice. So I hunched my shoulders and gave him my Cagney bit." Dane got to his feet, shook his hands at belt level, grimaced like James Cagney, and in a husky voice muttered: "Awright, Jocko, you and me are gonna have a little talk."

"That isn't all," Lobello said. "I was a witness. My dear roommate feinted a left jab, threw a right that missed by an inch,

38

and the junkie fell off the stoop. Collapsed. That's the last we'll see of him."

"I don't think so," Carrie said. "If it's the same man I saw this morning. A southern accent?"

Lobello and Dane exchanged looks. David looked searchingly at his wife. "What do you mean, honey?"

"He's the new super. Mr. McIsaac was fired by the mysterious Dukes. I saw him this morning when he moved in."

Loomis looked at her. "You didn't mention it."

"I didn't think it was important," Carrie said. She had decided to say nothing about the encounter with the bald man.

"I hope he was more civil to you," Dane said. "*Him*—a super? That bum, in his fake cowboy jacket? What will we do without McIsaac? He was a treasure."

Carrie was determined not to make an issue of what had happened in the basement. "He seemed a little stupid. He looked kind of blank when I asked him to fix one of our electrical outlets."

"Oh, brother, I'm getting bad vibes," Lobello said. "Come on, lover, the duck should be ready."

The roommates got up to leave. "I don't like the noises around here," Barri said to David and Carrie. "Or that dude Dukes, whoever he is. It sounds as if our landlord is up to something."

David walked them to the door. "Maybe we'd better do some investigating. Maybe it's time for us to flush Puttering out and find out what cooks."

"We're with you, David," Lobello said.

When they had left, and Carrie had brought their dinner to the table—feeling stronger, she had ambitiously sautéed a chicken with white wine and small onions—David tried to draw her out on her meeting with the new super.

"Didn't even give you his name? Or volunteer to come up here?"

"He seemed a little confused. Maybe moving in, and everything."

David's face was grave. She knew that beneath his relaxed exterior, he was a worrier. "Look, Carrie, that guy made some kind of indecent proposal to Dane. Okay, the little guy is a homosexual, but he's a citizen. That's all we need—perverts in the basement. I've heard about these supers. The landlords can't get anyone reliable to take the jobs, so they hire some junkie or wino and pretty soon he's inviting his friends in. I don't like it."

Carrie sipped the cold Riesling. It had been a long time since her aggrieved stomach could hold wine. Now that she was on the road back, she had no intention of having minor matters, like a superintendent, depress her.

"Don't sweat over it, sweetie," she said. "It's spring in New York and I feel great." Without warning she felt the salivary glands pumping. "Almost great," she added, speaking out of the side of her mouth—and sprinted for the kitchen sink.

Noncombatant, outsider, the coolest of cool black cats. So did Horton Sims, the schoolteacher in 2A regard himself. The dull dark suits, the soft-collared white shirts, the narrow maroon ties, the self-effacing, slow-spoken manner said to the white world: *this is an adjusted, no-nonsense, middle-class black man.* Deliberately Sims cultivated an exterior of blandness, of conformity, to contrast with his wife Leora's flamboyance. Leora also taught. She was a kindergarten supervisor in Greenwich Village. She was a flaming presence—an Afro bush, dangly ivory earrings, wild orange-and-purple robes, and braided leather sandals, perhaps fashioned of water buffalo or springbok.

Both were good-looking people—Horton in a diffident, retiring way, Leora in a lavish, extravagant way—and they made an attractive couple, he in a Rogers Peet vested suit, she in a flowing yellow jellaba from a head shop on West 8th Street. But they were private persons, and their façade, hip wife and square husband, was a fake, a grand deception. Both of them played the game with zest and cunning. Horton Sims—flattened nose, milk-chocolate skin, neatly parted hair, huge solemn eyes—

was presumably the ultimate Oreo, assimilated, reasonable. But he was not that at all. A hard intelligence worked inside Sims. He kept a great deal of himself secret, and invited no one, except his wife and his four-year-old son, Allard, to get close to him.

As for Leora, the aboriginal garb, the hoops, and the ivory bangles were for external use only. In truth, she was a middle-class woman with middle-class insecurities, and an honest interest in new vacuum cleaners and cheaper cuts of meat. She read the supermarket sales avidly, and could tell at a glance whether Brand A of coffee at 69 cents a pound (limit, one pound per customer) was a better buy than Brand B, two-pound can, $1.51, no limit.

On the morning after the eviction of the families next door, and the appearance of a new super, Sims sipped his orange juice, then poured himself a cup of black coffee.

"How come you don't eat the hearty protein-filled breakfast, like the black folks on the television?" she mocked. "You trying to undermine the economy, Sims?"

He rolled his sorrowful eyes. "Cease, woman. Not at eight o'clock." When she walked by, he embraced her full hips. They were very much in love; a couple who valued every moment of their closeness. But even in a moment of jesting passion, Sims retained his splendid neutrality—no emotion, no excess, no outbursts. He let her wriggle free. Placidity, Horton Sims knew, kept him alive and healthy in the jungle of Intermediate School 710, that stew of bad mothers and hard drugs on the Upper West Side. ("You a cool dude," Foster McBain, the leading fifteen-year-old pusher told Sims one day. "You so cool, you don't spook. Cain't spook a teacher like you.")

No, Horton Sims did not spook, or run, or tremble. Behind the narrow lapels and the sedate dark tie, there was an immovable force; he was uncommitted to anything but his survival, his welfare, the happiness and security of his wife and child.

"Pop-pop buy Allie a gun today," his son piped. "Allie

41

wants a big gun." The burnished brown face at rest on Sims' knee was unbearably beautiful. The skin was of some heavenly brown texture, the searching eyes enormous—odd, how they flashed with some kind of childish outrage now and then—the features those of Botticelli angel. The Simses were embarrassed by his beauty. Horton would retreat into his shell when someone complimented Allard. Leora, forgetting his camouflage, would smile to cover her unease and mumble, "Oh, we think he's good-looking also." Just a few days ago, the pregnant girl on the top floor, Mrs. Loomis, had ogled him and gushed: "I can't take my eyes off him. Oh, I'm sorry, Mrs. Sims. But it's true. He's irresistible."

"Gun, Pop-pop."

Allard, getting no answer from his father, retreated to his mother, clinging to the long robe. Like the old man, Leora thought. Not such hot stuff as he thought: a shy and reserved one. It was a good thing he was handsome, she mused. Sims had made it by being aloof, fenced in. But he had a sharp mind and a steel will. She worried about Allard. He was growing up as a middle-class kid in a West Side brownstone and he would never have to fight the way they did.

"What kind of gun do you want, Allard?" Sims asked. "Cowboy?"

"P'leeceman's gun."

"Hear that, Leora? Kid doesn't even know the right word. He's never heard 'pig' in this house."

"Can it, Hortie. There's four college degrees and steak twice a week in this house. I don't see you buying Black Panther literature from those bloods on Broadway."

"That's how I want it. Nobody got a part of me."

She hugged him from behind, kissing the top of his head. Allard, worried about who loved whom the most, leaned on his father's knee again. "Pop-pop. Pop-pop."

"Yeah, son."

"Das your wife?"

42

"You bet, Allard, Das my wife. And you my boy. And she is your mommy."

There was a soft rustling noise in the corridor. Sims walked toward the door. A single sheet of white paper had been thrust beneath the slit. He picked it up and switched on the hall light. Setting his horn-rimmed glasses, he read it swiftly.

DUKES MANAGEMENT COMPANY
612 West 74th St.
New York, N.Y.

May 7

Dear Tenant:

This letter is to advise you that the premises at 502 West 84th Street are now under the management of the Dukes Management Company, address above. Please send all payments for rent to that address, and not, as formerly, to E. J. Puttering & Sons.

Rest assured that the Dukes organization will maintain high standards in this building. Disregard rumors about any pending renovation or change in status for your building. Notices will shortly be sent out on various improvements that are planned.

Very truly yours,

RUDY DUKES
President

Above the name was Dukes' signature, in a large firm hand. Sims puzzled over it a moment. Leora, struggling with an outsized raffia tote filled with schoolbooks and art materials, Allard clinging to her skirt, walked into the hallway.

"What is it, Hortie?"

"Under new management, it seems."

"Hunh. Maybe things will improve. We've been after Puttering for a paint job for a half a year."

Sims opened the bolt on the heavy door, undid the latch chain, fiddled with the pickproof lock, and walked into the exterior corridor. He had heard men's voices, and he assumed they were the people who had put the letter under his door. Then he saw them at Schlossmann's door—a gray-haired, thick-bodied man and a lithe Puerto Rican, white-skinned but with kinky hair.

"Say," Sims called. "Hold it, there."

The gray-haired man—he had drooping features and wore enormous glasses—did not respond, but gave an order to the other. "Go on, Bolo. Give out the rest. Wait downstairs."

"Hoddya do, friend," he said, turning toward Sims. "Sharmak is the name. Call me Shlep. You're the teacher, right? That's nice."

Careful, careful, Sims thought. He watched the man named Bolo vanish—thin, leathery, a dude in a lavender shirt, assless in tight green pants. Warily, he pumped Sharmak's hand once.

"What's this letter all about?" Sims asked.

"Routine, Mr. Sims, routine. Dukes Management is takin' over a lot of these old brownstones. The landlords don't wanna be bothered. So we collect the rents, and so forth. Why, there's the missus."

Leora did not look at Sharmak. Her instincts warned her: *a phony, a liar.* "Horton, I'll be late today," she said to her husband. "I left a rib roast out. Could you put it in the oven, please? Oh, about an hour and a half at 350. And stick some potatoes and onions in with it."

"Sure thing, honey."

"That's nice, nice. Husband and wife working." Sharmak leered at Leora as she walked by him. "Both teachers. Nothing like a education."

"How did you know?" Leora asked.

"We make it our business to know our tenants. Dukes works that way. Knows all about you folks."

When she was gone, Horton held the letter out. "What does this mean? I heard Dukes handled the evictions next door. You going to throw us out also?" He smiled as he asked the questions.

"Naaah. Naaah. That's a dirty old dump. Renovation. Listen,

44

a landlord has a right to get more dough. Between you and me, Mr. Sims, there was a lot of filth in that building. Not like you people."

Hilda Schlossmann loomed in the dark hallway. She was waving the letter. "You. You, sir. I don't like this. I know these tricks. Pay the rent here, there, everywhere. We will have you in tenant-landlord court if you persist."

"Ah, Mrs. Schlossmann—"

"*Miss.*"

"Sure, sure. The professor. Would a nice *yiddishe* boy like me pull a stunt like that?"

From below Bolo shouted: "Feenish, Shlep. All done."

"Well, I got work, folks. Get in touch if you got questions."

With surprising vigor for an overweight man in his sixties, Sharmak ran past them and down the stairs. Hilda Schlossmann turned her severe face toward Sims. "They are after us, Mr. Sims."

"I hope not, Miss Schlossmann. We like it here fine."

She lurched past him—a strong brainy presence. Yet, Sims felt, she seemed vulnerable, a person whom a bully would single out. "Your likes, my desires, will mean nothing," she said.

Sims was silent. All that suffering—concentration camps, death, impoverishment—created Cassandras. More than ever he was glad to be the uncommitted man, the spade nobody knew.

"Tony, for God's sake, stop with Rudy Dukes," Lucy Paz pleaded. "Sit down and drink your milk. You haven't stopped talking about him since they stuck that letter under the door."

Tony suffered from too much energy, too many vibrations, in too small a body. He should have been six feet tall and weighed 210 pounds. Three jobs, minimal sleep, and a diet of sweet crackers and milk (he had a spastic esophagus, incipient colitis, and a pinpoint ulcer) failed to slow him down. Nights he was the manager of an underground garage near Columbia. Afternoons, he worked at Asmanoff's Fancy Fruit and Vegetable Store on Broadway and West 92nd Street. And weekends and

45

holidays he delivered flowers and steamer baskets for a florist on West 68th Street. Overworked, coiled, tense, he was nevertheless rarely tired. He drew sustenance, it seemed to Lucy, from his outrage. And nothing outraged him more than the thought of Rudy Dukes.

"He come back to get me," Tony said moodily. "I know. I know Rudy. Big car. Big dog. I know he got guns inside. To get me."

Lucy set a glass of milk and a plate of fig newtons, honey grahams, and Lorna Doones in front of her husband. Hunched over the kitchen table, his hands jammed below his knees, he looked about six years old. There were times when Lucy thought of him as her little boy. (She would never dare express this thought to Tony, with his mania for *machismo*, for male honor). He was a startlingly handsome man with his unmarked white brow, the firm nose, and the enormous, angry black eyes. Doll-like, carved from ivory, he moved about—hopped, or jumped, or darted—like an overstimulated kid, the sort who gave the teacher fits not by being bad, but simply by fidgeting and flying from his seat without permission.

"Maybe I better start on steak," Tony said. He nibbled at a graham cracker, sipped his milk, and sprung from the kitchen chair. "That lousy *pato*. He come back here to get me."

"He did *not*," Lucy said. "Listen, he's in the management business again. It was a coincidence he's got the house we live in."

Tony paced the apartment—into the living room for a peek into the street (would the Lincoln be cruising again?), into the bedroom with its wall covered with Sacred Hearts, Jesuses, Santa Rosalias, graduation photos, and then back into the kitchen.

"Lucy, it's me or Rudy this time. Me or him, that's it."

"Oh, cut it out, Tony."

She was always ready for his instant dramatizations. Tony was in perpetual combat. Bad guys were after him. His guard had to be up. Now that Rudy Dukes was back in New York—and managing their building!—Tony would be acting full tilt, parading around the apartment, imitating voices, anticipating scenes of conflict.

"Look, Tony, if he gives us trouble, I'll call Daddy and he'll call some of his friends in the city." She picked up the baby—he was not crying, but it seemed a good thing to do—and waited for her husband's response. Tony's feelings about his in-laws were a good gauge to his feelings.

"Hah!" Paz exploded. "Your old man got no friends in the city as tough as Rudy. Besides, your old man hates me."

"Oh, cut it out, Tony. He does not."

"Yeah, all your Italian relatives. They won't lift a finger to help us."

She was sorry she had brought up the subject of her father's assistance. When she, Lucy Cavatelli, daughter of a Sanitation Department supervisor, had married a Puerto Rican, the angry shouts filled the East Bronx. *A PR! A spic!* One of those roach-carrying immigrants who came to New York to sponge on welfare, sell drugs, cut throats, and murder each other, fifteen to a room!

"They like you now, Tony, honest they do." She appealed to him for a reasonable attitude, an acceptance of her peace offering. Lucy was tinier than her husband, a bird-boned girl with a mop of red upswept hair. Her eyes, like Tony's, were huge, dark, and shining—two ignored, misunderstood people, all of whose power and energies were concentrated in their magical eyes.

"Yeh, yeh, your old man makin' cracks about my three jobs," Tony sulked. He munched a fig newton, decided it was stale, and put it down. More and more, he realized, he ate less and less. "Well, we don' have to work for the city, us Puerto Ricans. We got pride. We do it on our own. And someday I have my own store, my own high-class Spanish delicatessen. We see who can make it big."

The baby wiggled inside his confining trundle-bundle, gurgling.

"Whassamatta?" Tony cried. "He okay?"

"Of course he is. Finish your lunch."

"Some lunch. One of these days, if my gut feels good, I start on meat. Steak and pork chops. When you got to fight Rudy Dukes, you need bellyful of red meat."

"No one's going to fight nobody."

But Tony was already dancing around the room, tossing quick jabs, holding the right cocked, snorting through his nostrils. Like most Puerto Ricans, he revered the memory of Sixto Escobar. At one time he had bought a leather-and-elastic "biceps developer" and had worked out with it every morning. It was no use. He was not only a squirt, too small for even a bantam-weight, and his tremulous stomach bent him double before every amateur fight.

"Pah! Pah!" Tony said—connecting with a right hook. Suddenly he stopped. "Better, better. I finish high school. Yeah, that's it, Lucy. I start night courses again. Once I get high school diploma, Rudy can't touch me. I be smarter than him."

Settling into a ruined armchair with Michael (he was not Miguel, or Mikie, but *Michael*), she wondered whether love or pity was foremost in her sentiments toward Tony. Forever, he would be a small boy, a worrisome, wild kid.

Outside, an automobile horn honked. Rudy was summoning him. Rudy would come for him. Rudy would try to break him. He gazed at the kitchen wall. The framed photograph of the Columbus Avenue Devils, PAL softball champions, 1948, gave him some reassurance. In the front row, a head shorter than anyone, legs crossed, was himself: Tony Paz, shortstop. He wondered why he had worn the baseball cap. It covered his eyes and made him look like the mascot, not a .356 hitter with a rifle arm.

Barri Dane was sensitive to noise. With Ron's help, he had installed soundproofing in the ceiling, heavy foam rubber padding under the rugs, cork on the walls, anything to muffle street noises. When the horn started blasting in the street, he

was reading his part for the television play. It was a good part
—a boutique owner who gets shaken down by hoodlums.

Setting the script down, Dane walked to the front window.
The auto horn—it was loud and harsh—was still violating the
morning air, with its shrill bleat.

"Hey, you," Barri shouted. "Stop that!"

The noise came from a white Lincoln Continental, Rudy
Dukes' ark. The blasting ceased for a moment, then resumed.

"Boy, I'd like to run down and tell that dude a few things,"
Dane said. "The nerve of some people."

Ron Lobello looked out the window. "*Quelle* coffin. It must
be the new pusher. Maybe a pimp. There aren't any hookers in
this building, are there, Barri?"

"No. Not counting amateurs. God, he's off again. And he's
got all the windows closed, so he can't hear us. Shut up, damn
you! Stop that honking!"

As they watched, Tony Paz came bounding down the front
steps. He stopped on the sidewalk, facing the car. Then he
made the sign of the horns with his right hand—pinky and
index finger extended. He did the same with his left hand, then
hit his right wrist over his left, and froze the insulting gesture.

"Good for Little Paz!" Barri shouted. "That's it, Tony. Give
him the double horns!"

"If that guy's a *paisan*," Lobello said, "he'll come out of the
car and strangle Tony. That's the worst insult you can give an
Eyetalian."

The roommates giggled. They knew Tony Paz slightly, and
they liked him, a crazy runt, full of fantasies.

"What . . . ?" Lobello asked. "Am I seeing things?"

"You're not, baby."

The rear window of the Lincoln was wheeled down. From
it there poked a long, shiny metallic rod, then a man's hand
curled over a chamber, then a wooden stock.

"He must be kidding," Dane gasped. "He's pointing a gun
at Tony."

"Hey! Hey!" Lobello shouted. "Put that damn thing back!"

"I'm calling a cop," Barri said. He ran to the phone on the baldachino.

"I'll go downstairs," Lobello said. "Hey! You with the gun! We're calling the cops."

Paz refused to budge. The barrel did not intimidate him. He stood his ground, arms folded, looking like a ten year old in long pants.

"Tony!" Ron shouted. "Get in the house before that maniac does something!"

With that, the barrel of the gun—it was a shotgun, Ron realized, and could scatter deadly pellets—jerked upward. Lobello saw the white hands, one under the barrel, the other on the trigger, and then the flash of a white face, curly dark hair. And laughter—a man enjoying himself.

Dane could not get through to the police. As usual, the emergency number did not respond. Nor the operator. Just a dead silence, a cavernous humming. He stopped his roommate. "Don't go down, Ron, don't get involved in it. It's some kind of Puerto Rican feud."

From the street, they heard a rough, hoarse voice: *"Hey, faggot!"*

Both men raced to the window again. The man was looking up at them, still pointing the shotgun at the window. "You're both in range, faggots. One blast and I get two birds. Ready?"

Lobello and Dane jerked their heads back into the safety of the room.

"He's nuts," Ron said. "Crazy. I'm going down and get his license number."

Barri frowned. "I don't know. It sounds like some kind of fight between Tony and that guy. Tony was in some racket once. He knows a lot of wrongos."

They peeked out again—Dane's clipped red head and Lobello's sleek black poll—laughing, mocking the gunner below, convinced it was a joke. The gun barrel was gone. The window was up. With a tearing of hot rubber the car roared away. There was a final blast on the ear-splitting horn, then silence.

"I knew it," Dane shouted at the vanishing Lincoln. "You're yellow. Tony, who's your friend?"

"You don't know?" Paz called up to them. His eyes were burning. He had inside dope, hot stuff. "You don't know?"

"No," Barri said. "Except he'd better keep that piece to himself."

"Tha's Rudy. Rudy Dukes."

"Who?" Lobello shouted.

"Rudy Dukes. New buildin' manager."

Lobello and Dane looked at one another. They shared these long, mirthful gazes, the two of them united in mockery, against cruelties, humiliation. "Manager?" Dane laughed. "That guy is a manager?"

Tony nodded. "Yeah, tha's him. Gun collector. You don't pay rent, *pow!*" Tony pantomimed the action, pointing his skinny arms at the boys, squeezing off the shot.

Inside, Dane made the cuckoo sign, twirling his index finger at his forehead. "He's nuts, that Paz," Barri said. "You ever see that look he gets in his eye?"

"I'm not so sure. He knew the man in the car. We saw the gun, didn't we?"

"But a manager? Collecting rents with a shotgun?"

"Darling, it's the culture of poverty, haven't you heard?"

Dane grabbed for Lobello's behind. They chased each other around the apartment.

One of the great boons of a teaching career, Horton Sims knew, was getting home early. A domesticated man, he treasured the walls, floor, and ceiling of his home—sound, secure, safe, *his*. Leora had to be after him not to be such a stick-in-the-mud. It was she who organized their summers—Sag Harbor, travel counseling at summer camps if they felt the need for extra income. The apartment, she argued, was dandy, a bargain at $185 a month, those huge rooms and lofty ceilings, but people had to *get out*.

Sims jogged up the stairs happily. He had a splendid afternoon planned. It was only four o'clock. (He had stayed late, extracurricular work with the eighth-grade class play. Sims did not like dramatics, but he stayed on to keep order so that Mrs. Shapiro could get the rehearsal started.) He could catch part of the Mets game on radio. He could switch to WQXR after that. He would dutifully prepare the roast as Leora had asked him to. In fact, Sims decided, he would make the entire dinner—tossed green salad with blue cheese dressing, fresh spinach, maybe a pudding dessert—cherry Jell-O with peaches, the kind Allard liked so much. The dinner working, he would settle into his lounge chair and catch up on his reading until Leora and the boy got home from shopping. She'd have nothing to do but change, have a drink, and relax.

He was whistling—a man at peace with the world, with his estate—when he reached the door. Carefully, he put his key into the tricky cylindrical lock. But the key would not go in.

"Damn," Sims said. "Am I using the right one?"

He squinted at it in the gloom of the hallway. Of course it was the right one. His classroom key, the key to the men's john, the building key, had different heads. He had only one key to the house, and this was it.

"What the devil," Sims said softly. He bent low and again tried to insert the key. It went in about a sixteenth of an inch then stopped. "They change the locks on me?" he asked. He paced the corridor, thought of knocking at Schlossmann's door for help. But that would not do. Schlossmann was an eternal victim, a charity case. He would help no one in the world.

Sims was not a man to panic. All kinds of freaks roamed the neighborhood. But to stuff a keyhole? To block it? A picked lock was one thing, a shattered chain. He made a third attempt to force the key through. This time, rotating it slowly with steady pressure, he felt something give slightly inside. But it was useless. The key could not enter.

He knew that McIsaac, the reliable superintendent, had gone. Paz had informed him of that. And he had only seen the new super fleetingly, a bald man in a fringed suede jacket. Sims did

52

not even know his name. But this was a super's job, and at four in the afternoon the man would assist him, or at least find a locksmith. After all, problems were surmountable. Everything mechanical was capable of solution, Sims assured himself.

Yet why was his heart pounding as he walked down the basement steps? He knew. It was the terrifying knowledge that someone—unknown, unseen, beyond revenge—had singled his house out for an affront. A crude vicious assault. A warning. Why? He paid his rent. He and Leora were model tenants. He would, as soon as the lock was fixed, call the new manager, that fellow Dukes, and let him know. They needed better security in the building. The super would have to be wary of derelicts.

He knocked at the wooden door leading to the basement. There was no response. He knocked again, then called in his soft voice. Then, losing his control, his vaunted cool, he kicked at the door.

Bending his head to the door, Sims listened carefully, then called: "Are you in? Is anyone there?"

There was no answer. He ran up the steps. Tony Paz's wife, the miniature woman—Sims was not sure of her name—was pushing a baby carriage toward Riverside Drive. He ran to her. Paz seemed to have some arcane knowledge of the neighborhood, of how to handle crises, disasters.

"Your husband home?" Sims asked, breathlessly.

"No. He's at the fruit store. Something wrong?"

"Oh, just a small thing." His voice shivered. "Some nut jammed something into my keyhole. Can't get in."

Mrs. Paz cocked her head. "Whaaat? What kind of a nut?"

"Kids, probably. Look, could you do me a favor? If my wife comes home, will you tell her what happened, and that I'm getting a locksmith?"

"Sure, sure."

He hurried toward Broadway, sorry that he did not know the woman's name. Endless, convoluted protocol governed his life. Should he have called her Mrs. Paz? Crossing West End Avenue he began to run, as if the locksmith were some beckoning wizard, a wise and resourceful healer. Then he began to worry: what would prevent someone from coming back and ruining the lock again? And again? He felt defenseless.

"The locksmith finally came," Carrie Loomis was telling the Allisters, "and he told Sims someone jammed wooden matchsticks and chewing gum into the keyhole. It took him an hour to replace it."

"Damn kids," Arch Allister said. "I don't trust those two Gilligan brats. I never have."

"You don't know it was them," David said. "Could have been anyone."

The Allisters had invited the Loomises over for after-dinner coffee and drinks. Arch had suggested that they ponder the meaning of the letter from the Dukes Management Company.

They sat around a plexiglass coffee table and sipped espresso. Carrie was vaguely envious of the Allisters' apartment. It was modern, daring, intentionally cold and barren—like Liz Allister's immobile face. The walls were white, but the ceilings were dark blue. The furniture was all metal tubing and inflated plastic. In one corner was a huge abstract welded out of Volkswagen parts.

"Why would anyone want to pick on Sims?" Loomis asked. "He's the most unoffending man I've ever seen."

"Kids, kids," Allister said. He poured brandy into four gleaming glasses.

They do things correctly, Carrie thought. After the baby came, after she had mastered the art of taking care of it, she would try to give their lives more elegance. She'd buy a collage and start an herb garden.

"I did some phoning today," Allister said, "and as usual, not a word from the Phantom Landlord."

"Has anyone ever seen Puttering?" David asked. "Is there a Puttering?"

"Oh, there is," Allister said. "But he keeps a low profile."

"Invisible," Carrie said.

54

"Right," Archie Allister said. "My contacts on the Real Estate Board tell me that the city has been trying to slap a subpoena on E. J. Puttering for five years. Unbelievable, isn't it? Some violations of the building code that resulted in injuries to tenants. Six years ago. They can never catch him. Our esteemed landlord lives on this walled estate in Scarsdale, or White Plains, and he never stays put when he comes to New York. Works out of a rented car so nobody can trace."

"He sounds insane," David said.

"Like a fox with a Ph.D." Allister shook his head. "Boy, he is something. And rich? My friend says he's one of the biggest owners in New York, but no one can figure how much he owns because he works through dummy corporations, fronts, relatives, what-not."

"Where does Rudy Dukes come in?" Carrie asked.

"Oh, there is a Rudy Dukes. And he has an office and a secretary. I called today. She said he'd call back but he never did."

David nodded. "I know there's a Dukes. I saw him the other day in his big white car. Rides around with a dog sitting next to him."

Allister cradled his brandy, then sipped it slowly, with a connoisseur's sensual touch. "In a way, you can't blame him. You know what it is to manage buildings around here? A lot of the rent collectors carry guns. You never know when one of those tenants will jump you."

"Did they say anything about the house next door?" Carrie asked. "You know, that poor crippled man is still in there, sitting in the ruins."

"Didn't occur to me to ask," Allister replied. "That dump really doesn't concern us. I know what he's after there—renovation, rent increases, a better element. Landlord's got to make a profit."

David frowned. "Wait a minute. There's a man living in there, and they're knocking the walls down around him?"

"He's some insane old Polack," Allister said. "You know,

sweetie." He looked at Liz. "That old guy in the wheelchair, who was always talking to himself. Scared you stiff one day."

Liz Allister arched her neck—a Modigliani column—and remained silent. It occurred to Carrie, with a twinge of envy, that women as beautiful as Liz did not have to talk, to contribute. It was unfair.

"Puttering is trying to upgrade the whole block," Allister said. "That's my guess. In the long run it will be good for us. Let him convert 500 to luxury apartments. He's probably going to do the same to 498. And if you ask me, if our rents didn't go up too sharply, I wouldn't mind seeing him clean that noisy mob of merengue dancers off the first floor. And that car washer in 1A."

"They don't bother me," Carrie said. "In fact they're pretty polite, the Escobars and the Fuenteses."

"You couldn't find a nicer guy than Tony Paz," David added.

"Hey, hey, no prejudice here," Allister said quickly. "I'm talking economics."

"But why should we want that?" David said. "Our rents would go up. These are sensational apartments, let's face it. And they're bargains."

"If you can stand the people underneath you," Liz Allister intoned. Her voice was low, fluty.

"I must say," Carrie said, after an embarrassed pause, "I wish I knew some of them better. Mr. Schlossmann and his daughter are scholars. One of these days I'm going to get up the gumption to ask the Simses over for dinner—"

"Be that as it may," Allister said, "the question before the house is, What does Dukes Management mean to us?"

David admired his direct way of handling discussion. Whatever he did on Wall Street, he surely did it efficiently. "What does it mean?" he asked.

"It can't be *all* bad," Allister said. "I asked some of my contacts and I have a feeling that Dukes is more than a manager. He may be what they call a net lessee. He's subleasing the building by paying Puttering a lump sum, and making whatever profit he can."

"How can that be bad for us?" asked Carrie.

"He may be willing to make improvements, fix up the halls, and throw out the marginal tenants. Of course we'd have a small increase in rents, but it could be worth it."

"How can Dukes make any money on a deal like this?" David asked. "And why does he want to assume all those headaches for a small profit?"

Allister scratched his chin and thought. "Dukes is a small operator. He can handle a bundle of these for several landlords and earn enough to make it profitable."

Carrie was looking uncomfortable. The baby kicked at her, and she felt the need to spit. She excused herself, carried her portable cuspidor to the hallway, and returned.

"I keep thinking of those men wrecking the building next door," she said, "and driving those Puerto Rican families into the street. What's to stop him from doing it here?"

"Lots of things," Allister said.

"Such as?" asked David.

"The Rent Administration. The City watches these things. We all pay our rent. We all have leases. He can't pull a stunt like that on us. Or any tenant who pays his rent and has a lease. Suppose he wants to renovate? He's got to file papers. He's got to get our agreement. When you get right down to it, this is a darn good building, with reliable people. He wouldn't dare try it, if he's got any brains."

Carrie shook her head. "I wonder if he isn't trying it already," she said.

"But he's just taken over," David said.

Carrie told them about the incident when she had called on the decorator, Ron Lobello—the obscene phone call from some whispering voice, ordering them to move out.

"Means nothing," Allister said. "Fags are fair game for dirty phone calls."

"And what happened to Horton Sims' keyhole?" David asked.

"Someone's got it in for him," Allister said. "Isn't he a teacher?

And his wife? School kids are little nasties. They'll think up all sorts of ratty things to get even with a teacher."

For a moment Carrie was tempted to mention her meeting with the superintendent. She had not told David about the man exposing himself to her. The incident had frightened her more than she would admit, and she had decided that if she ignored it, it would vanish. Moreover, it did not seem to bear on their conversation. If Dukes wanted to get people out, weren't there legal ways of doing it? Why resort to psychotics who showed their genitals to pregnant women?

"They got the people next door by not collecting rents for several months," David said, "then hitting them with a big bill."

"Yeah," Allister said. "Landlords do that when they have no alternative. They want to make repairs, but these people won't move. It's tough, but you can't blame them."

"Who?" Carrie asked.

"The landlords. I'm not sticking up for them, but they're in business also."

David shook his head. "I don't know. Something's out of whack. Just to toss people into the street—"

"Heck of a thing to be poor in this city," Allister said.

David studied the liquor in the bell-shaped glass: Remy-Martin. All four of them, he realized, were auslanders, invaders from small-town America, who had taken New York City on their own terms. They had interesting jobs, good salaries, education, white skin, spacious apartments with dramatic views of the Hudson, access to supermarkets, foreign movies, museums, the whole rich fabric of the noble city. But around them scurried the natives, the benighted hordes, the wild indigenous tribes, conquered dark people, pagans, struggling to preserve their lives with food stamps and rent subsidies.

Curious, he thought; *none of us are native to the city.* Carrie was from a village called Witherbee in the Adirondack region of New York State; he was an Ohioan; Allister had been born in

San Diego, a naval officer's son who had lived in a half dozen places, and Liz was from Emporia, Virginia. They were bedrock Americans, but more than that, they were the conquerors of New York.

An uneasy conquest, David thought. Colonial status that gave them no real control over the aborigines. The analogy fell apart. Who did rule the barbarian tribes? People like Puttering and Dukes, he supposed. And the police. The Allisters and the Loomises were more like corporate employees sent to a foreign place, living in enclaves, Americanized, unaware of the steaming jungle outside their air-conditioned compound.

". . . don't feel responsible for their problems," Allister was saying. "I'm sympathetic. I understand. But we didn't make the slums. We didn't create prejudice and poverty."

"No, we didn't," David agreed. "But it would be nice if we could do something about it."

"Come off it, Dave," Allister said. "Everyone's powerless these days. You do the best you can. What good would it do if you or I, or the girls, showed up twice a week at the West Side Parish House and told that minister—"

"Father Hasslinger," Carrie said.

"—yeah, that we wanted to help in the narcotics clinic or with the day-care nursery. He doesn't need us."

"I'm not so sure," Carrie protested.

"I am," Allister said. "He told me himself, when I met him at a church thing a few months ago, that those people have got to solve their problems themselves."

Allister filled the brandy glasses again. Carrie covered hers. She was feeling nauseous tremors. The discussion was troubling her.

From the back yard there rose the cries of the night: the Puerto Rican kids in 1B shouting at each other.

"*Mundito! Ven acca!*"

"*Carlos, que hay?*"

"*Mira, mira, Mundito!*"

Through the opened windows wafted the city sounds. The

weather was turning warm. It would get noisier each night—shouts, screams, the crunch of metal as cars collided, the crash of objects hurled down air shafts, and occasionally the unmistakable *crack-crack* of gunfire.

"Is something wrong, angel?" Allister was asking his wife.

Liz's bony face was the color of alabaster—translucent, stone-smooth. The aristocratic head was thrown back. The cords in her starved neck were straining against some invisible torture.

"Oh, oh," Liz moaned. "I just . . . smelled . . . something dreadful . . ."

Like rabbits, their noses began to twitch. Healthy, well-nourished noses, David mused, seeking out a slum stink. Naturally Liz would have sniffed it out first. She was a tender princess, a litmus-paper lady.

"God, yes," David said. "I just got a whiff of it. Seems to be coming out of the yard."

Carrie got up. "Not me. It's the pregnancy. I can't taste anything or smell anything."

"I just got it," Allister said. "Boy, what a stench."

Carrie bolted for the hallway again. "Sorry . . . I did too . . ." She spit into her cuspidor, gagged, and walked back to the room, her eyes tearing.

Allister opened the rear window wider and leaned out. "Mob of kids down there. Probably set off a stink bomb." He turned to the others. "And you tell me it wasn't kids who stuffed crap into Sims' door?"

"*Un perro! Un perro!*"

"*Muerto! Perro muerto!*"

"*Lanza, lanza, Mundito!*"

"They're tossing something around," Allister said. "Hey! You kids! Cut it out! Stop that noise!"

David joined him. He tried some of his dimly recalled high school Spanish. "Hey, *niños! Que pasa? Que tienes?*"

There were four or five boys in the yard. The object they had been throwing was on the pavement now—an animal of some kind. A huge rat?

"Dog, mister," one of the boys shouted. "Dead dog."

"Get rid of it," David called. "It stinks."

"What's the idea?" Allister shouted. "You're stinking up the whole place with that thing."

Carrie peered into the yard: a small circle in hell, boys dancing around a dead dog. Liz excused herself. Handkerchief pressed to her violated nose, she had to lie down, away from the offensive odor.

"Hey, mister," a man shouted. "My kids no bring here. That guy Bolo did it."

It was one of the men who lived in 1B—Fuentes or Escobar. He was a round fat man, tubbed beneath a yellow straw hat with a tiny brim.

"Bolo?" David asked.

"Yeah. That guy who work for Dukes. One of my kids see him stick *el perro* in the airshaft next to our apartment. That lousy *grifo*, he do it. The kids get it out with fishin' poles."

"Why? What did he do that for?"

"You know Bolo?" the man shouted.

"No."

"If you know him, you know why. He is big sonofabitch, tha's why."

"Okay, we believe you," Allister said. "Just throw the thing out. Far away. Go dump it in the river."

A window opened violently below. Hilda Schlossmann's braided head darted out. "Quiet, please. No noise. People must sleep here. There is an ill person here. *El profesor esta muy malo, per favor, non gritar!*" The window slammed shut.

"*Hijo, lleva el perro,*" the man said.

One boy threw the corpse at another. They shrieked. A third kid picked up the dog and began to whirl it around by its tail. The stench came to them in widening waves. The Puerto Ricans were inured, it seemed to David, to the misery. Or did they just behave that way, making the best of a bad deal?

The man in the straw hat smacked the boy twirling the dog.

61

Allister was furious. "Hey! Get rid of that damn thing, or must I call the cops?"

"Okay, okay, *señor*," the man said placatingly.

Another widow opened below. The Gilligan boys, awakened by the noise, were peering down. "Boy, what a stink," one of them said. "You see what Mundito done, Markie? He picked it up with his bare hands."

"Yeah. He'll stink for a week."

Amid much cheering, the Puerto Rican kids carried the dog off.

"How can they live like that?" Allister asked.

Carrie was annoyed with him. "They didn't put the dog in the airshaft. It was that Bolo, whoever he is."

"I don't believe there is anyone named Bolo," Allister said. "Those kids invented him."

"There is," Loomis protested. "Skinny guy with kinky hair. He's a sort of chauffeur."

"He's *another* Puerto Rican," Allister said, stretching. "These people are always after one another. Insults, taunts, challenges. They got something called *pundonor*. Like face with orientals. One of those tenants got smart with the guy and he paid them back with a dead mutt."

They got up to leave. "I hope you're right," David said.

Once Werner Schlossmann had read a feature story in the *Times* about a medical rarity, an Englishman who had not slept for seven years. Doctors were giving him all sorts of tests—metabolic measurements, studies of his heart, his brain. Schlossmann laughed to himself. He, Werner Schlossmann, had not slept (he was certain of it) since March 7, 1941. Should he have written a letter to the *Times*?

To the Editor:

Your account of a Mr. Henry Dunne in Worcester, England, who claims not to have slept for seven years interests me. I have not slept for over thirty years. I do not

62

even doze. Often my eyes are not closed. My mind is active and I sometimes write paragraphs while lying in bed. . . .

No one would be interested. Besides, it would involve getting into the events that started him on his sleepless life. Who cared about such stories any more? They were in Zurich, he and Hilda, visiting the Nunlister Hospital for children. Hilda was seven, a sickly, angular child, given to wheezing coughs, ridden with a persistent low-grade fever. The physicians in Berlin had advised a checkup at the Swiss clinic. On the last morning he was packing in the hotel room. He could remember Hilda, in a green flowered dress, sulking at the window, because they could not visit the amusement park. It was a miracle they had allowed him out of the country, with the war on. But Schlossmann was well connected with the conservative academicians at the *Historische Institut*. Favors could occasionally be granted, if you knew whom to see, how to phrase the request.

Then had come the phone call from Von Diemen, his colleague. "Schlossmann, do not come back," the old man whispered. "Stay in Switzerland. You are lucky. Stay with your daughter. Your wife and your sons were arrested today and are being sent to Theresienstadt. I cannot speak any longer."

"Impossible," Schlossmann said. "Our papers are in order. We have special clearances—" But Von Diemen had hung up.

He went back to Germany. A week later he and Hilda were arrested. Letters, contacts, Christian friends who could reach Goebbels, Speer. Nothing mattered any more. ("I assure you Schlossmann is a true German patriot, our greatest expert on the history of German mercantile systems in the Middle Ages and Renaissance. . . .")

The wanderings began. Terezin, Buchenwald, Gross-Rosen, Sobiber. He searched for his wife Babette and the boys, Karlheinz and Moritz, and he never found them. A word here . . . Babette had worked in this kitchen, in that barracks . . . and then silence.

Terezin was the "good" concentration camp—schools, libraries, plays, orchestra, a Potemkin Village to deceive the neutrals and the International Red Cross. When he had registered there, surrendering his scuffed valise, a huge Jewish truck driver from Prague, standing next to him, whispered: "Hey, Professor, stick your eyeglasses in your pocket, and don't admit you know anything. Work on the farm or the factory, not the school. These bastards hate anyone with an education." He had done so, and he had survived—planting potatoes, weeding gardens, shoveling dung. There was a joke there somewhere, but Schlossmann had never formulated it.

Gone, gone. Schlossmann was staring at the ceiling of the bedroom. In the room next door, he heard Hilda's labored breathing. Still a sick girl, still suffering from the ordeal of the camps. But Babette and the boys had vanished into the fiery furnace. Too late, too late. How much fear can we sustain? How much sorrow? How much hate? There are limits, Schlossmann told himself, turning on the hard mattress. The Nazis were the supreme psychologists of the modern age.

They not only understood their victims, they understood themselves. As for those they arrested, tortured, and murdered, the thesis was simple: human bodies are malleable, human nervous system are fragile. For their own part, the Germans realized that acts of evil can be justified only by greater acts of evil. Murder three men, and you must then murder thirty to convince yourself that what you did was morally correct. And so they prevailed.

Sachsenhausen: a United States Army camp, and Schlossmann, starved, stooped, in ill-fitting clothing given him by a British Red Cross team in Buchenwald, where he had been released. And in Sachsenhausen, he found Hilda, head shaved, eyes staring, whimpering, a child given to sudden starts and jerks, hiding in corners, wetting her bed, wailing over nothing.

When he tried to embrace her, she had punched him, bitten his hand.

All the strength that was left to Schlossmann, who was then in his late thirties but had always been frail, subject to colds and aches, he now dedicated to the child. And she survived, growing tall, angular, fiercely intelligent, wary of strangers. They came to America, and she graduated with honors from Columbia, wrote learned papers on language origins, became a teacher, an associate professor.

But Schlossmann had little left to sustain himself. What he had given her was nothing less than his blood and brain. A pensioner, he was reduced to piddling jobs—translations, editing scholarly manuscripts for small publishers, fly-by-night agents.

But he was alive. He breathed the air. He could eat a buttered roll, stroll down Broadway, buy a newspaper, joke with a neighbor. He always smiled and tipped his hat, said thank you, held doors open for women, and waited his turn in the food stores. These small courtesies were signs of gratitude for being alive. (But the sleepless nights . . . Babette and the boys . . . could he have saved them if he had not been in Zurich when they were arrested? Was his absence the cause of their death? Of course not, he assured himself. . . .)

"But, Schlossmann," his friend at the publishing house asked him, "in this lying-awake state, thirty years of it, do you dream?"

"No dreams. My body rests. My mind works. I am like a quadruple amputee, paralyzed, with an alert mind. It is amazing the original ideas I nurture in this state. Unfortunately, when I put them to paper in the morning, I find that Kant, or Buber, or Barth has already thought of them."

Eyes fixed on a crack on the ceiling—it resembled the curve of the Weser River as it passes through Bremen, Verden and Nienburg—Schlossmann was pondering a new thesis. Could the murder of Jews have been *central* to Nazi planning, more important to them than foreign policy, conquest, the economy? Witness the end of the war. *Götterdämmerung*, Eichmann commandeering trains to transport Jews to Auschwitz, when the wagons were needed to send food and ammunition to the front . . .

The telephone rang—relentless, loud. The phosphorescent glow of the clock on the night table read 3:15. With no fumbling, no uncertainty, Schlossmann reached for the phone. It was almost the gesture of a man awaiting a call.

"Yes?" he asked politely.

"Schlossmann?" The voice was muffled.

"This is Mr. Schlossmann."

"They should have gassed you also."

"Ah, ah. I see. Yes, some people might feel that way."

"You hear what I said, you old bum?"

"Most certainly. Is that all?"

The caller paused. Schlossmann's casual reaction appeared to have impeded him. *I have long ago used up my capacity for outrage, for fear,* he seemed to be saying.

"You're lucky you're alive, Schlossmann."

"I am not so sure."

The caller paused. Schlossmann's unoffended response had derailed his assault. "Schlossmann," the hoarse voice said, "I'm doing you a favor. Move out. There's gonna be trouble. Get out while you can, Schlossmann."

"But where shall I go? There are no more places to hide, my friend."

"Then drop dead."

The line was silent. The impersonal humming frustrated Schlossmann. He wanted to pursue the conversation. At times he felt the need to be threatened, punished. He lived. Babette and his sons were dead. He had no rights, no privileges.

"Papa, stop talking to yourself," Hilda called groggily from the adjacent bedroom. A hard, sound sleeper, his daughter. Her long, bony body nailed itself to the bed, and she closed out the world.

"I was merely looking for something."

"Is anything bothering you?"

"Nothing, my dear. I must have been dreaming. Imagine, the first time in years."

"What if there is no such person as Rudy Dukes?" Loomis asked his wife. He was on his knees, under his high drafting table, replacing the electrical outlet. It was the kind of work he hated, but the new superintendent refused to make an appearance.

"I can believe it," Carrie said, helping him out.

Loomis assembled his tools—he had borrowed them from Tony Paz, who seemed to have an unlimited supply of ancient hammers, pliers, wrenches, junk salvaged from trash cans and vacant lots.

"I'll get hold of that super and pay him off," David said. "I hate starting off like that, but what can we do? Think of what the winter will be like, depending on him for heat."

Carrie said nothing. She had made it a point to avoid the basement room. Not a notably adventurous woman, she had kept the secret to herself. David would have demanded a confrontation, a complaint to the police. It was easier not to talk about some things.

Every time Horton Sims locked the door to his apartment, he looked at the new cylinder with a faint shudder, an awareness of its vulnerability. It had cost him fifteen dollars to replace the ruined one. "Full of gook," the locksmith said. "Matchsticks and choon-gum. Smells like spearmint."

Sims minimized the incident to Leora. "I suppose some kid did it," he said airily. And he saw the consternation in her face, so he hid his own. But they were both thinking the same thing: why not again? And again? What was to stop them from jamming up their lock every day, ruining their lives, locking them from their home forever?

The more Sims thought of it, the more he connected the incident with the new management. He tried to reach Rudy

Dukes and failed. Once, he collared the new super and told him about it.

"Cain't help you, man," the super whined. "Cain't keep kids from runnin' around. Junkies. Winos." He leered at Sims. "You know, man."

"The front door should be kept locked."

"It is, man. But junkies and bums hang around till it gets buzzed open. Or one of you people leave it open and anybody can walk in."

"I'd appreciate your keeping an eye on the place. I can't spend the rest of my life paying locksmiths to let me in. By the way, what's your name?"

The bald-head smiled unevenly. His teeth were rotten. "O'Gara." Then he looked up from his mopping. "Hey, Mr. Sims. Gimme ten bucks."

For a moment Horton Sims found himself reaching for his wallet. A reflex: the business of the lock had made him uneasy, too ready to cry for help. "I will not," he said. "I'm going to get some action from Dukes."

Barri Dane was buying apples and pears at the fruit store on Broadway where Tony Paz worked.

"Listen, Tony," he asked him. "How's that friend of yours? With the white car? And the shotgun?"

Tony weighed the red Delicious apples, noted the figure on the brown bag, and stuck the grease pencil behind his ear. "I tole you. Tha's our manager. Rudy Dukes."

"He's crazy," Dane said.

"He ain't crazy. Rudy know what he do." His back stiffened, his eyes glinted. "I know him from way back. I once work for him."

"Really?" Dane, a good actor, was quick to gauge people's emotions. Tony Paz had ham in him, a natural tendency to dramatize. When he spoke of his past association with Dukes it was done with a hint of secret knowledge, dark deeds.

"Yeah. When he clean out the St. Charles Hotel. Other jobs."

"What kind of a man is that to be managing buildings?" Dane asked. "I mean, pointing guns at people?"

"Nah, nah. Rudy mean that gun for me, see? Only for me. He's after me. I think he get our building just to break me." Tony made change for Dane, and turned to wait on an elderly woman. "But he don't break me. No, he don't scare Tony Paz."

Cuckoo, Dane thought. He knew a lot of Puerto Ricans, and he liked them. But they fantasized, invented. Still, he had seen the shotgun and the big car, and he had heard the voice of the man in the car.

This was the way Rudy Dukes wanted it. A hint here, a move there. Let them find out slowly. He never gave the game away at once. It was better to let them work the thing out in their heads. Each move was calculated. Each victim was analyzed, and the best approach was used. Shlep and Bolo, those two halfwits, were not allowed to make the decisions. Like Mafia "button men," they took orders. Dukes studied the lists of tenants and told them what to do—whom to call, what to say.

Thus far, he was pleased with jamming up Horton Sims' keyhole. That would teach that smart boogie. They scared easy. Especially the educated ones, the teachers and mailmen and city employees. Give them an apartment and a job, and they spent the rest of their lives worrying if it would be taken away from them. The move against Sims (Bolo had done the job) was perfection itself. Cheap, effortless, untraceable, costing the tenant hard cash, and with the persistent threat that it could be done again—until he got the message.

In the first week of his stewardship, each tenant had been alerted in some way. The picture was changing at 502 West 84th Street. Something was in the works. No more McIsaac. No more Puttering. But Dukes was also a psychologist. He knew that a sustained assault was bad strategy. They caught on, they organized. All you needed was one or two smart lawyers, WASP or Jew wiseguys, to stiffen their backs.

"Lay off for a while," he told Shlep and Bolo, in his office on

West 74th Street. "No more phone calls. No more crap in that spade's keyhole. Tell O'Gara to start cleaning the lobby. And watch it with them people on the top floor. Allister. Loomis. I know tenants, and they ain't the kind who scare."

"When you gonna tell 'em they got to get out?" Shlep asked. He was an old-timer in the business. He had trained Rudy years ago, given him his first job. "I mean, like a notification, not the phone calls."

"That can wait," Dukes said. "Let 'em think about it. It helps if they ain't sure."

For a few days, all was placid at 502 West 84th Street. The weather was sublime—clear, warm spring days. A steady breeze from the Hudson blew away the accumulated filth of winter. Miraculously, one could breathe the air, walk the streets.

In the evening, the people who lived in 1B (were there ten of them? fifteen?) would gather on the stoop to listen to a quavering guitar and bongos and to dance. Fuentes, the fat man, the straw hat, played the guitar badly, but with spirit. Escobar, the other man of the house—they were distant cousins, from the same suburb of Santurce—rapped the bongos with somewhat more talent. At first they would merely sing—sad songs of doomed love, faithless women, broken hearts. Then, as the evening wore on, the children would dance. They favored the merengue. The men played, and the women, stout, mournful, in plain cotton dresses, sat to one side and listened.

Oi, Carolina, la miseria . . .

On Saturday nights, most of the other tenants were out. Those who remained in the building did not object to the stoop parties. The Escobars and the Fuentes were gentle people. They never played much beyond eleven o'clock, and the music was soothing.

Dane and Lobello looked out and called to the party. *"La Golondrina,"* Barri requested. *"Por favor."*

"Oh, you embarrass me," Lobello said. *"Golondrina,* God.

What corn. These people have their own songs, not that Mexican crap."

A ten-year-old girl in a green satin skirt was dancing with a boy of eleven. It was Mundito, one of the kids who had discovered the dead dog a few days ago.

"They say they start making love when they're six," Dane said. "It's not to be believed."

"Jealous?" Lobello mocked.

Leora Sims heard the music and nodded her head in time to the steady beat. Horton, reading his *Harper's*, watched her and could not resist a taunt. "They sure got that inborn sense of rhythm, hey, Leora?"

"Yeah man," she agreed, nodding her Afro vigorously. "But not like us darkies."

From his ground-floor window, Tony Paz looked at the Puerto Ricans with a solemn gaze. Public displays by his Latin brothers did not impress him. He was an American, a one-hundred-per-cent American, born at Columbus Avenue and 88th Street. So what if his family took him back to Arecibo when he was four, and he spent the next four years there? "I don' like dancin' and I don' like that kind of stuff," he complained to Lucy. She, an Italian-American, loved Latin music, and was always asking to be taken to La Paella or the Paramount.

"Hey, Antonio!" Escobar called. *"Ven' acca. Baila.* Dance."

"I don' dance," Tony said. He would not dance and he would not speak Spanish.

Lucy Paz watched the people on the sidewalk, swaying her tiny behind to the beat.

"Hey, you stop that," Tony said.

"I can dance if I want."

"In the back room, so no one sees."

"Boy, what a snob," she said. "They're your own people, Tony. Why do you have to be such a snob?"

Tony shrugged. He knew there was something different about him. Change, improvement, status—he strove for all these.

"Tha's a disgrace," he said to Lucy, "the way that little kid dances with her skirt all the way up."

"Oh, brother, I've heard everything. Rosita is ten years old."

Crazy, he thought, how Lucy was more *Borinquen* than he was, more of an islander. She might have come over on the *Marine Tiger* with a mob from San Juan, instead of being an Italian girl from the Bronx. Lucy liked rice and peas, cuchifritos, and fried plantains. Tony, with his ravaged gut, had to avert his head from the spicy food and nibble Lorna Doones.

"He come back," Tony said.

Lucy looked in the direction her husband was staring. "Oh, God, it's Dukes. Now don't start anything."

Shlep was driving the Continental. With a wild turn, he parked it next to a fire hydrant. Like footmen, he and Bolo got out of the front seat. Each carried a six-pack of canned beer. They moved sedately, craning necks, scratching crotches.

Shlep and Bolo distributed the beer to the men on the stoop.

"*Ai, amigo Bolo!*" Fuentes cried.

"*Gracias, padrón!*"

Suckers, suckers, Tony thought. Yesterday Bolo had thrown a dead dog in their airshaft, today he gave them beer. Smile one day, kick the next.

Rudy got out of the back seat. The dog began to whimper. It did not want to leave the golden interior of the car, but cringed against the seat.

"Come on, Angel, come on," Dukes pleaded. The dog made worried noises. Dukes yanked the chain leash. The animal slithered across the leather, then stumbled into the street, sniffing the air, its flat muzzle twitching.

"*Carai*, what a dog," the guitar player said.

It was a strange-looking beast—short-haired, buff-yellow, with thick chest and head. The sooty muzzle was wrinkled and speckled with gray, and the drooping eyes were red-rimmed. There was a hint of irrational violence in the animal—a dog that could not be trusted.

"There he is," Dane said to Lobello. "That's the fellow who pointed the gun at us."

"He's a squirt."

They studied Dukes as he crossed the street, and they were silent. Outsiders, they were good at assessing potential enemies. Dukes made them uneasy.

"He may be a squirt, doll, but he's a tough monkey," Barri said. "Dig that walk."

Dukes rolled lightly on small feet. He was not much more than five feet, seven inches, but his chest was thick, and his neck was like a heavyweight's. Waistless, hipless, his legs were spindly, perhaps too meager to support the muscled torso, sheathed in a powder-blue turtleneck sweater and a navy blazer. Daintily, his crocodile-shod feet stepped around dog droppings and sardine cans.

"Tony Paz said he was a fighter," Barri said. "Look at the way he moves."

"Oh, mother," Lobello moaned. "Don't get any ideas."

Leora Sims had also seen Dukes get out of the car and cross the street. "Hey, Sims," she called to her husband. "Dig the manager. Tough dude. How about them crazy shoes?"

Sims, scholarly behind horn-rimmed glasses, studied Rudy, who had stopped in front of the stoop and was applauding in time to the music. "Got the look of a JD," Sims said sorrowfully. "The kind ends up in juvenile court but never gets sentenced."

Dukes, tapping his feet in time to the bongos—the guitar player had stopped to sip his beer—rotated his head. Eyes shut in musical communion, his face tilted upward. The tenants saw a pale face—broad forehead, plug ears, a squashed nose, a cleft chin. A shock of chestnut-brown hair fell over his forehead and grew long in the back. Oddly, the sideburns had been cut short an inch below the ears. It was as if Dukes had not been able to decide whether he were Mod or hardhat.

"Hey, up there," he called to the Simses, and Dane and Lobello. "Hey, people." His narrow eyes opened wide—pale amber inside the slits. "Come on down. Free beer from Rudy Dukes."

"Thanks a lot, but no thanks," Barri Dane called.

"Afraid of the shotgun?" Dukes mocked.

"You know what you can do with it."

Dukes put a hand on his hip. With the other hand, he stroked an eyebrow. "Aren't we rough? Aren't we mean?"

Dane, inured to insult, said nothing. "A beauty, isn't he?" he whispered to Lobello.

"Not my type. I don't like prizefighters. And his pants are too tight."

Fuentes resumed strumming the guitar, a somber tune. The children did not dance. Dukes seemed to have frightened them, to have made them self-conscious.

"What's a matter?" Dukes asked. He ripped open a beer can and drank. "No dance? No *baila?* Don't be scared. I'm your buddy. Rudy Dukes, *panin.*"

"*Ai*, Rudy," Fuentes said. "You *panin.*"

"You bet, Rudy," Escobar, the bongo player, agreed. "*Panin.*" He tossed the aluminum sliver from the top of the beer can into the street.

"*Panin,*" Dukes said firmly. "But no *puerco.* What the hell do you mean throwin' junk in front of my building? This isn't lousy San Juan. Pick it up."

Dukes' voice was harsh, but he was grinning. Escobar, swaying on unsteady feet, got up, retrieved the top of the can, and put it in a trash barrel. "Sorry, Rudy. Keep clean."

"Damn right, keep it clean. Come on, let's have a fast number, somethin' we can dance to. You PRs love to dance, don't ya?"

Dukes looked at the women. They were sullen, unmoved. They were old-fashioned islanders, suspicious of landlords, loud *Americanos.*

"Scared of me?" Dukes asked. He spoke to Bolo. "Bolo, tell 'em who I am. Tell 'em not be scared."

Bolo spoke in Spanish to the group. The men nodded. They were impressed.

"You millaweight?" Fuentes asked.

"Welterweight," Rudy said. "You believe I went ten rounds with Rodriguez?"

"I believe," Fuentes said. "If I don' you knock me on my *fundillo*."

Shlep Sharmak pointed to the Continental. "You don't believe him, look at the license. What's 147? Welterweight. Champ of the Marine Corps. Don't futz with him."

Mundito ran over and grabbed Dukes' forearm. Rudy lifted him off the ground. "Jesus, he strong," the boy said. "Papa, look what he do to me."

Fuentes forced some quavering chords from the guitar. Escobar took up a faster beat on the bongos. Dukes looked at the women.

"Dance? Come on, dance." He walked up to Fuentes' wife—a shapeless woman with frizzy red-brown hair, a pitted face. He took her arm.

"No. I no good dancer." She pulled away.

Bolo walked up to his boss, whispered in his ear, and nodded at the Pazes' window. Tony had been half hiding behind a curtain, peeking out every now and then.

Dukes, spying him, opened his arms. "Hey, Tonito. *Buenas noches*, squirt."

"To hell wit' you, Rudy Dukes."

The people on the stoop turned to look at Tony. They would never dare talk to him the way Tony did. The music dwindled. Fuentes plunked the guitar a few times as if to signify that the party had ended. There was a final tap-tap of the bongos.

"You see that little guy there?" Dukes said to his audience. "He was once my buddy. Used to drive the car for me."

"He stunk as a chauffeur," Shlep said.

"Nah, nah, Shlep, lay off him," Dukes said. "He was my *panin*, my best buddy."

"I never your buddy, Dukes." Tony's glowing eyes turned to the people on the stoop. "Escobar and Fuentes, you drink this guy's beer one day, he throw you out the next."

Dukes put his finger over the opening in the beer can, shook it a few times, pointed the can at Tony's window. Removing his finger, he shot the beer out in a foamy stream that fell short of Paz.

The Fuenteses and Escobars laughed uneasily. They respected Paz. He was Americanized, had three jobs and an American wife, and he could read and write English. He made calls for them to *el Welfare*, went with them to the District Rent Office, interceded with their garment-district employers. He deserved respect. But Dukes was something else. Dukes was to be feared. With the instincts of the poor, they knew he had power, terrible power.

"Some funny guy, Rudy," Tony said. "I tell you people one thing. He never fight Rodriguez. He once fight some bum named Olmedo and Olmedo knock him out in first round. I read your record in the boxing book. You have six fights and win two."

"You hear him?" Dukes asked. He jerked a thumb toward Tony. "Buck Canel. Big sports announcer. *Que pasa,* Tonito? Why you wanna badmouth your old boss? What you got against me?"

"You no good, Rudy. You come here *suave*, free beer, jokes. But they learn about you. I learn."

"What did you learn, *panin?*"

"I learn you a lousy *cabrón.*"

Fuentes moaned. Everyone stared at Paz as if he were diseased. They knew that it was bad business to use words like that on people like Dukes. Such insults were reserved for other Puerto Ricans.

Lucy Paz appeared at the window. She put her arm inside Tony's. "Don't start nothin', Tony," she pleaded. "Don't talk back to him."

"The missus, huh?" Dukes asked. "How come we were never introduced? You done good since you left me. Wife. Baby. Still slicin' pastrami in the delicatessen, Tony?" He cupped a hand to his mouth and called: *"One corn' beef rye wit' cole slaw! And tell that counterman to keep his dirty thumb out of it!"*

Paz breathed hard. *"Maricón . . . puto,"* he muttered.

Pirouetting, Dukes moved among his audience. "He can call me dirty names all day. *Maricón, puto.* I don't give a damn. You people, you run for the *pistolita.* Get the *Gem* and cut. Not Dukes. I don't have to."

"Yeah, you got to believe him," Shlep said. "He ain't kidding."

"How it was in jail, Rudy?" Tony shouted. "You big *pato?*"

Dukes spun around. "They couldn't hurt me, Tonito. I'm back, ain't I? Bigger than ever." He walked closer to the window, the yellow dog shuffling at his side. "Tony, is your father-in-law letting you into that houseful of guineas in the Bronx? Is he talkin' to spics these days?"

A wild unshaped roar erupted from Tony's mouth—as if he had been jabbed with a hot poker. He burst from Lucy's restraining arm, flew through his house, into the foyer, and exploded out of the front door, scattering the Fuenteses and Escobars, bounding down the stone steps, and facing his tormentor.

"Tony!" Lucy shrieked. "Come back!"

Leora Sims called her husband again. "Hey, there's · going to be trouble down there. Sims, come here."

Sims sighed, put down his magazine and walked to the window. Other people's troubles did not move him.

"That guy Dukes is out for blood," Leora said. "Look at that dog. He'll kill Paz. Do something."

"Unh-unh. Us colored folks better off stayin' out, you dig?"

Dukes did not appear offended. He held one arm out. With the other, he tightened the chain leash. The dog lumbered to its feet, head down, sniffing an aromatic spot on the pavement.

"You stink, Rudy. You think you scare me? You insult me?" Tony's voice shivered and cracked. His spare body was trembling—from his dark hair to his toy shoes.

"Tony! Get away!" Lucy wailed.

He whirled around. "You beat it. This is man's business. Dammit, get away from the window. I handle this."

Lucy's mop of red hair vanished behind a drape. But she did not take her eyes off her husband.

Fuentes picked up his guitar. Escobar got up and drew the women away. *They knew.* Paz was about to be humiliated. It was wrong for women to watch.

"You say one more thing about my wife's family, I kill you," Tony said.

"Okay, okay. What a temper." Dukes patted the dog's flattened skull. It lifted its squashed muzzle and made small tearful noises. "Say hello to Angel, Tony. You like Angel?"

"I ain't scared of no dog. I ain't scared of no dog on two feet."

Bolo and Shlep had gotten up and were standing in back of their boss. It seemed terribly unfair, one-sided.

"I never said you was afraid," Dukes said. "In fact, I wanna give you your old job back. Bolo here is okay, but you know these *grifos.* His English stinks. You speak good. How about it?"

"I never work for you again."

"It's a chance for you. I got a big organization now. I'm operating on the whole West Side. Not just these dumps here. High-rises. I need help."

"Hah!" Tony Paz shouted. "You got some organization! Same as you had when you clean out the St. Charles Hotel?"

"Better. More muscle."

Paz turned to the Puerto Ricans, then directed his head upward, addressing the tenants who were watching—Horton and Leora Sims, and Dane and Lobello. "Hah! You see this guy? He is no buildin' manager. He is a blockbuster. That's all he is. They hire him for, for . . . you know what?"

"Tell 'em, Tony," Dukes said. "What am I?"

"You a blockbuster! That's all you are. Damn blockbuster! They hire you for one dirty job—*throw people out!*"

"Don't no one here believe that, do they?" Dukes asked. "That guy has a wild imagination."

"Yeah, you a blockbuster!" Paz shrieked. "And that's your goon squad. Shlep, Bolo. Who else you gonna hire? Lots of bums work for you, Rudy. Like the guy who got killed in the St. Charles. The Owl. Junkie shoot him dead. They find junkie in the river, hey Rudy? You know about that?"

He rattled on, waving his arms at Dukes, parading in front of him, detailing old events about some incident at the St. Charles Hotel. *Two people dead. Arrests. A trial.*

"I know about you, Rudy," Tony cried. "Don't you try no funny stuff here—"

The dog began to bark. Paz's hysterical shouts had aroused it. It lowered its enormous yellow head and bared its white teeth. The upper lip curled, and it bombarded the air with throaty noises. A ridge of tawny hair bristled on its back. Tony drew back. His face was white, his chest heaved.

"Tony!" Lucy screamed. "Come in! Get away from that dog!"

"Hey, you," Horton Sims shouted. "Keep that mutt on a leash!"

"I not afraid," Tony gasped. "Chicken dog. Chicken like his boss."

"Mastiff," Dukes said. "We use them on squealers. Also on boy hump. I always thought you was boy hump, Tonito."

Tony leaped forward. Dukes let the leash go slack. The dog reared, several inches taller than Paz, its slavering jaws working. With a swift, unhesitant move, Paz protected his body with his forearms, and then hooked both hands under the dog's collar, choking him with the metal links. They danced off, the dog gasping, Paz locking his hands into the folds of fur in the mastiff's neck.

"Jesus, let him go!" Lucy Paz screamed. She raced from the window.

"Ain't no dog!" Tony shouted. "He's a chicken! A chicken like his boss! You hear, Rudy Dukes?"

Dukes yanked at the leash, trying to pull the mastiff away. But Paz was a powerful runt. He moved like a ballroom dancer, stepping in and out of the dog's floundering rear feet, keeping

79

his hands locked into its throat, so that the jaws were pointed upward and could not hurt him.

"I kill this dog," Tony wheezed. "I tear his throat out."

"Stop them!" Lucy shrieked. She burst from the door, raced down the steps past the horrified Puerto Ricans, and leaped on Tony's back.

Impeded, he cursed her. "Get off my back, woman," Tony cried. "I handled this *puto* myself—"

A trio now, the couple and the dog waltzed into the gutter. The beast was like some underworld demon. Its chest heaved, and its thoat, clutched by Tony's hands, gave off whimpering noises.

"That's enough," Dukes said. "If I wanted to let him, he'd tear your stupid head off." With both hands he pulled at the leash. The dog coughed. Rudy pulled again. Aware that he was being given a chance to settle for a draw, Tony released his grip. He and Lucy stumbled backward. The dog fell to the asphalt, but made no attempt to attack again.

"Next time I stick a knife in his guts," Tony taunted.

"Shut up, Tony, shut up," Lucy wept. "You never know when to quit."

Horton Sims had appeared on the top of the stoop during the battle between the dog and Paz. "Mr. Dukes, is this your idea of building management? Siccing that dog on your tenants?"

"Sic him? I saved the punk's life."

Sims adjusted his eyeglasses. He had not wanted to get involved. It was Leora who had sent him down. "You provoked him. We all saw it."

The schoolteacher looked at the Puerto Ricans for support. But Fuentes and Escobar were neutral. Fear and gratitude governed their lives. Dukes had given them beer. He could decide whether they stayed or were thrown out.

"Sims, right?" Dukes asked. "Maybe you'd like to move farther uptown. You oughta be grateful we let you live here."

"I like it here. I have a two-year lease, Mr. Dukes."

Dukes' slitted eyes turned to the Puerto Ricans. "Hear that, *amigos?* The *moyeto* has a lease. He'll find out what Rudy Dukes thinks of his lease."

But they did not laugh. Escobar's wife drew closer to him. Fuentes plunked a guitar string and studied the pavement.

"Come on," Dukes ordered Bolo and Shlep. They followed him to the car.

Sims, walking down a few steps, called out: "We are unsatisfied with the super, Mr. Dukes. We want McIsaac back. There have been too damned many things happening around here. Someone jammed my keyhole the other day."

Emboldened, Sims hurried down the steps and began to cross the street. "The tenants aren't pleased about the way you refuse to answer the phone—"

Dukes, with Shlep behind him, had gotten into the Lincoln. Sims rapped on the window. The mastiff snarled at him. "Dammit, I have a right to talk to you."

The mighty engine roared, the car turned. Sims had to jump aside. The teacher stood in the middle of the street, frustrated, isolated. Bolo, the kinky-haired man, had walked over to the people on the stoop and was talking Spanish. Sims realized it was useless to register complaints with him.

Tony Paz had not entered the house. He wanted to miss nothing. When Bolo had left, Sims walked up to Paz. "What was that fellow saying to them?" he asked.

"Damn *grifo.* He say they got to move out in one week."

"Why?"

"No reason. Rudy want them out."

"But he just bought beer for them," Sims said.

"Free beer today, punch in the mouth tomorrow. He said he don' want no spics in here. This building is for decent people who can pay bigger rent."

Sims sighed. Leora was watching, straining to overhear their conversation. He thought of the brutal way in which the Puerto Ricans next door had been dispossessed. There was still that crippled man living in the ruins. Could people be mistreated that way, with no recourse?

"Can we do something to help them?" Sims asked. It was odd, he thought, the way he suddenly felt compassion for them. Horton Sims was a private person, a loner. He attributed his success, his ease with handling the delinquents in his school, to this marvelous aloofness. Why was he now concerned over the eviction of ten noisy Puerto Ricans whom he barely knew?

"I mean, the Rent Administration, the City," Sims said quietly. "Don't you have contacts at the Poverty Program office? That minister who helps people?"

Paz snorted. "Listen, Mr. Sims. Don't worry about Fuentes and Escobar. They be the first ones Rudy kick out. No money, no lawyer. You better start worryin' about yourself."

"I have a two-year lease."

"You find out."

"He'll need more than beer and threats to get me out. I am a tough *moyeto*."

"I hope you are." Tony saw Lucy gazing at him mournfully from the window. She was holding the baby, patting its fat bottom. Infuriated, he shouted at her. "What you standin' there for, watchin' me? What I need a wife who lookin' over my shoulder every second? You think I am some welfare bum? You get in and stop lookin'."

As he hurried up the steps, Fuentes grabbed his arm. "You no scare, Tony. You *muy toro*."

"*Sí*," Escobar added. He tapped his chest. "Tony—*corazón*."

Paz held his tiny head high. He welcomed the battles that would have to come now that he had challenged Dukes.

Shlep Sharmak put his hand over the telephone. "Rudy," he whispered. "Puttering."

Dukes put down the list of tenants he had been studying—biographies, details of leases—and tapped the new metal desk. His office occupied two large rooms that were part of his nine-room apartment in an old building on West 74th Street. The living quarters at the rear had a temporary, unsettled look. Plastic covers hid the chairs. Crates of unpacked household goods, unrolled rugs, disconnected appliances, littered the floors. It had the look of a place that would never be lived in, a place for which Dukes had bought objects doomed to gather dust. The office suite, however, was newly painted and furnished with new desks, chairs, filing cabinets, lighting fixtures. Almost all the equipment was rented, including the handsome framed prints of old New York scenes.

In the small reception room, at a shiny desk, sat Dukes' secretary, an elderly blond woman named Martha Hallweg. She had been hired from an agency, and knew nothing of Dukes' past or the nature of the Dukes Management Company. In the inner rooms, Rudy sat behind one huge desk, while Shlep Sharmak, in the smaller room, manned another. There was no desk for Bolo, who could barely read or write.

"Puttering," Rudy repeated. "Where is he?"

"Won't talk to me," Shlep replied.

Dukes picked up the phone. His slanted eyes took in the well-furnished room: an executive's room. He did not want Puttering's whispered voice to shake his confidence, so he stared at the refrigerator with its fake-grain finish, the enormous color television set, the expensive stereo with its twin round speakers. Angel, snoring at his feet, his flanks twitching, also reassured him. The mutt had cost him four hundred dollars.

"Dukes?" Puttering gasped.

"Yeah, yeah."

"Please meet me in half an hour."

"Where?"

"Broadway and 80th Street. I will be double-parked in front of the chink restaurant. A dark-blue Ford Galaxie."

Rudy rubbed his chin. Then he rotated the heavy ring on his left hand. Puttering made him irritable. The old man had some secret knowledge, some hidden power.

"You want I should go with you?" Shlep asked.

"Nah. He don't like crowds."

Angel got up on his haunches, lowered his head, and rested it on Dukes' lap. Rudy kneaded the dog's ears. Next time he'd let it tear a few pieces of skin off that madman Paz. He had been pleased to find Tony living in the brownstone, almost as pleased as he was to find Mary Gilligan there. A born mark, a loser, a natural pigeon. You could depend on Paz to snap back and put his skinny fists up. It made it more fun to destroy him.

"Take the mutt with you," Shlep said. He sensed Rudy's discomfort. Puttering seemed to Sharmak to be the only person in the world who had an edge on Dukes.

"He'll crap his pants," Rudy said. "Start coughing so hard he'll bring a lung up."

Dukes put on a double-breasted maroon jacket. It was flared at the sides, two hundred dollars' worth of fitted elegance.

"What do you want I should do about Paz?" Shlep asked. "I ain't sure."

"He's trouble, Rudy. He's crazier than when he worked for us. You see them eyes? He ain't afraid no more since he went bananas. We got to get him out or he'll poison the house."

Dukes nodded. "Bolo can give him a hot foot. I mean, *hot*."

Sharmak's eyes rolled behind the thick lenses. "Maybe we could do it easier."

"Is he still on welfare?" Dukes asked.

"Hell, no. The spic has three jobs. It's that guinea wife. She made a man out of him. He got to prove to his in-laws he's worth something."

Dukes walked to the door. "Wake him up at three this morning. Tell him if he don't move out, he better start worrying about his wife and kid."

Dukes walked uptown on Broadway. He needed time to think about Puttering. No one knew how much the landlord owned. Dukes had once heard a City official say that he was one of the richest property owners in New York. All over town there were old tenements, crumbling apartments, lofts, office buildings, tracts of precious land, attractive "parcels" that old E.J. controlled. Many were not in his name. Many were only

84

partially owned by him. He worked through dummy corporations, answering services, letterheads, relatives, an assortment of lawyers, ranging from lofty old Wall Street firms to neighborhood shysters in flyblown holes.

Puttering himself had no office. He was unlocatable. Dukes knew about the Westchester estate with the Dobermans behind the cyclone fence. But he had never been there. Puttering was said to pay a private cop to stand guard. For six years the City had tried to serve a paper on him and had never succeeded. Wraithlike, he moved through the city in his rented cars—never the same car, rarely the same agency—studying his buildings, avoiding rent officials, making sure that the money kept coming in.

"Old bum," Dukes muttered. He stopped in front of a crumbling welfare hotel to get his shoes shined. A black kid, no more than seven, knelt, snapped his cloth, and began to whistle.

"Cream, mistah?" the kid asked.

"The works. I'll give ya a buck if it's good."

Someday, Dukes thought, it would be a pleasure to smash Puttering's rotten face. Who the hell was he? A shrewd old hobo. He had his. He kept getting more. Dukes would get a piece of it. A big piece. Puttering was smart and knew the rent laws and the way real estate deals were put together—but he had to hire people like Dukes to get the tough jobs done.

He smiled, recalling how Puttering had gotten some bad publicity a few years ago, an incident that had scared him out of the city and into hiding. He had owned a group of middle-class apartment houses in the Bronx. They were rent-controlled, occupied largely by elderly Jewish couples. Puttering realized he could renovate and double the rents if he moved quickly, before the new rent laws took effect.

But to renovate meant emptying the apartments. Puttering hired a super named Dzyzyc, whose first act was to smash the elevator so that the doddering tenants had to walk upstairs. Not content to force them to make the arduous climb, Dzyzyc would stand in the lobby, and as the shaking old people began their ascent, he would shout, "*Get a heart attack! I hope you drop dead!*"

When the tenants found a lawyer and filed complaints, Dzyzyc, on Puttering's orders, cut off the heat and the hot water. Lobby furniture was removed. The ground-floor windows were tinned up. Finally, one old man *did* suffer a coronary after hiking six floors to his apartment. The City finally cracked down on Puttering, but it was too late. Fear swept through the old buildings. The tenants fled. Puttering vanished. They never proved anything, never touched him. Yes, the elevator was broken. It was old and creaky and it was impossible to get it repaired. The manufacturer was out of business.

"I told the truth," Puttering said in an affidavit. "The building was old, rotten, and needed renovation. I was only trying to help these tenants by getting them out of the place for their own health and safety. They would not listen, and a man is dead."

The shoeshine boy snapped his rag. Outside the hotel, two Negro drunks wavered in slow motion, the watery stride of the alky, the junkie. Human garbage. *Dreck.* They were ruining the city. He, Dukes, was a public servant. These people had to be cleaned out, to make the city safe for respectable people. Wasn't he part of it? How could the city progress unless the filth was cleaned up?

A few blocks away they had put up a luxury high-rise on the site of the old St. Charles Hotel. Did anyone in the city realize Rudy Dukes' role in helping create that beautiful tan building, sixteen stories of carpeted elegance? Sleek and rich, the tenants sat in air-conditioned rooms, with hi-fis and color TVs, antique furniture, fancy paintings—Hebes, WASPs, the usual kind who rented those places—and none of them were aware that it was Rudy Dukes who had scraped out the old St. Charles for them.

Ah, the crap he had had to handle. Kids eating the plaster off the walls. Whores in the corridors. Pushers in their expensive suits, and the bleary-eyed junkies, looking for the next fix, unafraid, uncaring, ready to strangle anyone weaker for a dollar.

And two men shot dead one night. A tenant, a hardheaded spade, fighting back when Rudy sent the Owl in to lean on him. "Just muss him up," Rudy said. "Tell him if he ain't out by tomorrow I'll come around personally." The gun had gone off. The tenant died. And his brother came back that night. The Owl, that halfwitted albino Negro whose white face was usually enough to scare the dinges, caught two slugs in the back. *Two dead.* The old hotel emptied in a hurry after that.

"Finish, boss."

"Not a bad shine. I seen better."

"You say you gimme a dollar." The boy said it hatefully, a threat from a seven-year-old.

"What would you do if I give you only a quarter?"

"I git you some day. Git my brother. He cut you up."

"Your brother is a yellow dude. He couldn't cut a pig's behind."

"Mebbe I cut you myse'f when I grow up."

Dukes smiled at the kid. "You talk like that, you ain't gonna grow up." He gave him a dollar. When the small black hand reached for it, Dukes pulled it away, then, laughing, gave it back to the boy.

Spades could be handled. But spics were something else. They were like mercury: changeable, alert, unpredictable, with their sense of honor, their codes, their bragging. You never knew which way they would jump. Like Tony. The night the Owl killed the tenant, and caught the bullets in his back, Tony had been there, shivering at the wheel of the Cadillac, so frightened that when the Owl came down and told him he had just wasted a guy, Tony took off—zoomed the engine, circled Central Park.

Paz would have to go. Like all PRs, he was driven by *machismo,* proving he was all guts. Rudy would never let him live down his old job as errand boy, chauffeur. And Tony would be just as determined to prove that he did not fear him. Dukes laughed as he walked south on Broadway. That was it. That was the key. If he frightened Paz, the rat would run—and the rest of the tenants would follow.

Anyway, he had four months, maybe half a year to do the job. Puttering had assured him of that. The package was not yet complete. Some problem about insurance or the interest rates.

Feeling confident, Dukes decided that he would make an effort to find a place for Mary Gilligan—the least he could do for an old girl friend. But wiseguys like Sims, or those two fairies on the second floor—*out*. No mercy. Dukes hated queens anyway. These two offended him. They did not seem to fear him. For that matter, he had some worries about the couples on the fourth floor—the Loomises and the Allisters. They were the kind who ran to lawyers. In a pinch, he might have to buy them off. It was against his principles. But there would be a bonus from Puttering when the place was empty and ready for the wreckers.

"And I'll get my cut," he said softly.

He cursed Puttering, and Haman, Lord & Fawcett, and all the landowners and developers and real estate agents and lawyers, the smart guys with their Park Avenue and Wall Street addresses. When the crunch came, when noses had to be bloodied, when people had to be scared, who did they come to? To Rudy Dukes, the blockbuster.

Just beyond the Chinese restaurant, he saw the landlord's rented car, the Galaxie, double-parked. In and out of the lobby of the welfare hotel on the corner, black kids chased each other, swatting each other with wooden crates. Well-dressed women ignored them, walked around them.

The doors of the car were locked. Rudy rapped at the window. Puttering looked around, peered past Dukes, and unlocked the right front door. Rudy climbed in.

"You are late, my boy," Puttering whispered.

"I walked."

"Not a good idea. People know you are working for me. People might be watching you, and would follow you. Take a cab next time."

"Hey, Puttering," Dukes said rudely. "Open the goddamn window. That whorehouse cologne you use is suffocating me."

The landlord grinned. His creased face reassembled, trying vainly to work itself into an agreeable expression. He pushed a button, and the window on Dukes' side lowered an inch.

"For a guy as rich as you, you sure use a cheap aftershave."

"Quite the contrary, my boy. Very expensive. My daughter buys it for me. The one who is married to the big heart specialist."

Dukes detested Puttering's references to his successful children. The rich lawyer, the richer manufacturer, the daughter who bought him cologne. It didn't help, Dukes could have told them. The old man had a diet-starved, indecent face, the thick gray hair groomed in loving waves and lush sideburns as if he were a young dude.

"One of these days, Puttering, you could take me to a fancy restaurant," Rudy taunted. "I'd even pay, just to see how you act in public."

"Impossible, my boy. There is no more freedom in America. My phones are tapped. I am trailed by people."

That was it: *cat's urine*. The cologne had an odor of pissed-in hallways, like the buildings he owned. Oh, he was a decrepit old bird. Yet there was something fear-inspiring about him. It was the money. The power. The ease with which he had eluded the law all these years. Secure in his fortress in Westchester County. Someday Dukes would have a few surprises for E. J. Puttering.

"Some new developments, Dukes," the landlord whispered. His lips barely moved and Rudy had to cock an ear to catch the breathy words. Dukes studied him, hating the artful haircomb, the perpetual summer tan on the ravaged face. Who was he kidding? He was in his seventies, at least. An old face, but a hard cunning face. And he had a habit of chewing all the time—on air, it seemed. His lips and his teeth moved and occasionally mysterious crumbs dribbled down his chin. But he never put anything in his mouth. It was as if Puttering were devouring his own dried innards.

"Some new developments, so I thought I would best speak to you personally."

"Somebody refuse a bribe?" Dukes taunted.

"Dukes, why is that necessary? After all I have done for you."

"Oh, you're all heart."

"No need to adopt a sarcastic tone." Puttering coughed into a green silk kerchief, studied it, then resumed. "How is it going, Dukes?"

"Better than I thought."

"They'll all be out?"

"You got to give me at least four months. Those people on the top floor won't scare. And the nigger schoolteacher. In fact, except for the spics they're all gonna give me a battle."

Puttering chewed his invisible cud. "Not good enough, Dukes."

"You told me I had four months."

"So I did."

"You said there wasn't a manager in the city could get the place empty in three months, so you gave me four. With the new rent laws, and the way the leases were written."

"I mentioned these new developments—"

Dukes was uneasy. Puttering was not only a liar, he was infinitely shifty, always thinking months ahead, covering all bets.

"What new developments? Haman, Lord & Fawcett backing out?"

"Not at all. They are more . . . interested . . . than . . . ever." Puttering, when making a point, tended to space his words, avoiding contractions, in the manner of old-time song writers. "This is their first big residential job. I think I told you. West Coast money, part of a conglomerate. They are new in New York."

"So? They found out about me?"

"No, no, my boy. I have made an effort not to tell them. To be frank, Dukes, they would rather not have the slightest idea who is handling the properties."

"If there's trouble, they'll say they didn't even know me. It'll be your ass, Puttering."

"Now, Dukes, listen to me. Far from backing out, they want the timetable moved up. Speed is essential."

"I thought you and them was going to hang on to the parcel. Wait for the values to go up."

"It's changed."

"How much?"

"You got to empty the buildings by end of the month."

"Less than three weeks?" Dukes asked.

"Actually, we want them even before then. I'm giving you a break."

Rudy's square face moved from side to side. "Can't be done."

"Oh, my boy. It must be done."

"Try it yourself, Puttering. Tell that West Coast outfit to get some West Coast blockbuster."

"Dukes, don't start with me. You are under contract. You got an obligation."

Rudy chuckled. Rubbing his knuckles, he mulled over the possibility of working the old man over. Of course he could not. He needed Puttering, perhaps more than the landlord needed him. Ah, someday . . .

"Pretty sharp, aren't you?" Rudy asked. "But maybe you outsmarted yourself. What kinda contract I got? I got a lease. All I did was rent that building from you for six months. Show me where it says I'm supposed to chase tenants out. Where does it say I got to clean the dump out by May 31—or any day?"

Up went Puttering's gray tufted brows. The mouth was pursed. "Dukes, Dukes. Of course it isn't in writing. But you and I have a gentlemen's agreement on what you are supposed to accomplish. The building was to be empty in four months. None of the vacant apartments rented. All I am doing is stepping up the timetable."

"Wanna take me to tenant-landlord court on it?"

"Oh, my boy. Don't play games."

"It ain't any game. I ain't sure I can deliver."

"But you must. A vacated building by May 31. So, it makes your job a little harder. But you are the famous Rudy Dukes. You are the last West Side tough guy, the man who cleaned the bums out of the St. Charles Hotel in three weeks, who emptied the brownstones on West 91st Street in four months. Not a single lawsuit, not a single action against the landlord sustained, no injunctions. An enviable record."

"It's different now. I been in the jug. They know about me."

"My boy, I will back you to the hilt."

Dukes looked out the window of the Galaxie. A prowl car rolled by. Cops. They were no problem. He knew them. They knew him. The Rent Administration was something else. All you needed was one eager kid trying to make a name. Thus far they had been slow to move on harassment cases. There were simply too many to handle.

There were other problems. That nosy minister, Hasslinger, would get into the act, or assign one of those creeps who worked for him, one of those freaks from Columbia or CCNY. And there were the newspapers. They could kill him if some wiseguy like Loomis or Allister went after him.

"What are you perturbed about?" Puttering asked. "I said we will back you. This is an important matter to me, and other influential people. We are not without resources."

"Use them."

"For what we need, only you can do the job."

"Because it's dirty? Illegal? Noses might be broken?"

"Possibly. After all, that would be nothing new for the great Rudy Dukes."

Dukes was not won over. He realized how desperately Puttering needed him. "Why the rush?" he asked.

"A matter of interest rates."

"You better explain. I'm just a dumb hustler."

"You understand more than you let on, dear boy. The principals involved have learned that the prime rate is going up next month, maybe as much as one percent. That will murder them. They can't afford to borrow at that rate. At least not to put up a high-rise with over a hundred units."

Rudy whistled. "Ah, that's it. Luxury apartments, right? Over a hundred bucks a room?"

"I assumed you would guess."

"Demolition."

"Of course. How else can we put up a multimillion-dollar structure? We are lucky that the old buildings on West 83rd are already empty. The parcel is ready. The money is there if we move. This is a marvelous opportunity for us."

"For *you*."

"I'm only assembling it, my boy."

"What's your cut?"

"That is of no importance to you, Dukes. Just get that building vacated. As quickly as possible."

"I'll tell you what is important," Dukes said. "*My* cut."

"There's big money here, my boy."

"I can imagine. Haman, Lord & Fawcett. And them Wall Street lawyers who tell 'em what to do. Not to mention E. J. Puttering, and his shysters."

"You needn't be personal." He leaned over and patted Dukes' iron knee, and the cologne made Rudy sneeze. "I'm just a fellow trying to make a living. I started poor, like you. Wrong side of the tracks. Don't tell me about that Wall Street crowd. They make me feel like dreck."

"It's rotten they make you feel that way," Dukes said. "But maybe you got to understand why."

"What is to understand?"

"That you *are* dreck."

A hard man to insult, Dukes knew. The look of outrage lasted a second on Puttering's actorish face. Then it vanished and he smiled. "You like to kid, right? A great kidder."

"I ain't kidding. Let me explain why you are dreck. You give me three weeks to clean your building out. I could get busted again. Suppose I do it. Suppose I give it to you clean. That land is worth a million and a half, right? You're fronting for big money. They make a bundle. You get your cut. Ten percent?"

"Everyone gets what they are worth in this world," the landlord said wispily. "I run risks. I run a risk merely hiring you."

"What about my risks? I ain't gonna get jugged again, Puttering. If I go down, I'll take people with me."

Coughing convulsed the old man. He buried his face in the handkerchief, emptied his throat, studied the oyster, and tucked the silk cloth into his pocket. "Dukes, that is no way to talk. You will not get into trouble, or get anyone else into trouble. This operation will be clean, quick, and within the law, as we discussed."

"Not in three weeks."

"Ah, but it must be. I have an obligation to the City to see that you behave. I told the parole board I would hire you and vouch for you. Now please oblige me and get those people off my property."

"No deal. I want something in writing."

"Never. That's how people get in trouble. Why do you think the lease is written the way it is? I don't want some lawyer finding out you are getting paid to drive people out. Never."

"There are people in that building who won't scare," Rudy said.

"Think of something that will scare them."

"I want an extra ten grand."

"Impossible."

"Goddamn you."

"Dukes, be realistic. If you want out of our agreement, say so. But think about it. You are a risk. Ever since that business in the St. Charles, people are afraid of you. Suppose you went to high-class persons like Haman, Lord & Fawcett? They would not talk to you. Oh, they are hard people, Dukes, harder than *shleppers* like me. After all . . . two murders . . ."

"I didn't kill no one."

"You armed him, my boy. You were lucky you got off so easy. Anyway, that's history. It is the future that matters, and you will ruin your future with this greedy attitude."

"You should talk. I want a cut."

Puttering coughed again, as if choking on the mysterious crumbs. "I know what you are thinking. Don't run to Haman, Lord & Fawcett. They would make me fire you."

"If I'm so much trouble, why don't you fire me?"

"I like you, my boy."

"I'm the only one you could find to do your dirty work. Puttering, I ain't so sure you're home free. Suppose one of these days I put in an anonymous call to the Rent Administration?"

"I doubt you would do that."

"I ain't afraid of you. I could bust you in little pieces."

"My dear Dukes. I am not afraid of you either. Look, my boy. I promise you a big bonus if you get that building empty by the end of the month."

It was amazing how controlled he was, Dukes thought. A million and a half dollars riding on an empty old building. It dominated Puttering, devoured him, kept him awake at nights, ruined his digestion, brought on fits of coughing.

"How much?"

"A generous one."

"Ten grand."

"Five."

"Not enough, Puttering. If them buildings ain't empty, you're dead. And who has the key? Me. Rudy Dukes."

"You are unreasonable. Dukes, I have promised you a thousand dollars an apartment to get that building empty, and I promise you some properties to manage."

"It's peanuts. I'm gonna have to bribe some of those tenants. I want a guarantee it don't come out of my pocket."

"Within reason—"

"I'll let you know before I pay off. But I want a guaranteed additional ten grand, and a guarantee I get back every cent I pay out." He grinned at the owner. "That includes miscellaneous things. Like kerosene for starting fires."

"Dukes, please. I don't want to hear about it."

"You want an empty building?"

"I'll speak to the principals. About extra money for you. Look, I have to go."

"Yeah. Process server might see you."

Rudy opened the door and started to get out. Puttering grabbed his arm. "Don't hurt anyone, Dukes. No beatings, or fires, or anything that will bring on the police. Subtlety, my boy, subtlety."

"Don't worry, I won't even leave no letters saying you put me up to it."

The landlord did not let go. "You're joking. I almost forgot. The Polack in 500. Get him out right away. He's been in contact with that minister. One of those poverty workers filed a harassment complaint. I'm trying to kill it, but the best thing is for you to get him out."

"In a hurry, ain't you?"

"I don't like this any better than you. But that's progress."

"Yeah, progress." Dukes yanked his arm away. Puttering slammed the door. He started the motor, looked about cautiously, and, satisfied that no one had been watching, drove away.

Disturbed, Dukes decided to walk north and look at the building. Perhaps he would get some new ideas about emptying it. A stroll on Broadway usually gave him confidence. It reminded him of how superior he was to the trash who infested the place. The neighborhood was a challenge. And he delighted in combat. When it got down to cases, he understood fear. He knew any man could be frightened. The trick was to find out what frightened him, and use it.

Squinting through the morning sunlight at the wobbly junkies, the winos, the occasional hooker, the old ladies, the dignified white-haired older people shopping for newspapers and a few oranges, the Puerto Rican women in cheap coats, he realized it was no contest.

As he crossed West 84th Street, he saw Tony Paz on the opposite side of the street, hurrying along in short, nervous steps. Paz was up early. Dukes made it a point to know his tenants' schedules, and he knew Paz worked late at the garage near Columbia. But here he was at 10 A.M., scurrying down Broadway. For a moment he wanted to call after him, buy him a cup of coffee, use the soft sell.

The he saw a tall bulky man in black appear, walking west on West 84th Street, as if coming from Amsterdam Avenue. The man had a pouchy white face and a clumsy gait. It was the minister, that nosy bum Hasslinger. Dukes was wise to every move of Tony's: he knew him from the old days. And the suspicious, sneaky manner in which the little man looked about him (not noticing Rudy, who had dodged behind a parked car) told him that it was a pre-arranged meeting, that Paz, in his scheming way, was going to rat to Hasslinger, to spill his guts to him about the house. *Coffee!* He would have to buy that dirty *pato* something stronger than java, something that would make his ulcers bleed so bad he wouldn't have the strength to squeal to those freaks in the West Side Parish House.

Dukes found he was breathing harder. It had started in prison. Whenever he was tense, he found his lips parting, his chest heaving. There was something about Tony Paz that infuriated him. Rudy had owned him once, sent him for cigarettes, played dirty tricks on him, called him every dirty name in the book. Yet Paz survived, worked, had a wife and a kid, and now he strutted about defying Dukes.

Instead of continuing, Dukes turned and headed back to his office. He'd pry Paz out, like digging a termite out of rotten wood. He'd scare that runt so bad he'd need more than a storefront committee. The conflict excited him. He would get the tenants out with lusty pleasure. He'd get his extra ten thousand from E. J. Puttering. He'd demand an apartment on the top floor of the high-rise. He'd run his company from there, hit it off

with rich Hebes and WASPs, and cut the pie. They'd know
who he was. They'd respect him.

Horton Sims had a recurring dream. He would catch the man
who had packed his keyhole with gum and matchsticks and
kill him. Throttling him, he would discover that it was his Uncle
Nate, a three-time loser, long-time con, dead over six years.
Uncle Nate had been the bad one in the family. As a kid
Horton had always feared him and been fascinated by him.
   "A simple dream, Sims," Leora said. "It's that old black self-
hate. I get spooked like that sometimes. Dream about my
mother begging, something she never did, something nobody in
our family ever did."
   On a warm afternoon, home a half hour early—there had been
a rumble in the cafeteria and school had been closed—Sims
ascended the stairs, and his head rose above the landing, he
saw a dart of lean lavender legs. *Bolo.*
   His heart sprinted. He had a premonition, a sense of a dream
being born, alive, kicking. Sims felt his hand tighten on the
handle of his attaché case. He turned the top step and saw the
lean figure of Dukes' assistant. Bolo was walking toward him. His
cake-eater heels tapped at the hard linoleum of the hallway.
   "Goo' afternoon," Bolo said—and moved to one side, anxious
to keep a space between himself and the tenant.
   "Hold it," Sims said. He moved to one side, blocking Bolo.
With his free hand he grabbed the Puerto Rican's right arm.
   "Hey, leggo."
   Sims looked owlishly into the *grifo's* face. The lips—thicker
than Sims', but a pale rose—moved slightly.
   "You like chewing gum, Mr. Bolo?"
   "Hah? Whah you, crazy? Leggo."
   Sims' hand locked on the wrist. "Juicy fruit? Spearmint?
Blackjack?"
   "I don' know whah you talk about."
   "I warn you not to chew gum around here. You know about
sticking gum into keyholes? Matchsticks?"

Bolo wriggled to release himself. His serpentine body twisted and jerked, and he broke Sims' hold. But the hallway was narrow, and Sims, armed with his leather case, braced his legs across the corridor and dared the slender youth to move.

"Go back to my door," Sims ordered him. "We're going to look at the keyhole."

"You crazy, man."

"I'll kill you. I am not a man to fool with, Bolo. Not when my home and my wife and my child are involved. I spent fifteen dollars replacing the lock because some *maricón*, stuck junk in my keyhole. Move back."

Bolo retreated. Sims reached for his door key, bent low, and probed the opening. The key slipped in easily.

"See? Whah you so angry for, man?"

"Because I think you were going to pull that trick again. Like you did the other day. Someone saw you."

"That's a lie. Who tell you that? Paz is big liar."

"Never mind." With a speed that belied his professorial air, Sims dropped his case, seized Bolo's right arm, and in schoolyard style spun Dukes' man around, yanking the arm up behind his back, bending the reedy body over the bannister.

"*Puto*," Bolo hissed. "Lousy *moyeto*. I cut you next time. Leggo, leggo."

Digging his knee into Bolo's lower spine, Sims began to rifle the pockets. His fingers found what he was looking for—a dozen kitchen matches. He released Bolo.

"You always carry these?" Sims asked. He held the matches up. "You light up with these, Bolo? You use these for your joints?"

"You make mistake, nigger. Next time, look out." He spit at Sims' feet, then walked away, hiking his pants, swiveling his behind.

In the apartment, Sims began to tremble. For at least a minute he could not stop his hands from shaking.

"Don't I know you? Wasn't you in this neighborhood before?"

"I been around," Rudy said.

The gray-haired Jewish lady bustled behind the counter of the Butternut Bakery, hefting her ungainly figure, sighing, picking at crumbs of cheese Danish, babkas, crusty rolls.

"So? What would you like?"

"Is Mary here?"

"Hah! Special people to wait on him!" Mrs. Jaffe wheeled her starched white bulk around and turned to a lumbering black man in mechanic's overalls who was pointing at a pistachio cream cake dotted with chocolate chips.

Mary Gilligan came out of the rear of the store, carrying a tray of hot rolls. Her blond hair was neat, not a hair out of line, and she held her head high. She wore her white uniform like a coronation robe. She had never looked more desirable to Rudy.

"Hi," Rudy said. "A rye bread, sliced very thin, not too many seeds, and not too dark or too light."

"What hand should I pick it up with?" Mary asked impudently.

"Hah!" the proprietress laughed. "Tell him, Mary. She's fresh. Like the pumpernickel."

"I know all about her," Rudy said. "A smart Ukrainian. And there ain't many of them."

Mary Gilligan put the rye bread in the slicing machine. She moved deftly, her figure tall and queenlike, a princess of salt sticks and corn muffins. Dukes watched her with admiration, affection. Even in a Broadway bakery she had class.

"Listen," Dukes said, as she gave him the white bag. "I'll take you out to dinner tonight. What time you finished here?"

"Who's next?" Mary's clear blue eyes searched the store.

An ancient lady, moving with a silver-handled cane, her fragile feet propped in high laced boots, moved toward the counter.

"Go, go, Mary dolling," the owner said. "Look, people get lonely. Your husband won't know. I won't tell."

"You heard Mrs. Jaffe," Dukes said. The heat of the bread spread through the bag, warming Dukes' hands. "Meet you at your place? What time you through here?"

"Late," Mary said. "Too late. I got to take care of the boys."

"You got a nice mohn cake?" the old lady with the cane asked. "A small piece, Mary?"

"Sure, Mrs. Bomeisler."

"Gimme a break," Dukes said, as Mary cut the laquered pastry. "I just wanna help out. You're gonna have to move, kid. I wanna help."

"Anything else?" Mary asked the old woman.

"Hmmm. Maybe two soft rolls for breakfast." The old woman lingered. Mary understood the appalling loneliness of their lives, the fear of going back to the silent apartment. Thank God she had the boys—noisy, alive, comical.

"Hey, mama," Dukes appealed to the bakery owner. "Tell her it'll do her good. You know from experience, right?"

Mrs. Jaffe nodded. "I know plenty. Too much by yourself for a pretty young woman isn't natural."

Dukes laughed, Sex amid the bagels. "Okay," he said to Mary, "so you don't want the kids to see me, right? Meet me at the Jade Inn at nine. Wear a red dress."

Mary did not look at him. She made change for Mrs. Bomeisler.

"Go, go, Mary," Mrs. Jaffe said. "A sociable evening with a nice young man, what harm?"

Tony Paz wondered how he got through the night at the garage. He could not sleep. There was never enough heat in the underground cave, and even in early spring it was damp and drafty. Lucy gave him a silk muffler to wear, but it was no help. Alone, shivering in the gray depths, he was never warm, never comfortable. Inside the glass cubicle, where he kept track of keys, stared at the time clock, and tried to study his English grammar, he thought a great deal about Lucy and the baby. Paz, unlike some of his compatriots, was blessed (or cursed) with visions of the future. The poorest, the most depressed of them did not give a damn about tomorow. Like the Fuenteses and Escobars who drank Rudy Dukes' beer—they lived for the next drink, the next meal, the next sex. Not Tony Paz. There was a tomorrow. There had to be. And his kid Michael would be part of it.

Tony watched two Columbia students—broad-chested, blond Americans—get into a Buick and blast out of the garage, upward into the night and a good time. "Michael can do that," he told himself. "Car, college. I see he gets it."

His trick was from eleven at night until seven in the morning. Sometimes he was able to doze, locking the door to make sure that he wasn't stuck up by some junkie, some bum.

Rapping on the dirty glass pane roused him. Tony was a light sleeper. He could go from deep slumber to wakefulness—the huge eyes staring, the mouth taut—in a fraction of a second.

Shlep Sharmak was standing outside the glass office. The garage was empty. The time clock read 4:25 A.M. What was wrong with Shlep, wandering around at that hour? But Shlep was a tough old rat. Nothing frightened him.

"Shlep? What you want? What you come here for?" Tony opened the door but did not come out.

"Wanna show you something, Ton'."

"What you got, wiseguy? You playin' dirty trick for Rudy? Go kiss Rudy behind, Shlep. Tha's all you good for."

Sharmak held up a brown-paper bag. Beyond him, Tony saw the dimmed headlights of the Lincoln Continental, its snout parked in the entrance to the garage.

"Free wine? You think you buy Tony off with free wine, like you do those Marine Tigers?"

"Nah, nah," Shlep said. "Rudy says you gotta get out. In one week. You got one week to move out, Ton'. You know what Rudy does if guys cross him."

"To hell with him. You too. Beat it."

Shlep pulled the paper bag off. He crumpled the wrapper and held up an empty bottle of Four Roses. Inside was a clear liquid, faintly yellow. In the neck of the bottle was a wad of absorbent cotton and stiff yellow cord. "You know what is this, Paz?"

Tony's body turned rigid. He opened the door and stepped out. "Yeah, I know. You good at that, Shlep."

"Rudy says if you ain't out in a week, you get one of these. Right through the front window. That's no crap. Pointin' the shotgun at you was a joke. But this time it'll be for real. *Pow! Pfffft!* Right in your house."

"You don' do that. You yellow."

"Rudy means it, Ton'. He saw you running to Hasslinger. We always figured you was a canary. You bring Hasslinger and his faggots into this, you stay in that dump, you get this. *Pow! Pfffft!*"

Sharmak laughed, feinted with the bottle as if to throw it, then walked up the incline toward the car.

"You goddamn brave," Tony shouted after him. "Burn up man's house. Woman and kid. You lousy bum. You don't scare me. Never."

He slept no more that night. When the relief man arrived at seven, he found Tony pacing the length of the garage, talking, cursing, jabbing at the air with his scrawny arms. But then, he had always regarded Paz as nuts. Who else could you get to take an overnight job?

"They killed my guts when I was in stir," Dukes said. "I shouldna ordered this hot stuff. All I can eat is the soup."

Mary Gilligan wondered if he was telling the truth. You never knew with Rudy. He lied as easily as other men bought a newspaper. Beneath the formica table, his knees reached for hers, and she drew back. When they were shown to the red-plastic booth, she refused to sit on the same side with him.

"No touch, hunh?" he asked.

"That's right. No touch. No kiss. I'll give you some more soup. Ten-ingredient Soup. Good for weak stomachs."

Dukes let the hot, spicy fumes drift up to his face. "It was them gray pork chops. And gray hamburger. I never knew meat could be gray. I swore when I got out I'd only eat first-class—

Pavillon, Caravelle. I knew those joints. So what happens? I can't hardly look at food."

"Champagne tastes, huh, Rudy?"

"I'm as good as any of them. Let's go to my place when we finish. I always keep a couple or three bottles of champagne on ice."

"Bad stomach, but not for champagne, is that it?" Mary asked.

"I force myself. Come on, be a sport. Wait'll you see the place I'm fixing up."

"Nope. It's bad enough I left the boys tonight."

Dukes studied her serene, well-formed face. There was a precision about it, a firmness and a coolness that intrigued him. She had a short nose, flat cheekbones, a good chin. A Slavic face, an honest face. Dukes knew about women like that—the Ukrainians and Slovaks and Poles he had been brought up with south of Pittsburgh. His own people were Croats. They always thought of themselves as a little more high-class.

"You got all these worries," he said, "and you look prettier than you ever did, Mary."

"Save it, Rudy. There's going to be no replay."

"That slob of a husband. You're too good to him. Got himself a sloppy girl friend. Some career. Running officers' bars. A pimp for the brass. When I did my time I was never no prat boy for officers. They knew Rudy Dukes and they stayed away."

Mary said nothing. She tried a mouthful of the shredded pork and ginger. It must have been loaded with MSG, that stuff the Chinese cooks laced their dishes with. It had flavor all right, but immediately she began to sweat, to feel a vague pain in her left breast.

"When's he comin' back?" Dukes asked.

"I don't know. He doesn't write much."

"And you stick up for that dude?"

"He was good to the boys. He sends them money. Rudy, don't push me, don't make me have to fight you all the time. You shouldn't of called me."

"You're my girl."

104

"No. I never was."

"My Mary. Mary Waslyk. I'm going bananas thinking of how we were together."

"Forget about it. Let's go."

Dukes made it a point never to reveal himself, never to tip his mitt, particularly when he wanted something badly. He cultivated indifference. When the time came to get what he wanted, he used force, guile, speed. But he was helpless in front of Mary. It had been almost a year since he had known her body, but he could recall each curve, each warm surface, each rounded hill of flesh. She was perfect. A strong, tall woman, small-breasted, narrow-waisted, but with full thighs, superbly molded legs. She was ageless, he realized. At sixty, she would be as well-formed as she was in her early thirties. It was this hardiness, this durability, that fascinated him. He was not a subtle man, but he understood that in a world where everything changes, crumbles, rots, Mary Gilligan was damned near eternal.

"I got to sleep with you, Mary."

"No, Rudy. It wasn't as good as you say."

"I was never happier."

"*You* were never happier. I got Frank to think of. He's a rat, but he's my husband. He'll be back. He knew I fooled around with you. There's no secrets around here. I don't want the boys thinking their mother is a tramp."

Dukes grabbed her hand and squeezed it. "You loved it. Don't fake."

"It was good." She looked at his brutal face—the hidden eyes, the mutilated nose. A hard man to love. "I was scared."

"What? Of that soldier? Listen, if he comes back and gets wise, he'll take a lesson. Nobody messes with Dukes. They learn that on the West Side."

Mary took her hand away. "I learned."

"What?" He looked affronted.

"I don't like getting smacked around. Some women, they say, do. Not Mary Waslyk Gilligan."

"I said I was sorry. I apologized."

"You'll do it again."

"I couldn't help myself. No dame ever made me lose control the way you did. I got on my knees. I used to cry. No broad ever made me."

"I didn't make you do anything."

"You were more than I could handle. That's why I belted you around. It wasn't too bad, was it, Mary?"

"Bad enough. Never again. I don't care how much you want me, or how many promises you make. I'm sorry you were jugged, and I'm sorry you never found a woman you enjoyed belting so much."

"Cut it out, Mary. I was in love with you."

"Yeah. You were nice enough to belt me on the body and behind anyway. So the bruises wouldn't show. You'd know about things like that."

"I didn't mean to sock you. I'll never do it again. You can divorce that soldier. We'll get married."

"No, Rudy. As bad as Frank was, he was—part of me. He gave himself to me. But you're different. You're by yourself. No matter how close you get to a woman. You're alone. You used to beat me up because you began to worry you couldn't be alone any more, maybe you had to give something away."

The image of her naked made him shudder—her long fair body, pliant, warm, strong. Rage replaced desire. He was murderously angry with any other man who had ever made love to her.

"You got a boy friend," Dukes said hoarsely. "You found some guy when I was put away, when Gilligan went overseas. I'll kill him."

"I know you could, Rudy. Nothing stops you. But there's no guy."

"You played around once with some spic dancer. Some guy with greasy hair and big eyes. I remember you told me once. Is it him? I'll strangle him." Dukes fists clenched and unclenched on the table.

"Shut up, Rudy. It was years ago. You have no right to talk to me like that." She eased her way out of the booth. "I'm going. I've had enough of this. It was a mistake."

"Come to my place. We'll open the champagne."

"Nope, it's all over, Rudy."

Yet a few minutes later, as they walked along Broadway, she let him take her arm, then held his hand warmly. On the street she felt the need for his protective assurance. There was always the threat of violence, especially at night. It was good to be accompanied by a strong fearless man. Mary, as cool and confident as she appeared, was always afraid. She would never admit it to the boys, but ever since Frank had gone back to Vietnam she had been uneasy.

Rudy was like that. Nothing shook him. In a doorway, two bleary-eyed addicts looked them over as they strolled by. Rudy returned their stare. Old-time pimps and pushers knew him and gave him room. He was a tough guy, the blockbuster who cleaned out the St. Charles. He packed a gun, and he had connections. They suspected—the street freaks, and peddlers of heroin, the numbers runners and procurers—that he was involved in a bigger racket than theirs.

"Wanna go uptown?" he asked.

"No. Just walk me home. I feel secure with you."

It was a warm night. Turquoise and beige cars were double-parked along Broadway. Most of the stores remained open late— the fruit and vegetable markets, drugstores, tobacco and news shops. The storekeepers, most of them elderly Jews, had that querulous look of people expecting the worst. A police car rolled by in low gear. A young policeman with long dark sideburns looked out the window.

"Hey, Ed," Rudy called. "Quiet night?"

"So far, Rudy."

Mary was impressed. "Big with the cops? Is that what a stretch does for a man?"

Dukes laughed. "They know me. The captain sent me a letter when I took this new job. He was glad I was in a legit business."

"I wish you luck, Rudy." She said it with affection, her pale eyes reflecting some sad lost connection. So rarely did Dukes hear these words, uttered with sincerity, that he was silent for a moment.

"Mary, in case you haven't got the word yet," he said slowly, "you're going to have to move out."

"I guessed that. Well, anyway, my lease runs another seven months. Maybe the Relocation Department can get me a place. I'm a soldier's wife with two kids, I should get a priority."

"You got no seven months."

"*What?*"

"I'll tell you, Mary, but don't tell any of the tenants. You got to get out by the end of the month."

She stopped short as they crossed Broadway. A careening taxi swerved around them. The driver cursed. "That's impossible," Mary protested. "Three weeks?"

"There's a million and a half riding on it. I'm getting a big piece of the pie. I'll be in business if I pull it off. They're gonna demolish the houses for a luxury apartment. Get out, before it gets bad."

"Bad?" She pulled her arm away. "Are you threatening me? I think you're crazy sometimes, Rudy. First I hear how much you love me and now you're telling me to clear out before it gets *bad*."

He yanked her arm rudely and pulled her close to him. "Come on, Mary. You know what I do for a living. I'll get you a new place. I'll be responsible for you. But anyone who gets in my way is gonna get it."

"Maybe they're getting it already," she said tersely.

"Like what?"

"Oh, I heard about the phone calls those two queers have been getting. And someone stuck gum in the colored school-teacher's door. And the dead dog. I know what's happening You got rid of McIsaac, the best super on the West Side. I know what's coming."

"I'll take care of you. Only you got to be more friendly."

"Never quit, do you?"

"That's right. I'm in business again. But no more blockbusting after this. I beat up my last spade. I scared my last spic. Once I pull this off for Puttering, I go on my own. Westchester, Long Island. Supermarkets, bowling alleys."

They approached the building. Three Puerto Rican girls from the first-floor rear were jumping rope. It was eleven-thirty. Puerto Rican kids weren't bothered by long hours. Didn't they go to school? And if they did, how did they stay awake in class? Mary wondered. On the stoop Escobar, Fuentes, and some of their friends passed around a gallon of cheap wine. They did not appear to be drunk, merely relaxed. Their voices were soft and liquid.

"Know something, Rudy?" Mary asked. "You'll never go respectable."

"I will. Like Puttering says, there's nothin' like a legitimate business."

She shook her head. "Not for you. You get your kicks hurting people. You're not happy unless you can belt someone."

"Mary, wait a minute."

She ran up the stairs, between the wine drinkers. "Don't bother about a new apartment. I'll find my own."

Escobar stumbled to his feet. Fuentes raised his straw hat to *la señora* Gilligan.

Dukes' face was ashen. "Whaddya drinkin' on my stoop for?" he asked.

"*Panin,* Rudy," Escobar said. "Drink, Rudy. Good wine."

"Drunken bums, lousy spics." He walked toward them. "Get off. Beat it."

They recoiled from him. One of the men staggered down the steps and vanished into an alley. Fuentes, held his arms out. "Oi, Rudy, you our buddy. We have party tonight, *sí?*"

Dukes snatched the glass jug from his hand. "I'll give you a party, you dirty greaser."

He raised the jug over his head, smashed it against the bottom steps. Shards of glass flew. The wine bled from a dark puddle, streaking the sidewalk.

"Jesus, he *loco*," one of Fuentes' friends said. He brushed bits of glass from his arm and started to stagger away.

"I'll show you who's *loco*," Dukes said. He grabbed the man— he was a slender fellow, a dishwasher—and yanked him upright. Unresisting, the man went limp. Dukes shook him a few times and threw him against a parked car. The man got to his feet, picking glass from his arm, murmuring some Spanish curses, and stumbled off. He was only mildly offended. Violence was part of his life.

On the steps, Escobar and Fuentes retreated slowly to the door.

"You move out!" Dukes shouted. "Outa my house!"

"Sure, sure, Rudy," Fuentes muttered. "Wha' you say, we gon' do."

They were not frightened. Escobar and Fuentes lived marginal lives. They were always on the edge of disaster. If Dukes was their *panin* one day, handing out free beer, it was not unthinkable for him to come back and bust their wine bottle. Life was not all free beer. Life was more often a smashed jug, lost wine.

From the basement steps, the bald head of the super O'Gara appeared. His eyes were shiny.

"You, you puke," Dukes snarled. "No more parties on the steps. You're my super, enforce it."

"Sure, Mr. D."

"Come to my office tomorrow. I got some orders for you."

"Sure thing, Mr. D." He came up the steps, in the uncertain gait of the addict. Light bounced off his shaved head, but his eyes now seemed to have vanished, burned out. Dukes wished he would close his mouth. He looked like some disgusting form of undersea life, a squid, an octopus.

"Can Ah get somethin'?" the super asked.

"So soon?"

110

"Ah tole you when you hired me, boss. Ah got a big habit. You said you could handle it for me, if Ah did a job."

"You ain't done a job yet. Talk to me tomorrow."

"Somethin' for tonight? Ah made a connection."

"You won't need a connection. I'll get it for you. Don't forget that. Just stay awake tonight thinking how bad you need it."

"You the boss."

"You damn right I am. Keep your nose clean and do what I tell you."

Shlep Sharmak had taught him the technique. A junkie super, dependent on you, ready to do anything to the tenants for the next fix. Personally, he could not abide creeps like O'Gara, a bald-headed hillbilly. Dukes never touched dope, nor drank excessively, nor smoked. He detested people who could not control their bodies, and he hated addicts most of all. But O'Gara would be useful.

The time had come to move Nordetzki out of 500 West 84th Street. Puttering had called again. The crazy old Polack had to go. With no family, no friends, no employer—Nordetzki had been a self-employed machinist, long divested of his shop— they had been able to draw up papers of commitment. He was a menace to himself and to the neighborhood. He was broke. He was not mentally competent. A certifiable case, the lawyers argued, the poor man carried as a charity tenant by kindly E. J. Puttering, and now endangering himself by refusing to leave a building scheduled for demolition.

Dukes waited in the Lincoln. At his side, the mastiff Angel dozed in the spring sunlight. He had sent Bolo and Shlep inside with firm orders: *get the guy out.*

Rudy looked at the adjoining house, 502. It was a good idea to empty 500, board it up, turn off the gas and the electricity, and let it go to ruin. It would help convince the people in 502. For a moment he was sorry about Mary Gilligan. He wished he could convince her of his affection.

"Rudy," Shlep called from the top step. "The guy won't budge."

"Drag him out."

"We can't. The jerk tied hisself to the wheelchair."

"Carry him out in it."

"But he tied the wheelchair to the radiator," Sharmak whined. "He must have a million knots in it. Someone brought him a hundred yards of nylon clothesline. It's like iron. We'll have to cut for a half hour to get him out."

"You got shivs. Start cutting."

"He says he'll kill us if we start. For an old crippled Polack, he's full of fight."

Dukes groaned. Losers were better off swallowing their mouthful of dirt and crawling away. He knew the Nordetzkis of the world—battling, protesting, running to court. They had to lose. Nordetzki's problem was that he was too honest, too trusting. Dukes knew that he had never been on welfare, never welshed on a bill. Where did it get him?

Rudy got out of the car. Angel growled, lifted his yellow head, sniffed the air. It was a weekday morning, the right time for a hard case. The men had gone to work, the kids to school, the wives asleep or occupied with household duties. Two well-dressed women—pants suits, long hair—strolled by. Dukes watched them walk toward West End Avenue.

"Let's go," Dukes said. Shlep and Bolo followed him in.

Nordetzki was enthroned amid rubbish—a madman in a wheelchair, surrounded by empty cans. He seemed to have lived on cold beans. Plaster, bits of studding, debris, littered the floor, the kitchen table, the sink, the unused stove. Laced to the cold radiator, bound a hundred times, knotted a hundred times, was the tenant.

"Why you do this to me?" Nordetzki asked.

"Tough noogies, Ignatz," Dukes said. "You'll be better off. We got you a nice bed on Welfare Island."

"I no go."

"You'll go." Dukes, Shlep and Bolo, sometimes getting in each other's way, began to slash at the ropes. Nordetzki tried to grab Bolo's arm. Rudy slapped him once in the face and he stopped.

"For Chrissake, cut, cut," Dukes said impatiently.

"Why you do this?" the old man persisted.

"Building coming down. You can't stay here with plaster on your head. You got no one to take care of you."

"Minister take care. Hasslinger, his fellow."

"He's a fink," Dukes said. "He's using you, because he wants to make trouble for me. All them fake priests use you people."

"I pay rent. I get it rent."

"Too late. You been evicted." Dukes waved papers under his nose. "All in black and white. Legal." They were old telephone bills.

"Jesus, this old guy musta been a scoutmaster," Shlep gasped. His gray face was splotched with scarlet as he hacked away. Two strands parted, and the chair began to roll away from the radiator.

The knives kept slashing at the tangle of ropes. Nordetzki began to weep, in a dignified way. His face did not contort. The tears dribbled silently down his unshaven cheeks.

"All my life I my own boss," he said. "Dukes, you believe me?"

"Sure thing, Iggy. Nothing personal."

"I got it own machine shop. Own business. Edgers, drills, shapers. Lose business, landlord make me sell machines. Five-thousand-dollar machines, I force to sell for four hundred dollars. Cripple. No family. I never late on pay bill in my life."

"Okay, okay, pop," Shlep said solicitously. "Bolo, get them knots, right under the bar there. Iggy, you're aces with us, but let's face it, you're a mental case."

"I not crazy."

"Close enough," Dukes said. "Okay, a few more and he's loose. Keep him tied in the chair. In case he gets any ideas."

"Dukes, please," Nordetzki said. "Untie it one hand."

"Why? So's you can make trouble? You can't go anywhere."

"No, no make trouble. Want to wipe face. Is disgrace for man to cry."

"Okay, boss?" Bolo asked.

Rudy nodded. Bolo slashed away with his knife and freed Nordetzki's left arm.

They bore him out of the ruined apartment, into the dark hallway. The severed ropes dangled like tentacles from the chair. Nordetzki slumped in the seat, his head lolling, as if drugged. Dukes walked in front of them, Shlep and Bolo each holding one of the wheels. They had tried rolling the old man out, but the ropes had been knotted countless times in the spokes.

As they approached the front door, it opened. A shaft of morning light painted the floorboards yellow. A slender figure stepped into the light.

"Nobody home," Dukes said. "Building closed."

"Excuse me," Danny Hart said. "Is that Mr. Nordetzki? Oh, good morning, Mr. Nordetzki."

"From the minister," Shlep whispered to Rudy. "Hiya, kid. Outa my way."

"Where are you taking him?" Danny asked. "Mr. Nordetzki, do you want to go?"

The old machinist cried on. "Ah, ah, too late. They got it papers."

"Father Hasslinger said they can't. It isn't legal. You have a right to stay—"

"One side, kid," Shlep said.

Hart placed his frail body in the center of the dark, narrow corridor. Dukes assessed him swiftly: faggot, long hair, 135 pounds, not a muscle on him, the kind he could break in half. Ah, those do-gooders, those block workers, and community organizers, and poverty program lawyers. They were all losers, born to go down, to fail, to be defeated by the very people they tried to help.

"It's legal," Dukes said. "Watch it, son. The guy is being committed to Welfare Island. Non compos mental. He's got no family, no job, nothing. We're his legal guardians."

"But he has a lease," Danny said. "Father Hasslinger had me

call the City this morning. This property has not yet qualified for demolition. And no certificate of eviction was issued for Ignatz Nordetzki—"

"I said one side, kid," Shlep bellowed.

Shlep and Bolo barreled forward, carrying the machinist like Hindu devotees bearing the juggernaut through the streets of Delhi. Sharmak stepped heavily on Hart's sandaled foot. They charged on, porting Nordetzki though the street door.

"Just a minute," Hart said. "You can't do this. Father Hasslinger said—"

Hart turned toward the door.

"Hold it, queer," Dukes said. He hooked a hand in Hart's belt, threw him against the crumbling plaster wall, and smashed the flat of his palm against Danny's nose. Tears flooded Hart's eyes. Blinded, he blinked in the darkness, wondering what would happen next. He saw Dukes' white face, the narrow eyes, the mashed nose, the jaw quivering. Dukes' lips exploded. Hart's eyes were filled with saliva. Shocked, humiliated, his hands went to his eyes, and as he wiped the spit away, he felt a sickening jolt in his groin. Dukes had brought his knee up and had walked away.

"What?" Hart gasped. "What was that for?"

"Stay the hell away."

Danny Hart rested against the wall. Outside he heard the motor of the huge car racing. The knowledge that he had failed again distressed him more than his injuries.

Horton Sims, on his way to school stopped to see if the mail had been delivered. In the foyer—it was aromatic with cat's urine ever since the new super had arrived—he went through a few bills, the usual throwaways, and then saw a letter with the return address:

City of New York
Housing & Development Authority
Department of Rent & Housing Maintenance

The schoolteacher ripped it open. The letter was dated two days ago and was signed by James P. Handley, Administrator for Special Projects. It read:

Dear Tenant:
   The premises in which you reside, 502 West 84th Street, New York City, has been condemned as unsafe. Demolition proceedings are to begin this month. You are hereby ordered by the City of New York to vacate the premises immediately. This office will assist you in finding new lodgings. There are also several excellent private relocation companies whose names we will gladly furnish. This is an emergency procedure based on reports by our Building Inspectors, which show that walls, roof and flooring in your building have been so weakened as to render said premises unfit for occupancy.
   This office has authorized Dukes Management Company to act in its behalf on this matter. All inquiries should be addressed to them, and they can assist you in moving. We emphasize that it is urgent to all concerned that 502 West 84th Street be vacant by the end of May.

Sims read the letter twice. It stunned him. It meant that Dukes had powerful friends in the city. He had gotten to someone, and they were taking his part. Worse, they had empowered him to handle the matter.

"Mr. Zimz! Mr. Zimz!"

Horton looked up and saw Hilda Schlossmann, lugging her briefcase, galumphing toward him. In her free hand she waved a letter.

"Good morning, Miss Schlossmann. I see you got one also."

"You got such a letter, Mr. Zimz?"

"I'm afraid I did."

She looked grim. Horton was intrigued with her. And the strange father inside, clacking away on his typewriter. That old Jewish gene pool, Sims thought. More brains than they know what to do with.

116

"Outrageous!" Hilda Schlossmann huffed. "How can the Zity do this?"

They walked outside. "It may be a mistake, Miss Schlossmann. I'll make some calls on my lunch hour."

"Yes, please."

Sims held her leathery arm as they crossed West End Avenue. A dreary spring day, Sims noted—bumpy iron-gray clouds, a threat of rain. A perfect day on which to be told you had no place to live.

"But I have a feeling, Mr. Zimz," she said loudly. "It will do no good. We will be thrown out. I have been through this."

Old mysteries, old secrets, old tragedies, Sims mused. They were full of them.

"Now, Miss Schlossmann, there's no need to cross bridges before we get to them. This isn't Germany, or Russia. This is a free country and the greatest city in the world. It has to be a mistake. That building is solid as a rock. Mr. Dukes gave us assurance that we were secure, didn't he?"

"Yes, so he did. And you are right, this is not Germany or Russia. Not at all."

Carrie Loomis ran her hand over the letter. It had a rough, mottled texture, the feel of official stationery. And the letterhead was convincing. As for James P. Handley, what better name for an "Administrator for Special Projects"?

Still, she was a shrewd young woman (one of her problems as an actress had been a tendency to see through the blatherings of directors) and she decided that the letter was a mistake. It was based on erroneous reports, she decided, or was intended for some other building.

Comfortable in the kitchen, her portable cuspidor at her side, she brewed a second cup of tea and began to study the New York City telephone directory.

First, she tried a number at the Housing Authority. All wrong. It handled *public* housing only. The letter was from an entirely different agency. After several wrong numbers, connections lost by inefficient operators, busy signals, dead lines, and intermittent buzzings, chimes, and recorded announcements, she reached a woman in "Rent and Housing Maintenance."

Carrie explained the letter from Mr. Handley. "Is that official?" she asked. "Do we really have to move in three weeks?"

"Sure. If the building is condemned."

"But this is the first notice. Surely we deserve more time, if this true."

"Wait a minute. I'll get someone for you."

There was more mumbling, a long wait, and then a man's voice got on the line. He had a thick accent, not ethnic, but distinctly New York, sprinkled with "foists" and "hoits."

"Ya better see ya District Rent Office," he said.

"Where is it?"

"In da phone book."

"But can't you give me any information? Can I speak to Mr. Handley?"

"Who?"

"The man who sent me this letter saying we have to move. James P. Handley."

There was a long pause. She heard the man shouting, as if to a room of fellow employes. *"Hey! Anyone ever hear of some guy named Handley? We gotta Handley here?"*

"Hello?" Carrie asked. "Hello?" For a moment she thought the line had gone dead.

"Yeah, yeah, lady. I was checking the directory list. I don't think we got a poison named Handley. Haber, Hackbart, Hannegan. Nah, no Handley."

"You mean there isn't a James P. Handley with your department? Administrator for Special Projects?"

"Soich me, lady. They make new jobs every day around here. It's possible the guy was appernted recently and ain't in the book yet. Anything is possible. Ya better come in and ask for yaself. Housing and Development Administration, 100 Gold Street."

"And who shall I ask—"

The man had hung up. She stared at the letter. Now she was convinced it was a fake. Someone had gone to a lot of trouble to fake it. Dukes, obviously.

Move in three weeks? With the baby due in less than two months? It was ridiculous. A hundred Rudy Dukes and a thousand of his goons, idiots like that grinning Shlep, and the slinky Bolo could not get her out. Not after the miseries she had gone through to save her child.

She raised her chin and announced to the empty kitchen: "*J'y suis, et j'y reste.*"

2

Two days after Rudy Dukes had sent out the forged letters, on stationery stolen by Shlep, who knew his way around downtown, the hot water was turned off.

"Dry," Leora Sims shouted to Horton. "Nothing."

Sims, rubbing his eyes, stared at the faucet. A wicked sucking noise issued from the tap.

Allard laughed. "No hot water, Pop-pop? No bath tonight?"

"Yeah, buddy, no bath."

Leora stamped her foot. "Damn. That honky Dukes means business. Don't tell me that suddenly on a May morning, the hot water stops. He's ordered that redneck in the basement to make life miserable for us."

Sims yawned. "Could have expected it. He must realize he can't scare us with phony letters." He washed his hands in frigid water, shivering. "Took me two phone calls to nail that lie."

"Hortie, see how long it takes you to nail down the hot-water situation. Maybe you ought to grab a few fellow tenants and make an assault on that creep in the basement."

Sims nodded. His teeth chattered as he gargled with icy water. Strange how he had gotten spoiled over the years. As a boy in Brooklyn, he never knew what hot water was.

David Loomis also turned on the hot water. The faucet gasped noisily, straining to produce, then sucked itself into silence.

"Dead," he moaned. He looked at Carrie's sleeping figure. There was no point in bothering her. He'd call Dukes' number and complain. And he'd drop by the super to tell him about it. Under the benign regime of McIsaac, hot water had flowed endlessly, steaming, comforting, abundant. He had kept the ancient boiler in beautiful shape.

It was depressing the way the lack of hot water could unnerve a man, Loomis thought. He rummaged through his dresser for the electric shaver. He never felt quite shaved with it. As he ran it over his beard, he wondered if he should phone Dukes' office. Would anyone be in? It was odd the way Dukes had conditioned them. People were reluctant to call. Besides, it *was* possible that the boiler was only temporarily out. Perhaps the water had been turned off for a few minutes.

Sims and Loomis met going down the stairs. "Join me in some community action?" David asked. "I'm suspicious about the water."

"Same thought here," the teacher said. "I believe this is what the City refers to as a temporary decrease in services."

The two men walked down the basement steps. They were filthy—littered with cardboard milk containers, tunafish tins, peelings.

"He gets no award for neatness," Loomis said. He rapped at the door.

O'Gara, his eyes hooded, his breath sour, came to the door.

"No hot water," Sims said.

"Yeah."

"What's wrong?" David asked.

"Intake valve. Cain't fix hit."

Sims frowned. "Can you show it to us? Take us inside."

The bald-head nodded and led them through his room. Dishes covered with dried scraps of food littered the table. A soiled mattress had slid halfway to the floor. The stench was laminated —unwashed body, unflushed toilet, congealed grease.

The three walked into the boiler room. The enormous rusted cylinder was silent, cold.

"Dang thing went clunk durin' the night," O'Gara said. "Then hit stopped altogether. Hit's this here thing."

He took a length of rusted metal pipe, threaded at either end, and showed it to Sims and David. "Intake valve. Hit's busted. Look inside."

David peered into it. He had only a marginal knowledge of plumbing. There was a loose hinged piece of metal flapping inside.

"Busted," O'Gara said.

"You can't call a plumber? Or a heating engineer?" Sims asked.

"Oh, yeah, Ah can. Got to call Mr. Dukes first."

"Well, call him," David said. "We need hot water. My wife is pregnant, and doesn't feel good, and I don't want her inconvenienced."

"May take some time," the super whined. They walked out with him.

"Why?" Sims asked.

O'Gara shook the pipe. "Had this happen oncet before. This here part is obsolete. Company don't make 'em. Mebbe Ah can find a used one."

Outside Sims shook his head. "This was deliberate. That fake letter should have tipped us off. Dukes ordered him to break that part."

"He isn't fooling," David said. "He means to drive us out. But to deprive us of hot water?"

"Be thankful it isn't wintertime and we're not poor. They could turn the heat off also."

Archie Allister called on the Loomises that night. "This crap has got to cease, Dave," he said. "Still no hot water. Threatening letters. Phony ones at that. Who does that guy Dukes think he is?"

Carrie was in bed, reading and listening to WQXR. Loomis closed the bedroom door while he and Allister talked.

"It's clear he wants us out," David said. "We've been kidding ourselves."

Allister winked. "Boards went up next door today. Two down and one to go. It sounds like a parcel."

David sat down. He was weary, and his mind had trouble focusing. A relaxed, diffident man on the exterior, he worked at a high pitch of concentration, and at day's end he was enervated, flaccid. The mounting problems with Dukes distressed him. He was no fighter, no competitor. On graduating from Cornell, degree in hand after five harrowing years, he had decided that he would never open his own office. Happily, he would work on some other architect's staff, letting him make the big money and worry about bills and expenses. Struggle was not for him; his father had done a great deal of useless struggling in Ohio, and had died young and broke.

"What's your guess, Archie?" David asked. Allister, with his Wall Street connections, seemed to know a great deal about real estate.

"I think he's been given a timetable to chase us out. Maybe a couple of months, something like that."

"But he can't. Unless he makes it worthwhile. And there hasn't been a peep out of him. Hell, he never even shows his face."

Allister pursed his lips. "He's a shrewdie. They do these things on a per-apartment basis. The less it costs, the more Dukes gets, or keeps."

David sighed. "We could call Haman, Lord & Fawcett."

123

"No way. They don't even know who he is. Puttering is handling it for them. Besides, I hear they're a new outfit. Los Angeles money. They can't be bothered with small-time stuff like Dukes and a few unhappy tenants."

David unloosened his tie and sprawled backward on the couch. A damned complication. He was a man who liked things to function properly. He detested shoddy work, poor drafting, a badly constructed building. Epstein, one of the senior architects, had complimented him several times on the precision, the fine details of his work. But life was not like a blueprint or a rendering; it was full of wrong measurements and sloppy drawings.

"What else can we do?" David asked, hoping that Allister would have some quick solution.

"There's the City. But we better move fast."

"Okay." David paused. Someone would have to bell the cat. Quite simply, he had neither the energy nor the desire to go chasing after civil servants downtown. He knew a little about filing architectural plans: a nightmare. The firm kept a special man on duty doing nothing but that, a clever older draftsman, wise in the ways of city offices. It was too Byzantine, too intricate, for David.

"We should get up a committee of tenants, maybe," Allister said. He eyed David—almost electing him.

"Hmmm." David was hesitant. "Maybe we could get up a letter signed by all of us, telling Dukes we don't like what he's doing."

Allister laughed. "He'll throw it away. The guy has been hired to do a job. No, we have to start somewhere. There has to be some kind of machinery in the City to handle these things."

Carrie, in a loose blue robe, walked in. She looked round, defenseless, pale. But she was approaching the end of her nine months in good health, a good frame of mind. She had even been spitting less.

"May I make a suggestion?" she said. "When I tried to track

124

down the nonexistent Handley, I had a terrible time finding anyone in the Housing and Development Authority. They're so inundated with complaints, its almost impossible to get through to anyone."

"But who else is there?" David asked.

"Let's use one of the neighborhood associations. Tony Paz knows Father Hasslinger. He's been to him about what's going on here. Why don't a few of us call on the West Side Parish House?"

Allister nodded. "I'm game. Of course, it'll have to wait till the weekend."

Loomis looked wary. Involvement, involvement. He didn't want to be on any committees, call on any activist ministers. There had to be an easier way of handling the mess.

"Heck, I'll go," Carrie said. "Tony Paz works at night, so he and I could go tomorrow morning. Maybe someone else from another apartment."

"You sure you want to, honey?" David asked.

"Someone's got to. I mean—no hot water, threats that we'll be thrown out. David, I'm not going to wait for those people to toss the next dead dog in our hallway. Or jam chewing gum into our lock."

"She's right, Dave," Allister said. "The hour has struck."

Loomis agreed reluctantly. Would it be easier to start looking for a new place?

Carrie could not help being amused by the committee of tenants (unofficial, unelected) that called on Father Hasslinger the next day. In addition to Tony Paz—silent, simmering, wearing a tight black suit and a white shirt—Barri Dane, the actor, agreed to go along. "He's a natural for the job," Ron Lobello told Carrie. "He'll cry on cue, and he'll recite the psalms to impress the priest."

"He's not a priest," Carrie said. "A minister. And from what I've read about him he isn't very big on psalms. He's more familiar with picket lines."

They were an odd bag—three undersized people, a homo-sexual, a pregnant woman, an angry Puerto Rican. She won-dered what the minister would think.

"It certainly sounds like a harassment campaign," Father Hass-linger said. "When the acts persist, it means one thing. They want the building empty so they can demolish, and they want it emptied as fast as possible."

The minister's mobile eyes sought the cracked ceiling, the toxic green walls of his office. It was a grim, barren place—a creaking mimeograph machine run by a crippled Puerto Rican woman, posters advertising rent meetings, adult education, wel-fare regulations, a series of old desks, a row of folding chairs against one green wall. Hasslinger looked perpetually distressed, preoccupied.

"But he has no right to do these things to tenants," Carrie said. "They're outrageous."

"There are lots of outrageous things going on in this city," the minister said. "You have to realize, Mrs. Loomis, that housing and land are the two commodities that are worth more as they get older. The building you live in is worth more empty than it is filled. Why? Because of the land it stands on. Your home can be knocked down and a high-rise put up. Millions of dollars are involved."

"But what about the people who live there?" Barri Dane asked. "What about us?" Carrie noted that, apparently in def-erence to the clergyman, the lilting femininity had gone from his voice. He sounded manly.

"You're in the way," Hasslinger said. "Poor people are thrown out every day, tossed into the street, or into welfare hotels, or doubled up, because they have no place to go. There are fifty thousand apartments kept vacant in New York City, for speculation, or for demolition. There is no place for the poor to go—especially the blacks and the Puerto Ricans."

Tony Paz stiffened slightly as if to say, *This* Puerto Rican can take care of himself.

"But why does the City let this happen?" Carrie asked. "They must know it's going on."

Hasslinger toyed with a souvenir letter opener on his desk: *Regency Ambulance Service.* "Partly ineptitude, partly indifference, partly corruption, partly—the nature of the beast. Private builders won't build cheap housing, landlords don't like blacks and the Spanish-speaking. The money is in speculation, highrises, office space. The action goes where the money is."

"But people can't be abused like this," Carrie protested. "How can Dukes do the things he does?"

"A landlord can do it legally. Some do. They file for a certificate of eviction. But it isn't always granted. It takes time, even when it is. So they resort to harassment, and it can take many forms. Sometimes it's a simple matter—no hot water, no heat, no elevator, no refuse removal. But it can get rough and dirty."

Danny Hart had been sitting quietly some distance from the minister. He padded over on his sandals and nodded at Tony. Tony introduced him to Carrie and to Dane.

"Danny here," Hasslinger said, "made the mistake of getting in Dukes' way the other day, when they got the last tenant out of the building next to yours. He got messed up a little."

"You mean he *hit* you?" Carrie asked.

"A few kicks and slaps," Hart said.

He spoke airily, not quite the martyr, but in an offhand manner. It bothered Carrie. He seemed to be saying, some get kicked, and some do the kicking, and little can be done about it.

"Mrs. Loomis," Tony said excitedly. "I know that guy Rudy from way back. He stop at nothing. He beat up. He carry gun. He start fires. Father, I told you how Sharmak show me a bottle of kerosene the other night?"

"Really?" Barri Dane asked. "To start fires? In our building? It can't be worth all that to get us out."

Father Hasslinger yanked at his collar. "Don't be too sure, Mr. Dane. The poor are allowed to freeze, get bitten by rats, catch diseases from stuffed toilets, uncollected garbage. Why should you be spared?"

"You must be joking," Carrie said.

"No jokes. I simply want to impress upon you that no one is safe, unless they're rich and resourceful. The first thing I learned when I started the Parish House was that they referred to Urban Renewal as Negro Removal. Nothing's changed much, except now middle-income people are getting it. Rudy Dukes is a symptom of the disease, a boil, a deadly one. But the sickness is in the city's blood."

Carrie was not sure she had too much confidence in him. He went on too long. And he had a curiously defeatist attitude. It was not what she had expected.

"Can you help us?" Barri Dane asked.

"I've asked Danny to take the case."

There was an embarrassing pause. All three appellants—Carrie, Dane, Paz—turned to look at the frail man in the faded field jacket.

"Danny has worked with tenant cases and he knows the procedure downtown," Hasslinger said. "I can't involve myself. Don't be insulted, Mrs. Loomis, but I have priorities and they concern truly desperate people. Your husband is an architect? Well, you'll manage. Tony knows his way around. Mr. Dane, you're an actor, you have a job. The other tenants don't seem too badly off."

Carrie was about to protest. But Hasslinger had gotten up and was moving his ungainly figure toward a group of black women, one screaming, one weeping, all of them surrounding an organizer's desk, unmoved by her Ivy League drawl and her icy manner.

"Now ladies," Hasslinger said. "One at a time, one at a time."

"She steal my baby carriage," one woman yelled. "I seen her. She and her junkie kid—"

Hasslinger put his arm on the woman's and led her to a chair. Yes, he had other priorities.

Danny Hart suggested that they go immediately to the Office of Rent Control and file complaints of harassment against Dukes.

"Can't we just phone in and report it?" Carrie asked.

The youth smiled. "Mrs. Loomis, you don't know how things get done in the City. Everything has to be in writing, in triplicate, filed, formal. It won't do any harm to meet the enforcement people. I suggest we all go."

They stood on the corner of Broadway and West 94th Street, blinking in the late-morning sun.

"I got to go to work," Tony said.

"And I have a rehearsal," Barri added.

Hart looked appealingly at Carrie. "I guess you're the little red hen."

"Is it far?" she asked.

"Half hour on the subway. It won't be crowded at this hour."

David didn't want her riding the subways. But she didn't feel queasy or weak. The "committee" had invigorated her. There was a challenge ahead, a job to get done.

"I'll go with you," Carrie said.

In the moments of quiet when the subway train was stopped at the stations, Hart divulged a few things about himself to Carrie. She had to draw him out, and he seemed relieved when the train would lurch off in a burst of noise and he could stop talking.

"Not much to tell," he said indifferently. "Nebraska. Farmboy. Good marks in high school. A scholarship to the seminary."

"Why did you quit?" Carrie asked.

"Oh . . . sense of nothing getting done."

The subway car rattled and groaned and his voice was inundated again.

"Were you trained for social work?" she asked as they got off at Times Square and walked through the malodorous, swarming station to the shuttle.

"Not exactly. I knew some of the men at the East Harlem Protestant Parish. A wonderful bunch. You know about them?"

Carrie had read a little about the dedicated ministers in Harlem; she was sorry she did not know more.

On the ride to Brooklyn Bridge the clangor silenced them

again. At one stop—Fourteenth Street—Hart disclosed that he was paid nothing for his work with Father Hasslinger.

"How do you live? I mean, with no money?" Carrie looked at his serene, fair face—a Midwestern boy, the kind who secretly read poetry in the barn. No good at athletics, shy with girls. Apparently in deference to their mission, he had gathered his hair into a ponytail.

"My needs are minimal," Hart said.

They got to the Office of Rent Control, were sent to another building, ended up in a third. By then it was close to one o'clock, and Carrie was weary. Each office they went to had the impersonal look of officialdom about it. A group of tenants or other pleaders huddled in anterooms. Brusque impatient receptionists. Officials bustling about. An odor of cigar smoke and disinfectant—the world of local government.

At the last office, in a gloomy high-ceilinged building on lower Broadway, a gray-haired woman told them it was lunch hour, and the District Rent Officer who could help them was out. Carrie suggested they have a sandwich in a luncheonette in the lobby of the building.

She offered to buy Hart something to eat, but all he wanted was coffee. He had two cups, while she, ravenous, ate a bacon-and-egg sandwich and rice pudding. It was standard luncheonette fare, but it tasted magnificent. Nor were her salivary glands at work. *Ptyalism, goodbye!* she thought. The mission was obviously good for her. Perhaps what had ailed her during the pregnancy was a sense of uselessness, of dependence on David.

"I hope this traveling isn't tiring you," Hart said.

"No. I feel fine. I feel I'm accomplishing something after so many months of being a drone."

The young man warmed his hands on the coffee mug. "Yes, that is important. One of the reasons I did so poorly at the seminary."

"You felt useless?"

"It was my own fault. It's a common disease among semi-

130

narians, ministers, priests, nuns. A sense that we're worse than irrelevant, as the kids like to say."

"I always heard that Union Theological Seminary was a progressive place," Carrie said. "Don't they turn out all kinds of radicals?"

"It was my own fault. I'd get these periods of despair, of inaction. The sense that nothing works. Some of my teachers admitted that was the case. They spend years in these slum neighborhoods and what do they have to show? Nothing. Addiction rate goes up. More buildings collapse. More lives ruined. I couldn't concentrate. Couldn't even read. Who cares about Luther when teen-age kids die of heroin?"

"But you're still in social work."

Hart smiled. He was not a bad-looking young man, his narrow pale face distinguished by a long crooked nose. "Hasslinger is tolerating me. He'd like to get rid of me, but he doesn't know how."

"Why? You have a lot of courage. Getting beaten up by that bum Dukes the other day—"

"That was an accident. I don't like getting beat up. I flopped anyway. They got Nordetzki out. The building's finished." He held his hands out. "I have a bad habit of not being able to find the handle on anything, to ever finish anything."

Carrie picked up the check. Hart made no move to pay and she respected him for that—no false show of generosity. He was broke, homeless, adrift. There was something admirable in him, but was he really what the tenants of 502 West 84th Street needed? Rudy Dukes had smacked him around as easily as cuffing a stray puppy. She realized, as they left the luncheonette for the Rent Office, that Hasslinger had sloughed him off on them. The minister had other priorities. And Hart was a pensioner himself, a charity case.

They waited for forty minutes in a small foyer. It was an ancient building with lofty tin-plated ceilings, the kind Carrie had not seen since her girlhood in upstate New York. The furnishings were old and stained, the linoleum-covered floor

131

bumpy and slanted. Several secretaries spent a great deal of time standing around and discussing a Bermuda vacation taken by one of them, a stunning Puerto Rican girl.

Finally an elderly woman beckoned them into a glass cubicle. A stout rumpled man was bellowing into a telephone.

"Whah? Whah? The landlord closed down the switchboard? He took the furniture outa the lobby?" He shut his eyes and ran a hand over his bald head. "Tell them to file a statement of violations, Moe. No, we can't send no one up on their say-so. They got to do it through channels. Whaddya think we got a system for?"

He hung up, started to get up—without looking at Carrie or Danny Hart—then sat down. "You are Mr. and Mrs. O'Neill, right?"

"No, I'm Mrs. Loomis. From 502 West 84th Street."

"Ah, violations, right?"

"Repeated cases of harassment," Danny said. "We want to file a raft of complaints."

"You're Mr. Loomis?"

"No, my name is Hart. I'm a community organizer. I work with Father Hasslinger in the West Side Parish House."

Was it Carrie's imagination, or did the man bridle slightly? Was he on guard? She looked at the small sign on his desk: MR. OBERLANDER.

"Hart, you know the procedure," Oberlander said. He reached into a basket on the radiator cover and took out a sheaf of pink forms. "Have the tenants fill these in and mail them to this office. We'll screen them and see if there's anything to them."

"You can't look into it right away?" Carrie asked.

"Sure, sure. Go outside, fill the forms out if you want, and leave 'em here. We'll get after it."

Carrie started to get up, then sat down. "But this is an urgent matter, Mr. Oberlander. A man named Rudy Dukes has taken over management of our building, and he's threatening tenants, putting dead dogs in the airshafts, pointing guns at people. He beat Mr. Hart up yesterday, and he sent out fake letters, using your stationery, and told us to move in a month. One tenant has had gum and matchsticks stuck in his keyhole—"

Oberlander was grinning. "Dukes. Dukes. Jesus, it must be Rudy Dukes. Never thought he'd be back in business."

"I'm glad you find it amusing," Carrie said. "It isn't amusing to us. The man's a psychopath."

"Lady, I'm just amused someone would hire that bum. Last I heard he was in jail."

"I wish he were," Carrie said. "Please, what can we do to stop him?" She glanced at Hart. He seemed calm. Probably he had been through the mazes of bureaucracy before. He was inured to the delays, the forms, the procedures.

"You'd better give me a lot more of these forms," Carrie said. "I think every tenant in the building will want to file one."

"Mr. Oberlander, the building is owned by E. J. Puttering, if that interests you," Hart said quietly.

The official rubbed his dome a few times. "No kidding? The phantom? Anyone seen him around?" He had cared little about Carrie's complaints. But the news that Puttering was involved moved him. His pouched, sagging eyes had come alive.

"No. No one's ever seen him," Carrie said.

"Boy, would we like to slap a paper on him. Imagine. Six years a guy avoids one of our subpoenas."

"I hope you'll be able to move faster to stop Dukes," Carrie said.

"Lady, if it's a legitimate harassment case, and not just violations, or a grudge fight between some people, we'll move. Landlords got rights also, and sometimes tenants bring charges that are grounded in malice."

"*Grounded in malice?*" Carrie asked, incredulous.

"I'm not saying in your building. But it's happened. Tenants aren't all angels."

"I didn't say we are. But there are a dozen people in that

building who have been threatened or abused by Dukes and his mob."

"Put it on paper," Oberlander said. He moved the pink sheets across his desk. "Remember, to prove harassment you got to prove that the landlord's conduct has the intent to cause the tenant to vacate his apartment or waive his rights under the rent laws. If you don't prove that, it isn't harassment."

"Well, my God, it's obvious that's what Dukes wants. He sent out fake letters. He keeps making threatening calls warning people to get out."

"You got to prove those things. If you do, fine."

Danny leaned back in his chair. "Hot water's been turned off. The new super says the boiler intake valve is broken."

A wary look passed over the man's face. "Yeah?"

"You know the trick, Mr. Oberlander. Landlords pull it every time they want to empty a place. Super deliberately breaks the valve. Then they get a letter saying the boiler is obsolete and can't be fixed, that a new part has to be specially made, usually somewhere in Wisconsin. It can take weeks. Meanwhile the tenants freeze or get no hot water."

"That a fact? Hasslinger teaches you a lot of interesting things. Yes, it sounds like the boiler stunt, but it isn't necessarily that. Boilers break down in old buildings. Supers sometimes *can't* fix them. I don't say you and Mrs. Loomis are making this up, but we have to act as impartial arbiters." He indicated the pink forms. "You could fill out a thousand of these A-60H forms, and unless we check them out and substantiate your charges, there's nothing to be done. Landlords got rights."

"Not this one," Carrie said. "Not Dukes. He has this monstrous dog he takes around with him, and he sicced it on one of the tenants last week."

Oberlander hunched his shoulders. Sympathy was overgrown with a hard callus. He had heard too many sad stories. "It's a rotten neighborhood. Lots of rent collectors have dogs. Maybe the guy provoked him."

Danny Hart leaned forward. "Suppose we have a clear-cut

case. Your investigators establish that Dukes is engaged in repeated acts of harassment. What can you do to stop him?"

"Easy. If the acts are of a minor nature, housekeeping details,
lack of heat and hot water—"

"Minor?" Carrie asked.

"Yes, as opposed to threats, beatings, bad stuff. As I say,
if it of this nature, we can telephone the landlord and tell
him to stop."

Hart laughed. "Mr. Oberlander, do you know any landlord
who'll stop after a phone call? When he desperately wants a
building vacated?"

The official pouted. "Some do. I mean, they're not all rotten.
If we don't like his response, we send our investigators to make
an on-the-spot inquiry. A copy of this pink form goes to the
landlord. If we are convinced the allegations are true, we ask
the landlord to sign an assurance of discontinuance, which has
legal force. He agrees, without hearings, or imposition of penalties, to stop."

"And if he refuses? If he says the allegations aren't true?"
Carrie was getting excited.

"We go into hearings. These hearings are quasi-judicial. If
the landlord refuses to attend, or delays, or gives us a runaround
—they're good at that—we serve a paper on him and he shows.
Usually with a lawyer. And the tenants appear, sometimes with
counsel also. It's like a court procedure. Witnesses are sworn, it's
recorded, and the presiding officer, someone like myself, then
decides whether there is harassment."

"And what then?" asked Carrie.

Hart was smiling again, stroking his upper lip, as if he knew
what the answer was going to be.

"Well, we like to give the landlord a chance to reform. If he'll
sign the assurance of discontinuance and in other ways indicate
a desire to stop, we give him a chance—"

"You mean Dukes and his goons can get away with all that
they've done so far? And can keep doing it?" Carrie's voice
rose. She felt the baby kick, almost in reaction.

"They usually stop."

"Suppose they don't."

"We have penalties we can impose. We can stop him from converting the apartments to other use. We can stop him from demolition. We can threaten to put any new building that goes up under rent control. We can fine him."

"How often is this done?" Hart asked.

"Not too often. I admit it. Usually the guy will stop once we get into the act. You see, if he wants to demolish and sell the land, or put up a high-rise, it's bad for him to have a finding of harassment in the record. The insurance companies, the banks, don't like it, and they may back out."

"What if none of these work?" Carrie persisted. "Warnings, second chances, findings, what then? Suppose he keeps on tormenting tenants?"

Oberlander opened his arms. "Rarely happens, my dear lady. Either he agrees—"

"Or the buildings are cleaned out by then," Hart said. "The blockbuster does his job."

"The what?" Carrie asked.

"Blockbuster. That's what Dukes is. Isn't that right, Mr. Oberlander?"

"I haven't seen any evidence yet, sonny."

Carrie frowned. "I thought that term meant moving in black people to scare whites out of a neighborhood."

"Originally, yeah," Oberlander said. "Today, it's just getting people out in a hurry, no matter how it's done, or who it's done to. Dukes got jugged for something like that, didn't he, kid?"

Hart could not resist the opening. "I imagine you would know the case better than that, Mr. Oberlander. Two men were shot dead."

Carrie gasped. Her heart thumped irregularly. The burden in her belly suddenly seemed too much for her to bear.

The official looked at her with concern, as if to ask why a woman in that condition wanted to get involved in such sordid matters.

"You should know what you're getting into," Oberlander said softly. "These things are exhausting. Hearings, investigations. We ask the guy to sign a consent injunction that he'll quit—provided there's evidence—and if he refuses, we go after a permanent injunction. That really scares them. They can't demolish, improve, build, convert . . . nothing."

"How often is that done?" Hart asked.

"Almost never," Oberlander said. "It's an extreme solution."

"What about extreme acts?" Carrie almost shouted. "Like throwing dead dogs into air shafts? Jamming up keyholes? Or Danny getting smacked around by that thug?"

"Mrs. Loomis, everything you say may be true. But we have to be an impartial agency. About ninety-five percent of the cases that come in here claim harassment. Would it surprise you that most of them are mere violations, or decreases in service? If you're going to get into this, I should warn you that harassment with intent to force the tenant to vacate is one of the hardest things in the world to prove. Wait till you try to collect evidence. Dukes is a tough guy. People will be unwilling to testify. It will be someone's word against his. He'll have his own witnesses. His lawyers will delay."

Carrie shook her head. "It sounds like you don't want us to do anything about it."

"Not at all. But I must emphasize. Maybe one case a week that comes in here is legal harassment. What are the others? Physical altercations. Grudges. A single tenant with some nutty idea the landlord is after him. Or simple breakdowns of services."

"Do I look like a nut tenant?" Carrie said. "Mr. Oberlander, I'm a college graduate and my husband is an architect. There's nothing nutty about either of us, or any of the tenants of 502 West 84th Street. We include schoolteachers, actors, designers, and one college professor. If I have anything to say about it, we're going to fight this thing down the line."

"We'll cooperate with you, dear lady."

"You know, my mind wasn't made up until you outlined the

interminable red tape we have to go through to get a little justice. But you've convinced me it's worthwhile."

"It is, it is. Goodness knows, there are cases that should be prosecuted. Yours may be such a case. I advise you not to waste any time, and fill the form out."

Carrie turned the pink sheet over. There were no fewer than twenty-two separate items to fill out, multiple choice.

22. Landlord has intentionally decreased, withheld or interrupted the following essential services: heat ☐; hot water ☐; cold water ☐; electricity ☐; superintendent or janitor ☐; garbage ☐; or elevator ☐; Give date and duration of each interrupted service in Part VI.

She wondered, as her eye scanned the complicated sheet, how the Puerto Ricans and blacks managed with such a form. Many, she was certain, tried to struggle through it, and gave it up.

"You could fill it out now," Oberlander said.

Hart got up. "No. I think we can wait a day. I'm going to get all the tenants together and we'll coordinate our reports. We'll send in a batch of these together, so you have them all at once."

"Good idea, Hart, good idea." Oberlander tried to sound enthusiastic. But Carrie, with her actress's ear attuned to these nuances, sensed that he had responded too soon and with too much *brio*. He was like a car salesman who has just been told that the customer will wait for next year's models.

Carrie and Hart got up, thanked Oberlander, and walked out of the office. In the street, she felt faint and suggested to Hart that they take a taxi. He, of course, was penniless. She willingly agreed to pay.

"It's maddening," she said, as the cab honked its way up lower Broadway. "They almost want us to clear out, just the way Dukes does."

Hart bit his lower lip. "They don't really. It's just that they're drowning in complaints, investigations, hearings. They care, but they're tired, tired of everything. Like everyone in this city."

"Well, I'm not tired," Carrie said. "And I hope you're not. That meeting got my Irish up. When can we have the tenants' meeting?"

"Let's try for tomorrow night. I'll ask Hasslinger to let us use the office."

The screams were indistinct at first—women howling, children shrieking. Then, as the residents of apartment 1A fled into the hallway, and to the street, the words became clearer, and the word that Werner Schlossmann heard (as usual, he had been awake) was *fuego*. There was a fire in the building.

Schlossmann's mind was swarming with images. When he heard the first screams of *fuego! incendio!*, he immediately summoned up a vision of Raphael's Vatican fresco *Fire in the Borgo*. How marvelous, the old man thought—as the noises from below grew louder, and orange light flickered on his window—if they were duplicating the scene! A Pope, he thought, there is a Pope standing at a distant window, one of the Leos, gesturing, miraculously putting the fire out. In the foreground, a young man bearing an old man to safety. Aeneas, mythic Trojan founder of Rome. And thick-legged Italian women carrying jars of water.

Schlossmann got out of bed. He was in no hurry. His feet shuffled their way into ancient felt slippers.

Mundito!

Carlos! Ven' acca!

Splendid, Schlossmann thought. A Latin tongue. How close to the street Italian spoken in Raphael's time, or even the earlier date that the fresco was supposed to represent? He awakened Hilda, tapping her shoulder.

"*Tochter, erwache. Es gibt Feuer.*"

Hilda's eyes opened. She heard the screams, sniffed the air, and leaped from the bed, grabbing for a bathrobe and her briefcase. Schlossmann, walking calmly, held the door open for

139

her. As they hurried down the stairs, toward the chaotic yells of the Puerto Ricans, Schlossmann announced: "Leo IV."

"Who? What?" she looked at him as if he had gone mad.

"Pope Leo IV. He is the one stopping the fire in Raphael's painting." And he held his right hand up. "With a gesture like this."

In the ground-floor lobby they ran into the Sims family. Horton Sims was carrying his son. Tony Paz and his wife were also in the hall. Schlossmann noted wryly that it was the minuscule Mrs. Paz who carried *their* child. A cultural footnote: Latin tradition, the women doing the hard work. But among Americanized blacks, the man hefted the child, a distinct departure from African cultures.

"What happened? Where is it?" Horton Sims was shouting.

Tony Paz was carrying a huge fire extinguisher with a long nozzle.

"Back. Fuentes and Escobar." The little man bustled past Sims.

"Can I help?" Sims asked.

"It's almost out," Paz said.

It amazed Schlossmann that the residents of the rear apartment, milling about in the smoke of the hallway, were barely upset. Two small boys chased each other up and down the hallway. A short fat man, naked except for a pair of trousers, and a straw hat, was conversing with a stumpy woman. Another man, a tall fellow with a mustache, was laughing.

Outside, they heard the clanging of an engine, more shouts, a siren. Mr. and Mrs. Loomis came into the hallway, then the Allisters. The men ushered their wives swiftly out toward the street.

"Mr. Schlossmann, you'd better get outside," Carrie said.

Schlossmann bowed, courtly as ever. The *Fire in the Borgo* was pleasing him. As perfect as a Raphael painting. The Puerto Ricans were the mythological Romans and their Trojan ancestors. He was Pope Leo IV. Had Raphael painted it as *IIII* rather than IV?

"One side, one side, everybody outa our way," a fireman bawled. A troop of rubber-coated giants tramped through the hallway. Hilda grabbed her father's arm. "Papa, outside, please. Stop staring."

The smoke in the hallway thickened. People began to cough. It did not seem to bother Mundito and Carlos. They flew about the corridor. On the bannister, the yellow heads of the Gilligan boys, Markie and Stevie, bloomed. "Hey, Mundito, what was it?" Markie called.

"Some guy t'rew a bomb," Mundito shouted. "Me and Carlos peed on it."

"Ah, you're lyin'," Markie said.

"No kiddin'. Me and Carlos took a leak on it, an' most of it went out, dint we, Carlos?"

There was a convulsive belch of smoke from the rear apartment doorway, as if the conflagration were in its death throes. Tony Paz, surrounded by the towering firemen, strode out triumphant, bearing his huge fire extinguisher. He was panting. His eyes were hot coals.

"Is out," Tony announced. "Lucy, take the baby back in. Is out."

A huge scarlet-faced fireman was smirking at Tony. "Where'd ya get that thing? I ain't seen one of them rigs in years."

"From the place I work. Garage. The boss let me borrow it."

"It did the job," the fireman said. From the Escobar-Fuentes apartment there were the sounds of axes smashing at walls, a room being reduced to rubble.

"I knew we would have a fire," Paz said loudly. "Rudy Dukes warn me. He said, you get it, buster, you get the Molotov cocktail. But he knows I ain't afraid of him or his goons. So he pick on poor people in back."

David Loomis and Archie Allister gathered behind the fireman. Horton Sims, leaving Leora and Allard on the stoop, joined them.

"You say some guy started it with a bomb?" the fireman asked.

141

"Sure. You send fire marshal around, I prove it. One of Dukes' goons threw it into the bathroom. Right into the back window. Easy, right from the yard. They ain't got no bathroom no more. Toilet is ruined, sink burned. It was for me, but Dukes knows I'll kill him if he try."

"Tony, please, come in," Lucy pleaded from the doorway.

"You stay out, woman. This is man's business."

Loomis wondered if he was telling the truth. Was it conceivable that Dukes would risk killing or burning people, jeopardizing the lives of the tenants? The man was a thug, a schemer, a liar. But to order a fire started in an apartment crammed with people?

"Was anyone hurt?" David asked.

"Nah," Tony said. "Fuentes was up. He just got back from his job and he was listenin' to the radio. The lights were out, so the guy who threw it figured they was asleep."

Tony gestured to Escobar, the tall man. He had been carrying furniture, boxes of food into the hallway. He seemed calm, conversing in normal tones with his relative, Fuentes, consoling the women, yelling at the boys to give him a hand. He and Tony spoke in Spanish.

"He says he heard someone in the yard and then *whoooosh!* There was a crash in the bathroom, then the fire. He started hollerin', threw some water in, closed the door. He knew I got this thing in my place, so he wake me up."

"Did he see the guy in the yard?" the fireman asked. The hacking, smashing noises in the rear increased. A hose had been dragged in, and they found themselves standing in cool water.

"*Carai,*" Escobar moaned. "*Agua. Mucha agua.*" He talked to Tony.

"No, he didn't see no one. But he find this. Show him, Fuentes."

The tenant opened his hand. He held the scorched neck of a whiskey bottle.

"Looks like the real thing," the fireman said. "Lemme have it. I'll give it to the marshal."

"Do these people have a place to stay?" Horton Sims asked. "I mean, with all that smoke and water. Can they spend the night in there?"

Again, Tony talked to Escobar. Little Fuentes came over. He was laughing. Sims found it scandalous.

"They say they manage," Tony said. "Only bathroom is wrecked. I let them use my place until it fixed up." He looked grim. "Only it ain't gonna be fixed. Rudy make them get out for sure. He wanted to get me, but I'm too tough. I ain't afraid of him, never, not him, or Shlep or Bolo, or super. He don't get me out."

They stood in the half light, obscured by the malodorous smoke, their slippered feet soaked. Loomis and Allister looked at each other, concerned, puzzled.

"I guess we can collect our wives and go upstairs," Allister said.

"Yes, it's safe enough now," David said. He began to cough. They walked outside to summon Carrie and Liz. Horton Sims was behind them. "But for how long?" the schoolteacher asked.

The following evening Danny Hart called on the Loomises. He had not telephoned in advance, and when the buzzer sounded shortly after eight—David had finished drying the dishes, and Carrie was about to turn on the television—they both looked startled. Ever since the fire in 1B, they had been edgy.

Carrie was delighted to see the long-haired young man. He carried a large yellow envelope.

"I hope I'm not bothering you, Mrs. Loomis," he said. "But I heard about the fire, and I think we'd better make sure we have that meeting tomorrow night."

Carrie introduced him to David. She laughed to herself as she noticed the way her husband studied the community organizer. David was not antagonistic to long hair, sandals, the casual way of life of young people. He was merely confused by them. An essential middle-of-the-roader, a moderate man, he was puzzled by any departure from the norm.

"Your wife was great yesterday," Hart said. "She really put it on the line with the Rent Administration."

"Carrie is a clear thinker," Loomis said. "Would have made a great lawyer. In fact, it was one of her troubles as an actress."

"I can imagine," Hart said. "I had the same sort of trouble at the seminary. The day I told my professor of Christian ethics that the Honorable Elijah Muhammad's theories made as much sense as the Trinity, or transubstantiation, or the afterlife, something ended for me."

"I can see why you're in this line of work," David said. "Not much time on the Upper West Side for theology, is there?"

"Not with people like Dukes around."

They discussed the fire. The Fuenteses and the Escobars were still living in 1B, using the kitchen sink for washing, availing themselves of Tony Paz's toilet. Hart had called Dukes' office to see about getting the bathroom fixed. The secretary had promised to have Dukes return the call. No one did.

"I finally got Dukes a few hours ago," Hart said, in his gentle, vague voice. "I told him that if he didn't have that bathroom fixed at once, I was going to file a complaint with the Rent Administration tomorrow."

"Good for you," Carrie said. "What did he say?"

Hart ran his hand through his hair. "He said, 'How would you like to find yourself in the gutter with an ice pick in your chest?'"

Carrie gasped. "He didn't! He's . . . he's . . . crazy!"

"Not so crazy," Hart said. "It's important to him to keep me out of this case. I'm an outsider. I can work full time at it. He can scare tenants, because he's got this power over you. He can drive you out, and he can hurt you while he's doing it. But all I need is my cot at the Parish House."

Loomis's placid face was furrowed.

"This thing is getting ugly," he said. "I'm not sure I want Carrie involved any more."

"David, we're perfectly safe."

"Maybe we are. But you're a month away from delivery. After the miseries you've been through, why have to worry about that hoodlum?"

Hart opened his envelope and spread some papers on the coffee table. "I don't think Dukes will bother people like you, Mr. Loomis, or your wife. He knows who can be abused and who can't. Dukes has a strong sense of the social order."

"You're saying he'll pick on people like the Puerto Ricans downstairs, but not on us?" David asked.

"Yes. He'll attack people where they're vulnerable. A threatening phone call for one tenant, a punch in the nose for another. But he knows you have resources. You can hire a lawyer, and find out what your rights are."

"We've done that already!" Carrie cried. "We're building a case against him right now!"

"Carrie, honey, I don't like this. You aren't Joan of Arc."

"I've never felt better!" she shouted. "David, I want more than anything to get that bastard!"

Loomis looked amused. Unlike most actresses—successful or frustrated—Carrie did not not use profanity. She was in many ways, still an innocent from upstate New York, a land of deep snows and Protestant probity.

"We'll need everyone's help," Hart said. He looked at David. "We'll need a tenants' committee chairman, other officers. It'll mean going to hearings, drawing up papers, doing a lot of legal work ourselves."

"Well . . ." Loomis hesitated. "Is it—"

"Is it what, honey?" asked Carrie.

"Is it worth it?"

Hart studied the papers on the table. "I think it is. It's not just a hoodlum named Rudy Dukes. It's the whole rotten structure—the way the landlords, the city, the big companies can do what they want to people. If we make a stand here, we can get some attention."

"But I don't know if I'm up to being enlisted in a crusade," the architect protested, "if it means harming my wife. We've had a rough time. Frankly, if it gets any worse here we may move out."

"No!" Carrie said. "I like it here!"

Hart stared at his papers. "You'll have to move sooner or later, Mrs. Loomis, so your husband has a point. If Puttering and Dukes can't force everyone out, if we get the courts to enjoin them, they'll wait a year, or until the leases run out. So you'll go eventually."

"That's what I mean," David said. "Why prolong it?" He looked at Carrie. "I thought about this, Carrie. Ever since that fire. If Tony Paz is right, Dukes set it. That's nothing to fool around with. Waiting here to let that murderous bum fry us in our beds. I'd be ready to move us into a hotel tomorrow. Until you had the baby, and were up and around."

"David, that's a fink's way out."

Loomis laughed. "Well, I'm sort of a fink. I'm not flinching or anything, but I think when you've got a pregnant, shaky wife on the premises, you don't start looking for fights."

Hart saw the look of tenderness that passed between them: the yeasty, lively little woman with her distended belly, the affable, good-natured young man. He sensed a vague guilt.

"I can't make your minds up," he said softly. "But if folks like you move, Dukes will win hands down. The panic will be on. But if you can hang on a little and let me organize a counter-attack, we might have some fun, and we might do some good."

Loomis was a compassionate and understanding man. At his office, he had devoted a great deal of time to a voluntary survey of a block in Harlem, with an eye toward on-the-spot rehabilitation. Without fee, he had served as a consultant, the firm's representative, to a neighborhood group in South Jamaica. But these were tangible, measurable projects, things he understood. What loomed ahead was far more upsetting. Dukes was a bad actor, a cruel adversary, a man who abided by no rules. He would not respond to the wisdom of slide rules and T-squares. Worse, Hart was in no way a man to inspire confidence. David

146

admired his impoverished dedication, his innocent desire to have justice done. But was he totally reliable? Was this starved reject, this dropout, this frail boy in sandals the kind of champion they could depend on? And he knew Carrie. She liked a good fight. Burdened, weary, she would take the toughest jobs. And a visionary like Hart would not, he feared, hesitate to make her the building's Molly Pitcher.

"Fun," David said cynically. "Like fires? Threats? Dead dogs?"

"I think we can make him stop," said Hart. "He's afraid we'll organize. That's why he's putting so much pressure on. If he can get a few families to leave quickly, he'll be on his way. I want to hold everyone."

"What can we do to start?" Carrie asked.

David said nothing. Clearly he had been overruled. Hart held out a sheet of yellow paper. "I drafted a letter of invitation to the tenants. If you could type these up tonight and get them under everyone's door it would help. A personal visit would be better. Remind them how important it is."

When he had left, Carrie sat at David's portable typewriter and started writing the letters. She decided to make them all personal. It would mean a little extra work, but it would be worth it.

"Don't look so distressed," she said. Loomis was pacing the floor. Every now and then he glanced down to the street. He had become almost like Tony Paz—anticipating an assault from Dukes.

"I'm not distressed," he said. "Just distraught."

"Well, what is it? Aren't you in the spirit of this thing? Can't you feel adventurous?"

"I've got the spirit," he said. "I don't mind putting Dukes in his place."

"Then what is it?" She pecked away efficiently. Acting had never produced any income to speak of. In her early years in New York, jobs with Manpower and Temporaries had sustained her.

"I wish we had a more encouraging leader."

"You don't like Hart?"

"He's a slender reed, honey. Dukes will eat him alive."

"He'll have to eat all of us. And I'm indigestible."

Loomis walked over and kissed the back of her neck.

"Move, faggot."

"Drop dead, Dukes," Lobello said. "Come around and say that. With your dog and your gun and everything."

"For God's sake, Ron hang up on him," Dane called from the couch. He had been memorizing his lines when the phone rang.

The daily call—the manager muffled his voice, but they were certain it was Dukes—had become part of their routine.

"I don't like fags in my building," the thick whisper said, "I can't stand their perfume. How'd you like me to cut your belly button out so you can wear it like a ring in your ear?"

"You stink, Dukes," Lobello said.

The door buzzer sounded. Barri Dane got up from the couch, still pleading with Ron to hang up. But Ronnie was a hard-headed Sicilian. He could not resist a vendetta. It was sometimes very hard for him to be a homosexual. Challenges to his virility demanded responses. He could not roll with the punches the way Barri did.

David Loomis was at the door. "Running errands for his wife," the architect said. "We're having a tenants' meeting to-morrow night. Please try to come. We hope to get some action going against this character Dukes."

He gave Barri a typed sheet of information. Dane glanced at it:

IMPORTANT—TENANTS' MEETING—IMPORTANT

Dear Messrs. Dane & Lobello:

The time has come for the tenants of 502 West 84th Street to make a stand against repeated acts of harassment, violations of the building code, and decreases in services, designed to drive us from our apartments. . . .

148

"It sounds terrific," Barri said. "One of us will be there, for sure. Ron? You hear that? Mr. Loomis is heading up a tenants' committee."

"No, no. I'm not heading anything. It's just that my wife and I—" The last thing he wanted was to be propelled into leadership of the crusade.

"Tell that to the goon," Dane said to his roommate. He handed the sheet to Lobello. "Give him something to sweat over."

"You're finished, Dukes," Ron said. "We have a few surprises in store for you. Maybe you can be as slippery as Puttering at ducking subpoenas, but I doubt it."

There was a muffled noise from the phone.

"And yours too, baby," Lobello said. He hung up.

Carrie and David decided to walk to the Parish House. The meeting had been called for 8 p.m. It was still light when they left the building, and the weather was mild. They had knocked at the Allisters' door. Archie said he would grab a cab and make it as soon as he could. Liz wasn't feeling too strong— a long day of modeling hosiery, backbreaking positions, hot lights.

In front of the house Tony Paz was wrestling huge rusted metal sheets from a small battered truck. They looked like the enormous metal plates used to cover street excavations, but thinner.

"You'll be late for the meeting," Carrie said.

"Take a minute," Tony said. "Wait. I drive you over."

Paz set the rectangular plates against the side of the house, beneath his two front windows.

"What are those for?" David asked.

Paz's wife, the little Italian girl—Lucy? Lily?—appeared in the window, holding a baby in a trundle-bundle. She looked distrustfully at the sheets of rusty metal, shaking her head.

"Protection," Paz said. "Dukes gonna bomb me next. But I fix him. Tomorrow I nail up."

Loomis and his wife stared at the ugly sheets. Apart from the esthetic affront—the building would look abandoned—the notion that a fellow tenant had been driven to hide behind a fortress appalled them.

"But . . . you don't mean it, Tony," Carrie said. "Why don't you tell the police?"

Paz dusted rusty powder from his hands. "Police don't believe me. They say I'm nuts, I got grudge against Dukes and tellin' lies about him."

Lucy Paz shook her head and walked away. It was too much for her, Carrie could see.

"But they know about the fire the other night," David said.

"They laugh in my face," Paz said. Elegantly, he held the door of the pickup open. "They say spic arguments. So, I don' need them. I make my own protection. Dukes try to throw fire bomb at me, I be waitin'. Right behind the iron, with my guns."

Loomis felt he was dreaming. This was his home as much as Paz's, as much as Dukes'. He had a wife one month away from parturition, a wife who had been bedridden for seven months. He was David Loomis, thirty-one, architect, citizen, university graduate. How had he suddenly been enticed into this fort besieged by a psychopath, protected by a violent midget? Now he was convinced he had been right last night. They should move. Get out. Go to a furnished room, an apartment hotel. Let the child be born in peace. It would cost them more, but they would have their tranquillity.

"Is safe," Paz said. Carrie had hesitated in front of the truck. "Good truck. I borrow from my boss at the garage. Okay, I drive slow. I'm ace driver. U. S. Army license for all kinds vehicles."

Carrie climbed up. David got in beside her. Tony handled the truck smoothly. He was good at mechanical things, he knew machines, and he liked them.

"Why does Dukes do these terrible things to you?" Carrie asked.

"He knows I ain't afraid," Paz said. He braked the truck

gently at the corner of West End Avenue and 92nd Street. "I know him from way back. I used to work for him. I think he was legit, but I soon find out Dukes is a crook. Police record in Pittsburgh. KG."

"KG?" asked David.

"Known Gambler. Dukes ain't his real name. Rudy is a Polack, or Hunky, something like that. Different name, something like Rudy Dukes, but different." Paz laughed. "Boy, some guy. He is biggest liar whoever lived. When he hire me—way back, four years ago—he say, 'Listen kid, you be tough, you tell people you killed a guy, you got prison record, see.'"

David smiled. Paz was imitating Dukes' voice and doing it with skill—the hoarseness, the clipped words, the secretive quality.

"I say, nuts to you, Rudy, I never kill no one. He say, 'Well, I have, three guys already, and I am tough. I got metal plates in my skull from shrapnel in war in Korea, I shoot lieutenant who bust me, right in the back, I beat up MPs. I am welterweight champ, First Fleet.'"

"How much of that was true?" David asked.

"Most of it is lies. Rudy is tough. He is pretty good fighter, but he stink as a pro. I ain't sure he ever killed anyone. Beat plenty of guys up. I seen him. He knows how to use his fists. Dirty tricks."

As much as Tony Paz hated and feared Dukes, there was yet an edge of admiration in his voice, a fascination with the man. Suddenly Loomis himself was sensing the same magnetic pull. There was unquestionably something intriguing about such gratuitous ingenious evil.

"I quit his lousy job after two guys get killed in the St. Charles. He call me yellow. I say I fight him any day, with knives, fists. But Rudy get put away. Now he is back. Big shot. Puttering hire him. Nobody else would do the dirty job."

"He was hired from the start to drive us out," Carrie said.

"Sure," Paz said. "They gonna put up high-rise. Poor people no place to go, but rich get apartments."

Abruptly conversation halted. The gulf between them had widened. They lived in the same building, but they were light-years apart. Paz was poor. He made do with three jobs, and his wife probably got help from her parents.

Tony parked on West 94th. They walked toward the West Side Parish house. A man selling coconuts and avocados from a pushcart called to Tony. He answered him in Spanish. Both laughed.

"My turf," Tony said. "Everyone know me around here. When I was little kid I work here. Sellin' ices, bananas, soda."

On the sidewalk outside the opened door of the community office, Danny Hart was talking to a huge black woman. She was bespectacled, dignified, a churchgoer and hymn singer. Her hair was plain and straight and her dress was a homely gray cotton. Neither Afro nor dashiki would ever adorn her figure.

"We need fifty dollar," she was saying. "We promise the chilren that Memorial Day picnic, and we gonna have it. But we need fifty dollar. Otherwise no picnic."

"Did Father Hasslinger say he'd get it for you?" Danny asked.

"He do."

"Then we'll get it. I'll go out and raise it personally, Mrs. Hall. I promise you the children will have the picnic."

"I git your word?" As she said this, she looked him up and down. Ponytail, sandals, soiled denims, and old army shirts did not fill her with confidence.

"I'll have the money for you a week before the Memorial Day weekend."

Horton Sims, hiding behind dark glasses and Hilda Schlossmann, walking with him, but a half stride ahead, approached them.

"Let's go in and get started," Hart said. "Father Hasslinger cleared the place out early for us."

"Will he be here?" Carrie asked.

Hart shook his head. "No. Low priority. He's involved with people like Mrs. Hall."

"Will you be able to get that fifty dollars?" Carrie asked as they entered the office, exchanging greetings with Sims and Hilda Schlossmann.

"Maybe from some local merchants. The main thing is not to worry about it. The one thing I've learned about working with the poor is not to identify with them. Sounds cruel, but it's true."

Inside, Hart walked to a small desk. The large front room was used for meetings, in full view of the outside world.

The tenants took seats in front of the desk. Carrie looked over her shoulder. Sims was there, but not his wife; Hilda Schlossmann, but not her father. Ron Lobello walked in. No sway of the hips, no camping, Carrie noticed. He was lean and mean for the meeting—blue jacket, matching slacks. The blond woman from the third floor arrived, wearing her white bakery uniform. In the harsh overhead light of the storefront office, Carrie saw that she was extremely good-looking, a handsome Slavic face, a tall shapely figure.

"Just about everyone is here," Carrie said. "Except the people from 1B. Maybe I should have sent them a notice in Spanish."

Tony Paz leaned over the back of his seat. He was sitting in the first row, looking like an elementary school student. "I tell them. I translate into Spanish."

"Are they coming?" she asked.

"I don't think so. Stupid people. Don't know enough to stick up for their rights."

The only other tenant missing was their neighbor Archie Allister. Probably Liz's illness was delaying him.

Hart, shuffling his papers—he had a stack of A-60H forms from the downtown Rent Office—looked at David.

"Mr. Loomis," Hart said. "I want to do as little as possible. For a tenants' council to be successful, the people involved have to make the decisions. Would you mind being temporary chairman? Just until we can elect officers."

David's tweed jacket seemed nailed to the back of the folding chair. He edged away. Carrie tugged at his sleeve. "Go ahead. It's just temporary."

"Go on, Mr. Loomis," Tony Paz said. "People respec' you. If no respec', this never work."

Reluctantly Loomis walked up to the desk. He looked at Hart. "What do I do?"

"Ask for nominations for officers. We need a chairman, a vice-chairman, and a secretary. No need for a treasurer."

Loomis hated himself for agreeing to the meeting. Old Schlossmann had the right idea. Let the world go by. He'd paid his debts to society, he'd had his involvement. As he thought this—looking at Hilda Schlossmann's grim face—he realized how selfishly he had been acting. Schlossmann and his daughter had seen the edge of hell. Even Sims, the black teacher, and Tony Paz, the three-job man, and Mrs. Gilligan, raising her children without a husband, knew what it was to suffer. He and Carrie were the lucky ones.

David began: "I guess you know why we're here. Mr. Dukes wants us out, and we want to stay. I gather all of us want to stay."

"Or be relocated," Sims said. "In comparable nonsegregated housing. Or be reimbursed for costs involved in moving."

Loomis looked around helplessly. "I gather that we have certain courses of action. Mrs. Loomis and Mr. Hart made some inquiries, they have some forms, they have some information, and I think we can start tonight. Okay?" He looked at Hart.

"Go on. Nomination for the chairman of the 502 West 84th Street Tenants' Committee."

"Right, right. Okay, we're open for nominations."

"You're doing fine. Stay with it."

The loud voice was Archie Allister's. He had come in late and was standing at the rear as if hesitant to take a seat.

"Oh. Hi, Archie, come sit down."

"Hey, Mr. Loomis," Tony Paz called. "He is right. You stay up there and be chairman."

"It's okay with me," Horton Sims said. The black man got

to his feet. "I move we move unanimously to elect Mr. Loomis chairman."

"No, really . . . I don't have time. I—"

Before Loomis could protest any further, the vote had been taken: *unanimous.* Carrie and Tony Paz applauded.

"I can't see how I can refuse this honor, but I'm not much of a fighter. I'll be glad—"

"Don' you worry!" Paz shouted. "We got fighters on this team!"

"You said it," Lobello added. "I'm fed up with that Dukes and his mob."

There was some angry mumbling, some rising argument.

"Call them to order," Hart said. "Bang with the chair."

David did. They quieted down. Nominations were asked for a vice-chairman. Horton Sims was unanimously elected. When no one wanted to be secretary, Sims volunteered his wife for the job. "She'll hate me when I tell her," the teacher said, "but she is a good organizer."

"So, we have our officers," Loomis said lamely. "Now, I'd like to call on Mr. Hart, who has worked on other harassment cases, to outline a plan of action."

Hart held up the pink forms. "These are called A-60Hs. We are going to fill them out tonight. I will help you. They are formal complaints of harassment against Rudy Dukes. We will sign them and—"

He had stopped and was staring at the back of the room. "Yes?"

"Go on, go on. Don't let me interrupt."

The tenants turned around. Lounging against the rear window of the office was Shlep Sharmak. The lights glinted on his lenses.

"Hey, Shlep!" Tony Paz shouted. "You get the hell out!"

"Shaddap, punk. Please, go on with the meeting."

Hart cocked his head. It was pitiful, Loomis thought. No contest. Sharmak, rent gouger, arsonist, strong-arm man. And their knight-errant, Hart, a man without a permanent address.

"I'm sorry," Hart said, "but this is a private meeting." He lowered his head—almost as if expecting a blow thrown from thirty feet away. "This is a tenants' meeting. I don't believe you qualify."

Sharmak opened his hands. "I'm here in your innarest. I'm representin' Mr. Dukes. You folks got complaints, I'm here to hear them."

"You liar!" Paz shouted. "You are Rudy Dukes' spy! Get out, or I knock you out!"

"Tsk-tsk," Shlep muttered. "I am surprised at high-class people like you, Mr. Loomis and Mr. Allister, associating with such trash. Did you know Paz used to be a knife fighter?"

"Please leave—" Hart was saying.

Tony Paz leaped from his seat. "I show you who is a knife fighter, you lousy *pato!*" There was a knife in Tony's hand, a blunted carpenter's tool of some kind.

Lobello blocked Tony's way. He held him tightly. The little man struggled, but he wanted to be held. "Come on, Tony, cool it," Lobello said. His grip was potent. Lobello worked out with barbells twice a week. "That slob wants to break the meeting up. He'll go."

Carrie called to her husband. "David! It's your job. Chase him out."

Vaguely David remembered a political convention some years ago: an angry audience hooting and cursing Nelson Rockefeller, and the governor coolly informing the chairman, (Morton somebody?) *"It's your job, quiet them down."*

"Mr. Sharmak, you'd better leave," David said. He was delighted with the firmness in his voice. "Mr. Dukes will be informed in due time of the decisions taken by this council."

"Sure, sure. I only wanna help."

"I'm not so sure of that. Now, please go."

With the painstaking precision of an illiterate, Shlep had begun to scrawl notations in a dog-eared copy book. He was counting the house, noting each attendant, scribbling names

156

down, licking the blunt pencil. "Yup. Almost a full house. Not bad. I give yez credit."

"You give us more than credit when we get you into court, *maricón!*" Tony shouted. "We gonna make you sweat."

Sharmak turned. At the doorway he stopped. "Whaddya gonna do? File them statements of harassment? Don't you know you can't prove a thing?"

When he had gone the room was silent for a while.

"I guess we got them stirred up," Horton Sims said. "No secrets from Rudy Dukes."

Hart resumed. "I'm glad he's concerned. He wouldn't have sent his man here tonight if he felt secure." He held up the pink sheet again. "Now these are easy to fill out. Why don't we start with you, Mrs. Gilligan."

Mary looked around, as if there were another Mrs. Gilligan in the room. "Me?"

"Yes. Come up here, and we'll fill out the form."

"I'm not sure I want to. I mean, I have no real complaints. I mean, the hot water turned off. And the dead dog. Only it wasn't in my apartment."

They all looked at her. A bad start, Loomis realized. "Maybe Mrs. Gilligan wants to think it over," he said. "Look, why don't we distribute these, read them over. Mr. Hart can explain what each section means."

David passed the pink forms around. When Tony Paz got his, he held it up. "Dukes laugh at this. He got downtown with his lawyers and tell lies, make up stories, frighten some of us."

"What do you suggest?" Sims asked.

"Oh, is okay to fill these out. But Dukes only understand this." Paz made a fist out of his miniature hand and shook it.

The meeting ran longer than anticipated. Everyone completed a form. Sims, acting for his wife, the newly elected secretary, gathered a list of names and telephone numbers. Leora Sims would type them the next day on her lunch hour.

They would each get a copy and thus be able to contact one another at all times.

Hart collected the completed forms. Under an open section at the end of each sheet ("Part VI—FURTHER STATEMENT OF TENANT—OTRAS DECLARACIONES DEL INQUILINO"), he made the same entry on each:

Repeated acts of harassment by Dukes Management Company demonstrate a deliberate campaign to drive tenants from building by any means.

"The City likes things in packages," Hart said. "They'd rather deal with a group, a few of us doing the talking for the rest. That's why they include number 13 under Part IV."

David nodded as they checked the forms for proper dating, signatures. Under number 13 was the question:

Is there a tenant's committee in your building? ☐ yes; ☐ no. If Yes, indicate Name, Address and Telephone Number of the Chairman of the Committee_____.

They all made the notation: David Loomis, Apt. 4A, 764-8990. He was anointed, enlisted, a reluctant captain. How had he been dragooned into this? It was Archie Allister with his cavalier "You're doing fine, stay with it." Clever Archie, that broker, or customer's man, or whatever. He had guessed that the job of heading the tenants' group would fall either to himself or to Loomis, the two WASP lords. So he had euchred Loomis into it.

"Well, that's all of them," Hart said. "Except the Escobars and the Fuenteses. It'll be the most important. The dead dog, the fire." He gave some forms to Tony Paz. "Tony, could you get these filled tonight? It's okay if they are in Spanish—"

"English, English." Tony was annoyed. "I translate for them."

"Get them to me as soon as you can. Before the weekend, so I can take them downtown first thing Monday."

"If there's no more business," David said, "the chair will entertain a motion to adjourn."

Carrie made an admiring *moue* with her lips, as if to say, *That's my chairman.* She moved to adjourn, Sims seconded and the meeting ended. Then all lingered in their seats, as if anxious to talk some more, know one another better, enforce their new-found unity against Dukes.

Tony Paz did not believe in delays, excuses. As soon as he had returned the truck to the garage, he got on a Broadway bus and hurried back. He would sit down with Escobar and Fuentes and fill out the form, just the way Hart and Loomis wanted it. *Carai,* he would show that bum Rudy!

He looked approvingly at the rusty plates stacked in front of the house. Tomorrow, his day off, he would nail them up. Too bad if people didn't like the way the house looked. This was war. It was Dukes against the tenants, but mostly Dukes against him, Antonio Paz.

There was a light on in his apartment. He decided not to enter, but go directly to 1B, tear the Escobars and Fuenteses away from the television, and have them fill the sheet out. He would put it into good English. That would give Hart a terrific file to take downtown. Rudy's phone would start ringing. If he refused to cooperate, they'd call him to a hearing. Once he had to start with lawyers, and be sworn, and give testimony, he would be in trouble.

Tony knocked at the door of 1B. There was no answer. He tried the knob and it swung open. The apartment was dark, silent. Tony called in Spanish for Fuentes, then for Escobar. He flicked on a light switch. The living room was deserted. It had the look of sudden abandonment. Most of the furniture was gone. The stuff that had been left was broken. Tony flew into the kitchen. It was empty. The door of the scorched bathroom dangled on one hinge. The bedrooms had been emptied.

"*Dios mio,*" Tony muttered. "He clean them out. Nothin' left. *Nada.*"

A Spanish-language comic book lay on the floor, a photograph postcard of the San Juan fortress. Oh, how Dukes had hustled them out! The *hijo de puta!* He knew everything. He knew the other tenants were meeting. With the building empty, nothing could interfere with his eviction. Ten or eleven people (no one knew how many lived in 1B) swept out in the night! And he had done it in *less than two hours,* while the others were sitting in the Parish House, planning to fight back! They sat around filling out pink forms, talking about how they would appeal to the City—and Dukes had muscled two families out of his building!

Tony walked quickly to his apartment and rang the bell. "Lucy. Is me, Tony. Open up." He heard Lucy working the combinations of locks on the door—the Medeco Cylinder, the Eagle Kno-Pic, the Supersecurity.

"What happen in 1B?" he asked.

"Dukes and Bolo came. With a big truck. And a caseworker."

"Caseworker?" Paz shouted.

"They *said* he was. Some little guy who spoke Spanish. He said they had to get out, the building was unsafe. He had papers to put them in a hotel in Brooklyn. They started moving all their stuff out. Tony, in fifteen minutes they had the place empty, and those people on the street. The caseworker gave them carfare to get to Brooklyn."

Tony knew that caseworkers could be bribed. It didn't happen often, but when the stakes were high, when the landlord wanted the building emptied, anything went. Dukes must be desperate. Of course he ran small risk with people like the Puerto Ricans. Those poor Marine Tigers, those dumb *Borinquenos.*

"So. He clean them all out." Tony began pacing, in and out of the living room, the front room.

"Tony, maybe we oughta move," Lucy said. She looked like a defenseless child, a tiny woman in a green kimono. Her eyes were round with fear. "I mean, he'll start on us now."

"I know what you thinking!" Paz shouted. "I know what is

in your mind! He go floor by floor and he pick on the weakest ones. First, Fuentes and Escobar, then Tony Paz! Just the way he clean out people next door, Rios and that bunch."

"I didn't say that, Ton—"

"Tha's what you think! Stupid people! Dumb sugar cane cutters, dishwashers, lousy spics! Like what your old man think about me, high-class Italian garbage collector!"

"Tony, please."

"*Ai*, please, please!" He was screaming. "I never move now! I am not like Fuentes and Escobar and Rios, I am a tough American! I got rights! I got jobs! No damn caseworker come talk to me. If he do, I throw him on his *fundillo!* You understand, woman?"

"I understand, sweetheart, I understand. But what kind of way is this to live? Are you gonna put up those metal sheets to protect us? To keep out the sun and the light, because Dukes threatened you? I mean, Tony, it's crazy. It isn't normal."

"Be just for a little while. Until Puttering fire Dukes and we win. We gonna win. We gonna beat that rat."

"We'll have to move sooner or later," Lucy said plaintively. She sank into an easy chair. "You know these buildings are being demolished. So why don't we see how much money they'll pay us to get out, and start looking for a place?"

Paz raised himself on tiptoes. "No. No. Is not just where we live or when we move. How much money, no. Is war. Me against Dukes. Someone gonna lose. Maybe die."

Had she not been accustomed to his outbursts, his vision of the West Side as a stage, himself a leading actor, she would have been more shocked. "Tony, cut it out. You'll make a nervous wreck out of me."

But he had flown out of the apartment. Voices on the stoop told him that some of the tenants were coming home from the meeting. He ran out the front door, almost bumping into the Loomises and Archie Allister.

"Hey, hey, Mr. Loomis," Tony gasped. "You know what just happen? That Dukes. He throw people out of 1B. All gone.

Empty apartment in back. Now he start working on me. I know Rudy. He pick us off one at a time."

Loomis frowned. "You mean . . . in that two hours we were gone . . . he got all those people out?"

Tony jabbed a finger on David's tie. "On purpose. Special for us. He tellin' us, here is what I think of your committee. Here is what I do to my tenants, when you are meeting, making resolutions, filling out papers. Dukes is tellin' us, here is how I do things. No meetings. No committees. No papers."

"Well . . ." Allister stammered. "How could he . . . ? Hadn't they paid the rent? They must have had a lease. We know he hasn't filed for eviction certificates."

Paz began to laugh, a sour noise. "I am next," he said. "He gonna start on me *next*. But I don't move. I stay. You help me?"

"Of course we will, Tony," Carrie said.

"Darn right," Allister added. "We're with you, Tony."

As if playing fish on a line, Dukes had the hot water turned on after the tenants' meeting. Inexplicably, the broken valve was replaced—on a weekend, no less—and the water ran again.

"I think that bum got our message." Ron Lobello said, shaving artfully with his straight razor. "A little community action, and he came around."

"He didn't come around with those PRs," Barri said. "Paz tells me he threw them out so fast they didn't know what hit them."

Lobello shrugged. "It's the breaks of the game. Those spics were born to lose. If it isn't Dukes, it'll be someone else on their backs." He looked at Dane. "You know, I wish he'd come around with that gun and that mutt. Now that we've organized, I bet he'll be nicer."

"You never know," Barri said. "He might even be gay."

Tony Paz took no reassurances from the hot water. Mid-morning, when he felt reasonably certain that most of the tenants were awake, he began hammering up his protective metal plates. When he had finished, the red-brown façade of the old building had a bleak look. The huge rusted sheets blinded the house.

Leora Sims, wheeling Allard in a stroller, shaded her eyes and studied the depressing sight. Tony had just driven the last nails into the thin metal barrier.

"What's the big idea?" she asked. "You moving?"

"Protection," Paz said. "Rudy says he gonna bomb me. He find out. I be ready for him."

Leora wheeled Allard away. Who was crazy? She tried to be tolerant about Puerto Ricans. Little brown brothers, and all that. But Paz had that gleam in his eye. Horton had had some weird conversations with him. But still, he had a point. Someone had started a fire in 1B. And 1B was now abandoned; the people erased, swallowed up in the heartless city. She shivered. At least she and Sims could take care of themselves. They had good jobs, a union, security, and they were tough.

"Bang, bang," Allard said. He pointed his brown finger, shooting stray cats. "Pop-pop buy me a gun?"

Maybe he should have it, she thought. It was a bang-bang world, a bang-bang city.

Liz Allister had a Sunday job. Some photographer, some nut in Greenwich Village, had botched a series of her hands he had taken a few weeks ago. Could she come to his place for a few hours? Overtime, and all that.

Mrs. Allister didn't mind. Like many exceedingly beautiful women she was interested in virtually nothing. She did not care for sports, books, theater, good food, or conversation. Archie worried about her at times; too fragile, too sensitive. Her beauty was a burden, a cross to bear. People stared at her on the bus, in supermarkets. Her blood pressure was low and she was short of thyroid.

Carrying her embroidered Greek tote, Liz walked sedately down the stairs. Again, her supersensitive nose sniffed out something foreign, noxious, in the corridor air. Descending toward the ground floor, she saw two black men entering the building. Neither was Sims, the only black tenant. They were shabbily dressed, stooped, one wearing an outsized green cap, the other a black fedora pulled low over his eyes. They did not quite walk, but seemed to float on silent feet.

The two men came through the inner door, saw Liz and stopped. It was not unusual for people to stare at her—starveling thin, chalk-white, huge pale eyes. When the men stared, Liz halted. She was halfway down the stairs. If she turned and retreated, and asked Archie—deep in the financial section of the Sunday *Times*—to accompany her, it might be worse. She worried about offending the menacing poor of the city. Seated next to a mumbling madman on the subway, she was fearful of leaving. He might be insulted and follow her.

"Git on, she live here," the man in the green cap muttered.

"I goin'. I goin'. Wheah it? In back."

"Back. It open."

They glided past her, two lost souls of the West Side, shuffling, malodorous, deep in narcotics, or wine, or booze. Cautiously, Liz walked down. The two men, without a backward look, walked to the end of the corridor, and entered the opened door of apartment 1B.

That night she told Archie about the incident. He consulted the list of phone numbers that Leora Sims had typed for the members of the committee and called the Loomises. They knew nothing about it. They had not seen the men.

"What do you think, Dave?" Allister asked. "Should we call Dukes? As if that would do any good."

"Maybe we should knock on the door," Loomis said. "If they're drifters off the street, they have no right to stay there."

"Discretion is the better part of valor, Dave. Don't fool around with those types. Maybe we can call the cops. People can't just drift into vacant apartments. And why did that jerk of a super leave the door open anyway?"

164

Loomis pondered the new headache. There were women, children in the building. How had the vagrants managed to walk in? Wasn't the front door supposed to be locked all the time, responsive only to a tenant's key or the interior buzzer? As chairman of the tenants' committee, he had to take action.

"I'll call the police," David said. "You might check with Tony while I do. He knows everything that goes on."

Loomis dialed the nearest precinct. An offhand New York accent, identified as Sergeant Cudlipp, spoke to him.

"Coupla bums off the street? A tenant saw them in the lobby? Well, chase 'em out. They do that alla time. You got to keep doors locked. We can't send men after every wino who wanders into an open house. You people got to be more careful—"

"But the apartment was just vacated. They may have broken the door—"

"Go on down and see for yourself. You wanna file a complaint? Waddya want, Jack?"

"My name isn't Jack. It's David Loomis. Before I ask for anything, I'd appreciate a civil attitude Sergeant." He felt like the good little boy "Gallant" who always said the proper thing in the children's magazine.

"I can be civil all night, mister," the policeman said, "but it's a simple matter. Most of those bums are harmless. They're so doped up they can't see straight. You and some of your fellow male tenants go take a look in the apartment. Tell them to get lost. If they go, okay. If they won't go, I'll send a car over. Fair enough?"

"Fair enough. Except these people can be dangerous. There are women in this building. And little children."

"So? It isn't any different from other buildings. Everyone runs a risk living here. What'd you say the address was?"

David repeated the address. There was a slight pause. Did he imagine things? "Oh, yeah. One of them brownstones. The ones coming down."

"How did you know that?" he asked.

"Landlord told us a few days ago. Sent us a form letter."

Loomis paused. Surely he and Allister, both reasonably strong, intelligent men, were capable of knocking on a door, confronting two derelicts, and ordering them to leave. He thanked Sergeant Cudlipp.

"I'm running over to Allister's, hon," he said. Carrie, knitting in bed, had not heard his conversation on the kitchen phone. He did not want to alarm her.

"Playing chairman?"

"Big executive decisions. I just got the police on our side. They'll toss out those bums Liz saw. If they're still there."

He rang Allister's bell. Archie greeted him, scotch in hand. "Nightcap?" he asked David.

"No, thanks." Allister drank a good deal, but like all serious drinkers he rarely showed the effects. "I guess we have to beard the lions in their den," David said. "Some sergeant told me to tell our visitors to leave. If they refuse, they'll send a police car."

Allister was grinning. "Won't be necessary."

"Won't?"

"Tony Paz chased 'em out."

They looked at each other warily, each gauging the other's thoughts. Here they were, two successful young men on the make, educated, white, happily married. And they had hesitated—*hell, they had been frightened*—at confronting two stumbling blacks. But Tony, that shriveled child of the streets had done what they had feared to do.

"Tony did?" David asked.

"Yup. He says he was ahead of Dukes on that one."

"What did Dukes have to do with it?"

"It's a standard blockbusting ploy. Tony didn't phrase it that way. Empty one apartment, preferably on the ground floor, break the locks, and fill it with undesirables. The rest of the tenants get the message."

"But how did they get in?"

"Dukes or the super opened the front door. Tony threatened

to cut them into minced meat if they didn't get out pronto. They went."

David leaned against the doorway. "But how do we keep them out?"

Allister tapped his forehead with his index finger. "I've been mulling that one around. The key to it is that tramp in the basement, O'Gara."

Again, David had the notion that the battle was not worth it. For Allister to conclude that the hollow-eyed ghost who put out the garbage and occasionally swept the lobby was the key to their security reinforced his own doubts about the operation. Why not just get out?

"Really?"

"We could assess the tenants. Pay the guy something extra to make sure the front door is locked and that 1B is locked all the time."

"It's a thought. But according to Tony, Dukes is calling the tune. He's probably told O'Gara to let these bums in."

Allister pursed his lips. "We'll outbid him. That guy is an addict, I'm sure. He'll do anything for money."

A shiver of Puritan righteousness ran through David. "I wish we didn't have to do it their way—"

"It's a lousy war," Allister said. "Anything goes."

Danny Hart called David the next morning. He wanted Loomis to meet him at the Rent Administration on his lunch hour, to submit the statements of harassment.

"It would be a good idea if you went with me," Hart said. "They're impressed with tenants' committees."

"And short hair?" David asked, smiling.

"It helps. I may have to trim mine before we settle with Dukes. Those enforcement officers always look me over suspiciously. Anyway, I'll see you there at noon."

Loomis rested his arms on the drafting table. On it were revised plans for a middle-income complex—garden apartments, supermarket, stores, schools, civic center—in western New

Jersey. How uncomplicated it would be to live in such a place! He wondered: perhaps, after the child is born, he and Carrie would move. New York, as everyone in his right mind knew, was unlivable, unmanageable, hostile, filthy. They had been suddenly plunged into the midst of all the city's malignant misery. It was almost as if punishment had been visited on them for daring to challenge the city.

The large formless man Oberlander, the official with the haggard face and offhand manner, studied the pink forms. "Nice job," he said to David. He tended to ignore Hart. "Lots of information."

"Now what can you do about it?" David asked.

"I'll check them over with one of my field men."

"And then?"

"I'd say they look pretty good. A lot of tenants who file these are cranks, minority-type people—I'm not prejudiced, mind you —who have grudges against landlords. But these look legit."

"So you can stop Dukes?" Hart asked.

"We'll telephone him and advise him of this, and we'll ask him to stop. If he's nasty about it, we'll ask him to sign an assurance of discontinuance."

"May I make a suggestion?" Hart asked.

Oberlander did not acknowledge the request. David could see that the community organizer was not welcome in the office.

"May I suggest," Hart went on, "that you telephone or send a registered letter to Mr. Puttering. He hired Dukes."

"Yeah, there's some kind of arrangement there," the official said. "Puttering is a hard man to reach."

"A message left with his answering service will do the trick," Hart persisted.

"What if Dukes won't stop?" David asked. "While we were having our tenants' meeting he evicted ten or eleven people from an apartment. Moved them out in an hour."

Oberlander's eyebrows arched. "We know about it. Welfare

agreed to it. People hadn't paid rent. They were creating a nuisance."

"That isn't all," Loomis said. "Since we made these out, he's broken the locks on that apartment, and derelicts have been wandering in."

"Oh, he's a bad boy, Rudy Dukes," Oberlander agreed. "Look, I got other people waiting outside. I promise you we'll act on it. If he doesn't agree to stop, we'll have our inspector up there in a day or two."

"I'd be happier if he were there today," David said. "I have a feeling someone's going to get hurt if this goes on."

When they had left, Oberlander had one of his assistants, a stout dark man named Labato, bring in a thick file.

"How come you couldn't find it?" the official asked.

Labato grinned. "It was filed under his real name." He read the lettering on the manila folder. "Duzich, Ratislav. Sounds like a Polack."

"Croatian," Oberlander said. "I never figured he'd start block-busting again after those people got killed. Used to be a strike-breaker in Pittsburgh. Gambler, strong-arm hood, Navy, dishonorable discharge." He shuffled through the papers. "He's tried everything."

"How come guys like that keep beating the rap?"

"Well, he didn't forever. He did a stretch."

"You gonna lean on him?"

Oberlander nodded. "We'll try. Trouble is, a guy like Dukes covers his tracks, makes sure there are no witnesses, scares the tenants. Besides, he's a psycho. Guy like that is harder to handle than a legitimate businessman."

Oberlander, sighing, reached for the phone and dialed the number of the Dukes Management Company.

Shlep Sharmak took the call from the secretary.

"Whah? Oberlander? Enforcement Division of the Rent Administration? Hoddya do, sir. Yes sir. No, this ain't Mr. Dukes. This is his assistant, Mr. Samuel Sharmak." Shlep looked across the office at Rudy. The boss's eyes were almost closed. He gave no signal. "He just went out the door. Wait, I'll see if I can catch him. . . ."

Rudy paused a few seconds, then nodded his head.

Shlep also waited, yelled for Rudy with his hand half covering the telephone, then, breathlessly, said, "Here he is, Mr. Oberlander, and a pleasure making your acquaintance."

Rudy was the essence of politeness. His hoarse voice assumed a confidential tone.

". . . filed a stack of complaints against me, huh? I'm sorry to hear that Mr. Oberlander. I hate to make this charge but it's the work of that homosexual, that kid Hart who works in the West Side Parish House. You know how these queers are. He made a pass at me once, and it's a personal thing. . . ."

Shlep smiled at the boss's ingenious mind. Not only did he concoct a great story, he made it sound believable.

"How do I explain that the tenants went along with him? Mr. Oberlander, I am not one to deny there have been differences between my firm and some people in 502. You been in the Rent Administration long enough to know what can happen. I lost my super, a wunnderful black man, and I can't get a good replacement. When the boiler broke, I had it fixed. About the fire? It's a dirty lie. I am not an arsonist. I know I got in trouble once, but that's all over. I do not start fires. You know what spics are like. They probly began it themselves. Thank God they're gone, those animals. The other tenants should thank me for getting them out."

Shlep thought: *A genius, a mind like a trap.* If he had had education, he could have been anything, anything at all.

"Threatening calls? Never. Maybe there's some nut loose in the neighborhood. I got queers for tenants also, and spades, and all sorts of trash. They imagine things."

Shlep listened carefully, Oberlander could barely get a word in.

"A dead dog? What dead dog? Do I have to get blamed for every piece of garbage? One of their kids did it. So why

170

are all the tenants after me? Mr. Oberlander, it is no secret that these apartments will not be rented once they are vacated. On Mr. Puttering's instructions. I have been authorized to make settlements with the tenants to get them to move. I'm a reasonable guy. But you always get a couple hardheads, like Loomis, or that teacher Sims. All they need is for some outsider like Hart to get in on the act. He makes them think it's a crusade or something."

"Will you give me your guarantee these acts, alleged or real, will stop?"

"Cease? How can I stop what I haven't been doing? All you want is I should say okay, I'll say it. Okay. You won't hear no more from these people, I guarantee that."

When he hung up, Sharmak was laughing. "You told him good, Rudy. Those guys are all alike. They don't wanna be bothered."

Dukes was not smiling. "Damn freak, that Hart. I shoulda hit him harder." He spun around in his swivel chair, rubbing his forehead. It was getting messy. It was on paper now. They had an organization. They were in touch with the City, and while the City moved slowly, it moved. The inspectors would be around. Suddenly he snapped at Sharmak: "Get the hell out of here. Find that bum Bolo. Give them something to worry about. Tell O'Gara to bust the lock on 1B permanently. He can invite some more friends in."

Ten minutes later his phone rang again. It was Puttering— breathy, trying to camouflage his anger.

"Dukes, what are you up to? Exactly what do you think you are doing?"

"Something wrong, Puttering?"

"What is this with the Rent Administration calling me? How can you let this matter get out of hand?"

"Puttering, you want action. I have to get rough. Leave it to me. I'm going to—"

"No, no, no. I don't want to hear one word about what you intend to do. And remember this, my boy, if they question

171

you, I have given you no instructions of any kind, none, and I have no idea what you are up to."

"Don't worry. I'll keep you clean."

"Get that building vacant, Dukes. And do it so no one gets hurt, so these stupid committees and people like that architect don't make trouble. You can't fool around with these educated types."

"How the hell would you know?" Dukes sneered.

"Listen to me. Break up that tenants' group. You only have seven apartments to work on. Offer money."

"Whose money?"

"I'll share it with you."

"No good, you cheap louse. Empty the buildings yourself."

"All right, all right. Go as high as two thousand dollars for the Loomises and the Allisters. The others, keep working on them."

Puttering began to cough. Dukes was tempted to advise him to choke on his own phlegm; but he needed the landlord. And now that Puttering had agreed to pay off some of the tenants—something the landlord refused to do except in emergencies—he felt better about the operation.

We warned you not to marry his kind. See what you got now?

Her mother's accusing words hummed in her ears. Lucy Paz tried to concentrate on the baby. She talked to him, teased his fat cheeks, watched as he sucked at the nipple, and his eyes crossed slightly. (Normal, the doctor said, a result of concentrating.) He was a fat brown infant, but he was intense, alert, and loud, like Tony. While his lips sucked, he jammed his tiny fists against his cheeks, in fierce commitment to eating.

See what you got now?

Lucy had called Mama Cavatelli in the Bronx. She tried to make it sound like a joke, another one of those crazy things Tony was always getting involved in. But when she told her about the metal plates blocking out the light from the front

172

room, Mama had blown. *A crazy man. Only a crazy man would do that to a wife and child!*

What good did it do to explain that it was a point of honor, *pundonor*, for Tony? How explain his own friendship with Dukes, and Dukes' determination to make Tony bend? Impossible. Her parents had their secure niche. No one pushed them around. Her father was a retired inspector for the Sanitation Department. Mama, with her huge family of Sicilian relatives, including one doctor, one real estate operator, and one bail bondsman, feared no one. They stuck together. Mama could not understand Tony's vulnerability to a landlord. It made no sense to Lucy's parents. *Like I always thought,* Cavatelli would say, *he's a weak-a-ling, deep down that element are all weak-a-lings.* Lucy's recital of their troubles with the building manager elicited only those maddening repeated words from Mama: *See what you got now?*

"Oh, poor baby," Lucy crooned. "Oh, you don't know anything yet. You're lucky."

It was the innocence of the child that terrified her. As soon as he was old enough he would learn that there was never enough money to go around, that his father worked at three jobs, and had visions of glory that could never be fulfilled.

In the hallway, there were shuffling noises as if someone were hauling things along the floor, brushing against the walls. More and more, she was reluctant to go out—even with the apartment engloomed by Tony's fortress. *"Tony, do we have to live this way? Can't you go to the police?* And she knew his angry response before he uttered it: *Dukes got them fixed also.* Whether it was true or not, she had no idea. What mattered was that Tony believed it. Dukes was unbeatable.

The noises in the hall were louder. Feet running? Then they ceased. Gently she set Michael down in his crib, suspending the plastic bottle from the holder. He sucked away, fists pressed against his cheeks.

Cautiously, Lucy opened the door. The corridor was empty. The stairs appeared to be empty also. But the door to 1B was ajar. She was fearful to go near it. The apartment which two days ago housed the Escobars and Fuenteses had become a pad for tramps.

As she stepped into the corridor, a penetrating odor assailed her. She recoiled. The stench was like a presence, a force. She remembered the dead dog thrown into the airshaft. But this stink was different—vile, thick, giving her a faint headache.

Then she saw the brown streaks on the faded yellow walls of the hallway. And more brown streaks on the wall alongside the steps. They had smeared the stuff all over the place. *Dog's*. She wanted to scream. The house was strangling her. And then, abruptly, she grew angry. What as there to fear? She was part Sicilian, of a blood that knew how to take care of itself. Her ancestors managed. They fought back. And they survived.

Raging, she strode down the corridor—the brown streaks ran the length of the hall—and into the vacant apartment. One of the black men Tony had thrown out was sitting on a soiled mattress, an empty wine bottle in his lap.

"You . . . ? You . . . ?" Lucy sputtered "Did you just put that crap all over the hall? You bum! You lousy bum!"

He did not hear her. It had to be someone else. She ran out, made sure she had her keys, locked the door, and raced down the steps to the superintendent's door.

She banged it, fear giving way to rage. There was no response inside. More and more the basement door was locked—O'Gara gone, or lying in a stupor. Lucy raced into the house, muffling her nose and mouth with a handkerchief.

In the kitchen she filled a plastic pail with hot water, poured in a liberal amount of powdered soup, found a scrubbing brush, and went into the hallway. "Dirty, rotten bums," she said. "Lousy bums. I'll murder them, murder them. . . ."

She began to weep, not out of sorrow, but because of the choking odor, the malicious intent that had motivated someone to defile the corridors. With vigorous strokes, she began to scrub the walls. The filth spread, vanished, and the clean chemical odor of the soap asserted itself. "I'll show you, you rats," Lucy wept. "I'll never move now, never, *never.*" She understood Tony's iron-headed refusal to budge.

When the tenants came home, the halls still retained a faint reek. Lucy had cleaned the brown streaks as best she could. Toward the end, her small arms gave out, and she left traces on the wall. The old plaster had been so infrequently washed over the years that her applications of hot water and detergent left long irregular splotches, pale cream, gray-yellow.

The story spread quickly. One of Dukes' people had done it. Tony Paz recalled that it was a trick perfected by Sharmak, Rudy's mentor. Usually it was reserved for blacks and Puerto Ricans, on the theory that they would be too lazy to clean up, would live amid the stink until they could no longer bear it, then move.

At a gloomy dinner, Loomis thought again about leaving.

"You want to chuck it," Carrie said. She offered him a second serving of pork roast with prunes. Now that her stomach had settled, and her salivation all but ended, she was more ambitious in her meals. But David held his hand up.

"No thanks, honey," he said. "That business in the halls. Killed my appetite."

"Since when are you so sensitive?"

"It's not my stomach. It's my mental attitude. I have the feeling it's a lost cause. That guy Dukes is insane. He's driven by something. He's like a virtuoso, trying out new themes. Why should we have to fight it?"

"Because it's right. No one has the right to abuse people the way he and his mob do. And we haven't even caught the worst of it."

"We've been lucky. Let's get out before he murders all of us in our beds."

"David, we sat by smugly when they threw those people out next door, and when they let the building crash down around poor Mr. Nordetzki. We let him burn out the people in 1B. We always assume we're untouchable because of who we are. It isn't right. People like us and the Allisters, and the Simses for that matter, and the boys in 3A, have to fight the rottenness in this city. I'm sorry if I sound like a Girl Scout troop leader, but dammit, I'm aroused."

He patted her hand. She got up, waddling, proudly bearing her load, and sat in his lap. They kissed. It began as a simple act of affection, and in seconds they were passionate. David stroked her legs, her firm rump.

"Sorry, buddy," she said. "Short rations for the chairman."

"I know. Maybe it's why I'm getting uneasy."

"Call a meeting. Tonight. I'll go around and knock on doors. We'll have an emergency meeting right here and decide what to do."

Loomis's face drooped. He was exhausted. His neck and back were screaming for rest. He'd had no lunch hour, and had worked too long at the drafting table.

"I suppose we could—"

The phone rang. Carrie got up and walked to the kitchen. "Maybe somebody got the same idea," she said.

But it was not a call from the tenants' committee. It was Rudy Dukes, asking for David.

Carrie held her hand over the mouthpiece. "Good God, David. It's as if he heard us talking. As if he knows what we're thinking every minute."

Loomis got on the phone. He nodded, said yes a few times, then hung up. "He wants to meet with me and Archie tonight. Says he's ready to make a deal with us."

"Just the two of you?"

"That's what he said." He scratched the back of his head. "I can't figure the guy out. He sounded nice as pie. He said this whole thing was a misunderstanding and he wanted to clear it up."

"Hold on to your wallet."

Dukes met them in a bar at the corner of Broadway and West 107th Street. It was a dingy place, with one booth occupied

176

by solemn Puerto Ricans, and another by some shock-headed Columbia students. It was dimly lit, conducive to low voices and slow motion. Even the elderly bartender seemed stupefied.

Allister and Loomis sat opposite Dukes. He was drinking imported beer. Allister and Loomis ordered scotch. They made some embarrassed small talk. David had never had a chance to see Dukes at close range; he found him oddly impressive in appearance. It was a tough, cold face, but not unintelligent. The slanted eyes and the thin mouth gave him a wary look, but the man smiled easily, and he talked well. He talked a great deal, in fact. Strange, David thought, for a fellow who had been so hard to reach on the phone, who had proved so elusive.

"You people I can talk to," Dukes said. "I know my tenants."

"I don't know," Allister said, feeling impelled to defend the other tenants. "Miss Schlossmann is a college professor. The Simses are schoolteachers. Lobello and Dane are bright guys."

Dukes crinkled his nose. "*You* know what I mean, Mr. Allister. You dig me, don't you, Mr. Loomis?"

"I'm not sure I do," David said.

"You guys have it made in the real world. Not crummy teachers, people worrying about their phone bills. But real guys. You both got futures."

Allister nudged Loomis's knee. What was it? Warning? Amusement? There was something faintly pitiful about the hoodlum's effort at conciliation. He was a crude man, but there was something subtle and evasive in him. He wanted to be better than he was, but the means of elevating himself seemed to confuse him. It was as if he realized that beating up losers like Danny Hart, threatening midgets like Tony Paz, ordering halfwits like Bolo and Shlep around, were no substitutes for status, for power, for the respect of his fellow men.

"We won't have very pleasant futures," David said, "if you keep smearing filth in the building and starting fires."

Dukes raised his eyebrows. His oriental eyes were almost closed.

177

"I played rough, hunh?"

"Rough and dirty," Allister said. "Dukes, you don't seem to understand. Mr. Loomis and I are family men. We have wives to worry about."

"I ever threaten you or your wives?"

"No," Archie said. "But others—"

"Who? Who? That lunatic Paz? Don't you know he's nuts? He'll say anything to make himself sound important, to add a few inches to his heighth."

David sighed. "You're pretty quick to condemn people."

"Look, Mr. Loomis," Dukes said. He was confidential, sincere. And the incredible thing to David was that he *believed* Dukes. The manager had turned his head, pushed his jaw forward—the essence of truthfulness. "Look, if that building wasn't coming down, let's say I was looking to renovate and raise rents, make it a classy place, you two men would *thank* me for what I'm doing."

"For what?" David asked. "Starting a fire? Tossing dead dogs around?"

"I never did either of them things."

"Tell us about this big favor you've done," Allister said.

"You know what I mean," Dukes said. "The rest of the people in that house are garbage. You wanted those spics playing *bolita* and having bongo parties on your stoop?"

"They didn't bother me," Loomis said.

"I got complaints about them," Dukes said.

"Dukes, my wife isn't feeling so hot," Allister said. "Could you get to the point? What do you want to tell us?"

The shrewd eyes studied Allister, and Allister was uncomfortable. He wasn't sure why. Dukes had been obsequious, almost servile. But now that Allister mentioned his wife, a cunning glaze had come over the manager's face. It was as if Dukes were saying: *I know your kind of wife, and I know the troubles she makes for you.*

"I'll level with you," Dukes said. "Whaddya wanna fool around with this tenants' committee? What'll it get you?"

178

"It might get you to treat us decently," Loomis said. "For openers, you could fire that creep of a super. Keep the front door locked and the bums out."

"Housekeeping," Dukes said. "It's hard to get good help."

"That won't do," Loomis said firmly. "You want to force us out of the house. We might have listened to you, but you came on like a hoodlum. People don't like being pushed around."

"Nobody woulda moved. There's no place to move in this town, not for slobs like Paz and those faggots and old guys like Schlossmann. Stupid people like that refuse to budge. They're scared to go. I had to shake them up."

"That's why we have a tenants' committee," David said. "And that's why you're going to have an inspector around tomorrow, and hearings at the Rent Administration, and if any more dog crap is smeared in the hallway, a trial in tenant-landlord court."

"You won't beat me."

"I'm willing to find out," Loomis said. "How about you, Archie?"

"I'm with you, Dave."

"That's how it is, Dukes. You see, some people have a sense of outrage. You succeeded in doing what no one else could do with such a mixed bag of people. You united us."

"Ah, come on. So you're chairman of the tenants' committee. So you'll haul me down to hearings. I got lawyers also. Puttering has lawyers. You can't lick us. Even if you do, it'll drag on and on. I been through these things. We can dodge you and fake you and give you trouble, and what happens in the end? When we want it, that building will be empty, people will get hurt—"

"Wait just a minute," Allister said, his handsome face turning crimson, "wait a minute. Did you ask us here to threaten us?"

"Nah, nah." Dukes laughed. "I know who to hit. I hit plenny a guys in my time. You know I almost killed a lieutenant in the Navy? Tony tell you that? I already leaned on that faggot Hart. Maybe I might drop one of those nances, or that jigg Sims, with the commie wife. But people like you—I know better. I have a respect for high-class people."

He was damned near unbelievable—street-brawling hoodlum and social climber combined. "What do you have in mind for *us*, then?" David asked.

Dukes showed the empty bottle to the bartender. "Once again, Jack." He dusted the bottom of his squashed nose with a thumb, fighter style. "Since you wanna go through with this committee —why I don't know, all them hearings and paper work for a buncha slobs—I'll make you my best offer."

Allister nudged Loomis again under the table. Dukes missed nothing. He saw the knowing look that passed between them. The fake joviality on his face, the familiar manner gave way to a dull stare. "Don't trust me, hunh?"

"We haven't heard what you have in mind. What's your offer?" David pushed the second scotch away.

"I'll pay you to get out."

"Really?" David asked.

"I got to get seven tenants out. You two are the only ones I'll make the deal with. The rest of the scum there'll get out when I tell them to get out."

Apparently the thought of Sims, and Dane, and Lobello, and Mrs. Gilligan and the others defying him, lingering in their weakness, cowering in the high-ceilinged rooms, filled Dukes with rage.

"So, once we're out, you can concentrate on them." David was sweating.

"That's my business. They aren't anything to you."

David did not respond. Dukes saw the hesitation on his face. Yes, he had told the architect the truth. They weren't anything to him, or to Allister, or to their high-class wives, the little blonde ready to drop the baby, and the tall cool glass of ginger ale. Dukes knew his people. Those four, those dwellers on the fourth floor, had little in common with Tony Paz.

"There's a moral issue involved," Loomis said.

"Why? I'm a mean bastard? I did some lousy things? Listen, this is a tough racket. You can't stop progress. I'm helping upgrade the city."

"A public servant, is that the idea?" Loomis asked.

"That's it. Only it's the kind of service damn few people are willing to do." He grinned. "You'd be surprised how many big shots know what I'm doing. You'd be surprised how many cops know me. They're on my side. I handle a lot of cruds the way *they'd* like to."

"Cruds like old Schlossmann?" David asked, feeling the anger rising in him. He was faintly dizzy. "Or women like Mrs. Paz?"

"They're in the way," Dukes said. "I made you guys an offer. That's all we got to talk about."

Allister looked flustered. Before David could stop him he blurted out: "How much?"

"Okay," Dukes said. "Now we're in the ring." He sat up straight in the seat. He was wearing an expensive blue turtle-neck shirt. In the darkness of the booth, his square white face appeared detached, isolated, like King Charles' head.

"Wait a moment," Loomis said. He had wanted to get Archie aside, perhaps talk it over with him, with their wives.

"What's to wait?" Dukes knew it would go this way. People like Allister and Loomis were lousy bargainers. They felt it was dirty, beneath them, to negotiate with the likes of Rudy Dukes. "It's money outa my own pocket," he said, with a pained look, "and I'm gonna lose money on this whole thing unless I can clean the dump out soon. But here it is. One thousand five hundred bucks for each of you."

"Ridiculous," Allister said. "Won't even cover moving expenses." He seemed to be deflated.

"It doesn't seem like much," David agreed. "I've heard of cases where landlords paid as much as ten thousand to get a tenant out. Not that we want to hold anyone up."

"There was a case of a lady who owned a bar over on Lexington Avenue," Allister said quickly. "I heard she got two hundred thousand to move out."

"That's all there is," Dukes said. "You're gonna get out anyway. It'll get worse before it gets better. Once the ground floors are empty, I can't be responsible for what kind of trash moves in. Your wives ain't safe. Take it, last time around. I'll go to one thousand seven hunnert and fifty."

"Dukes," Allister said uneasily. "You call us in here for some big deal, to straighten out this mess, and what is it all about? A payoff, and not a very big one."

"Would a big one make a difference?"

Allister lowered his head. Dukes had him. Yes, anyone could be paid off. All that noble stuff—tenants' committees, the organizer from the minister, the inspirational meetings where spics and WASPs got together—all that garbage, Dukes was telling them, could be canceled with cash.

"It might," Allister said nervously. "I'm speaking for myself, not Mr. Loomis. My wife isn't happy. You've helped make her a nervous wreck."

"I told you people. Get out." The hint of bloodied noses was pronounced now. Dukes' square fists—Loomis marked the blockish ring on his right pinky—rested on the table.

"We're back to where we started," David said. Was he afraid of this illiterate galoot? No, it wasn't fear. How could he describe it? A sort of fascination. He understood why Tony Paz could not shake the man or his memory. One looked at Dukes and one got a glimpse of another world, subaqueous or extraterrestrial. He was a throwback, a vestige of an older race, some tracery of man, a giant before the flood, one of the vanished Anakites of the Bible.

"Forget about the two-hundred-grand payments," Dukes said with finality. "You got the offer. It'll help. There's no more money around. I got to make a profit. I'm just a hardworking Bohunk from Pittsburgh trying to make good." He jerked his head back. The change in lighting turned his eyes into black holes, accented the gouges of his cheekbones. "Never had the advantage of no college education. Old man was a coal miner. Ever been in the mines?"

Loomis shook his head. "Dukes, we appreciate your problems. I'd like to see you make good. But not at my expense. Besides—I think Archie is with me—we have a sense of justice. I'm against threats and beatings and arson. Before you take any more jobs for Puttering, maybe you'd better get some medical help. You take too much joy in tormenting people."

"I got enough of that from the shrink at Dannemora. Free association. Inkblots. I was three steps ahead of him."

"I don't doubt it," David said. "You're not stupid."

"Yeah. With an education I could join Haman, Lord & Fawcett. Or be an architect. Or a broker."

The man was pitying himself. He was not acting, not threatening anyone. Loomis found him even more offensive when he asked for sympathy.

He looked at Allister. "I guess we'd better go, Archie."

They got up.

Dukes was rubbing his fists. There was no mistaking the gesture. He would have enjoyed using them on these two job-holding, wife-loving, soft-handed jerks. It was not their resistance that infuriated him—in the long run, they would spook—but what they *were* that aroused his hatred. In a way, he detested them more than he did a frustrated hood like Paz, or a smart spade like Sims. Paz and Sims were closer to him. They had known the gutter, the taste of blood in the mouth.

"Let us pay for the drinks," Loomis said. "From the tenants' committee treasury."

"Forget it. You'll be paying for a lot more than booze before I'm through. Both you guys better wise up."

As they rode back in a cab, Allister was visibly upset. "That goon, that gangster. There must be some way of putting him in his place. We ought to go to the police."

Loomis was shaking his head. "I don't think it'll help. He covers himself. There are never witnesses. And the cops aren't interested in fights between tenants and landlords."

"Somebody'd better be interested. I don't know how long Liz can stand this." Allister was trembling.

"I'll call Hart tomorrow morning. We need some action from the Rent Administration."

When Allister got to his apartment—there was the usual wait in the hall while Liz fiddled with the locks—his nose sniffed the lingering stench of Dukes' latest outrage. Liz must be suffering. He dreaded the confrontation.

In a white crepe gown, she was so staggeringly beautiful that he coud not stop staring at her. Too much for him, too much. Liz had been courted by a Broadway director, an international vice-president for a cosmetics manufacturer, a Greenwich Village artist who had parlayed personal eccentricities into big money. Yet she had married him; handsome, articulate, ambitious, but no real competition for the others. He wondered why. Perhaps it was because Liz was essentially a passive, fearful woman. Not very bright, Archie realized, and not aware of much beyond the right way to hold her head—oh, what a head!—or her hands, or her reedy body.

He told her of Dukes' offer.

"I assume you accepted," she said wanly. She was barely able to talk.

"No, we didn't," Allister said. "Loomis and I feel an obligation to stand together with the others and put that rat in his place. He simply shouldn't be allowed to get away with the things he's done."

"Darling, need it concern us? I mean . . . those other people . . . what do we have in common with them?"

"You have a point. But let's be honest. One thousand seven hundred and fifty is peanuts. We'll have to double our rent to get anything like this—these huge rooms, the view. I wish to heck Puttering *had* renovated and raised the rent, instead of just tearing the place down."

"But suppose you ask him for more."

"More?"

"If that monster Dukes wants us out so badly, let him pay for it. Don't tell Loomis you're negotiating. Just do it."

184

Allister looked vaguely pained. "I suppose I could. If he got up to five thou—"

"He will, Archie, I know he will. Darling, I have to tell you, I can't live here another week thinking we may be burned in our beds. The odor in the hallway. I found that Paz woman scrubbing . . . filth . . . off the walls—"

Tears rimmed Liz's huge white eyes. The Delft-blue pupils seemed to have been obliterated. Oh, she was too precious for him. Too much beauty, too much independence with her high-paying modeling jobs, too much exquisite weakness.

Allister walked to the phone, paused a moment, then dialed Dukes' number.

There was no answer. Somewhat relieved, Allister did not try again that evening.

"Move, nigger."

"Drop dead, Dukes."

Leora Sims, having completed the litany, kept the phone off the hook. The nightly telephone calls had become part of their routine. Horton had argued for keeping the telephone disconnected all night. But Leora had refused. "I won't admit to that honky that we're scared. Sims, once we do that, he knows we have been spooked. And this big mother doesn't spook."

But they were unable to sleep after the interruption. The clock read 3:25 A.M. Didn't Dukes ever sleep? They were sure it was Dukes—a whispered threat. He was a caricature of a bad guy, a self-created hood. The gangster intonations, the swagger, the bragging. How could anyone take Rudy Dukes seriously?

Unable to sleep, Sims lit a cigarette, turned on the all-night news radio station and sat up in bed. In the adjoining bedroom Allard mumbled—*Hraarh! Hraarh!*—then gnashed his teeth a few times. Was the child a secret worrier? Sims wondered about the exquisite boy. They had not pampered him, but he was surely a middle-class child—well-fed, well-dressed, raised in a home with books, music, art. He heard whole sentences and a variety of words. *Ergo,* a middle-class child. No brawler, no curser, no wild racer through crowded streets like the Puerto Rican kids down the block.

Sims worried (he would never tell Leora) that Allard would miss growing up with a certain toughness, a cruel dexterity, a useful slipperiness, traits that might prove more valuable in New York than a rich vocabulary. They were raising Allard properly and he might be unprepared for a world populated by Rudy Dukeses and Shlep Sharmaks.

"What are you moping about, Dad?" Leora asked.

"Life in the Big Apple. Does anyone call the city the Big Apple any more?"

"Old folks like us'n." She nestled close to him.

The cigarette roiled his stomach. Sims extinguished it on an ashtray on the end table. The butt stank immoderately, and he got up and emptied it into the toilet. Leora watched him, slender, slightly stooped, his pajamas bagging. He seemed defenseless. Horton Sims the peacemaker, the one black teacher who got across to the worst of the bad mothers, hiding his fear with a blank face.

"Maybe we should take that dude's advice," Sims said. He sat in a stuffed chair at the end of the bedroom, and she saw only the black oval outline of his head.

"Dukes?"

"Yeah. Maybe we are dumb hanging around."

"Hortie, we are officers of the tenants' committee. Mr. Vice-chairman and Madame Secretary."

"You don't sound thrilled by it either."

Leora sat up in bed. "Seemed the proper thing to do. Brotherhood of man. Loomis and his wife, they're okay. No big liberal pitch, just decent people. Funny. It almost seemed like we owed *them* something, that *we* were obligated to go along with the united front against the landlord."

"I don't mind chipping in. But, Leora, I have never been a joiner, an organization man."

They were silent a moment. She sighed. "Ah, shoot, Sims. We're both scared."

"I guess we are."

"Not scared stiff, just unnerved. That bum Dukes has done it. He just wants us out. Ever since that fire, I get nervous every night."

Sims nodded. "I know. I've seen you at the Nembutal twice."

"The rat. We could have stayed here till Allard grew up. It's the best place we've ever had. He could have gone to Columbia and lived with us. And the bookshelves we wanted to put up. That secondhand Steinway we looked at—"

He got up and sat on the bed, embracing her hip, leaning over her. "We'll get it, Leora, we'll get it. It's just we got caught here. In the path of progress. We've been redeveloped out of existence."

"But where to, Sims? Where do black schoolteachers go? Out to Queens, in South Jamaica, where Allard can learn to mainline heroin? Or Fresh Meadows, if we can get in? Dammit, I am a New York girl."

"I'll start looking. Maybe the union can give me some leads."

"I keep thinking a miracle might happen. The banks might run out on them or something."

"I still got hopes." Sims patted her leg. "Fellow told me if these cases of harassment are proven, they get an injunction put against the landlord and he can't do a thing. Can't demolish, can't build."

Leora embraced him. "Hang in there, Lefty. They haven't laid a glove on you."

"Love you, Leora."

Dukes had driven a wedge of terror into their lives.

An urgent meeting of the tenants' committee was called the following night in the Loomises' apartment. Every apartment was represented. Barri Dane attended for 3A. David was surprised to see Mr. Schlossmann himself, rather than the awesome

187

Hilda, come shuffling into the room, proper in a black suit and a black tie, bowing to everyone.

"Dan Hart won't be able to come," David said. "Father Hasslinger has him out working the welfare hotels tonight."

"Where we all may end up," Barri Dane said.

That morning Tony Paz had been appointed a one-man committee to contact the police and the Fire Department. Tony knew the neighborhood. He claimed to know the cops. But David wondered if he was the right man for the job. Tony often hinted at dark deeds in his past, a record for minor offenses. Would they laugh him out of the station house?

"The cops don't know from nothin'," Tony reported. "They say, if he make phone calls, contact the phone company. He start a fire, see firemen. He stick stuff in keyholes, complain to Puttering, he is the owner. We got to file a complaint." Paz paused dramatically. "I tell you, he is payin' them off. Rudy pay off everyone before he through—inspectors, caseworkers, cops, firemen, anyone who take a buck."

David saw an opening. He had decided to tell the others about Dukes' offer. Allister had resisted the idea. "Is it necessary, Dave? Maybe he'll up the ante, but if all these people start pestering him. . . ." But David felt they were obliged to tell the committee.

He disclosed the details of Dukes' meeting with them. He even mentioned the sum of money—one thousand seven hundred and fifty dollars. There was a breathless silence, a whistle from Barri Dane, an arch look from Mary Gilligan, an exchange of glances between Horton and Leora Sims.

"What are you saying, Mr. Loomis?" Sims asked.

"That any of you are free to ask Dukes for money to move out," he said.

"I doubt he'll appreciate that. He'll never go that high for *us*. I don't mean that insultingly, but Dukes is a fellow who feels he knows everyone's price." The teacher smiled.

David was uneasy. He saw Carrie blushing. "I don't know that Archie and I are valued so highly."

"Don't get me wrong. Dukes thinks so."

"I never ask that bum for money!" Tony Paz exploded. "I die before I go on my knees to him for a nickel!"

"Not everyone's got your pride," Mary Gilligan said. "Some of us got money problems. Some of us don't like the idea of getting burned out. Or living in a house boarded up with tin in front."

Paz was ready to sail into orbit. "Whah? Whah? I protectin' everyone here with my metal! You don' know what I do to protect this house!" He bobbed his head. "I got more than metal. I got surprise for Rudy Dukes when he come around."

"Yeah," Mary said. "You'll get us all killed."

Paz bounced up, his arms jerking. "But not you. You got better things for Dukes. I know from before."

There was an embarrassed silence. Mary Gilligan brushed her hair back. Her ears and her neck darkened, and she looked as if she had sustained a blow.

"Tony, that's enough," David said. "I spoke to the Rent Administration today. They talked to Dukes on the phone. He denied everything. He says this is a grudge fight, that it's a conspiracy to put him out of business—"

There were hoots, laughter. "I bet he say I am responsible!" Tony shouted. "He blame me!" He sounded ecstatic. It would be an honor to be named Dukes' prime adversary.

"Oberlander didn't go into detail," David said. "He's cagey. But he is sending an inspector up tomorrow. So please, anyone who is at home—wives, Mr. Schlossmann, Barri—cooperate with him and give him the details of what we've been living through."

"What happens then?" Allister asked.

"The Rent Administration assured me that they'd have Dukes on the carpet for a hearing as soon as the report is filed."

"We could all be dead or driven nuts by then," Leora Sims said.

"Not if we stand together," David said. "If we refuse to budge Dukes will have to let up. Let me be mercenary about this. If he wants us out so badly and sees we won't run, he may pay us to get out. I mean, pay us well, to cover moving, interim expenses and so on."

The looks of disbelief on their faces disheartened him. Paz was shaking his head. Mary Gilligan had covered her eyes. David had the feeling that after the way Paz had insulted her she would not attend any more meetings.

"We are going to file another form A-6oH, a statement of harassment, concerning the filth in the halls yesterday. We are going to bombard the City with these. Every time Dukes strikes, we will strike back."

David spread the pink form on the coffee table and offered his pen to Barri Dane, who was sitting alongside him.

"Mr. Loomis, sir, please," Werner Schlossmann was saying.

It was so strange to hear him speak that everyone stopped and stared at him. Schlossman fiddled with his frayed black tie. Mourning?

"My daughter has a late class and has sent me as her proxy," Schlossmann said in professorial cadence. "She has asked me not to speak, but I am impelled to. I know a little about tyranny, and we are here involved with a small tyrant, a fascist of hallways, a commissar of airshafts."

There was an absolute dignity about the man, a wry wisdom. Up to that moment, they had regarded Schlossmann as a cracked hermit, pecking away at his typewriter, forever doffing his hat, opening doors for ladies, mumbling to himself as he took his constitutional along Riverside Drive.

"Now these interesting papers Mr. Loomis has," Schlossmann said, "are helpful. But they are only paper. And tyrants do not respect paper. Please recall Herr Hitler's references to the Treaty of Versailles."

It was marvelous, Carrie thought. He was lecturing them, treating them like students. Suddenly the apartment was transformed into a lecture hall. The uncomprehending looks on the faces of Tony Paz, Mary Gilligan, and Barri Dane were immaterial. If they did not understand him, they respected him.

"So with our oppressor," Schlossmann said. "More than these reports is required, if we are to survive."

"What do you suggest, Mr. Schlossmann?" David asked.

"I have given a great deal of thought to the matter. We require a community action directed against him."

"But that's what this committee is," Allister said.

"The committee is a structure. I speak of a direct action."

"But what can we do?" asked Leora Sims. "Hold a party?"

"In a sense, Mrs. Sims, yes." Schlossmann stood up. He hooked his hands on his ragged lapels. "Consider. The hallways, the stairs are in deplorable condition. In deference to the ladies, I will not go into details. In spite of Mrs. Paz's courageous efforts the walls are dirty and are redolent of ordure. Mr. Dukes' storm troopers were thorough. Sadists and hoodlums are of a thorough nature, since they derive erotic pleasures from torturing innocents."

David darted a look at Carrie. She was wide-eyed. The Simses were smiling. Leora nudged Horton. It was as if the committee had discovered a jewel, a resource of good sense and courage. Who would have believed it of Schlossmann?

"But what do you suggest?" asked Carrie. "Should we picket his office?"

"No, my dear Mrs. Loomis. Picketing is symbolic. It is not a direct attack."

"Should we start calling *him* in the middle of the night?" asked Leora Sims. "Threaten him?"

"No, that would be what he wants. He thrives on childish confrontations. We must attack him with the simplest of weapons—an affirmative cooperative effort."

"Such as?" Sims asked.

"Painting."

"Painting?" David repeated.

"The hallways. The corridors. Mrs. Paz, that lovely Italian girl, gave me the idea. When she took it upon herself to clean the walls, I realized that they had needed cleaning even before Mr. Dukes perpetrated his deed. Then I carried it a step further.

Let us join together and paint the hallways. All of us. A combined effort, a statement to him that we like this house, we intend to stay, and we will make it attractive and livable."

Everyone mulled over Schlossmann's notion. David noticed that people were smiling at one another.

"Listen, everyone," Barri Dane said excitedly. "My friend Ron, he'll get us everything at cost—paint, primer, rollers, whatever we need. He's a decorator, you know. I'll see him tonight."

"Hold it, hold it," David said. "We're still a committee. Is there any more discussion of Mr. Schlossmann's proposal?"

"Good idea!" Tony Paz shouted. "Mr. Schlossmann is right! This kind of thing drive Dukes nuts! He don' understand why we do it, and he go crazy!"

"Will someone put it in the form of a motion?" David asked.

In seconds they passed the motion unanimously. The halls would be painted. Dukes would be put on notice that they did not intend to move, that they would fight him down the line.

A few minutes after Markie and Stevie Gilligan had left for school, Dukes, who had been waiting outside in the Lincoln, entered the building, the leashed mastiff shuffling alongside him, whimpering stupidly.

He ran quickly to the third floor and rang Mary's buzzer. She came to the door, drowsy, her hair uncombed.

"Got a cup of coffee for a friend?" he asked.

The bolt chain was hooked. She made no move to unfasten it. "Rudy . . . go away."

"I got to see you."

"No. And what's with that mutt? I don't like his looks."

"Gentle as a kitten. He's scared of his shadow."

"Yeah. I heard what he did to Paz. Almost tore him apart."

Dukes smiled boyishly. "Anything connected with me comes out bad. That spic started it. He wasn't even touched. I should of let Angel tear his head off. Come on, Mary, let me in. Just for coffee."

Reluctantly, she undid the chain. He knew how lonely she

was. He knew everything about her. As soon as he was inside, Dukes grabbed her, drawing her close, digging his hands into her back, reaching for a breast. He kissed her feverishly, but she refused to respond, going slack, turning her head, closing her eyes.

"Stop. I don't want it."

"Sure you do," Dukes said. He undid the belt on her robe, but she moved away from him, and he did not pursue her.

"Forget it, Rudy. You won't like it because I won't be interested. And if I'm not, you won't want to beat me up."

"I promise, none of that."

"Your promises are for the birds. Sit down."

Breathing heavily through his mashed nose, he sat at the kitchen table. She brought the percolator over and poured coffee for both of them.

"If I can't get any love," he said slyly, "give me the dope on the meeting last night."

Oh, he was shrewd. Mary shook her head. "Unh-unh. Secret. We're sworn not tell you anything."

"Okay." He took out a thick roll of bills. "Need dough? Wanna buy something for the boys? It's a loan. Five hundred?"

"How about fifteen hundred, huh? To move out?"

"Loomis and Allister told everyone? I better get to my office and wait for the calls. Every jerk in this building'll want his share. You know what they'll get from Rudy Dukes, sweetie."

"I don't think anyone'll call," Mary said. "We made our mind up. We're staying."

Dukes sipped his coffee. His eyes tried to mock her, but she was in command. "Real community stuff, huh? You ain't that type, Mary."

"I'm with them."

"To hurt your old stud? Your main man?"

"Nothing personal, Rudy. It's just we're sick of being treated like dirt."

Dukes leaned over the table and began to stroke her hand.

She had tantalizingly smooth skin, strange in a woman who had led a rough life. "I haven't bothered you."

"You will when you're ready. Besides, I have no place to go."

"I told you. I'll fix it up with a relocation outfit. I'll pay the fee."

"I know all about them. Those people next door—that Mr. Rios with the kids. They're still wandering around. I heard from Lucy Paz. They can't find a place."

"Spics. No one wants 'em. But a good-looking dame like you with two nice boys. Any landlord would want you." He puffed out his chest. "Move in with me, Mary. All of you."

"Forget it, Rudy." She got up and the motion of her tall body shivered his throat.

"You better go," she said.

He grabbed her arm. "What are those people up to? Loomis and the rest, and that queer Hart?"

"Make up your mind, Rudy. Either rape me or try to make me turn stool pigeon. Now let go."

She tried to shake loose, but he was terribly strong. "What the hell are they up to? Why you against me? Why are you scheming with them?"

"Because I don't like what you're doing to us! I won't be your whore and get favors from you! I'm through with all that jazz, Rudy! Get out!"

He spun her around, pulled her toward him, tearing at the thin robe. He was a small engine of a man, quick and hard. "I got to have you, Mary," he gasped. "I'm in love with you . . . always. I hate that bastard Frank and all the others. Who? Who'd you sleep with?"

She struggled to get away, but he hugged her close, his grip like a mechanical press, one arm across her shoulders, another below her waist, while his mouth bit softly at her neck, her ear, her cheeks.

"Damn you, Rudy, stop. I won't."

They thrashed about the kitchen, Mary slightly taller than her assailant, her strong legs providing her with balance. When he saw he could not subdue her, he punched her once, a swift professional jab with his right fist against her lower spine. It was a coward's trick, the technique of a professional goon, a strikebreaker.

Mary screamed as the pain radiated, but she did not cry. Momentarily abashed by his act, Dukes released her.

Freed, her pain intensified. He had struck some vulnerable area, and she felt as though voltage was scorching her back.

"Damn coward," Mary moaned. "You dirty yellowbelly. That's all you were ever good for. To hurt people. To get your kicks watching people suffer."

Dukes' face was gray. His jaw dropped and he rubbed his mouth. "I ain't through with you," he whispered.

"The hell you're not." She seized a bread knife from the sideboard. "I mean it, Rudy. I'm not afraid to stick this in you. I wouldn't care what happens. With your record they'd never do anything to me."

He began to giggle. "Wanna see me disarm a dame? You didn't know I was busted outa the Green Berets for socking a lieutenant? Broke his jaw."

"Save it, Rudy." She held the knife forward, braced her feet on the linoleum. "Last week it was the Navy, the week before the Marines. I don't think you ever served anything except time."

He made a sudden move, his arms wide, his head lowered. But it was only a feint. No sooner had he moved—she responded in terror, backing off, her buttocks striking the edge of the stove—than he backed away.

"I could take it off you in five seconds," Dukes said. "But you're too beautiful. Put it away, Mary Waslyk. I'll be back tomorrow morning. I'll keep coming till you say yes."

"You'll be too busy answering subpoenas. You're gonna need lawyers."

He turned to leave. Then, unpredictably, he whirled about

and kicked over the kitchen table. Percolator, cups, saucers, scattered and bounced.

"Get out!" Mary screamed. "Get out, you lunatic!"

Oberlander's aide, Labato, wore a dark brown suit, and a dark brown hat glued to his head. He wore it low over his eyes and never removed it, a cagey man.

When he arrived at 502 West 84th Street in the late morning, the painting project had gotten under way. Ron Lobello had gone out early and come back with a load of paint, primer, turpentine, brushes, and rags. Tony Paz had borrowed two ladders from the garage where he worked. Schlossmann, donning an ancient stained smock ("Probably wore it as a student at Heidelberg," Carrie said to David), was put in charge of the stores. The gear was stowed in the foyer of his apartment. He immediately drew up a schedule, an inventory, and a work plan.

Because it was a weekday morning, only a limited force was available. Tony and Lucy Paz were able to work—Tony was not due at the fruit store until three o'clock—as were Carrie, Schlossmann, and Barri Dane. The latter had memorized his part for the TV film, and was eager to get started. "Isn't it a scream?" he asked Lobello. "We'll knock off Dukes by decorating his dump, for God's sake."

In the dim corridor, Lobello, who came from a family of plasterers and painters, assembled the party. "Now I won't be able to watch you today, so don't let me down. The first thing is, the walls should be fairly clean. Lucy did a good job but they should be gone over again, lightly with soap and water—"

Carrie, in jeans and one of David's old work shirts, was sitting on the bottom rung of a ladder. She had never felt better. "I'm forbidden to swing a brush, Ron. Just a helper."

"Good. That's all we need, our painters passing out. Okay, we'll give the primer a day to dry, then move up. One team can work on the second coat, the other team can go ahead to prepare the next floor."

196

"Enough," Tony Paz growled. "I paint more house than you ever do, Lobello. Only I don' get your kind of money."

"Tony, baby," Lobello crooned. "I'm only helping out."

"Paint must be well stirred," Schlossmann announced. "I refuse to issue paint unless it is properly stirred."

"Of *course*, Mr. Schlossmann," Lobello said. "And everybody—don't knock yourselves out. Painting is tiring work, and we want to make it last to upset Dukes. If you get dizzy from the fumes, go outside."

"Let's go, where is the buckets? Where is the soap and water?" Tony was leaping from his skin. He was the most professional of the group, in a Hi-Lo Paint Company cap, coated white coveralls. He had, for some months, worked at painting before Dukes had hired him with the promise of big money and a reputation as a hard guy.

When Adriano Labato walked into the dim hallway, he saw them at work—two men and two women washing down the walls, ladders, paint buckets, drop cloths neatly spread. He had entered with O'Gara. This was the first inkling that O'Gara had that the tenants had decided to paint the corridors.

"Ah," Labato said, "I see the landlord is fulfilling his pledge."

"He ain't doin' this," O'Gara muttered. "Them's tenants.

Labato was an old hand. He spent his life dodging curses and brickbats from irate blacks and Puerto Ricans. Suspicious, cynical, he kept his hat tight on his head as if ready for a fast getaway, and he trusted no one—tenants, landlords, community workers. They were all fakes, and he, A. Labato, understood them with cold clarity.

"How come they're paintin'?" Labato asked.

"Beats me."

Tony Paz, scrubbing the caked walls vigorously, recognized Labato. Paz nourished his memories of battles with the City.

"Hey!" Tony shouted. "You buildin' inspector! Ask that guy with you why he break boiler, hah?"

Labato's oily face did not react.

"Ah tole him hit's fixed," O'Gara said. "He seen it." The super started to leave.

"Hey, make that guy stay while you look around," Paz shouted. "He is in with Dukes. Dukes put him here to throw us out."

O'Gara, slithering in his fringed jacket, left. The inspector made no move to stop him. Carrie, sighing as she stood up from her perch on the ladder, walked toward him. "I'm Mrs. Loomis. My husband is the chairman of the tenants' committee. Can I help?"

"Yeh," Labato said. He did not sound interested.

"I tell you everything!" Tony cried. "Dog crap in halls! Why you think we paint? Gum in tenant's lock. Dirty telephone calls. No hot water—"

"He says he fixed that," Labato said indifferently.

"After we complain and go to your boss. How is your boss, Labato? What is his name?"

The more Tony talked, the further Labato withdrew into his dark-brown shell. He had learned one thing: *say very little.* Carrie saw that he had to be diverted. She prevailed upon Tony to remain with his scrub brush and took the inspector down the hall. She showed him the broken lock on the empty apartment, and told him of the evictions and the recurrent appearances of drifters.

Labato made a notation when he saw the smashed lock, but he said nothing. Inside the empty rooms, Carrie was surprised to discover two urine-stained mattresses on the floor of one room, and several orange crates. A half dozen empty wine bottles were strewn about.

"It's worse than I thought," she said. "I didn't know there were mattresses here."

Nodding, Labato wrote again in his notebook. Carrie then showed him the bathroom—the ruined sink and toilet, the walls hacked and gouged as a result of the fire.

"I seen the fire marshal's report," he said cryptically.

"He said it was a Molotov cocktail," Carrie said.

"T'rown by parties unknown."

"Dukes threatened to throw one at Mr. Paz, the tenant in 1A."

"The little guy I talked to out there?"

"Yes."

"Hmmmph."

Carrie led him upstairs and showed him the Simses' door, telling him about the jammed keyhole. He asked if either of the Simses were home, and seemed relieved to learn that they were not. Then he followed her up another flight, checking the halls, the locks on all doors, the cleanliness of the floors. On the way down, Werner Schlossmann, standing amid his buckets, beckoned to them.

"Sir, I am the tenant in 2B, second floor back. My name is Schlossmann," he said. "You represent the civic authority?"

Ai, another nut, Labato thought. "Yeh," he said. He was on guard.

"This person Dukes is determined to drive us to the street," Schlossmann said. "He has called me in the middle of the night. Once he told me to drop dead, and on another occasion he informed me that the Nazis should have gassed me."

Carrie gasped. She had not heard this.

"Well, didja know for sure it was him?" Labato asked. He put his notebook away. He was not paid to deal in phone calls, only building violations.

"It is of a pattern, sir. I am not the only one to be threatened. He varies the technique, changes his voice, sometimes has his storm troopers do it. To Mr. Sims he says, 'Move, nigger,' to others—"

"Yeh, yeh. Sounds like some nut is loose. You can testify under oat' at the hearings." Labato started to back away.

"Is there going to be a hearing?" Carrie asked.

"Probly. Don't say I said so. I didn't promise nothing. It's a possibility."

He rolled on oiled bearings, away from Schlossmann and Carrie, down the steps. Carrie walked after him. "It's all part of a scheme, Mr. Labato," she said earnestly.

"Yeh, yeh."

The inspector studied the people working in the hallway, shook his head (what did it mean? Carrie wondered) and walked out. She walked to the door. On the street Shlep Sharmak, eyes buried in the *Daily News,* was lounging against a trash bin.

"You seen enough?" Sharmak asked.

Labato said nothing, waddled down the stoop, and shook hands with Sharmak. Carrie was horrified.

"Want I should tell you anything?" she heard Shlep ask.

Labato shook his head.

"You got time for lunch? There's a new chink place opened." They walked off. She felt anguished. But was it unnatural? The inspector came as a neutral party to resolve disputes. Perhaps one of them should have offered to take him to lunch. Sharmak was an old hand in the neighborhood. It was logical that he knew Labato from prior investigations. But where did that leave them?

She walked back into the hallway and felt dizzy when the first whiff of primer hit her. As Lobello had warned, it stank dreadfully. She walked the stairs slowly, feeling the need to rest.

At night, David phoned Danny Hart and told him about the inspector's visit.

"Doesn't sound encouraging," the community worker said, "but all of these fellows come into cases that way. They don't believe anyone. The problem isn't that we'll look like liars, it's just that there's so little evidence."

"What can we do?" David asked.

"Get all the tenants, as many as you can, in your apartment in half an hour. I'll be over with some new ammunition."

When Hart arrived, he had brought a stack of legal-size forms, with the heading:

STATE OF NEW YORK } SS.
COUNTY OF NEW YORK }

Carrie recognized them from her secreterial jobs. "Affidavits?"

"Yes," Hart said. "If we do them now, we can hit the Rent

Office with these at the same time Labato files his report. It'll show them we mean business."

"They'll have to be notarized," David said.

"I have a friend at the cigar store on West 86th Street. If we hurry, we can get over there and have them notarized. I'll hand-carry them to Oberlander in the morning."

Mary Gilligan was not present and the tenants of 1B were no longer party to the case. The main complainants were Paz, the Simses, the Schlossmanns, Lobello, and Dane. The Loomises and the Allisters would also file affidavits, summing up the inconveniences and assaults of the past weeks.

Leora Sims brought her typewriter to the Loomises' apartment, and she and Carrie, with Hart drawing up the texts, went to work. Tony Paz proved irrepressible. The notion of getting something on paper, something official, something with which to clout Rudy Dukes, inspired him.

"I tell plenty! I tell how that *hijo de puto* try to give me gun to threaten tenants in St. Charles! I tell how he brag he kill a lieutenant once!"

"No, no, Tony," Hart said. "That's all fine. But all we want is an account of what's happened here since Dukes took over."

The depositions were carefully drawn up, David and Hart writing them out in longhand on pads, Leora Sims and Carrie transferring them to the legal forms. Tony Paz's proved to be the longest and most dramatic, and began:

ANTONIO PAZ, being duly sworn, deposes and says:
For 16 (sixteen) months I have resided and continue to to reside at 502 West 84th Street, New York City, in a five-room apartment, number 1A, on the ground floor of this walkup structure. On April 30, Mr. Rudy Dukes, previously known to me, appeared on the street in an automobile and pointed a shotgun at me, while I was watching from the window, accompanying this threatening gesture with a variety of threatening exclamations, such as, "Move, squirt," or "Get out, fink," or "We'll get you, pigeon. . . ."

There followed, in the quasi-legal prose at which Hart seemed skilled, an enumeration of the outrages suffered at Dukes' hands: the fire, the affair of the dead dog, the smearing of filth, the threatening phone calls, the breakdown of the boiler. David and Carrie were impressed with Hart's expertise.

"Comes from studying for the pulpit," Hart laughed. "There isn't much difference between legal lingo and the average sermon. Hasslinger taught me this. He perfected this business of the affidavit. It impresses them downtown, and it scares the landlord when he sees a notarized paper."

The other affidavits ran in the same vein. The Simses' was particularly condemnatory, although Hart insisted that the dry tone be maintained no matter what the outrage.

. . . one Enrique Torres, known in this area as "Bolo," an employee of said Rudy Dukes, was found loitering in the corridor on the second floor. He was chewing gum, and in his pockets, deponent found dozens of large kitchen matches. Two days prior, the Simses' exterior keyhole had been jammed with a mixture of chewing gum and identical kitchen matches, necessitating replacement of lock, costing fifteen dollars and causing concern and inconvenience to aforementioned tenants, Mrs. Sims suffering a recurrence of insomnia and headaches. That night, and two nights following, the telephone rang sometime between 3 and 4 A.M., and a voice, believed by deponent to be that of Rudy Dukes, threatened tenant with words, "Move, nigger."

When it came the Schlossmanns' turn, Hilda Schlossmann appeared reluctant. She kneaded her large hands and looked sternly at David and Hart. There was a hint that they were dragooning her into something dangerous.

"I am not sure, Mr. Loomis, I am not sure we should be involved," she said. "I am wary of putting my name on legal papers."

Her father waggled a finger. "Ah, please, my dear. We do the right thing. The united front against the aggressor."

They chatted with each other in German. Schlossmann patted her hand.

"Miss Schlossmann," Hart said patiently, "I know it's selfish of us to make these demands. Who knows? Every tenant in this building may be out, one way or another, in a few months. But the issue has gone beyond harassment, or legal rights, or even Rudy Dukes."

"I know, Mr. Hart, what you will say." Her long, intelligent face (odd, David mused, she might have been pretty with makeup) was concentrated. "You are going to tell me about the morality involved, the need to inform our hearts, as the psychologist said."

"Exactly," Danny said.

Hilda Schlossmann shook her head. She did not trust Hart with his long hair, his freakish oddments of clothing, his cavalier attitude toward their safety. "This man Dukes is a Nazi in spirit," she said. "His associates are storm troopers. They do not have the sanction of government, but—"

"In a sense they do," Hart said quickly. "Not that anyone in the City approves of a hoodlum like Dukes. But he is permitted to get away with everything short of murder because of laxity, laziness, red tape, and worst of all, special interests that require someone like him when vast sums of money are involved. In a sense I'm giving you and your father a second chance to hit back."

Had he gone too far? Carrie and David exchanged apprehensive glances. They had not realized how much of a moralist Hart was, how intense he was about Dukes. More so, it seemed, than Dukes' victims.

"Very generous of you," Hilda Schlossmann said, with sarcasm. "Perhaps we are not interested in what may be only a second chance to be murdered."

Carrie cried: "Oh, no, Miss Schlossmann, no. No one wants any harm to come to you."

David appealed to them. "The odds are better this time, Miss Schlossmann. Your father could phrase this better than I can, but if democracy means anything, it means people can work together to improve society along humane lines. The violent don't necessarily bear victories away; governments should be called to account when people like Dukes are turned loose."

"Excellently put, young man," Schlossmann said. Again he spoke in German to his daughter. When he had finished, they both nodded their accord. Schlossmann would file an affidavit under his name.

Hart sat next to him and began to take notes:

. . . resided and continue to reside at 502 West 84th Street, in apartment 2B on the second floor. Starting May 8, a series of incidents leads deponent to conclude that a concerted campaign of terror to drive him from his apartment exists. Repeated telephone calls in the middle of the night have disturbed and agitated tenant, himself a graduate of three years in Nazi concentration camps. Unidentified caller has on various occasions said to deponent: "Move, Jew," or "You should have been gassed," or "The Nazis missed you, but we won't," or "Drop dead." Deponent further states that presence of derelicts on ground floor has caused concern to himself and his daughter. . . .

None of the tenants (or Hart) had known of Dukes' nocturnal threats to Schlossmann. There was a vague assumption that the homosexuals and the Simses were obvious targets. A bully like Dukes would direct his fire at them—and at Tony and the people in 1B. But Schlossmann was something else. Schlossmann had suffered more than any man deserved to suffer. And to subject him to such vileness seemed beyond the capabilities of even the blockbuster.

When Schlossmann had finished his deposition and Carrie had typed it, Hart ticked off the people he wanted to accompany him to his notary public on West 86th Street.

"I need Tony, Mr. Sims, Mr. Loomis, Mr. Schlossmann, Barri, and Mr. Allister. We can get these notarized in a few minutes. I'll take them to the City tomorrow."

They disbanded. David sensed a heartening new unity, a new courage in the group. It was amazing how putting something down in writing could invigorate. The power of the word, David concluded, the strength of the sentence. Would it give them an edge over Dukes, that preliterate huntsman?

The men were talking animatedly as they descended. As they turned on the second floor, they heard an undulant wailing. Tony Paz, arguing with Danny Hart about the wisdom of hiring a lawyer, let out a shout.

"Holy Jesus! Holy Chris'! Look what they do!"

The corridor walls of the second floor and the old linoleum flooring had been splashed with paint. They had intended to work with two colors—a chocolate brown for the lower part of the wall, a creamy beige for the upper part. Now, someone had hurled the paint, from the cans, onto walls, floor, bannisters, in huge, streaking, sticky puddles. Three empty cans lay in the hallway, and Tony tripped on one.

"*Hijo de puto!*" he shouted. "Oh, that *maricón* Rudy!"

The wailing had come from Hilda Schlossmann. She had left the Loomises' apartment a few moments before her father had finished dictating his deposition. She stood, her shoes sopping with dark-brown paint, on the threshold of the apartment, her hands clapped to the sides of her head. She turned her desolate rage on Hart:

"Look what you bring us with your crusades. They smashed the locks on our door. They threw the paint over everything. Not just out here. But inside. On our furniture. On Papa's work. Oh, we are fools, fools, to stay and fight this monster. Papa, do not go in, please—"

But Schlossmann, the gray peaks of hair seeming to rise, his shoulders drooping, walked across the paint drenched threshold into the ruined rooms.

"Such stupidity, such waste," Schlossmann said. Loomis followed him into the room, weathering Hilda's baleful stare.

In Schlossmann's living room, the large cluttered chamber in which every available space was covered with books, magazines, papers, scraps of evidence, cans of brown paint had been thrown, helter-skelter. The sticky liquid, staining everything impartially, lay in dripping gobs on his reference works. Only haste had prevented the raiders from doing a more thorough job. But even in a few minutes they had despoiled hundreds of books, magazines, papers.

"We'll help you clean them," Danny Hart said. "We'll hold up on the painting until we clean your books, Mr. Schlossmann."

Schlossmann did not hear him. He was, in a slow rhythm, clapping his hands together silently, shaking his head from side to side.

"It is beyond my understanding," he said.

"I understand it, Papa," Hilda said. "We are being tormented by madmen, and we will not stay."

Hart started to say something—as if to plead with her—but David cautioned him not to pursue the matter. Dazed, Schlossmann wandered amid the slimy puddles. When he saw his Olympia typewriter, drenched in paint, the interior machinery coated with viscous stuff, he seemed to lose control of his legs, and collapsed into a chair.

Barri Dane appeared at the door. He had gone up to his apartment and gotten his Polaroid camera. "Look," he said to David. "I think we should take some pictures. Evidence."

"Is it all right, Mr. Schlossmann?" David asked. "Can Barri take some photographs for the hearings?"

Schlossmann did not respond. He had extracted some smeared sheets from the desolation on his desk, and with the sleeve of his jacket was trying to blot up the paint.

When Danny Hart left the Rent Office, Oberlander summoned Adriano Labato. "We heard from Dukes yet?" he asked.

"He won't answer the phone," the inspector said.

"You finish your report?"

Labato nodded. "Plenny evidence those people are bein'

harassed. But provin' it will be somethin' else. No witnesses. Nobody. Their word against his. The guy who started it, Paz, used to work for Dukes and hates him. Know what I mean?"

Oberlander riffled the stack of affidavits on his desk. That morning Hart had typed a new one for the Schlossmanns, including the incident of the paint smearing. "That guy is working to drive those people out," the official said. "He was a no-good hoodlum before he got put away and he's worse now. Puttering is twisting his arm."

"I ain't saying he ain't," Labato said. "But proof . . ."

The morning mail was dumped on Oberlander's desk. Among them was a letter with DUKES MANAGEMENT COMPANY on the return address. "Ah, some business," Oberlander said. "Maybe he agreed to the assurance of discontinuance. If he has, and they still complain, we can sock him."

The functionary read the single sheet of paper from Dukes. Then he gave it to Labato. Expressionless, the inspector saw that it was a form that had been sent to Dukes—an "answer to application." It was notarized at the bottom, with Dukes' large, assertive signature, and it read:

I, Rudy Dukes, manager and net lessee for the premises at 502 West 84th Street, submit this answer in opposition to the various allegations of harassment claimed by tenants at said address.

Your deponent denies categorically all the charges made in their applications, and charges, in turn, that said accusations are grounded in malice.

Your deponent reiterates and states unequivocally that there has been no harassment of any type, manner, or form against any tenant.

"Kind of overdoes it, don't he?" Labato asked.

"Got himself a smart lawyer." Oberlander tapped the desk a few times. "Send him a telegram, make sure it's delivered and signed for. We'll hold a hearing in two days, 10 A.M., right here."

Leora Sims, grasping Allard by one hand, balancing her huge tote with the other, crossed West End Avenue on her way to the subway. When she got to the east side of the street, and began the climb toward Broadway, Shlep Sharmak stepped out of a doorway and fell in step with her.

"Mrs. Sims," he murmured, sneaking the words out of the side of his mouth, "get out, get out of the house as fast as you can."

"Go to hell. Get away from me, you old bum."

"I'm tryin' to be nice. I'm warnin' you. Get out. Dukes ain't fooling."

She stopped, released Allard for a moment, and swung the tote back, ready to smash at his seamed, eyeless face. Revulsion swept over her as she recalled his smarmy friendliness when they had first met. "You hoodlum. You coward. Don't ever talk to me again."

Shlep, an old street brawler, backed away. His arms were slightly raised, ready to ward off the blow. "It ain't you or your dinge husband, you should worry about, Mrs. Sims," Shelp said. He nodded at Allard. "It's the kid. If I was you I would worry about the kid."

Before she could respond—fear clotted her throat—Sharmak spun away and waddled around the corner.

Over Hilda Schlossmann's objections, the painting of the corridors was resumed. But first it was agreed that the Schlossmanns' possessions be cleaned. It proved somewhat easier than anticipated. Tony Paz brought a drum of paint remover and a bale of rags, and a team of volunteers—Hart, Loomis, Tony, Dane, Lobello, and Horton Sims—went through Schlossmann's documents and books, under the scholar's eye. The old typewriter was beyond salvation. Carrie lent Schlossmann hers.

"A dreadful affair," Schlossmann said to David, "but in a sense, a rewarding one. I am finding papers I had no idea I possessed. They shall be of great use to me. I had no idea this was still in the house." He fiddled with his steel-rimmed glasses and translated the German title. "Hmmm, a bit abstruse, but perhaps the only thing of its kind extant. *Some Aspects of Rural Mercantile Systems in Swabia in the Early Fifteenth Century.* I am not always in accord with Grossbardt's conclusions."

While the men helped clean Schlossmann's apartment—Hilda sulked in her bedroom, correcting examination papers—the women resumed painting the first floor. Dukes' goons had not had time to mar the first-floor walls. Now they were cleaned, primed, patched, and ready for the first application of paint.

Under overhead droplights, Lucy Paz, Leora Sims, and Carrie Loomis began, starting near the vestibule door, Lucy and Leora working on the high stepladders, and Carrie, in deference to her condition, painting below. Both the street door and the inner door were opened to disperse the paint fumes. It was a refreshingly mild and clear night, and there was a sense of optimism in the air. That afternoon, Hart had brought word of the hearing. Dukes had been summoned to appear. Once and for all they would confront their tormentor, frustrate his scheme, throw Puttering and his secret masters into retreat. Later that night, Hart and David would draw up a format for the presentation of their evidence.

"Here comes trouble," Leora Sims said. Her Afro glinted with silver lights under the harsh bulbs. She nodded at the door. O'Gara was shuffling into the house. Two young men were with him; each carried a knapsack and a rolled sleeping bag.

"More bums," Lucy Paz said. "Boy, I shiver every night thinking about them."

"Evening, ladies," O'Gara said.

They did not respond. Carrie shrunk away. What a wreck of a man! And how did he manage still to inspire fear in her? She shuddered inwardly whenever she saw him.

O'Gara ushered the two men toward the rear. Carrie turned to look at them. They were not the wino types who had been lodging in 1B ever since the Escobar and Fuentes families had vanished. Both men were white, with a look of intelligence about them. Carrie assumed they were students. It was odd that O'Gara should know them, even more odd that Dukes should. They smiled shyly at her. One was a tall youth with orange hair that did not fall to his shoulders but defied gravity and grew out sideways from his head, in wiry horizontal waves. He was sickly pale, and he seemed to stoop under the burden of the loaded olive-drab pack and bag. The other youth was dark and squat, with something of a cave-dwelling animal about him. Carrie could barely see his face. It was hidden by a mat of black swampy hair.

"Hit's in the back, fellas," O'Gara said. "Hit ain't much, but y'all can have hit for a while."

"Creeps," Lucy Paz said. "Dirty hippie bums."

"They could be students," Carrie said.

"Boy, if that's what college students are today," said Lucy with resonant Bronx rectitude, "I hope Michael never goes to college, unless it's a good Catholic one where they teach them manners."

"Lucy, honey," Leora said, from her perch, as she worked the roller professionally and admired the clean new coating, "they got that long hair and marijuana on every campus in America, including the best Catholic ones."

"Hmph. I don't believe it. The priests wouldn't permit it."

"You kidding?" Leora asked. "The priests are all out looking for wives. They haven't got time to make the students get haircuts."

Lucy was appalled. But she did not get angry with Leora. They had become hesitant friends in the past few days.

At the rear of the hallway, sounds rose—O'Gara's whining voice, the mutterings of a drunken black. The women listened. They had become attuned to disaster. Even the matter of leaving Allard alone behind locked doors, while she painted and Horton worked at Schlossmanns', upset Leora.

"Git," O'Gara said. "Ah said git. If you don't, Mr. Dukes gon' come around and sic his dog on you. Look, he let you in heah, he can throw you out. Go on, move out."

There were mumbled curses, the flooded voice of a drunk. A black man in a tattered overcoat and a cap two sizes too big floundered into the hallway, took a final swig from a bottle of wine, then dropped it on the floor. Fortunately it did not smash. Wheezing, he lurched down the corridor in search of his next place to flop. Carrie drew back under the safety of Leora's ladder as he stumbled by, redolent of sweat and alcohol.

"It's crazy to say it," Carrie said. "But it's almost as if we're the selfish ones complaining about those men, and Dukes is the good guy letting them stay there—"

"You think that way," Leora said flatly, "you'll be sorry."

"And how," Lucy said. "I hate bums. I hate those dirty kids he let in. He has no right to. He's trying to kick us out, and meanwhile he lets all kinds of bums and hippies into the house. It's a disgrace."

"It'll all come out in the wash," Leora said. "Thank God the City is on our side."

Loomis was impressed with the hearing. There was an air of officialdom about it, of people who knew what they were doing, a sense that justice would be served. His employers, young architects, had given him the day off to appear. They were successful men who believed that the city's ills were susceptible of solution, if only reasonable men could sit down and talk. "Go on, Dave," his boss had said. "We'll be most anxious to hear how it goes."

The room was in the old building on lower Broadway—high-ceilinged, airy, light. There was a long dark-brown table, at the head of which sat Raymond Oberlander, the enforcement officer. He displayed his usual weary air. No doubt he had sat through hundreds of these. To one side sat a shorthand reporter, and at the other was Adriano Labato, the building inspector, looking denuded without his tight brown hat.

"This is enforcement case two seven slash five eight zero one

211

slash letter C," Oberlander began. "A hearing by the Legal Enforcement Division of the Rent and Rehabilitation Administration into complaints by various tenants of 502 West 84th Street, New York City, against Dukes Management Company and its employes . . ."

His voice dwindled away. David, seated at the long table, looked puzzled. He nudged Danny Hart, at his side, his pale hands resting on stacks of affidavits, letters, the mounted photographs of Schlossmann's apartment. "How can they start?" David asked him. "Dukes isn't here."

"Whadja say, Mr. Loomis?" Oberlander asked.

"Excuse me, Mr. Oberlander, but Rudy Dukes isn't here. You aren't starting, are you?"

"No, no. He'll be here. Just to get it on the record." He nodded at the stenotype reporter, who was tapping at the keys. "This is a quasi-judicial hearing but we tend to be informal." He yawned. His tired gray face became all mouth.

They waited. Ten minutes. Fifteen minutes. David began to shift his legs, feel his collar compressing his neck. He looked at the rows of folding chairs at the rear of the room. A corporal's guard of tenants—Tony Paz, fuming; Werner Schlossmann, reading a salvaged tract, its cover caked with dried brown paint; Barri Dane, studying his lines; Carrie, in her Saks maternity suit. Archie Allister had begged off—the brokerage house was behind in paperwork.

Archie's absence was tolerable, but what David found difficult to accept was that the Simses had turned him down. They had made no effort to get time off from their schools. Leora Sims had frozen when he pleaded with her to attend. "I'm sorry, but I've done my share," she said. "Let some of the others confront Dukes. Horton and I feel we can do better in school, with our own folks." Something had happened, David realized, some threat, some new fear engendered by Dukes, or Shlep, or Bolo. What made their absence painful was that they were both officers of the committee. What kind of a committee was it, when two of the officials failed to attend the hearing?

212

There was also the matter of a lawyer. Hart, in his usual breezy way, assured David that none was necessary at a preliminary hearing. Father Hasslinger told him what to expect. But when David had insisted, Hart said he would try to get Gary Feldman, the Parish House attorney, a man noted for his shrewd, tough handling of rent cases, to represent them. Somehow word had never gotten to Feldman—an overworked, much-in-demand fellow, it developed—and so they had come to the City without counsel. "Don't worry about it," Hart assured David. "The whole thing is routine. It's Dukes who has to defend himself, not us. Our case is all on paper."

"Hey, Mr. Oberlander," Tony Paz erupted. "Where is Dukes? You sure you serve paper on him?"

"No paper was necessary. We sent him a telegram."

"Hah!" Tony shouted. "He stick it in garbage can!"

"As a matter of fact, his secretary called after receiving it and assured us he would attend."

"Why in hell he not here?" Tony insisted.

"He's got a point," David said to the official. "Here are seven people waiting for a half hour for one man. It doesn't seem fair."

Oberlander smiled. "That's the way these things go, Mr. Loomis." He nudged Labato. "Go call Dukes' office. See if he's on his way."

Paz began to talk, not quite shouting, not addressing anyone in particular. There was an edge of nuttiness to his voice, but as they listened, it was evident that he was the sanest person in the room.

"I know how landlord work," Paz orated. "I know for long time. He can drag you aroun' the block fifteen times with these hearings. Excuse. Lawyer. Subpoena. He got advantage because he don' care."

Hart whispered to Loomis: "He's right. God, I hope Dukes shows. We've got a strong case."

"I don't understand this," Loomis said to Oberlander. "Can he disregard that notice? Thumb his nose at everyone? While he delays, we can all be thrown out."

"Wait, wait," the enforcement officer said. "Here's someone." The green door to the hearing room opened. It was not Rudy Dukes who came in with Labato, but a dark young man in a flared electric-blue jacket, bell-bottom trousers, a navy shirt, and a gold tie. He carried an engorged briefcase and he moved swiftly, looking at no one except Oberlander.

"Hiya, Ray," the man said. "Sorry I'm late." He walked up to Oberlander, pumped his hand and nodded at Labato.

A finely honed awareness of protocol, David thought. The newcomer had to be a lawyer—Dukes' lawyer.

"How you doin', Al?" Oberlander asked. There was between them that bantering familiarity of the courthouse crowd, and it made Loomis uneasy.

"This is Mr. Tremark," Oberlander said. "He's representing Dukes Management."

"How do, folks," the man said airily. He had mobile eyes and a wide, red mouth. "Is your committee represented by counsel?"

"No," David said. "I'm the committee chairman. Mr. Hart helped us prepare the case against your client."

"What case?" he asked. "A few complaints. I'm sure reasonable people can resolve their differences."

Tony Paz could contain himself no longer. "Where is Dukes, hah? Why he is not here?"

Oberlander stared at the ceiling. "Please, Mr. Paz. I'll conduct the hearings."

"Okay," Tony persisted. "Ask where he is."

"I have an answer for the gentleman," Tremark said. "Mr. Dukes regrets that he cannot attend." The lawyer took a letter from his briefcase. "Last night Mr. Dukes suffered severe attacks of dizziness brought on by head wounds he sustained in Vietnam, where he served with distinction with the United States Navy—"

"He is a damn liar!" Tony cried.

Oberlander rapped the table.

"—and I have here a letter from Mr. Dukes' physician, Dr. Arnold Seploff, of 1195 Park Avenue, attesting to the fact that Mr. Dukes is in no condition to attend hearings."

"Counselor," Oberlander said, "how long does Mr. Dukes' physician estimate he will be out of combat, so to speak?"

Tremark shrugged. "Oh, a few days. No more than a week."

Danny Hart had been making notes on a pad. "Mr. Oberlander, if I may?" The enforcement officer nodded. "It's possible that Mr. Dukes is ill. He certainly hasn't seemed sick the past few days pointing shotguns at tenants and setting fires—"

"Not proven," the lawyer said. He looked deep into his treasure chest of a briefcase, perhaps for evidence that Dukes was afraid of guns, or disliked fires.

"—or for that matter when he slapped me around. These tenants, who have been terrorized, will be the first to swear that Mr. Dukes' health appears to be very good."

"You doubt the doctor's word?" the attorney asked. "An eminent New York specialist? One of the biggest neurological men in town?"

"It's in writing," Oberlander said.

"I've been through these before," Hart said. "And you have, too, Mr. Oberlander. Dukes is trying to force these people to vacate by the end of the month. It might be worthwhile investigating why there is all this urgency. Maybe E. J. Puttering, or Haman, Lord & Fawcett could shed light on the reason. Or Mr. Tremark."

The lawyer opened his hands, pushed out his thick lips. "Don't look at me. I have one client in this matter. Dukes Management." But he sounded defensive. And he was studying Danny Hart now with an unsettled look, as if confounded that this hippie jerk could be so shrewd.

"What's to keep Dukes from endless delays?" Hart went on. "He can give us a runaround for two more weeks, and by then, who knows what will happen at 502 West 84th Street? We've had one fire already. Tomorrow, Mr. Dukes may have to attend his grandfather's funeral in Pittsburgh. Two days later, he may decide someone should be subpoenaed. Or he may forget to bring records. Or lose them. These people work and cannot take time off while Dukes evades this hearing."

"Come on, come on, Hart," Tremark said. "You make a big deal out of a simple medical postponement. Dukes has nothing to hide. Or to fear, for that matter."

"How about this?" David asked. He held up the Polaroid photographs of Schlossmann's apartment, the books, papers, furnishings daubed with paint. "This is the way your client works. This is what he did to Mr. Schlossmann's place."

"Hold it, hold it," Tremark said. "Ray, are you going to let these innuendos go into the record? My client is sick, he is under medical care, and I won't let him be slandered. I don't know anything about those photos, who took them, when. They could be fakes. I request that these hearings be adjourned."

"There is only one fake!" Tony shouted. "That bastard Rudy Dukes!"

"Mr. Paz, please," Oberlander sighed. "Mr. Loomis, you and Mr. Hart have a point. I am going to reschedule this hearing for three days from now, in this room, at 10 A.M. That's Friday. Mr. Dukes will be served with a paper. Since he has, in formal answer to application, already denied all charges of harassment, all accusations brought by the tenants"—Oberlander looked directly at the attorney—"he should have no qualms about appearing and giving testimony *under oath*."

"Under *oath?*" the lawyer asked. He seemed surprised. "It was my understanding that in preliminary hearings, parties need not be sworn."

"We have *had* our preliminary hearing," Oberlander said flatly. "This is it. See to it that Mr. Dukes is here on Friday."

"In three days," Danny Hart said, "Dukes can burn the whole house down."

"He won't if he's smart," the official said. "Mr. Tremark, you had better convey that sentiment to him."

Abruptly the hearing ended. The officials swept out of the hearing room. Tremark gathered up his papers, avoided the faces of the tenants ("Shyster!" Paz yelled after him. "Dukes will cheat you also!"), and left.

In the vast gloomy room, they gathered around Hart—Tony, Loomis, Carrie, Schlossmann. David saw the unhappy faces, the frustration. They had come to confront the blockbuster. And he, with the subtlety of a schoolboy getting a note from his mother claiming that he had a bellyache, had evaded them.

"How long can he do this?" Schlossmann asked. "How long can such a man avoid retribution?"

"Hah! Forever!" Paz sputtered. "Dukes is not human. Dukes is not like us."

"We're not through yet," Hart said. "David, you feel up to calling on Haman, Lord & Fawcett? If we can't find Puttering, maybe we can get some action from them."

"Whatever you say." But he was wondering: was it worth it? Would it not be simpler to take Dukes' money and run?

The morning of the hearing, Leora Sims discovered that the kitchen sink was stuffed. She was a tidy housekeeper, but she was terrified when things went wrong. Neither she nor Horton was mechanically inclined; they lived in dread of short circuits, clogged drains, leaky radiators.

"Damnation," she said, as she watched the eggshells and crusts floating in the pool of dirty water. She ladled out the breakfast scraps from the sink, moved her finger in the drain, removing bits of grease, and groaned. The sink had backed up once before and she recalled that she had some liquid drain cleaner in the house. It was lethal gook, the label warning users to protect eyes and hands, to stand back, and to be wary if anything bubbled out of the drain when the cleansing agent was poured in.

Horton, coffee cup in hand, wandered in to survey the operation.

"Here goes nothing," Leora said after emptying the sink with a pot. She poured in a cupful of the brown liquid. There was a

217

wicked hissing in the bowels of the sink and a foamy exudate bubbled up. "It's alive," she said.

"Stand back, honey," Sims said. "It don't like us."

"You think Dukes is hiding down there?"

Ten minutes later, following the instructions on the plastic bottle, she filled the sink, hoping to see it run clear. It did not. The violent chemical sizzled again but the water remained in the basin.

"Must be the grease trap," Sims said professionally. "Sometimes they got to replace that elbow gimmick down there."

"Hunh. Plumbers' union? Since when did they open the apprentice program to deserving blacks?"

Things material disturbed Sims, so Leora agreed to request repairs from O'Gara. The man had proved so inept, so secretive, that none of the tenants bothered with him any more. Tony and Lucy Paz had taken to sweeping the vestibule, stoop, and sidewalk.

With Allard clinging to her skirts, she walked down to the basement and rapped at the door. More likely than not, O'Gara was in a daze and would not bother to respond. But this time she heard shuffling, and he opened the door—a spectral night creature, blinking in the sun.

"Kitchen sink is stuffed in 2A," Leora said. "My husband says it may be the grease trap. Can you fix it?" Ah, for the days of old McIsaac, who could repair anything!

"Ah cain't, but Ah'll call the boss."

"Its badly clogged. I used some drain cleaner, but it was no help."

"Ah'll try."

She turned, and in the fractional moment when her field of vision still included O'Gara, she saw him undo his fly and expose himself. She dragged Allard up the stairs and did not look back.

There was a damp odor in the apartment when Horton Sims got home that afternoon. At once he was afraid, trembling with expectation. The sink had been ripped from its rusted moorings and lay, cracked, on the floor. The various drain pipes had also been removed, but rather than having been unscrewed with a wrench, they had been broken, the old strained metal coming apart in jagged hunks. The refrigerator had been knocked on its side. The trays and shelves had been removed and smashed, the food thrown on the floor.

The garbage can had been emptied, the contents strewn about, and on the kitchen table, a sheet from Leora's monthly calendar had been ripped, and across it, with a black felt pen, someone had lettered: MOVE, SPADE.

Again his heart began to flutter and he felt driblets of sweat forming in his armpit. *When you git scared, you smell like a nigger,* they used to taunt him. But it was less fear than hate that Sims was experiencing. How easy to maim and kill! If he had had trouble understanding the galoots he tried to teach and reform, the wild kids to whom he was Mr. Cool, he had no trouble now. Leaving the door open, Sims walked to 2B. No, old Schlossmann had seen no one. Men to fix Sims' sink? Maybe. He couldn't remember.

Barri Dane had seen them. The actor listened in horror as Sims described his kitchen. "Bolo came here around noon," he said. "With some big dude carrying a plumber's bag. I didn't recognize him. O'Gara was with them, I think."

Sims ran downstairs and knocked at O'Gara's door. There was no response. Damn! If he could catch his breath he could think clearly. Of course. They had gone to get spare parts for the sink. It would be fixed later. Panting noisily as he climbed the steps again, he understood he was deluding himself. If they intended to repair the sink, why the strewn garbage, the wrecked refrigerator, the threatening note?

He telephoned Dukes' number. A woman with a tired voice answered. "He isn't in," she said. And Sims could hear the uncertainty in it, the poorly delivered lie. His ear was sensitive to these. He lived with them every day at school.

"When will he be in?"

"He's sick. In bed."

"But his apartment is the same as the office," Sims said.

"He isn't here. The doctor told him to get some rest. In a hospital."

"Where?" Sims felt isolated, denuded, alone in the desert, pleading for help from uncaring Bedouins.

"I'm not sure."

"How about Sharmak? Or Bolo?"

"They aren't here either."

He cursed his heart. It pounded so violently that it interfered with his words. "Tell Dukes they wrecked my kitchen. He won't get away with it. He won't frighten me. I'll stay in that apartment forever, till it rots, and till he rots. Tell that to the son of a bitch."

Rudy Dukes had succeeded where all the JDs in Junior High School 710 had failed; he was no longer Mr. Cool.

Leora Sims returned a few minutes after the phone call. She surveyed the wreckage and rubbish in the kitchen, sank into a chair, and wept.

"Mom-mon don't cry," Allard said. "Mom-mom is gonna be all better."

She embraced his small, perfect head. "Yeah, all better, Allard." How had this happened? They were the lucky ones, escapees, with careers, incomes, professional pride, and a child who would go to Columbia. "Sims, I'm licked," she said, dabbing at her eyes. "The honky's got me licked. Let's find a place."

Horton sat opposite her. There was a dulled look in his eyes. "Where?" he asked.

"I don't care. We'll go stay with my sister in Jamaica until something shows up. Hattie'll put us up. I can't take any more of this. If it's the sink today, it'll be the john tomorrow, then a fire, then—" She stopped, wondering whether to tell him everything that was tormenting her.

"Leora, we shouldn't chicken out. There's an issue here. More than that sink. If we run on that hoodlum, we let the others down."

220

"What in hell do we owe them, Hortie?" she cried.

"You know. That Loomis is okay. Old Schlossmann. Paz. They're people like us."

Leora shook her Afro. The gold hoops under her ears clanked. "You are a beauty, Sims. Mr. Involved. Mr. Committed. Since when? You were the loner who never joined the NAACP, let alone the Panthers. You didn't go to meetings of the UFT, you sometimes don't even vote. And what happens? A bunch of ofays rope you in to fight their battles with a crazy landlord and you're gung-ho. I say to hell with them. Let's move."

"South Jamaica," Sims said sourly. "Hoods and winos and bums. You'll have to keep Allard under armed guard."

She wanted to withhold the worst from him but now she had no choice. "What makes you think we're so safe here? Yesterday that creep Sharmak came out of an alley and told me to keep an eye on Allard. And just this morning—Sims, I didn't want to tell you but you forced me—"

She struggled to keep back tears, peered across the kitchen to make sure Allard was not listening.

"What, what?"

"That hillbilly in the basement exposed himself to me. Gave me a full view, a treat. You like that?"

Sims made a noise as if he had been struck in the abdomen. He got up and took off his tie and his jacket.

"What are you doing? Stay away from that degenerate. Don't go near him."

He had become thoughtful, a thoroughly ordered man. "No, not him. I have to visit Mr. Dukes."

Leora grabbed him. "No. He's a criminal, Hortie. He's got that damned shotgun, that dog. He'll have those goons beat you up. Hortie, please."

"Of course he won't," Sims said. "The last thing Dukes wants is a case against him. He can't push me any farther than he has. I'm ready to move. Call Hattie."

"Then why bother with him?"

"Dukes has to be punished," he said. "Now that the City is

in on the act, and there's hearings scheduled, he'll watch his step. I want to make him sweat a little."

But as Sims walked along West End Avenue, he wondered why he was bothering to track Dukes down. Oh, he knew. He wanted to kill him, of course. But that was out of the question. What, then? Tell him to his face he was a bastard? Threaten him with a lawsuit?

It was almost—he could not quite describe it to himself— almost a *fascination* with Rudy Dukes that drew him to West 74th Street, a compulsion to stare at the bad man, to look at the torturer, hear his harsh voice. And perhaps feel his fists?

Strange, Sims thought. All his life he had stayed out, kept quiet, avoided trouble. Maybe that was the way to do it. And the one time he had entered the arena, helping form the tenants' committee, he had been licked, crushed, cowed before the game was barely underway.

Loomis had no difficulty making an afternoon appointment with a representative of Haman, Lord & Fawcett. Danny Hart, bearing copies of the allegations of harassment, the affidavits, and the photographs, accompanied him. Carrie was eager to go along, but David sent her home. Each day, he marveled, she looked rounder, healthier. She was thriving, and had been eating so heartily that she had retired the portable spittoon.

The real estate firm's offices in the financial district were sober, elegant, staffed by slender girls, vested young men. A Mr. Cathcart—dark-haired, dark-suited, firm-jawed—took them into a small dark-walled office.

"This has to do with the premises at 502 West 84th Street?" Cathcart asked. "You're both tenants?"

"I'm chairman of the tenants' committee," David said. "Mr. Hart is with the West Side Parish House. He's helping us with the hearings at the Rent Administration."

"Oh. There are hearings?"

David felt hopeful. Young Cathcart could not hide the concern in his well-modulated voice.

"Dukes managed to duck the one this morning, but he's been subpoenaed to appear at one on Friday. As you can see, we have a full file on his operations. They include arson, assault and battery, physical and verbal threats, destruction of property—"

The young man held his hand up. "I know, Mr. Loomis. You gave me the details on the phone. But why are you telling me all this?"

Danny Hart replied: "Your firm's name appears on the adjacent buildings. We have been told you're involved with this one also. Obviously it's a package, including the houses on West 83rd Street."

"We want you to force Dukes to stop," David said. "We want you to fire him."

Cathcart laughed. "Gentlemen, until you called me today I had no idea that a person such as Rudy Dukes existed. I assure you no one at Haman, Lord & Fawcett knows who he is. From what you say, he appears to be a manager engaged by Mr. Puttering."

"You admit there's an E. J. Puttering?" Hart said.

"Of course. He is the landlord of record. He's the one to see."

David tapped the elegant desk. "Come on, Mr. Cathcart. You must know about the Phantom Landlord. Even the process servers can't find him."

Cathcart did not respond. He opened a manila folder on his desk. Then he said, "Mr. Loomis, I know what you're up against. This matter of vacating old buildings can get messy. It's possible Puttering has hired a bad apple. But we have no responsibility in this matter. None whatever. We can't even pressure Puttering into doing anything about it. We're mere brokers. Not only that, we're new on the New York scene. We're still learning."

David was getting edgy. It was maddening the way no one would take responsibility for Dukes, no one could be brought to book. "Mr. Cathcart, would you like it if we went to the newspapers, or the TV reporters? Your firm's name would be mentioned."

"We wouldn't like it, but so what? I repeat, we have no idea who Dukes is, and, despite all you've told me, no idea whether he has actually harassed any of you. Obviously we don't approve of those tactics, but we're not a law-enforcement agency, or part of the poverty program."

"What are you?" Hart asked.

"Landlords. Real estate agents. Building managers. Let me add one thing, as politely as I can. Don't contemplate any legal action against us. You wouldn't stand a chance."

Horton Sims walked purposefully toward Dukes' apartment. He had no idea what he would do, what he would say. But he was drawn there inexorably. On the corner of West End Avenue a black drunk bumped against him and tried to back him against the news stand. "Gimme a dollar, brother," he mumbled.

"Go to hell," Sims said. Ah, the reminders of what he might have been. Maybe better off, Sims thought. Panhandling, sleeping in doorways, living from pint to pint of Zinfandel, Muscatel, Pinot Noir. He had made it in the white world, escaped from that brotherhood of self-hate and despondency, and now he had his reward.

The door to Dukes' apartment was open. Sims was cautious. He reached to straighten his tie and was dismayed that he was not wearing one. Divested of his school uniform, he felt unprotected.

A stout woman was sitting at a reception desk. "You must be Mr. Sims," she said. "I'm sorry, but Mr. Dukes can't see anyone. He's in conference."

"I'll wait." Where was his voice?

From the inner room, the *grifo* Bolo drifted into view. Sims recalled the time he had bent him over the bannister and taken the matches from him.

"Whah you wan'?" Bolo called. He lounged against the door, insolent, the kind who, ten years younger, Sims had to face down at knifepoint in the hallways, the boys' room, the schoolyard.

"I want your boss."

"He busy."

"I can wait. I can wait all afternoon. He'll see me." Silently, Sims cursed his good breeding, his dedication to civilized behavior. It came of ambition, a copycat slavishness toward the world of nice white teachers, conscientious union members, concertgoers, liberal voters. Oh, for a leavening of whatever it was gave the bad mothers their terrible daring!

In the inner office, Dukes, dyspeptic, embittered, had taken a call from Puttering. The landlord's voice was barely audible, a man calling from the bottom of a well.

"Dukes, Dukes," Puttering said, "you got to wind this thing up, before the hearings."

"I'll duck them. Puttering, give me some more dough to buy people out. You cheap bum, you made me go in there swinging—"

"I made you do nothing. Do you know what kind of trouble I am in? That architect and that other fellow were at Haman, Lord & Fawcett and gave them an earful of the things you are doing."

"For you, Puttering, for you. When I go down, I drag you with me."

"Don't bet on it, my boy. I'll authorize you to go as high as twenty-five hundred for those people on the top floor. I'll pay. And I'll raise the bonus on everyone you can get out by May 31. Fifteen hundred dollars an apartment. Is that a sign of confidence?"

Dukes paused. Puttering was beginning to panic. He said: "Okay. Maybe I got one on his way. The nigger."

Bolo had come in and whispered in Dukes' ear. Rudy nodded. With his lips he formed the words: *Get the cops.* Then he repeated the Puerto Rican slang for police: *La hara.*

"All, my boy. Out. Do you know what it is to have a million-dollar deal fall apart in your hands because of some stubborn, stupid people? Is it any wonder landlords go crazy? Dukes, I am ordering you, get them moving. Or it's the end of our relationship. And who else will touch you?"

Puttering's voice dwindled to a gargle. He hung up.

"I said he's in conference . . . please . . ." Mrs. Hallweg, Dukes' secretary, was pleading with Sims. The door to Dukes' office burst open and the teacher walked in. "I told him, Mr. Dukes—"

"It's okay, Martha. Come on in, Sims."

Face to face with the manager, Sims was at a loss. Then he blurted out: "Your man Sharmak wrecked the sink in my apartment. The other morning he threatened my child's safety. And that pervert you hired showed his privates to her. Dukes, what is wrong with you? What kind of an animal are you? Is the phrase 'Move, nigger,' or 'Move, spade,' your notions of a tenant-landlord relationship?"

"It's good advice, Sims. I can't be responsible for what Shlep does. You better get out. We'll fix it up for the next tenant, someone who don't leave pork-chop bones and watermelon seeds on the floor. Now beat it."

"I can't take any more of this," Sims said weakly. "Yes, we're moving. But I'm going to make all the trouble I can for you. I'll go to court, I'll testify against you, I'll go to the newspapers—"

"Ah, calm down Sims." Dukes got up from the desk. He looked past the angry tenant. In the outer office, he saw Bolo and a policeman entering. It was Dattolica, one of the new men in the neighborhood.

"I'll get you, Dukes," the teacher said. Rudy was walking toward him, his fists clenched, his short thick arms in classic boxer's stance. "Sims, I'll give you two hundred bucks to help with the moving expenses," Rudy said. "To show you how glad I am to get rid of a nigger. That's my special price for MF's. That's all you're worth, ain't that right? You and your spade wife and the little smoke—"

Fury clouded Horton Sims' eyes. He lunged for Dukes, not throwing punches, but reaching for the mocking face. He knew it was a doomed effort. He was in poor shape and Dukes was a pro. Strangely, the manager barely resisted. Sims' hands were on Dukes' throat and the hoodlum was stumbling backward, over his own desk, crying in a pained, voice: "Help. Help. The guy is killing me. Get him off—"

I can kill him, Sims thought. *No remorse. No guilt.* He tried to tighten his grip on Dukes, but he had the feeling he was being controlled.

"Leggo, leggo," Dukes moaned.

"Hey you!" Patrolman Dattolica shouted. "Git off that guy! Git off!"

"Jesus, he killin' the boss," Bolo cried.

"Help. Help." Rudy wriggled on the edge of the desk, locking a leg inside Sims.

The teacher understood too late. He had been trapped. The instant he released Dukes, he felt the hard crack of the policeman's billy across the small of his back. A fire burned in his kidneys. He gasped. Bent double, holding his back, Sims staggered away.

"That spade attacked me," Dukes cried. "One of them crazy tenants, know what I mean, Officer? I want him arrested. It's a disgrace what goes on around here. A man can't sit in his place of business without some bum attacking him."

"Ah right, ah right," the policeman said. He had whipped out his pad and was taking notes. "Wanna file a complaint?"

"You're damn right I do," Dukes said. "This guy assaulted me in my office. Look at my neck. See them marks? He tried to kill me."

Sims, panting, had fallen against a wall. "Officer . . . Officer," he said. "This fellow has been tormenting me for three weeks. He is a blockbuster, trying to scare us out of our apartment. I came here to discuss it . . . and he—"

To his horror, Sims found himself confronted by four smiling faces. Why? Why did they think it so funny? Bolo was grinning. The elderly secretary, peering in, looked elated. And Dukes and the cop, head to head, were enjoying his misery.

"This man goaded me and taunted me . . . he has threatened me . . . ruined our kitchen sink—"

"*Kitchen sink?*" the policeman asked, incredulous. "For this you wanna kill the guy?"

"It's more than that—"

"Suppose you shut up, huh, buddy?" Dattolica asked. "When Mr. Dukes gives me his version, it'll be your turn. And siddown. No funny tricks, like runnin' for the door, unless you wanna get belted."

"May I call my wife?" Sims asked.

"No," the cop said. "You can keep your mouth shut till I'm ready for you. What happened, Mr. Dukes?"

"This guy came in threatening me. I got witnesses. Martha heard him. So did Bolo. He said he'd kill me for what I done to his place."

The scratching of the policeman's pen in the notebook sounded to Sims like the recording angel's goose quill. Some awful judgment had been rendered; unjust, unfair. In a way it served him right for getting involved.

When Horton failed to return for over an hour, Leora Sims became panicky. She had already called her sister in Jamaica and received some advice on a cheap and reliable mover.

After an hour had passed, she was trembling. She called Dukes' office. There was no answer. She thought of calling the police, but to what end? Allard began to whine. He wanted Pop-pop. He was hungry. She gave him a cold dinner, set him in front of the television set, and wondered to whom she could turn for help. Loomis, surely. He was emerging as the dependable man in the building. And yet how could she, now that she and Horton had let him down by running, by showing their cowardice?

When the phone rang, she thought her heart would burst from her breast. "Yes?" she asked.

"Leora, honey, don't get scared. I am in the police station. A small altercation with Dukes. No one's hurt. Can you get down here?"

"My God," she moaned. "Hortie . . . I told you not to . . . Should I get a lawyer? Someone?"

"See if Loomis can get down here."

Leora rushed up to the Loomises'. They were having a predinner cocktail, but they responded immediately. Carrie would babysit with Allard. Leora and David would go to the precinct house and find out what had happened to Horton.

"I warned him not to go," Leora said, as she and David hailed a cab. "I told him Dukes was too much for him."

"He can't be hurt," David said. "Dukes is supposed to be sick. That's why he didn't show at the hearing."

But the hearings, the tenants' committee, the struggle with Rudy Dukes, no longer interested Leora. She had left that battle.

In the precinct, amid the odor of Lysol, unwashed bodies, and despair, they saw Sims, unruffled, standing in front of the sergeant's desk. To one side, at a table, Dukes was seated, chatting amicably with two police officers, and the dapper lawyer whom David had seen at the hearing, Alvin Tremark.

"Sick?" David asked. "He looks healthy. Wait till I tell that lawyer a few things."

"Plaintiff step forward," the sergeant intoned. "Rudy Dukes? You wanna continue your complaint? It's up to you."

"Sergeant," Sims said. "I feel I have a right—"

"Wait yer turn. Dukes?"

Tremark nudged Rudy, whispered in his ear, then spoke. "Sergeant, as an act of generosity Mr. Dukes will withdraw his complaint, even though this man Sims tried to strangle him."

"Okay, okay let's wind it up. Sims?"

"Sergeant," Sims said, "I did not try to . . . I did not."

"The policeman saw you, Sims," the sergeant said. "You had your hands on Mr. Dukes' throat. Didn't you?"

Of course he had. And of course he had wanted, deep in

his heart, to murder him. How explain it to the uncommitted face of the law? Sims had seen the arch glances, the knowing winks in the station house: *a smart dinge, one of them educated spades, the worst kind.* And now they were ogling Leora, with her shiny ebony skin, the rising Afro, the gold hoops, the yellow dashiki.

"Let me talk," Leora cried. "Dukes is a thug. He's been abusing people, threatening us. We couldn't take it any more."

"You Mrs. Sims?"

"Yes, Sergeant."

"That your lawyer?"

"I'm David Loomis. I'm the chairman of the tenants' committee at 502 West 84th Street, and I know the history of this feud. What Mrs. Sims says is true. Dukes was asking for it. And he doesn't look badly hurt to me."

The sergeant was impeded for a moment. Loomis's manner, voice, bearing had set him off. Blond, soft-spoken, neatly dressed, educated. No fag, no radical, no troublemaker. "So? What do you want?" he asked. "You heard the plaintiff's offer. He'll let bygones be bygones."

Tremark raised his hand. "That's right, Sergeant. We'll withdraw the complaint, provided Sims agrees to vacate his apartment by the end of the week. The man is an agitator. He and his wife are the moving forces behind a plot to shake down my client."

"Okay!" the sergeant thundered. "Enough. Settle that among yourselves. This isn't tenant-landlord court. Dukes, I'm gonna let this guy go. You stay outa trouble from now on. And you, Sims, you better move out if you're not wanted."

The attorney and Dukes started to leave. David stepped across the room. "You don't look very sick," he said. "Those dizzy spells must have stopped in a hurry."

Rudy looked at him with an eyeless stare. He knew when to keep quiet.

"None of your business, Loomis," Tremark said. "It so happens Mr. Dukes disregarded doctor's orders and left his bed.

And all because of the trouble you shakedown artists are making for him. Wise up, Loomis. Take a lesson from what just happened."

David followed them. Dukes, hitching his belt, got to the door, turned, and *sotto voce,* said to him: "Loomis, I got two grand for you. Take it and get out. Call me and we'll make a deal."

"No, Dukes. Not after this."

David turned and had the feeling that he was looking at a stage set: the gloomy gray room with its overhead lights, the ruddy-faced sergeant behind the desk, the lesser cops lounging around, the police stenotypist staring at his machine.

Sims had surrendered. He was crushed, David could see, beaten. Dukes had played him like a fish, hooked him, given him his head, worked the line, then gaffed and boated him, a glassy-eyed victim.

But if the scene was dreamlike to him, how must Leora and Horton Sims have felt? Loomis wondered. They were aliens in the house of the law, and he could understand why they did not pursue the case, did not protest the injustice. They accepted the decision (had not Dukes been the soul of magnanimity?) and walked out.

"You want something?" the sergeant asked.

"May I speak to the captain?" David asked.

From bland contempt, the sergeant's eyes now registered an amused respect, as if he were saying, *Not such a dumb guy, not such a pigeon.*

"What about?"

"This matter of the fight between Dukes and the tenants. It doesn't involve only Sims and his wife."

The officer sighed. But he reached for the intercom. "What'd you say your name was?

"Loomis." David reached in his wallet. He handed the sergeant his card.

"A Mr. Loomis," he muttered on the phone. "Tenants' group at the place on West 84th where they had the fire."

David was suddenly inspired. What motivated the police, he realized, was a desire to *stay out of trouble*. He saw it with the Sims-Dukes confrontation. Police sought the amicable solution; anything that would cut out paperwork, trials, involvement. They simply had too much to do, too much to worry about. The best citizens were the ones who looked the other way, did not report crimes, settled things with a handshake.

"Tell him I want his help in cooling the feud," David said. "I want to make sure no one gets hurt, and that the police won't have to be called in. Precautions, that's all."

The sergeant repeated the words. Then he looked at David, with shrewd appreciation in his sour eyes. "Go on in. Captain Gossett. First door on your right."

Loomis caught the cunning smile that passed between the sergeant and the other policemen. They had a world of their own, and he had the disturbing feeling that he was not a part of it. Nor were Sims and his wife, nor Danny Hart. The cops existed on some middle earth, some central kingdom, where people like Rudy Dukes also enjoyed quasi-citizenship. He tried to argue against the curious concept, but he could not separate Dukes, in some maddening way, from the lawmen who were supposed to protect people from him.

Dukes should have been exultant when he got back to his apartment after taking care of Sims. But he was not. The kicks had gone out of it. Sims had been too easy. All along, Rudy suspected that the educated spade would fold. And he knew why. They would resent running interference for a bunch of ofays. Had they been stupid drunks, welfare cases, they would have been flattered to be made officers to the tenants' committee. They might have stuck it out, hung tough. But having achieved what they had, they had no desire to lose it all in drawn-out combat with Rudy Dukes. And the beauty part, Rudy told himself, was that Sims would not even get his lousy two hundred dollars! A saving all around.

But he could not savor the victory. There were still six

apartments to go, and two weeks in which to get them out. He thought of calling Puttering, giving him the good news, and asking again for more money to buy people off. But Puttering would refuse, until the very last minute. Payoffs were against his principles.

He would probably have to do it with the resources he handled best—terror, threats, fear. Loomis had turned down two grand and he was worried about him. A hardhead. A Boy Scout. Maybe the technique would be to drive everyone else out, and let Loomis and his pregnant wife hold the fort alone. Give the snooty bastard a lesson, teach him what it was like in the real world, where his college degrees did not mean a damn. Teach him how it worked with cops and city stooges and building inspectors. Teach him . . .

That damned hearing, Dukes thought. Tremark had told him that he had to show up on Friday. No more delays. No more doctors' letters. "Deny everything," the lawyer said easily. "There are no witnesses that count. No evidence. The hardest thing in the world to prove is harassment."

And how would it end? Dukes had demanded. "Worse comes to worst, we'll sign an assurance of discontinuance," he said. "In the meantime, put the squeeze on Puttering for more cash, so you can wind this up before someone gets hurt. You know what I'm talking about, Dukes."

He was alone in the office. Angel, snoozing at his feet, yipped and jerked in a dream of doggy terror. The mutt was the only one around him when the working day was over. Bolo and Shlep left in a hurry. In a crazy way, he now felt close to the tenants in 502—buddies, pals. Their very enmity, their fear and hatred of him were comforting—like knowing you were *thought* about all the time, that you were on people's minds. He realized now why he enjoyed his work so much. It kept him close to people, deep in their minds, etched in their hearts. "Like an ice pick in the gut," Dukes whispered. Tony Paz understood this best. He knew what Dukes meant to him. With

Dukes persecuting him, he could be a big man. Paz licked up his bowl of fear like a street mongrel.

Dukes dialed Archie Allister's number. "Mr. Allister?" he asked in a buoyant voice. "Dukes. You wanna talk some more? I got an interesting offer."

Archie looked at Liz—ivory-pale, drained from weeping. How could he cope with such beauty? How dared he endanger their fragile marriage? He understood—the awareness pained him— that he did not possess Loomis's courage. But then, he did not have Loomis's wife either.

"All right, Dukes," he said. "The Arriba Bar? Amsterdam Avenue and 87th Street? Right. In a half hour."

David pressed the Simses' buzzer. He walked in after Leora came to the door, and found them packing suitcases, dismantling furniture. Carrie was helping Leora fold slipcovers.

"Listen," he pleaded. "Change your mind. Stay. There's no reason for you to move now."

"Isn't there?" Sims asked. He led David into the kitchen and showed him the wrecked sink, the message: MOVE, SPADE.

"But you're quitting," David said. "I got the captain at the precinct to agree to a meeting Thursday. He's calling Dukes, and Puttering, and even Haman, Lord & Fawcett, and asking them to come down to see if we can work things out. And he wants all the tenants to come. Not that it should matter, but he's black."

"No, it doesn't matter, David. You saw what happened. Dukes has those cops in his pocket. He's bragged about it."

"I'm not sure he has. That cop who arrested you could have honestly believed you were assaulting Dukes."

"Hell, I was. He trapped me. If I don't agree to move he goes ahead with his case and I get mugged and fingerprinted. And there were witnesses. So I get out. What Dukes wanted. Maybe it's what I want also."

"You don't mean that," Loomis said. "Look, let me get Dane's camera. We'll get this all on the record."

"Forget it. The way he *handled* me. Like a kitten. I never hurt him a bit. He controlled everything I did. Almost led me to his throat, then prevented me from getting a grip. That boy is a professional."

"Even if you've decided to move, you could come to the hearings," David said. "It'll be a chance to state your case against Dukes. We're getting some action out of the City."

Sims shook his head. "Too late. Get yourself another vice-chairman. I broke my rule. I got involved and I got burned."

They walked back into the living room, where the Sims child sat on the floor, coloring a picture book. Loomis understood their fear, their refusal to face Dukes any longer. If it meant waking at night to worry about the boy, the fight was not worth it.

Sims began asking his wife about the moving arrangements, the living quarters at her sister's house, various unpaid bills. He sat at a small desk and began looking at his checkbook, taking documents out of a folder. Carrie nodded to David. They were no longer needed, their presence was an embarrassment.

"I'm sorry," Carrie said. "I wish it hadn't come to this. I wish you could have stayed."

Leora, studying the stacks of books and magazines that would have to be packed, nodded sadly. "Yes, I'd hoped we could have also."

"I want you to know what I'm truly sorry about," Carrie said. "It's that we never got to know each other."

Leora blinked behind her eyeglasses. It was all behind them; all over. "I am also," she said. "Maybe we'll see each other again."

But they all understood that they never would.

Tony Paz got off the Broadway bus at 110th Street and began walking uptown to the garage. To an undiscerning pedestrian, he would appear to be a scrawny twelve-year-old. The scuffed briefcase in which Lucy packed his lunch added to the impression. Only when people saw the choleric face did they realize that the fast-walking, hunched figure was that of a man.

Paz had heard about the Simses' decision. Too bad about those *moyetos*. He thought Sims had *corazón*, that he was a gutsy guy. But he had been faked out. Rudy had gotten him, screwed him up with *la hara*. Tony could have warned him. It was an old trick of Rudy's. To let you make the first move when the fuzz were around. Yeah, he was paying them off, Tony concluded. He could not wait until the meeting with Captain Gossett. He, Tony, spoke the cops' language. He would tell them plenty about Dukes.

Then they would have the Rent Office hearings and Dukes would be sworn. That was the way to get the rat! Oh, they had him, they were closing in. Dukes did not know what kind of tiger he had by the tail. Let him try to burn Tony Paz out, buy him out, scare him out! They were all together now in the building and they had him scared! Sims should have hung on. But these *moyetos* . . . especially smart ones like Sims—

"Hey, squirt."

As Tony crossed 111th Street, he heard Rudy's voice. On silent tires, the Continental had sneaked up on him and was cruising north on the almost deserted street.

"What you want, Rudy? You can't wait until hearing?"

"Move out, Paz," Dukes called from the car. He was seated in front. Bolo was driving. "This is a good weekend to move in with your ginzo in-laws in the Bronx. I hear they like spics now. Get your wife and kid and beat it before I bomb you."

Tony stopped. He walked to the curb. There was a parked Volkswagen between them. "I cut your heart out, Dukes," he said. "You touch Lucy or the baby, I swear your heart come out in one big red piece. Raw meat."

"Get smart, Tony. I give you two hundred bucks right now, American dollars, if you move."

"Stick it in your nose."

"Don't want my money, *panin?*"

"I don' wan' your money. I wanna see you on witness stand

on Friday when you got to answer questions. You better get more lawyers than you got now, because we gonna make you eat dirt. You are dead, Dukes, but you too dumb to know it."

Dukes and Bolo were grinning at him. Two oriental students passed, ignoring the confrontation. It might have been a nocturnal conversation between a king pusher and one of his local runners. A dignified elderly man—a Columbia professor?—strolled by, oblivious to the drama.

"Stand up, squirt," Rudy whispered.

The long shiny double barrel of the shotgun poked itself out of the car window.

"You gon' kill me now, Dukes?" There was a soaring, thrilling pounding in Tony's chest. Damn, he was not afraid! He knew Dukes would not dare, never, not with the rewards Puttering must be dangling before him. "Kill me the hard way, Rudy, *a la canona?*"

Dukes caressed the stock, sighted down the barrel, cupped his hands under the smooth metal. "In the sights, kid," he said. "One more dead spic. Think I care?"

"I think you care." Flights of sea birds fluttered in Tony's starved chest: the seagulls over El Morro. "I got good lawyer now."

"Yeah?"

"Here he is, Rudy." Tony opened the briefcase, and from amid the assorted Oreos, Lorna Doones, and fig newtons, the chilled half quart of milk, he took out a dark-handled automatic and pointed it at Dukes' forehead. "You like my lawyer, Rudy? His name is 7.56 magnum. Double clip."

Bolo murmured something and ducked. But Dukes kept his shotgun on Paz's white glowing face. All he could see were the huge hot eyes, and he was momentarily upset by them.

On the deserted street they were alone in the world, despite the passage of students, lovers, losers.

"This my lawyer, Rudy," Paz said slowly. "I never afraid of you, with or without shotgun. I got more guns in apartment.

You come around for me, you get nice greeting from my lawyers."

Dukes laughed and pulled in the weapon. As soon as he did, Tony, with a furtive look around, put the automatic into its nest of crackers, and, hunched over, as if under the whip of a wind from the Hudson, moved on to the garage.

3

"My men can't be everywhere at once," Captain Gossett said. He was the color of a fine walnut piano, a smooth-skinned, drowsy-eyed man with a shaved head, and a musical West Indian accent.

"I realize that," David said. "But if we could get a little extra patrolling around the house, checking the doors now and then. We're at the mercy of this man."

Gossett made a tent of his hands and closed his eyes. A Buddhalike black man, full of serene wisdom. Carrie, watching him with fascination, had read about him in the *Times:* a tough cop, a born leader.

"Not easy," Gossett said.

Tony Paz shifted in his seat. This was his arena—cops, crooks, violence. As a kid he had hung around the precinct house running for "coffee and." Many of the old-timers knew him. But this slick *moyeto* cop was hard to figure. Not that Rudy Dukes had any trouble figuring him out; he had just stayed away from him and greased a few dumb rookies, the few rotten ones. Ah, that Rudy. Of course he had not come to the meeting. What did Gossett expect? Nor had Puttering. Nor had anyone from Haman, Lord & Fawcett. Only the tenants—the Loomises, Hilda Schlossmann and her father, Dane and Lobello, and himself. And Hart. Allister was not there, nor the Gilligan dame. Tony had his suspicions about her. That *puta* was probably in bed again with Dukes, informing on the committee. Leave it to Rudy to use a woman like that, make a spy out of her.

"We know Dukes' record," Gossett said, "but we can't hold that against him. He did his time, and several persons of repute have vouched for him. What you folks need in a case like this is evidence."

"Evidence?" Carrie asked. "Captain, last night at 3 A.M., Dukes' goons ran through the corridors pounding on doors, yelling to us to move out or get thrown out. Everyone at this table heard them. Everyone had his sleep disturbed. This sort of thing goes on daily."

"Right!" Tony shouted. "He point his shotgun at me again! Right on Broadway, say he blow my guts out if I don' get out."

"Look what he did to Sims, that man your police arrested," Carrie said.

"There were witnesses that Sims attacked him," Gossett said.

"If he do, he have a right to," Paz cried. "If I go for Dukes throat, I finish the job. I don' care how many cops come."

Gossett smiled—compassionate, resigned. "Ladies, and gents, I have to repeat what I said. You will have to file complaints against Dukes. Do you want to? Please do. But remember that if you do, you will need evidence."

"But here's some evidence," Danny Hart said. He patted the stack of Xeroxed affidavits and A-60H forms. "I think these should be on file here, so you know what you've been up against."

"I know about them," the captain said. "Suspicious fire. The marshal says it looked like arson. But who? Who saw anyone?"

"Bolo!" Tony yelled. "That *grifo!* Enrique Torres. He got a record too."

"All right," the captain said. "Who wants to file the complaint? Where are your witnesses? Where are the people whose apartment was burned?"

David laughed drily. "They've moved. Dukes chased them out on the night we organized the committee."

"Well, you should have moved faster," Gossett said. "And the assault, the alleged assault on Mr. Hart. You should have reported it if it was so serious."

"Maybe I'd have gotten the same results Sims did," Danny said. "I might have been charged with attacking *him.*"

"Maybe you did," Gossett said. His subtle eye lingered on Hart's anemic face, the long hair, the bent nose.

"Captain, we want your *help,*" David said. "We know Dan. He's a former seminary student. He doesn't throw punches. Dukes is a strong-arm man."

"Yes, and he makes sure he has witnesses," the captain said. "Who saw this fight? Who saw the fire being set? Who saw Dukes or any of his mob throw the paint in Mr. Schlossmann's apartment? Who saw him point the gun at Mr. Paz?"

"Wait a minute," Barri Dane called. "I did. We did. We were at the window the first time it happened. He pointed it at us also."

"That's right," Ron Lobello added. "And called us every dirty name in the book."

Carrie noticed they were both dressed sedately and that the feminine inflections were missing. They knew how to behave inside the temple of the law.

"So you blew your chance." Gossett looked satisfied. "You should have called us and we'd have looked into it."

"But would you?" David asked. "Dukes started moving derelicts into the vacant flat on the ground floor and one of your men told me to throw them out myself. He said it was the kind of thing that happened all the time."

Gossett tapped the table gently. "Mr. Loomis, I know about

that. I've briefed myself on the Dukes case. Sergeant Cudlipp said if you couldn't get them to leave, he'd send some men over. You never called."

"I admit it," David said lamely. "Your man discouraged me."

"*I* throw them the hell out," Tony said. "I ain' afraid of Dukes or any bum he bring in."

Gossett was studying Tony with the intrigued eye of a herpetologist who has sighted an exotic snake. "See? Things work out. Have they come back?"

"Not really," Loomis said. "There's a couple of kids in there now. I guess they're students. They're quiet and we never see them. But that doesn't change matters."

"Look at how he thumbed his nose at this meeting," Carrie said.

"He is above the law, sir," Werner Schlossmann announced. "He makes his own, and until he is brought to realize that all men must obey laws and honor the agreements of a civilized society, he will continue to persecute us."

The captain looked sympathetically at Schlossman. Then he asked: "What can I do to help?"

Loomis looked at his notes. He had gotten into the habit of jotting things down. "First, increased car patrols on the block. Regular checking of front-door locks. Second, a faster response to our calls for help. The tenants' committee wants to take you up. The next threat from Dukes, the next attack, and we'll be on the phone at once, and we'll file a complaint. Third, an awareness on the part of your men that we are in a state of siege on West 84th Street, that as the pressures mount on this man, he'll do anything to force us out—"

A sergeant poked his head into the captain's office.

"Cap'n Gossett, excuse me. There's a two-alarmer on West 84th Street. Fire Department's en route. I sent over three cars."

"Where? Where on West 84th?" Tony yelled.

They all knew his answer before he spoke. "Your place. Don't worry. It's under control.

They all got up. In their terror, they were unable to run. It was pure Dukes, an essential Dukesian act. He had snubbed the meeting. And while they politely talked with Gossett about ways of containing him, he had struck again. It was the same technique he had used when he had ousted the Puerto Rican families: at the moment they met to unite against him, he had thrown some of them into the street.

"My wife," Tony Paz said. "My kid." He was trembling as if seized by epilepsy. He burst from the room, shrieking curses.

Loomis gathered up his notes swiftly. Hart collected his affidavits. The paperwork seemed more futile than ever.

"Shall we file a complaint?" David asked Gossett. "How much evidence do you need?"

By the time they reached the building, the fire was out. It was not nearly as serious a blaze as the one that had ruined 1B.

A large crowd, including many children in pajamas, stood around the two fire engines. Police pushed them back. From the window of 3A, the apartment of Dane and Lobello, smoke billowed in black gusts.

"Oh, Christ, Ron," Dane moaned. "Ours."

"Ah, the bastard," Lobello said. "Why us? Baby, we should have gotten out. Who needs this?"

Tony Paz shot through the crowd and ran to Lucy. She was holding a bawling Michael. "It was in 3A, Ton'," she said. "It burned a little while, and we sort of heard a *whoosh!* The Gilligan kids were the heroes."

Markie and Stevie Gilligan, strutting, wearing only their shorts were talking to a fireman. They had heard the explosive noise, smelled smoke, and run out of their apartment. They had been alone. Their mother was at the bakery. They saw a man running downstairs, but the hall lights were out and they didn't recognize him. Then they saw the smoke issuing from underneath the locked door of 3A. At once, Markie, the eleven-year-old, ran to his flat and called 911. Stevie started on the top floor, rousing tenants. The Allisters were not at home and most of the other people were at the meeting at the station house. No one was hurt, but the apartment was damaged by smoke and water.

"Dukes can't wait," Paz shouted. "He gonna burn us all. You see, you see."

A cloaked fireman called from the window. "Look out below. We're throwin' it out. This is the thing they boined."

The crowd moved back. A charred square form sailed from the window—closet? table?—and landed in the gutter with a terrifying crash, an explosion of hot smoke.

"My baldachino," Lobello moaned. "The bastard burned it."

Dane put his arm around him.

"Was goin' like a bonfire," the fireman above called down. "Like it was doused with something."

A fire chief called up. "Anything else?"

"No, all out," the fireman responded. "Like they put the torch to that. Picked it out. What is it, anyway?"

"He's desperate," Danny Hart said to David. "To leave himself open like this—"

Loomis shook his head. "They haven't laid a glove on him yet. Why should he stop?"

In the gutter, Lobello's antique piece, that curious table-phone stand, crumpled into black chunks. *They must have doused it with something.*

Over on the stoop, a policeman was interrogating O'Gara. The super looked stupefied. "Didn't see no one," David heard him say. "Hell yes, Ah keep the front locked. But some bum can break in. They do, y'all know they do. . . ."

Hart was watching him narrowly, trying to get a reading on him. Was Dukes using him to start the fires? Unlikely, he thought. People like O'Gara were undependable, lacking in courage. He had worked with addicts in the Parish House. They could act only when driven to act. But what if Dukes were playing Fagin with him, withholding drugs, then forcing him to set the fires to get his reward?

A fireman, bearing an ax, came out the front door.

"How bad is it?" Lobello asked. "Can we sleep there?"

"Not unless you're a helluva swimmer."

Ron walked back to Barri. "Well, sweetie, we're done in. We ought to collect some things. Where to?"

Hart came over. "The Parish House can put you up. I'll call Hasslinger. I'm sorry about this."

Barri turned a hip toward him. "Oh, go to hell, go away. Who needed this crusade? Who needed it? Look at what it did for us."

Hart started to say something, thought better of it, and halted. They had a point.

Carrie Loomis whispered to Tony Paz: "Is that Dukes? I can't even recognize him."

"Is Rudy all right. He is like an actor. Look different, fool people."

It was incredible. When she had seen Dukes on previous occasions, a fleeting glimpse of him in the car, walking the streets, he had a swagger, an I-dare-you look about him. His clothes told you something—the expensive blue turtlenecks, the tight trousers. Now, he wore a sedate dark-gray suit, the kind favored by bank clerks or insurance salesmen. His shirt was white, with a soft collar, and he wore a dark-blue tie. In addition, he seemed to have had his curling chestnut hair trimmed. It no longer reached his collar, and the forelock was neatly combed. And his face simply *looked* different—repentant, reasonable.

"What's he wearing in his lapel?" Carrie asked.

"Purple heart," Tony sneered. "Lot of baloney. He never get it."

Raymond Oberlander looked at the stenotypist, muttered something to Adriano Labato. There were a stack of manila folders in front of the enforcement officer. Whatever the outcome at 502 West 84th Street, the record on Rudy Dukes was piling up.

"I take it you are still not represented by counsel?" Oberlander asked David.

"Mr. Hart and I will speak for the tenants." Again Hart had let him down. Feldman, the Parish House lawyer, had not been contacted.

In one of the folding chairs facing the long table sat Carrie, Tony, Schlossmann, and Barri Dane. Mary Gilligan was unable to attend. And Allister, after his enthusiastic start, had dropped out of things. Last night, during the meeting at the police station, and at the fire, the Allisters had been absent. Carrie had heard something about their going to the theater.

It was a time of small triumphs, David thought. And the triumphs so far were twofold—Dukes had actually shown up, and Barri Dane, after his tearful attack on Hart of the previous night, was remaining on the committee.

"All right, folks," Oberlander said. "We're ready. This is a resumption of hearing two seven slash five eight zero one slash letter C, in the matter of complaints by tenants of 502 West 84th Street against Dukes Management, Rudy Dukes, and employees. Presiding, enforcement officer Raymond J. Oberlander. I remind you that all witnesses will be sworn, and these hearings are quasi-judicial in nature."

"Mr. Oberlander," David asked. "Can we interrogate Mr. Dukes?"

"Not in these first hearings. I shall conduct the interrogation of all parties." He fussed with some notes on his desk. "Oh, before we begin, Mr. Loomis, I think I should put this letter in the record. It arrived this morning, and it is from a Mr. A. R. Allister, a tenant at 502 West 84th Street. Do you know Mr. Allister?"

"Yes. He's a member of the committee."

Oberlander's eyebrows rose. "No more." He read swiftly, slurring words. "Dear Sir, et cetera, et cetera . . . please remove my name from any communications concerning events of the past weeks. . . . I am no longer associated with aforementioned committee of tenants, and I wish that the various allegations of harassment and the affidavits I filed be stricken from the record, and that I in no way continue as party to the dispute between Dukes Management and the other parties . . . et cetera, et cetera." Oberlander looked at David. "You know about this?"

"No, sir."

Behind him, he heard the tenants stirring. Paz was mumbling to himself, and he could hear Schlossmann loudly tsk-tsking. In his own chest there was a weighted despair. Dukes was picking them off one at a time. It was like an old film, *The Lost Patrol,* that he and Carrie had seen at the Museum of Modern Art—a British Army patrol in the Mesopotamian desert in World War I, being shot dead one at a time by invisible, relentless Arab snipers. The Puerto Ricans were gone first, easy victims. Then poor Sims, hounded, framed, driven from his home. And now Allister.

"All right, we'll move ahead," the official said. "Mr. Dukes, you are aware of the charges against you. You have been sent copies of the complaints, and you are here to respond to them. You understand?"

"Yes, sir, I do." His voice was faint.

"Ray," Tremark said lightly, "I should like to request that I make a statement on behalf of my client before any interrogation takes place, and I would like it in the record."

"If it's pertinent."

"It is. My client has already denied any allegations by this group of tenants. He will do so today. Further, we will charge that this tenants' association is motivated by malice, greed, and selfishness. And while he has agreed to participate in this hearing, he registers his disapproval of it, and regards it as an invasion of his privacy and a denial of his rights."

The brazenness of this statement, uttered with evident indignation by Dukes' attorney, stunned everyone for a few moments. Even Oberlander, a thick-skinned functionary, a man

247

who had heard innumerable lies, every evasive technique, seemed disoriented.

"We will let that go into the record. It is pretty much what Mr. Dukes said in his answer to our application. But if you want it twice, that's all right. Mr. Dukes, will you please come forward and be sworn."

Labato placed a Bible on the table. Dukes came to the head and was sworn.

"Rudy Dukes maybe drop dead from the Bible," Tony Paz said to Carrie loudly. "You know. Like vampire. Like devil. He can't take holy book."

Dukes returned to his seat. Oberlander stared glumly at some papers in front of him and began asking basic questions—Dukes' name, the name of his company, how long he had been in business.

"You are managing this building? And you managed 500 West 84th Street when it was occupied?"

"That's right."

"But aren't you more than a manager?"

"Huh?"

"You are also a net lessee, are you not, Mr. Dukes? I have a copy of your contract with Mr. E. J. Puttering, and it is called a lease. 'This agreement between E. J. Puttering, Inc., et cetera . . . as landlord . . . and Dukes Management Company, et cetera, et cetera . . . as tenant. Landlord hereby leases to the tenant the following premises' . . . and they are specified."

"Yeah, that's right. I rented the buildings."

"And paid Mr. Puttering the sum specified as rent?"

"That's right."

"And the idea was, you collect the rents and make a small profit on them?" asked Oberlander.

"Sure. It's done. When a landlord don't wanna be bothered with small properties."

Oberlander rubbed his chin. "May I ask how you hoped to realize any profit on such a short-term arrangement?"

Dukes looked hurt. "Well, I was in trouble. It's no secret.

Those people there keep hollering about it, like a man can never make good again once he's in trouble." He directed a rueful look at Loomis. "But I'm trying to make a comeback. Mr. Puttering was nice enough to give me a break. He promised me some bigger jobs—I mean bigger rentals, and maybe a chance at building. I admit this thing is peanuts, not worth my time, unless it could lead to something better."

"Mr. Dukes, I have read this lease between you and Mr. Puttering and I find nothing in it about your obtaining the removal of tenants," Oberlander said.

"Sure. That wasn't part of it."

"Is there any understanding between you and Mr. Puttering, of any kind, written or verbal, to remove the tenants from the building mentioned in the lease?"

"None whatsoever."

Tony Paz hooted. "Yah! You believe that you believe anything, Mr. Oberlander! He is lyin'."

"Mr. Paz, let me conduct the hearing. Mr. Dukes, did anything pass between you and Mr. Puttering, any advice, any hint, that he wanted the building in a vacant state?"

Dukes affected a puzzled expression. "I'm not sure I follow you."

"Did Puttering tell you to—"

"Look," Tremark intervened swiftly, "if what you're driving at, Ray, is does Puttering desire an empty building, does he not intend to rent apartments once they are vacated, the answer is yes. Is that what you're driving at?"

"Yes. That's part of it."

Tremark waved his manicured hand. A whiff of expensive cologne sailed across the table. "Of course Puttering wants them out. We've never denied it. But these people have been unreasonable. They've formed this group to hold up my client and Mr. Puttering. They hope they'll get fat cash settlements—"

"That isn't so," David said.

"You know it is, Loomis," the lawyer said, and for a second, David saw the fang and claw, the bloody thrust of street-level legal work. "Loomis, everyone who has moved out has been paid. Those Puerto Ricans on the ground floor were rewarded by Mr. Dukes—"

"With a goddamn fire that almost kill them!" Tony shouted.

"Just a minute, just a minute," the lawyer said. "We don't have to listen to these wild outbursts from that man, a man who goes around armed."

"Armed! You bet I am armed! I am ready for Dukes next time he threaten my wife, next time he point shotgun at me!"

"See what I mean?" Tremark crowed. "See the kind of people my client has to contend with?"

"Mr. Paz, I beg of you," Oberlander pleaded. "I don't want to ask you to leave."

"Okay. I shut up."

"Now in the matter of these families who were in apartment 1B," Tremark went on, "I have located them, and I have secured affidavits from both men, Mr. Escobar and Mr. Fuentes, to the effect that they were in no way harassed by Mr. Dukes, and that upon their departure, he paid them each the amount of five hundred dollars, for which they signed receipts. I offer these as proof of the falsity of the charges against Mr. Dukes, and with the hope that you will end these hearings which are wasting everyone's time."

The attorney shoved the papers across the table. David glanced at them. Two could play the game of affidavit and Dukes' lawyer had moved shrewdly. Paz had warned him how Dukes worked—a different scheme for everyone. After terrorizing the people in 1B, chasing them out with dead dogs, threats and fire, he had bribed them into silence. (With a lot less than five hundred dollars, Tony was certain.) And in so doing he had severely damaged the tenants' case.

"Adriano?" Oberlander asked. "You wanna add what you know?"

The inspector nodded. "I can support Mr. Tremark's statement. I was unable to locate Carlos Fuentes, but I did find

Mr. Escobar in Brooklyn. He is satisfied with the arrangement Mr. Dukes made with him and he did not want to testify."

Hart appeared relaxed—even as a good part of their case went up in smoke. "It is possible they were intimidated by Mr. Dukes," he said.

"You stop that," Tremark said. "Or you may have a slander case on your hands. Just watch that talk."

Oberlander was studying the signed affidavits from the Puerto Ricans. He knew how Dukes had gotten them. Some money, the show of fist. The long-haired kid from the Parish House was probably right. But there it was in writing, as worthy of his attention as the affidavits submitted by the tenants.

"Mr. Dukes," Oberlander went on, "you are aware of the charges made by these people, and it is my hope that, whoever is in the right, we might resolve this by having you agree to sign an assurance of discontinuance, so that these people's minds may be put at rest."

"I can't discontinue what I haven't been doing," Dukes protested.

"If I may, Mr. Oberlander," David said, "our committee will not be satisfied with such a paper, whatever its force, and Mr. Hart says it has virtually no force. We want more than the stoppage of future acts. We want Mr. Dukes, his hoodlums, and Mr. Puttering called to account for the way they have maltreated people, and we want a finding of harassment brought against them, so that they are punished."

"What did I tell you?" Tremark shouted. "Malice. Pure malice."

"Just hold it," the enforcement officer said. "All right, we'll proceed. I shall work my way through these statements of harassment, give Mr. Dukes a chance to respond, and then we'll see where we are at. I had hoped to begin with the matter of the fire in 1B—"

"Those people never filed A-60H forms, Ray," the attorney said.

"I know. But the fire was a threat to other tenants and is

mentioned in all the reports. Mr. Dukes, what do you know about it?"

"Nothing. I didn't see the house till the next day."

"Did you or one of your employees set it?"

"No."

"Did you order anyone to set it?"

"No."

"Are you aware that an employee of yours named Enrique Torres, known as Bolo, was reported seen in the building carrying a bottle some time before the fire was set?"

"I heard that report," Dukes said. "It's a lie. These people will say anything to discredit me."

Paz, squirming in his chair, struggled to contain himself. *Carail* Escobar and Fuentes had both told him, told him to his face, they had seen Bolo! But what good did it do? Dukes had scared them stiff, bought them off.

What about the daubing of paint in Schlossmann's apartment, the destruction of his books and papers? Dukes knew nothing about it. If Shlep and Bolo were involved, they would have to speak for themselves. He would never authorize that sort of thing.

Threatening phone calls? Do I look like that kind of person? Dukes responded. Tremark pointed out that his client was a veteran with a distinguished war record, a purple heart, a man who respected his country. Such a man did not make obscene threats to people.

And the faked letter?

Here Dukes paused. Contritely, he lowered his head and told the official: "I admit it, I made a mistake. I shouldn't of done that. I'm sorry. But it didn't do no harm. No one believed it, did they?"

Oberlander twiddled his pencil. "It certainly indicates a desire to get the people out, doesn't it, Mr. Dukes?"

"I never denied I wanted them out. I just say I never did anything illegal." He paused, and his slanted eyes appealed to

Oberlander. "Except maybe that crazy letter. And I'm sorry, I really am."

Hart looked at Oberlander. "Doesn't this admission establish the existence of *intent*, Mr. Oberlander? What could be clearer than this illegal letter, this theft of stationery from your office?"

"That's true. But we must have actual evidence that these specific incidents took place. What it really boils down to is Mr. Dukes' word against the tenants'."

Paz groaned—rude, mocking. "Wha' you want? You wan' we should bring in the first dead body, when that guy shoot someone? You wan' blood?"

"Mr. Paz—"

"Excuse me, Mr. Oberlander," Hart said, "but Tony is right. The City means well. But the laws are so worded as to give the landlords every out. You admitted that a finding of harassment was very rare, that you try to resolve these disputes by having the landlord call off his goons, stop his violent acts. Anything, apparently, to save the landlord the possibility of fines, punishment, the kind of rude justice that is usually reserved for the poor."

"Look, Hart," the official said irritably, "I don't need any radical speeches. You have no actual status."

"That's why I can say these things," Danny said quietly. His voice was low, but David noticed a cold light in his eyes. Loomis had the uneasy sensation that Hart was determined to bring Dukes down, or die, or get them all killed. For a moment, he was almost as fearful of Hart as he was of the scowling thug across the table.

"I remind you," Overlander said, "to prove harassment we must find a continuing course of conduct, as distinguished from an isolated incident or a group of incidents, like a boiler breakdown—"

"Which, incidentally," Tremark shouted, "was fixed in a few days by Mr. Dukes, after these people, led by that agitator, raised a big stink over it, and accused him of all kinds of plots. Ray, let's wind this thing up. We haven't seen a bit of objective supporting evidence—that's the way the law reads—*objective supporting evidence*—that my client's conduct has resulted in tenants moving."

"What about the Sims family?" Loomis asked.

As he asked the question, he felt the worms of doubt eating at him. Dukes was too smart for them, too tough. He could get away with everything up to murder, and perhaps murder itself. The blockbuster was untouchable, beyond the law, a creature functioning with his own rules.

"What about them?" the lawyer cried.

"Since we're on that, let me ask Mr. Dukes," Oberlander said. "Mr. Sims claims in his A-60H and in his affidavit that your man Torres jammed his keyhole. Did you tell him to do that?"

"Absolutely not. He never done it. Sims said he caught him in the hall, chewing gum and with kitchen matches in his pocket. What's he gonna do, accuse everyone in New York who chews spearmint and likes wood matches? It's phony, like this whole case."

"You wrecked Sims' kitchen," David said.

"Like hell I did," Dukes responded. "He chickened out. We were going to fix it, but he couldn't wait."

Tremark slammed his palm on the table. "This is idiotic. This is disgraceful. The tenant Horton Sims attacked my client and tried to strangle him, with witnesses and a policeman present, and we sit here arguing whether Mr. Dukes harassed Sims. I do not like the trend of this hearing, and I intend to file a protest with the commissioner. I don't like the idea of a group of crackpots and agitators trying to wring an honest businessman's neck. The Sims thing is the last straw. The man attacks Mr. Dukes, and suddenly he is a martyr, and we should shed tears over his departure."

Tony Paz was on his feet. He shook his fist at Rudy. "Why you call him every night and say, 'Move, nigger'? Why you send Shlep to threaten he beat up Sims' kid, hah?"

There was an unsettled look on Oberlander's lumpy face. He seemed too tired to censure Paz any more. Loomis saw it and

254

took momentary hope. It was as if Paz were the unquenchable voice of truth, and the enforcement officer knew it, even though Dukes and his lawyer had every legal advantage.

The official turned to Labato. "Did you contact Sims?"

"Yes. I talked to him."

"What did he say?"

Labato squinted at a small notebook. "Former tenant Horton Sims says he has no desire to participate in the hearings concerning Dukes Management, has no desire to bring charges, and wants to forget the whole thing."

"There it is, Ray," Tremark cried. "There's your tenants' committee and its martyred people."

The hearing moved ahead, into the matters of the super, the filth in the hallways, the derelicts in the back room, but the heart had gone out of the tenants. David appeared confused. Hart's pale eyes were concentrated, but on more remote matters, it seemed.

When Oberlander adjourned the hearings till Monday ("Is this really necessary, Ray?" the lawyer whined. "Can't we wind this up here and now?") and Dukes and Tremark had left the room, the tenants huddled around the table. For a few minutes no one spoke. Then, Werner Schlossmann sighed, an old European sigh, laden with despair, and said, "I am afraid we are beaten by this man."

"No, no," Hart said. "I can see Oberlander believes us, but he needs something concrete—"

"I say to hell with it," Barri Dane interrupted. "Look, Hart, this Christian Endeavor bit is great for your soul, but what about our bodies? I had to twist Ron's arm to stick this out, and now with the fire he's ready to chuck it. And so am I."

Carrie touched his arm. "Barri, you can't. Not after all we've been through."

"So what? What does it mean? You saw what that goon did to us with his slick lawyer. He'll do it again, and again, because he's good at it."

"And," Schlossmann said mournfully, "I am afraid, because he has powerful interests working for him. They would not approve of Mr. Dukes and they would never admit to knowing him. He is part of the technological machine. And we are only bits of dirt that get in the way of the machine. He is in the mainstream, and we are not."

"You're wrong, Mr. Schlossmann," Hart said. "He isn't. And he can be stopped—"

"Stop him yourself, sweetie," Dane said. "I've had this knight-errant shtick. I won't get burned alive. Joan of Arc was never my idea of a good role."

"Nor am I in favor of self-immolation," Schlossmann said. "I had thought that I was strong enough to resist these forces. I disobeyed Hilda when I suggested our great painting scheme, our united front against the tyrant. It was a fool's plan, like the stagings of *Rosenkavalier* and *Carmen* in the Terezin concentration camp. But we were shipped to Auschwitz, *Carmen* or no *Carmen*. So it is with Mr. Dukes. He appears to be beyond our powers of resistance."

"The Nazis were beaten, Mr. Schlossmann," Carrie said. "Hitler's dead. People were liberated."

The old man smiled indulgently and patted her arm. "Oh, my dear innocent child."

David said nothing. He looked at the bleak faces of his corporal's guard; Schlossmann and Dane announcing their imminent surrender, Carrie looking pained, sitting awkwardly to accommodate her load of life, Paz so white with rage, so that he seemed on the verge of some irrational act.

"What do you say, David?" Hart was asking him.

He did not know what to say. He had come into the struggle mildly committed. Allister had euchred him into it, the same Allister who had now run out on them. And Hart with his bleached distant eyes, his hesitant voice, that congenital loser, failure, fumbler, a pensioner without home, bank account, woman, or future. Why had he listened to Hart?

Loomis did not respond. He knew that if he agreed to pull out, to bow to Dukes' will, to take a bribe and move, it would leave Tony Paz. And what would Paz do? Paz, who had seen guns pointed on him, a dog sicced at him, his wife and child threatened?

Yes, he wanted to get out. All along he had talked to Carrie about it. The hotel until the baby was born. Small, clean, neat, efficient. Why fight Dukes? He had never been a scrapper, a moralizer.

"Oh, honey, don't you think we should try to see if we can beat him?" Carrie pleaded. But her voice was empty of confidence. "At least go through one more hearing?"

"Damn," David said. "I don't know. I just don't know."

Paz had been waiting for the cue. He buried his head in his hands. "Me. I don' know either. I cannot give in to Dukes. I never look myself in face again."

"If you keep fighting him, Tony," Barri said. "You won't have any face to look at."

Hart leaned over the table. "Give me another few days," he said. "Give me the weekend to try to get something on him. If I can't, you're free to do what you want."

"Ach," Schlossmann said. He made an impatient European gesture with his right hand. "It is useless. An exercise in futility."

"We've come this far," Hart said. "What's two more days? One more hearing?"

"Jesus, Hart," Dane moaned. "Over the weekend that hood may bomb us. They haven't touched him for anything he's done so far; what's to stop him?"

"We can stop him," Hart said. He stood up, and for a moment, Loomis saw him as a daft preacher, and he understood the concern of the doyens of the seminary. "We can stop him and we *will* stop him. I know I can get some evidence, if I work all weekend. But even if I can't—"

"Hedging, hedging," Barri mocked.

"—I know we can win. The point is, even if Dukes gets off he'll be in trouble, and he won't be able to do it again."

"So what is that to me?" Dane said.

"A great deal, Barri," Hart pleaded. "How often can people

like us get together and do something constructive? If we stop Dukes, it will make the landlords go easy, it'll alert the City to people like Dukes, it will be a warning that ordinary citizens can't be persecuted just because of greedy interests."

"Ah, who the hell cares," Dane said. "You know nobody's listening. Nobody ever is in this town."

"We'll make them listen," Hart said. And again, Loomis saw the fire in his eyes, that light of mission, of preaching to the Gentiles, of visions on desert roads, shimmering images dimly seen and imperfectly understood. The man was dangerous in his own private way, and yet there was nothing illogical or contemptible about anything he had said.

"Don Quixote," Schlossmann said, "accomplished nothing, my dear boy. He was laughed at for his pains. Drubbed. Beaten. Mocked."

"But he succeeded, Mr. Schlossmann."

"Oh, your musical-comedy notions," the German said. "Read the work carefully. It is a gloomy book beneath the *opéra-bouffe*."

"You all think I'm crazy, don't you?" Hart said.

"You not nuts, Hart," Tony cried. "I go with you. I know what you mean."

"See? See?" the community organizer cried. "Tony understands. We're on a collision course. We can make Dukes sweat if we don't give in. I know he's got a deadline. "There's a lot of money on the line. Let's keep at it till we knock Dukes off."

"Oh, mother," Barri Dane said. "Are you going to tell us now that God's on our side?"

"No," Hart said. He smiled. "I don't make those decisions for people, not any more."

"Well, you sure make a lot of others," Dane said.

"How about it?" Hart asked. "Do we stick it out a few more days? At least till after the next hearing?"

"I am with you," Paz said. "I am with you till me or Rudy Dukes is dead in the street."

Carrie gulped and squeezed David's hand. David nodded at

her and spoke. "Well, I won't make it so dramatic, but as chairman, I suppose I have to give it a whirl. Okay, Danny."

Barri pouted. "I'll have to ask Ron. I guess so."

"And I will ask Hilda," Schlossmann said. "But I am afraid we have become *Mussulmen*—the walking dead of the camps."

Despite Dukes' victory at the first hearing—he had read accurately the despair in the faces of the tenants—he was not in a buoyant mood. Alone in the apartment, Rudy sipped champagne, feeling it soothe his gut, and watched television. The job would get done. That did not worry him. And he would not be badly hurt by the hearings. He'd sworn off blockbusting. No more goon stuff. No more arson, threats, beatings. He'd get his money from Puttering, get some decent properties to manage, and then branch out on his own.

In the dark (he liked to turn the lights off and stare, his mind dulled, his nerves gentled, at the colored screen) he reviewed the status of the house. Three down, five to go. Allister was the latest to agree. It had been easy, but expensive. He had been forced to go the limit, give Allister the full five thousand that Puttering had put up for both the broker and David Loomis. But things were getting desperate and Loomis was a Boy Scout. And his wife was no help. Dukes disliked small, stubborn, intelligent women like Carrie, with shrewd eyes and good manners.

Lobello and Dane were ripe fruit, overripe. He snickered at his own joke. The fire had broken them. Dane showed up at the hearing, but only because the Loomis broad buttered him up. But Lobello, the guinea, was shaking in his suede boots. They'd be out in a few days, ahead of Puttering's deadline. That would leave Schlossmann, the old Hebe (what was he hanging around for?), and the Loomises and Paz. He sipped the champagne slowly: Paz and Loomis. They would have to be bought off.

"I forgot Mary," he said aloud. "Mary Waslyk."

He knew why. He had forgotten her because she was not

another pigeon, not another mark to be driven from the building to satisfy Puttering, and Haman, Lord & Fawcett, and the builders, and the expense-account creeps who would come to live there, soft-bellied, suntanned, gin rummy-playing creeps, who did not know how to throw a left hook, or handle a shiv, or sight down the barrel of a Winchester.

Again, a turbid sensation struck his guts. Left out. Out of it. A bum, a hood, a hard-nosed ex-con with a bad reputation. It was the outs and the ins. And those who would build the white apartment with its uniformed doormen and television security system and carpeted rooms and glass walls were in, in, in. And he and Mary were out. Raging, he turned off the television, went to the refrigerator in his office and poured himself another glass of Mumms.

He would hold Puttering up for a bundle. Enough to get Mary out in style, five grand, the same as he had shoveled out to that yellow fink Allister and his bony wife. Mary was worth at least that. It would help her move. He'd never ask for it back. With Mary gone, and the fags on the ropes, it would be just Paz, Loomis, and Schlossmann. Ten days to work them over. Enough time. More than enough. And the big bonus from E.J.

But his cut was too small. And for what he had done? For the risks he took? Dukes, in his half-sodden fury, the champagne splashing from his tumbler, stumbled over Angel, kicked the dog ("Bastard cost me four hundred and can't scare a faggot"), and fell into an easy chair still in its Pliofilm cover. It reminded him: nothing was paid for, almost everything rented. The few items he had purchased had been bought on time. His father never would have approved. "Pay cash, get cash, Ratislav," the hardfisted old Hunky used to tell him.

He had lied to Loomis and Allister about his father. He'd never been in the mines, nor had Rudy. The Duziches ran a saloon, a mining-town saloon, and Rudy, without the old man's knowledge, had started the fixed Blackjack games in the woodshed. He was fifteen then. A few years later, after he'd beaten two dumb Polacks unconscious for insisting on a new deck, he'd been labeled a KG, a Known Gambler. He was now Rudy Dukes, a.k.a. Ratislav Duzich. A lousy life, a life for stupid Hunyaks. He was determined to be better, to show the world. The Lincoln was part of it, the apartment, his clothes. All these were important. And style, class.

They were afraid of him on Broadway. Before he'd gone off to stir, a couple of smart Jewish writers, frustrated tough guys, with apartments in the Belnord, racetrack nuts and baseball bettors, had been introduced to him, and their dark eyes glittered as he crushed their mitts. "So you're the legendary Rudy Dukes?" one asked. He liked that. *Legendary.* "You're the guy who walks around these welfare hotels collecting rents and keeping order?" the other asked. "I hear you never use a rod."

He admitted that was the case; showed them his fists, gave them his usual spiel on the fleet welterweight championship, and the time he went four rounds with Rodriguez. A real hard guy. "A vanishing American," one said, "a real unique type." "Boy, Dukes," the other said gratefully, "I didn't know they made them like you any more. Ever hear of a guy named Harry Bennett, who cleaned out unions for Henry Ford?" Rudy hadn't, but he nodded, studying them with thick contempt. Writers. Fakes. Soft-handed mama's boys, wanting to meet an old-fashioned nose-busting hood. "He's no Mafia sneak, that Dukes," one said, "he's the real thing, an elemental man."

Yes, he'd get the five grand for Mary from Puttering. That would be part of the deal. And whatever extra he needed to work on Paz and Loomis. All of the rough business was over, and he felt good about it. And the good deed to Mary. That would make everything perfect. He had decided he loved her. Or if it was not love, he needed her, craved that ageless, long-legged Ukrainian, with her blunt nose and yellow hair, seamless skin, and brave eyes.

Impulsively he dialed her number.

She answered, her voice coated with sleep, faintly afraid. "What? Who? Rudy . . . are you crazy? God, it's three-thirty in the morning. What is this, a Dukes special? Dirty words to scare me?"

"Mary," he said hoarsely, "I'm giving you five thousand dollars to move. You got to get out in a week. Think of it, kid, five grand. Because I love you, Mary."

"You're a liar."

"No, no, I mean it."

"You're drunk, then."

"I'll bring you the check tomorrow. Free and clear, all yours, when you sign the letter and release me from any claims. It's all in legal lingo."

"I don't believe you."

"It's true. I decided. I gave that bum Allister—"

"What? What'd you give him?"

Careful, careful. Why tell the truth when a lie will do as well? "He got three grand. You get top price. The last payoff. Because you're my girl. Mary Waslyk. We got to talk. That soldier is finished but he don't know it yet."

"Rudy, Rudy, let me go to sleep. Tell me tomorrow . . ."

He tried to be tender, to say something endearing, but he could not. The words stifled in his throat. All his life he had believed in the show of fist. That was why they valued him, the Putterings, and the operators in the Wall Street offices. They'd know about Rudy Dukes, and they'd be sorry when he went straight. Straight, married, respectable—and rich.

"It's got me bugged," David said to Carrie after they had watched the seven-o'clock news and sat down to dinner.

"What, sweetie? The way Dukes manhandled us?"

"Oh, no. Not that I'm proud of the way I sat there like a fixture and couldn't argue with him. About Archie Allister."

"What has you bugged?"

"Well . . . he ran out on us. He took whatever it was Dukes was offering, and he finked out. But I'm the one who feels ashamed. I can't explain it. I'm afraid to look the guy in the face. Why is that?"

262

"Maybe *you're* sorry you led all of us into this uplift movement. I'm not sorry, David. And I'm glad we're still in it." She served him veal piccata with lemon sauce. Now that her last few weeks had found her healthy, fat-cheeked, nonsalivating, she had turned again to the *Times* recipes.

"Get more conviction in your voice, Carrie," he said. "I feel sorry for Allister. I'll be damned if I'll know what to say to him. We went into this as buddies, the two bright guys on the top floor. So I end up a flop, a patsy for that oddball Hart, and Archie is King Fake, who did just what Dukes wanted him to do."

"I never had much faith in him. Liz wanted to get out."

"Maybe they're right. Why did we get those grand ideas that we could fight Dukes?"

"My fault, David. I thought it was like a play. A leading role, at last. And what a villain!"

"That's it. He's too much for any of us. Too smart. Too mean. And I can't help feeling he fascinated us. Look at Tony. I think his life wouldn't mean as much if he didn't have Dukes on his mind. Allister was intrigued with him. Schlossmann. And we are, for that matter. Have you noticed the way Oberlander studies him every now and then, as if he's not quite certain how to handle him?"

Carrie poured the coffee. "It's the violence, David."

"Violence?"

"He's not afraid to use it. He doesn't care about hurting and maiming people. Ever see the way kids love movies about Nazis, and want to know all about them?"

"But should that make it more difficult to catch up with a guy like that? Is part of his success the fact that people secretly admire him, or are envious of him? I can't believe that. There's some justice in the world."

Carrie sighed, shifting her position. She sat clumsily, legs apart. Every few minutes she felt a violent kick. "There has to be. It would be nice to leave this place knowing we did him in. It would be even nicer if they let us stay on here, and bring the baby up. I don't think I'll ever like any home as much as this one."

He got up from the table, came to her, kissed her hair. "We'll start looking for something like it. I have a feeling the battle of West 84th Street is almost over. We look like good losers."

Later that night, when Carrie had gone to bed, David worked at the drafting table. He often saved such parts of his work that he particularly enjoyed for the night. Alone, with the gooseneck fluorescent light spreading its glow on the cluttered surface, the radio softly humming, he felt at peace. He had always been able to work well, think clearly, find a gratifying spark of energy before retiring.

In the midst of some painstaking measurements, Dukes phoned him. He sounded drunk, but conciliatory. He offered David $2500 to move out. David refused. "It'll be your ass, Loomis," he growled. "You ain't any better than me. You'll learn. When the bomb is dropped, you'll all go."

The man sounded irrational, a crazed note in his threats, as if some crisis were imminent. And then he realized that Dukes was a good actor. He was no less unsure of himself now than he had been the day he started wrecking the house next door, with the frightened tenants still in it.

What amateurs we are! David thought. He should have rigged a tape recorder to the phone. *Evidence, evidence,* Oberlander kept saying, *objective supporting evidence.* They should have worked day and night to trap Dukes, record him, take pictures of him. And now it was too late. What a pitiful group their committee had been! What a comic failure! They had organized it with courage, a sense of a grand campaign against the personi- fication of all that was rotten and cruel in the city. And Dukes had mocked and beaten them from the very first.

David stopped drawing, straightened his back, and kneaded the muscles in his neck. He'd flipped all right. But he never claimed to be a fighter, a leader. He had been the wrong man for the job. But someone had had to do it. And they weren't quite finished yet. There was still Tony, and Schlossmann, and the Gilligan woman, and maybe even Dane and Lobello. Not a terribly encouraging group, but a group. Danny Hart, that misfit of misfits, wanderer, *Luftmensch*, the Prince Myshkin of West 94th Street, was dropping hints that he had new leads, some way of getting evidence. Did he hear the community organizer asking Barri Dane if he could borrow a tape recorder?

There was a buzzing at the door, and David, in spite of himself, started, feeling his heart accelerate. It was past eleven. He got up slowly, convinced it was Dukes or one of his thugs. What could they do? Beat him? Threaten him again? Surely, with the case now before the City, with the documents on Oberlander's desk, with another hearing imminent, Dukes would not dare. Loomis glanced at the bedroom. The light was out. Carrie was asleep.

He walked down the corridor. At the door he undid the double locks, slid the bolt, but kept the chain anchored.

Archie Allister was standing in the hallway.

"Hey, Arch," David said. "Come in."

"No. No, thanks, Dave." He hesitated. His face was splotched with red. At the bottle again. "Listen, I just wanted . . . wanted . . ."

Loomis was embarrassed. It would have been better for Allister not to have come around.

"Please. Come on in, Arch."

"Nah." The Wall Street man smothered a belch. "You think what you want about me, kid. It's okay. I couldn't stick it out. Not with Liz so upset. No way."

"No way," Loomis found himself repeating. What did the man want? "Well—we do what we have to do."

"Right. Right, buddy." He punched Loomis playfully on the shoulder. "You hang in there, Dave. You and Carrie, hang in there. It's important. Sorry I couldn't. The way it crumbles."

The man's mumbled clichés, his fake assurance, Loomis decided, was more bothersome than his defection. He accepted a few more of Allister's soppy good wishes, then shook his wet hand and closed the door.

Danny Hart slung the tape recorder over his right shoulder. It was a simple affair, and Barri Dane, who used it to play back his readings of lines, had given him instructions: start button, record, playback, erase. In the scuffed black leather case, it might have been a transistor radio, camera gear.

Hart was in search of O'Gara. He would get O'Gara to talk. Recorded, they would have the "objective supporting evidence" that the City wanted. He had also brought along an affidavit for O'Gara to sign. Armed with these, they would confront Dukes and nail him.

With his long hair, tattered denims, and sandals, Hart could have been any of the drifters of the West Side—students, quasi-students, dropouts, street freaks, failed artists, radicals, the whole mixed grill of young people, the committed, and the dazed. Because of his appearance, he had always enjoyed good contacts with street people. Father Hasslinger's office, particularly the narcotics clinic, was well known, and if the results they showed were meager (the minister was the first to admit this) their reputation was good. They never turned anyone away. The Parish House had a good name; the human wreckage of the neighborhood was often willing to talk to its people.

It was a warm sticky night, hot for late May, and Hart felt expectant. After long years of floundering, indecision, failures (none of them had bothered him especially), he felt he had a fix on something, he had grabbed the handle, as the kids said. Dukes had been a godsend. He had been waiting for a Rudy Dukes all his life, an embodiment of what was cruel and destructive in the modern city. You could argue, as Hasslinger had argued, that Dukes was a mere symptom, a boil on the civic skin, induced by a fever in the blood, but that was no comfort to the victims who had to feel his wrath. Hart recalled the first time he had seen the blockbuster, the cocky little man with the square pale face, the slanted eyes, the hoarse voice. Dukes had presence, style. It was as if he understood his role and dressed for it, acted it, nourished it. Hart had been drawn to him. Some divine providence had supplied him with Rudy Dukes, at this time, in this place.

In his boyhood, Hart, raised on an impoverished dirt farm in Nebraska, was given to daydreaming, inventions, long half-waking hours in the hayloft. For a while he thought of a career in politics, as a brave reformer, friend of the poor farmers. But his parents discouraged him: too shy, too feeble. At college in Omaha, he had turned to social work, going into the black slums in a work-study program, trying to reach the angry poor. They had mocked him, rejected him, and he failed. At the seminary in New York, he had sought reassurance from the ancient faith. The trouble was, he realized, the answers were too obvious, apparent to anyone who took the trouble to walk down Broadway on a summer's night. Who needed libraries of theology and stacks of scholarly works to explain why the air crackled with hate and fear and greed? It was the very simplicity of the human condition that made solutions difficult.

Small things might be accomplished. A dreaming farmboy, too weak to work the fields, too impractical to make a go of anything, might yet make some mark on the city. And he had found his cause. The building and its tenants were important to him. They had been ever since he had seen the white car, the miserable Puerto Ricans being hustled out. The whole sorry state of the world summed up: the white ark, the furniture on the sidewalk, with the oleograph of an effeminate Jesus staring from the cracked mirror of the dresser . . . The situation was good, but the protagonist was perfect. Dukes had surfaced, the beast with seven heads and ten horns, like unto a leopard, with feet of a bear, and mouth of a lion, given his power by the dragon, the blasphemous beast of Revelations. Hart smiled as he thought about it. Long ago, he had stopped reading the Bible, but the old book was useful sometimes. Dukes and he would arrive at their own Armageddon. They had already played a rehearsal in the corridor of 502 West 84th Street, when the blockbuster had slapped him. Ah, the overpowering evil fragrance of the man, the cologne that filled the air when he swung his thick arms!

After all his failings, Hart mused, one victory. He tried not to be too arrogant, to depict himself in his mind too thoroughly as the sole force for good. If this were the battle between the Prince of Darkness and the Teacher of Righteousness, the teacher had some avid pupils. But he had led, he had organized, he had kept them going, even now, when their army was reduced to a pitiful rear guard. Just the other day, after Dukes had wiped them out at the hearing, he had stiffened their backs, begged for and gotten a vote of confidence. Now he would have to deliver.

A Puerto Rican prostitute who sometimes came to the Parish House for advice on a rent war with a landlord had told Hart that O'Gara had been hanging around a bar, La Finca Vieja, on Columbus Avenue, near the rehabilitation area. He evidently had a connection there. O'Gara was known as a big user, one who often had the cash to buy his deck, but still begged and connived and, when necessary, stole, to satisfy his habit. He was unmistakable with his shaved head, haunted eyes, and fringed jacket.

Danny found the bar and squinted through the broken neon sign in the window. At the bar were a few Puerto Ricans, a huge man Hart recognized as one of the dark princes of the welfare hotel around the corner, a serenely ugly hooker, and O'Gara. He stared at the dismal scene, but he was not frightened, not downhearted. They knew him in the neighborhood.

But as he entered, the whiff of stale beer and sweat, the moist heat, the appalling sense of loss and misery, shivered him. Was it wrong to use O'Gara, to force him to commit himself to Dukes' revenge? And what could he offer him?

With or without O'Gara's help, Dukes would have to be brought down. Dukes would have to be trapped, made to pay for what he had done. In the dank, half light of the bar, Hart shuddered as a revelation came to him: he would let Dukes kill him and pay the price if necessary. All the failures of the past canceled, all the frustrations annulled! But before the final scheme of glory, that eschatological climax, he would try to enlist the superintendent.

"Hi, O'Gara," Dan said. He climbed on the stool next to him. "Can I buy you a beer?"

"Why sure. You the preacher's boy?"

"I work with Father Hasslinger."

"You still fussin' with the tenants at mah place?"

"Haven't you heard about the hearings? Dukes is in trouble. We've got him on the carpet."

"Hit no skin off mah back. Ah just doin' a job."

Hart studied him. Where from? What kind of life? He had thought, from what the tenants had said, that the man was menacing, violent. But all that Danny saw in the haggard face of the super was a muted terror.

"Dukes is dead," he said. "Even if the City doesn't act on the hearings, nobody'll hire him again."

"Don't give a damn." O'Gara leaned toward Hart. His breath was foul. "Gimme ten dollars."

"You kidding? I don't have enough for your next beer."

"That minister got money. Gimme five."

"I don't have any dough. I'll tell you what I'll do. I'll take you down to the narcotics clinic at the Parish House. Ever try methadone?"

"A preacher down deep."

"What are you going to do, O'Gara? Be a sucker for people like Dukes all your life? How old are you? Thirty? Thirty-five? You can be helped."

"Listen, boy. Ah take care of myself. Ah git what Ah need. Ain't no minister gonna git me on methadone, or cold turkey, or what."

"What'll you do for a fix when Dukes gets rid of you?"

"He ain't gettin' rid of me."

"He's finished at 502. One way or the other. And he's got

strong-arm men like Shlep and Bolo. They'll go out and get him a dozen like you."

An offended look on O'Gara's face told Hart that the man had some kind of warped pride. As the lowest of Dukes' soldiers, he needed some reassurance. "Bolo is a spic yellowbelly. Afraid to start a damn fire. I showed 'em how. I done it."

"Nobody believes that. They all think Bolo was the torch."

"Bolo got crap in his blood."

"Want to tell me about it?"

"Reckon you'd like that. Ah seen the recorder on your back. Gonna use it to hang Dukes?"

"Maybe. I can't force you. If Dukes is keeping you supplied, I don't know what I can offer. Methadone doesn't sound too great, I suppose."

"Supplied. Huh. He ain't come acrost in two days. Ah got to stay on beer and butts. Through with him. When he gets that dumb empty, what about me?"

"Look, there's one thing we can do at the Parish House," Hart said. He could be convincing in his bland way. "We get jobs for guys. We know how to zap the City for welfare, hospital benefits. Give us a try."

"Have me singin' hymns. Quit that when Ah left Waycross, Georgia."

"I quit when I left the seminary. Let's go over to the Parish House. If you don't like what we're doing, you tell me stop it."

O'Gara got off the bar stool, with the creaking rhythms of an ill man. How long would he last? Danny wondered. And what had destroyed him?

"Let's go, Wayne."

"How in hell you know mah first name? Ain't no one called me Wayne since high school."

"I don't know what to say, Rudy," Mary said. She stared at the pale-blue rectangle of paper on the kitchen table. "Why?"

270

"It's a start."

That morning he had drawn a check for five thousand dollars from his savings account on Broadway. It had just about cleaned him out. But with the building empty, Puttering would owe him a bundle—a bonus, the refund on the rental he had paid, and the extra five grand that he was giving Mary. Puttering would be so grateful, so obligated to him, that he would have no choice. And deep in Dukes' mind was a last wild stratagem if Puttering refused. He would sing. He would tell Oberlander and his people everything, all that had passed between them. He would admit he had lied at the first hearing in denying that there was an understanding to drive tenants out. He would admit it freely, say he saw the error of his ways, and that that had been his job from the start. Oberlander knew it, but he needed it from Dukes.

That would murder Puttering. The penalties for proven violations, Tremark told him, for being found guilty of harassment or illegal eviction (they had indulged in both) could be a year in jail or a five-thousand-dollar fine. It might also mean a permanent injunction, and that would hit them where they lived. It would mean that 502 West 84th Street could not be demolished, the tenants would have to be serviced, the empty apartments rented. That would kill for a long, long time E. J. Puttering's plans. It would also mark him double lousy, and the important people would think twice before getting involved with him.

"Rudy, I can't thank you enough. I'm humiliated. After some of the things I said . . ."

In the living room, her two sons thudded and slammed off the sofa, onto the floor, against the walls. Dukes watched them narrowly. He didn't care for the blond kids. They looked the other way when he tried to butter them up. He was no good with kids.

"I want you to come stay with me," he said. "I got that big place with no one in it."

"And Markie and Stevie?"

"Stick them on your old man's farm."

"Frank would find out. I got to be with them. Rudy, you have to understand that."

"Try it for a while. Leave them there and you come stay with me. If it works out, then we'll worry about Gilligan."

Every now and then a towhead would flash past in the arch of the living room. It seemed to Dukes that the snots were looking in, catching the conversation, missing nothing.

"Rudy, let me think. I'll move out the middle of the week. Give me a few days at the farm with my parents. Give me a chance to think."

Dukes looked at her serene face, and he wanted her more than ever. And he was determined to get her. What was the five thousand? Nothing, since he was now certain that Puttering would pay him. When he left he tried to kiss her, but she moved her head away, indicating the boys.

"You like that guy, Ma?" Stevie asked, when Dukes had gone.

"He's an old friend. Do you?"

Stevie blew a loud raspberry across the room. "He's a fink. He says he was a champeen boxer, but Charlie Diaz says he got the crap kicked out of him by Rodriguez."

"Ma, why you so nice to him, if he's tryin' to throw us out? He beat up on a coupla people here."

"He's helping us move, Markie. We're going to Grampa's for a while."

"No school?" Stevie shouted.

"For a few days."

"Woweeee!" They pummeled and cuffed each other, hitting the couch with a soft *clunk,* and the floor with hard *thlunk.*

Mary stared at the check. She was not being fair with Rudy. It would never work out. He and her sons would never get along. But she could not stay, and perhaps something would change. She began to construct a familiar imaginary sequence in her mind, beginning with the letter from Frank saying that he wanted a divorce, that he wanted to marry his girl in Saigon . . .

"Genuine *Cinquecento,*" Ron Lobello said morosely. He pointed to the charred ruins of his baldachino. He had salvaged it from the street and stuck it in a corner of the ruined living room of what had once been their handsome apartment. "I could kill that bastard, I mean tear his eyes out."

David and Carrie had come to ask the roommates if they would attend the Monday hearing. The apartment was a wreck, barely livable.

"Oh, this is dreadful," Carrie moaned. "All those lovely chairs. And that lamp, and the drapes."

"It's insured," Lobello said. "But that isn't the half of it. That baldachino kills me. Everything else I can duplicate, but I gave a part of me to get that thing, and look what Dukes leaves me with. The bloody stumps."

"Come on down to the hearing," David said. "It'll be do or die. We still want to see if we can get hunk with him."

"Didn't we tell you?" Dane asked. He served them red vermouth with a twist of lemon. "We're getting out in two days. We can't take any more of it. I really think he's going to do something awful, like blast poor Tony and his wife. He's been working up to it."

"I doubt it," David said. "He's going to watch his step for a while."

Lobello wagged a finger. "Don't bet on it, David. The guy is desperate. I was at a party with some real estate operators last night. They say this thing is getting hot, some kind of money deadline. Puttering has to deliver or he loses it."

"Then stick around," said Carrie. "You don't want to miss high noon, do you?"

"I'm as yellow as they come," Lobello laughed. "Barri and I found a dump down on Hudson Street. It's got possibilities —old brick walls, two-story living room, huge windows. It was a bakery once, but I've got ideas for it."

"I'm sure you have," she said, "and we'd love to see it when it's ready."

Dane was looking guilty. His freckled face appeared contrite. "Look, I'll come to the hearing tomorrow. Can't let him reduce the ranks. We're out of it, but I guess we owe it another try. Okay?"

David thanked him, and they left.

"Nicest straights I ever met," Lobello said. "But they're headed for trouble. Dukes is getting ready to unload."

On Sunday afternoon, the Loomises, strolling through Riverside Park, met the Paz family. Lucy, the little redhead, was pushing the infant Michael in an elaborate carriage. A midget's parasol was attached to the side of the carriage to protect the sleeping child from the warm spring sun. It looked European, possibly Italian, maybe a gift from her family.

The women exchanged small talk—the baby, Carrie's imminent confinement, the weather. Carrie liked the diminutive woman—her hands were like a six-year-old's!—but she felt Lucy withdrawing from her, vaguely antagonistic. She could guess why. The Loomises and Hart had kept Tony in the battle. She would have been happy to avoid it. Now she lived in a darkened flat boarded up with great metal sheets, and waited for Dukes to attack them.

"You hear from Hart?" Tony asked.

"No. Has he gotten anything?"

"He got a tape from O'Gara. He don' wan' talk on the phone about it, but he tell me tonight at the trial."

"Trial? Who is on trial?" Things were moving faster than Loomis imagined. But what kind of trial was held on a Sunday night?

"No. Is not a real trial. Housing Crimes Trial. At Columbia. Poverty people, community organizers, all gonna make speeches against City, landlords, real estate people. I gonna make a speech about Dukes."

"You are?"

"Sure. Gonna be TV there, reporters. They print in paper what a son of a bitch is Rudy Dukes, then let him try to get me."

David wondered about Tony's plan. Would it not give Dukes' lawyer ammunition? Proof that the charges against the manager were indeed "grounded in malice"?

"Listen, you come, you and Mrs. Loomis. Will be fun."

Carrie decided not to attend the Housing Crimes Trial. She found, at the end of the day, that she became comfortably sleepy, and she had to rest her unwieldy load. But to David's surprise, Werner Schlossmann was waiting for him on the stoop with Tony. As usual, the German wore his lumpy black fedora and his black tie. He bowed to David, and said, "Señor Paz has kindly invited me to this evening of communal action. Are you familiar with such matters?"

"I'm afraid not, Mr. Schlossmann."

"Well, we shall all learn something. One's education never stops. Mass meetings have always intrigued me. Ever since the thirties. Will there be violence?"

"I doubt it," David said, as Tony, hurrying down the steps, joined them, and they walked toward Broadway. "Tony says Father Hasslinger is one of the sponsors, and he runs a tight ship."

The Housing Crimes Trial was held in the Wollman Auditorium at Columbia. David wondered why the university allowed it, and then realized it was part of their community-relations program. The university was regularly denounced, insulted, abused, and vilified by pressure groups. The least it could do was supply a forum and a theater for the denunciaions.

The meeting room was about two thirds filled. Most of the audience was black or Puerto Rican. The whites did not look like poor people, but rather like activists, students, poverty workers. The blacks seemed hard and purposeful; the Puerto

275

Ricans soft and vulnerable; the whites embarrassed and out of place.

On the stage, under a badly lettered banner reading WE WANT GOOD HOMES—WHO ARE THE CRIMINALS? sat a panel of "judges." David recognized a Puerto Rican youth leader in beret and field jacket, and the stout black woman he had seen with Danny Hart on the night of the committee meeting, Mrs. Hall. There were black-jacketed Afro-bobbed men acting as stern ushers along the aisles, and a security guard of young Puerto Ricans in berets at the rear door. The quasi-military security arrangements hardly seemed necessary. The audience was eminently mannerly.

At one side of the stage, seated in the front row, David saw Father Hasslinger and Hart. The minister, David knew, was a firm believer in letting the poor do their own work. He gave them guidance, but he let them run the show and make the decisions.

A fat black woman with an attractive face was at the microphone testifying.

"And so he turn off the heat. He turn off the hot water. I got to go to work, leave six o'clock every mornin' from Brooklyn to go the hospital in the Bronx, an' I must leave my son Harris, who is fifteen, in this rotten place with roaches and filth and a toilet what won't work. Harris is diabetic and need his insulin shots and he is weak. How can I leave him in a place like that? The door lock is broke and there are junkies and bums who come in and beat up Harris and steal his needles . . ."

She burst into tears, the words convulsing, losing shape, and she sobbed unashamedly. "Ah . . . ah . . . my poor son . . . he can't defend hisse'f . . . and he cold all the time . . ."

"It's all right, sister," Mrs. Hall said. She appeared to be a leading judge. "Take your time. We all know what landlords do to people . . ."

The woman was excused. There was a flurry of activity in

276

the center aisle. One of the black ushers was pushing a wheelchair toward the stage.

"For goodness' sake," David said. "It's Nordetzki. I thought Dukes had him committed to Welfare Island."

Paz winked at him: inside dope. "Hasslinger spring him to testify."

Black arms lifted the wheelchair to the stage. The microphone was lowered. The machinist, the tough old bird who had bound himself to the radiator, seemed to have shriveled in the past few weeks. But his voice was loud and firm, the voice of outrage.

"I am Ignatz Nordetzki, machinist," he said. "Live now in ward, Welfare Island, but I am not crazy, not bum, no drunken man. I am hard worker all life, got own shop, own business, until lousy landlord sell it my machines. Next lousy landlord throw me out of place West 84th Street—"

"Tell it, brother," Mrs. Hall said.

David felt dazed. Here was Nordetzki, fighting, taking on his enemies again. It seemed ages ago that he had heard about the dreadful business at the house next door—the crippled old man carried out, spirited away in Dukes' car.

"I want to sue it these people," Nordetzki shouted. "But got it no place to go. District attorney don't care. Mayor's task force say I am troublemaker. Rent Administration say landlord got it papers from caseworker, I am not able take care myself. Listen, people, Nordetzki take care of himself all life! Pay bills! Pay rent! Work with hands! Not crazy! But no way to get back at people who throw me out! Where is justice? Where is decent people?"

"Tell it, Nordetzki!" a Puerto Rican youth shouted.

"They screw us all!"

"Right on, brother!" Mrs. Hall thundered.

The machinist gripped the arms of the chair. "Yes, I brother to all people who get dirty deal. I try to sue, try to go to court. No one listen. No one interested."

"Story of this city, brother," the Puerto Rican boy shouted.
"But Mr. Hasslinger listen. We make big trouble before we through. We find it caseworker who say I crazy. We get him. I thank all people who listen to me."

There was applause for Nordetzki. Loomis, watching him being carried from the stage, felt a bond with him. He was among the first of Dukes' victims on West 84th Street. But the old man had not quit. He was still demanding justice.

"If he can fight back," David said to Schlossmann, "why can't we?"

Schlossmann threw his hands up. "I am not sure he is fighting very hard or will get anywhere. He is to be admired, but that is all."

Tony Paz had taken Nordetzki's place at the lectern.

"A born actor," Schlossmann said. "Look, look at our colleague."

Eyes wide, arms open, Tony shouted:

"What Nordetzki says is true. He is talkin' about the same guy who is tryin' to throw me out. I am Antonio Paz, 502 West 84th Street, and I am here to denounce a yellow, rotten, lousy blockbuster named Rudy Dukes. He is usin' fires, dead dogs, threats, dirty words, crap inna halls, busted boilers, and every dirty trick to make me move out. But I no move! I am here to tell Rudy Dukes I ain' afraid of him, not afraid of his goons, Shlep Sharmak and Enrique Torres, or his guns, or his dog!"

"*Arriba!*" a boy in a black beret shouted.

"Never mind that," Tony said. "I am good American, good as anyone, raised on Columbus Avenue. Know my rights. I hope there are reporters here so they print what I say about Dukes in newspapers!"

"Now, brother," Mrs. Hall said, with judicial calm, "are you tellin' the court that this goon has threatened your life if you don't move?"

"Yes. And we ain't gonna move. We gonna stick it out and make him sweat, and ruin him, so he can't go around throwin' people in the street!" The applause was thunderous. Tony acknowledged it with an Eisenhower upward thrust of his arms, then, encouraged, returned to the microphone and shouted: "And we gonna get the landlord, Puttering, and all the big shots who are behind this!"

He stalked off the platform, and was replaced at the microphone by an elderly black man on crutches.

In the lobby, Danny Hart joined them.

"Was reporters there?" Tony asked. His face was flushed with excitement.

"I think the *Times* sent a man," Hart said. "I'm not sure I want to see it in print. Let's get out of here. I have the tape O'Gara made. He told me everything. He set both fires."

David looked at Hart with admiration.

"Excellent," Schlossmann said. "The evidence the official wants."

Hart nodded. "I have an idea Dukes will find out. There's no way of keeping anything from him. Maybe I should stay with one of you tonight."

"With me," Paz said.

"We've got an extra room," David offered.

"But you ain't got this," Paz said. He opened his briefcase and showed them the automatic. "Let's go."

Schlossmann mopped his forehead and looked at David inquiringly, but Loomis said nothing. The meeting had unsettled him. They had gotten too close to the miseries of the poor. No one understood the curse of poverty until he experienced it. It was another country, another set of structures. How in a million years could he compare the secure and happy life that he and Carrie and their child to come had, with that of the woman who rose at six to ride the subway to a hospital job in the Bronx (cleaning kitchen floors? scrubbing bedpans?) and left her diabetic son alone in a roach-ridden apartment, where addicts and hoodlums preyed on him? She might have been living in a Kaffir kraal, and he and Carrie in Camelot.

"Hey, Hart," Mrs. Hall shouted. She had temporarily left the bench and was waddling after Danny as the four men walked down the steps of Ferris Booth Hall.

"Yes, Mrs. Hall?"

"Where's the money for the Memorial Day picnic you promise me?"

"I'm sorry. I forgot. I hate to tell you this, Mrs. Hall, but I don't know where you can get that fifty dollars. And don't ask Father Hasslinger. He's as broke as I am."

"Well, ain't that a rotten yam. You promise me."

"I didn't. I said I'd try."

"All them children gonna be heartbroke. Because of you."

Hart would not be moved. David could see that he had listened to many such appeals. It did no good to burst with pity if you could not help. "I'll try again. But I'm busy this week."

"Yeah. You always the same. You don't give a hoot."

"I do, I do, but—"

"But, nothin'."

She turned her great injured figure, and started back to the trial. David called after her. "Mrs. Hall . . ."

"Yeah?"

"I'm a friend of Mr. Hart's. I'll advance you whatever I have. You can pay me back when you can. This is the church picnic, is that right? For Memorial Day?"

"Yeah. But I don' even know you. Who you?"

"Mr. Loomis," Hart said. "A friend. I'll get you his address."

David looked in his wallet. He had thirty-nine dollars. He took it out and gave it to her. "I'm sure the children deserve a good time," he said, sounding patronizing.

A wary look hooded her eyes. Behind the steel-rimmed specs she was on guard. "Thanks, brother."

In the taxicab Paz looked quizzically at David. "You never see that money again," he said authoritatively.

"Want to bet?" Hart asked.

Loomis sighed. "I felt I had to do something. I'm not sure why."

The driver cursed. "Bastard in backa me. Got his brights on."

David turned around. It was Dukes' Lincoln.

"He's after us," Tony said. His hand went into the brief-case.

"Tony, keep that briefcase locked," David said sharply. "He won't do a thing. He's trying to shake us up. There's four of us. Dukes never tries anything with witnesses around."

"But why is he following us now?" Schlossmann asked. The old man was not afraid, merely curious.

"The tape," Hart said. He patted the breast pocket of his denim jacket. "He knows I have it. Bolo probably found out from someone in the bar where I picked up O'Gara."

David thought a minute. They would have to call his bluff, stay together, dare him to make the first move. "Driver, let us off on the corner of West End Avenue and 84th Street." He paid the hackie with the remaining change he had, hoping that Carrie had some household money. He was broke.

The four men got out. Schlossmann stooping low, needing help. As they started down West 84th Street toward the house, the Lincoln rolled by. Dukes grinned at them from the window. On the back seat the mastiff stuck its head out the window, its tongue dangling.

Then the car lurched through the red light—Shlep was driving —and turned down West 84th Street, apparently to make the swing around Riverside Drive and come back on 84th.

"He be there," Tony said.

"But why do we not call the police?" Schlossmann asked.

"He hasn't done anything," Hart said. "Would they come?"

"Hah!" Tony shouted. "It be worse for us if they come. Rudy fix them all."

"Captain Gossett promised us protection," David said. "Maybe I'd better phone."

The white car was parked alongside the house. Moby Dick, Loomis thought, our own white whale.

Schlossmann studied the car with European calm. He had never been afraid of Dukes. What distressed him primarily about the affair was how his plan to paint the hallways had fallen apart. He decided, looking at Dukes lounging against the side of the car, the huge dog sitting at his side, that he would resume the painting himself. He alone would venture into the hallways and daub at the flaking, sloping walls. (The first floor had been almost completed, and it looked splendid.)

"Hey, Hart," Dukes called. "You been botherin' my employees."

"Have I?"

"Yeah, you fag. Stay away from them. You threatened O'Gara. Don't you know he's mental? A junkie with a record? Who's ever gonna believe anything that moron says?"

"It's always your word against the world, isn't it, Dukes?" David asked. They were on the steps. All four had turned to look at the manager. Inside the car, Sharmak, with that eternal mocking grin on his face, was staring at them.

"Loomis, you had your chance. You can still get out while it's safe. You wanna talk now?"

"No, Dukes. I'm sticking it out."

"A holdup, huh? Keep hearin' about those settlements · for twenty thousand?"

David said nothing. He wondered why Dukes did not go after Schlossmann. Possibly the old man confused him. When you inform a man that he should have been gassed at Auschwitz and he does not react, you have to measure your next insult very carefully.

"Beat it, Rudy," Paz said. He moved down a step. Alone, apart from the others, he would face Rudy Dukes.

"Go on, squirt, get inside. Go behind your fort. I got some surprises for you."

"Me too." He patted the briefcase. "In here."

How in God's name, Loomis thought, *did I get into this?* He was certain that Dukes' shotgun was inside the car. A flash of temper, an insult, a challenge—and the sidewalk could explode in bloodshed.

"All of yez, go on," Dukes said. He scratched his elbow and looked toward the river, disgusted with them for fighting him so long, and to no purpose. "Only Hart. Listen, Hart, you got something I need."

"I know."

"I'll pay for it. Wanna come to my office?"

"No. Besides, it won't help. I made a dubbing of the tape." Dukes scowled. "Huh?"

"A copy. It's in a place you can't reach, but it'll get to Oberlander tomorrow if you get the one I have on me."

"You're lying, you puke." Dukes got up from the car. The mastiff got to its feet and began to growl uneasily.

Paz stiffened. "Watch your step, Rudy. I swear I kill you right now."

"For God's sake, Dukes, go away," David pleaded. "Tony, go inside. Dukes, I'm calling the police as soon as I go in. This lunacy has got to stop. No house, no property, is worth people's lives. Now why don't you leave?"

"He leave because I got my gun. I use my gun."

Loomis saw Sharmak shifting in his seat. He was surely reaching for the shotgun, getting ready to put it in position. Schlossmann watched in fascination, a smile turning his lips.

"All right, Tony, he's leaving," David said. He took Paz's arm and led him up the steps. Hart went along, Schlossmann following, looking over his shoulder, not with fear but with a historian's concern. Was this the way of the future? Was this the pattern for the great cities of the world, grown unlivable, overcrowded, poisonous, full of irritable people?

"Moving in, Hart?" Dukes asked.

"I think I can get some evidence."

"I thought you had all you needed."

Hart shrugged. "You're a hard man to pin down. I want to be around for the next fire."

They heard Dukes cursing, fouling the air. David decided he would call the police as soon as he got to the apartment.

Lucy Paz was waiting up for her husband. "How was the speech? Was there a big crowd?"

"Yeah. Headlines in newspapers tomorrow. I denounce Rudy in public. Wait till he see."

She looked, with something less than warmth, at Hart. "Hi. Were you there?"

"He help organize it, woman," Tony said. "He stayin' here tonight. Maybe a few nights. Till we get the goods on Rudy. Dukes can't make a move because Danny be here to catch him."

Lucy extended no welcome to the youth. To her, he was more trouble. She did not care for the way he dressed or spoke. What was he? Some kind of crazy minister? He had egged Tony on, organized the committee, and now they were all suffering for it. And to have him in the place, with the baby around! That made two of Dukes' favorite targets—her husband and this skinny nut.

"Don't worry," Hart said. "Dukes doesn't dare try anything. He knows I'll be watching for him every second."

She sighed. When would it end?

Hilda Schlossmann scowled at her father. "Why are you at these meetings? What are those people to you?"

"Nothing human is alien to me."

"Your philosophizing makes me ill. Papa, I have decided we must move. It is no use waiting. What are we waiting for? To prove a point? To show how courageous we are?"

Schlossmann shuffled into his bedroom. With methodical, careful movements, he began to undress. "As you wish, *teuere Tochter*."

"The university is getting new apartments for faculty. I shall talk to someone. I shall ask this fellow Dukes what he can give us to move. I am told that Allister was well paid."

Schlossmann moaned comfortably and settled into his bed.

Had the Allies marched, would Hitler have dared seize the Rhineland? Would the next step be their Munich? And would the floodgates open, would the barbaric hordes overwhelm the civilized world?

Loomis did not tell Carrie about the confrontation on the doorstep. Instead he described the Housing Crimes Trial, and Tony's denunciation of Dukes. "In a crazy way," he said, "it was impressive. Those people organizing, trying to get some attention."

"Will it do any good?" she asked.

"Tony's speech? I doubt it." He got into bed, holding her gently, running his hand lightly over her abdomen.

"Hershkowitz says two weeks to go," she said. "I feel marvelous."

"Great." He wondered where they would be in two weeks. It hardly seemed likely that their child would come home to this apartment. Dukes would get them out. They might undo him—Hart seemed convinced that the tape would be the clincher —but what would it accomplish? The building had become a nightmare—doors open, vacated apartments attracting derelicts, filth on the stairways, Tony's metal sheets.

Loomis stretched, yawned, hugged his wife again. In a half mumble he told her about the confession on tape that Hart had gotten from the super.

"I'm glad," she said. "Maybe now we'll get somewhere. That miserable super. I hope nothing happens to him."

She was gratified that O'Gara had a decent side. It was an act of considerable courage to inform on Dukes. Neither Sims nor the Puerto Rican families had shown any desire to testify against him. She decided she would never tell David about the incident in the basement.

Hart slept on the sofa in the Pazes' living room. Lucy had offered him sheets and blankets, but he preferred to rest on the pillows without anything. She registered her disapproval:

what else from a freak? Oh, he was not her type. Her father would punch a creep like that in the nose as soon as talk to him.

In the bedroom, she tried to calm Tony down, but he was seething. "Rudy come back for that tape," he said.

"Tony, go to sleep. What can he do? The doors are bolted. He can't float through the house like a ghost."

"He come back."

At two-thirty in the morning Hart heard noises below the living-room window. There were curses, muffled cries. And then an ugly thudding noise. It sounded as if a man was being beaten, but that someone was covering his mouth to keep him from shouting for help. Hart stumbled to the barricaded windows.

"O'Gara," he said aloud. "They're getting him."

Paz had left a peephole in the metal sheeting, and by squinting, Hart could see part of the street, and the steps leading down to the basement. He heard more of the choked animal sounds. Then he saw a man stagger up the steps. The harsh yellow street light illuminated the man's face. It was O'Gara. He was covered with blood and he was crying like a spanked child, a bitter contained weeping. At the top of the steps he collapsed.

"Move, junkie," Hart heard Shlep say.

"Go on, canary." It was Bolo's voice.

The super got to his feet, leaned against the wrought-iron railing, and spit a stream of blood. Then he straightened up and, making strangled noises, as if his nose and mouth had been flooded, walked toward West End Avenue.

Hart was frightened. He feared violence. He hated getting hit. And he knew he would be next. Perhaps not that night, secure behind Tony's armored apartment, but whenever Dukes decided to even scores. And as terrified as he was (Hasslinger had tried to teach him never to waste time on fear), it was guilt over what he had done to these people that truly wracked him. O'Gara had been beaten because of him. Paz lived in terror because of him. Schlossmann and his daughter endured these humilations because of him. Loomis had been suckered into a role he never wanted. There were others: Sims with his hard-earned black dignity exposed, forced to turn tail; Lobello watching his prized antique burned; all of them victims of Rudy Dukes.

They should have given in to Dukes' superior force. What nonsense he had sold them! The tenants' committee, the complaint forms, the affidavits, the hearings, the communal painting! As if these could prevail against Dukes' savage will. The problem, as Hart saw it, was that Dukes delighted in violence, believed in the power of fear. They could never be any match for him. They appealed to reason, law, discourse. And thus far these had proven useless.

"I hear what happen," Paz said. He was standing in the living room in his underwear. In his right hand was the automatic. "They beat up the junkie, right?"

"Yes. It was my fault."

Tony jerked his left hand sideways. "Tough. We in jungle. He work for Rudy, he get hurt by Rudy. Tha's the way he do it."

"Tony, for God's sake, put that gun away," Hart said.

"You think they finish? They come back."

"Call the police," Hart said.

"*Chinga* police. Mr. Loomis call already. I seen prowl car before we go to bed. They see Rudy's car is gone, they ain' gonna come back."

"Then let's go to bed," Hart said.

"No. You crazy, Hart? They ain't through. Rudy is outside. I know. He waiting. I can smell Rudy Dukes. Smell like fire, like devil."

"No he isn't. He can't get in."

Tony held a finger to his lips. Then he gestured to Hart to follow him to the front windows. Paz pressed his ear against the peephole. "He is outside. Listen." Hart obeyed him and heard soft voices. It was Dukes. The hoarse whisper was unmistakable.

"Hey, squirt," Dukes called. "You in there? I hear someone walking around."

"Is me, Rudy."

"Tell Hart to give me the tape and we'll go. I make a deal with you tomorrow. Two grand to get out."

"Stick it in your *fundillo*, Rudy. You don' get nothin'. We gonna hang you, *pato*."

"Get smart, Tony. You can't beat me. Tell him to throw it out."

Danny shuddered. Once again, he was forcing one of the tenants, to do his fighting for him, to suffer for his principles. Was it so important to defeat Rudy Dukes? Was it truly a life-and-death matter? Had he the right to encourage Paz in his resistance, his obsession with Dukes?

"Never," Paz said. "You come in. Try and get it."

Lucy walked into the dark living room. "Oh, Tony, please, please give it to them. You know Rudy. You know what he'll do."

"Go away, woman," Paz said. "Go where you belong. Lock the windows. Take the baby and get under the bed."

Hart was dizzy, disoriented. He knew now why Tony had refused to call the police. The contest had to be between himself and Rudy, a battle to the end, a *mano-a-mano*. But it was insanity, an invitation to bloody death. Why not give them the tape? As he fingered the small plastic reel in his pocket, he wondered if he should throw it out to them. That would end it. They would never get any evidence on Dukes. He had lied about the duplicate tape.

"All right, Paz, you had your chance. I'm gonna pay you a visit."

"I shoot you in your heart, Rudy."

"You'll go too, *maricón*."

Lucy ran to the telephone and dialed 911. She was trembling, her hands like ice, her feet numb. Too frightened to cry, it was a few seconds before she comprehended that there had been no signal when she dialed. She hung up, picked up the phone again, and realized that there was no response at all, nothing. "Tony," she cried. "The phone's dead."

"Sure. Rudy cut the lines in the basement. I tol' you it is no good. Between me and him."

"You're nuts," she wept. "The two of you, you and Dukes, two of the same. Tony, put the gun down, get away from the door—"

There was a loud rapping at the door. Tony straightened up, pointed the automatic and walked toward the noise. High noon, Hart thought, a lunatic's high noon. The little man was walking on his tiptoes, his back straight as a board, his head elevated, his handsome profile turned toward the door. In his white underwear, the shorts drooping baggily in the seat, the undershirt garnished with holes, he seemed to Hart the ultimate in comic despair. It was not the imminent violence that terrified Hart, it was Paz's utter vulnerability. He would die in his underwear, mocked, derided, a comic legend among his people.

Danny grabbed his arm. "Tony, I'm going to give him the tape."

"Go 'way. I don't care what you do. Tape, hearing, Oberlander, that is all crap to me now. Is just between me and Dukes."

"Open up, Tony," Rudy called from the door. "I'll made a good deal with you. Relocation. Four nice rooms in the project on Columbus Avenue."

"I pee on your project."

"Two grand to get out, Tony. More money than you ever saw. You go free, with cash, no sweat, and to hell with Hart. He got you into this. He made you the sucker for him."

"It ain't him who is fightin' you, Rudy. It is me, Tony Paz."

"No deal?"

289

"No deal. After you threaten my wife and kid, I cannot make deal with you."

Hart walked to the front window. Through the view hole he saw Shlep Sharmak standing on the sidewalk, holding the shotgun. Why? What did they intend to do? Even if they wanted the police now, they could not call them. *Rudy cut the lines.* Rudy knew everything, could do anything. Maybe it was true. Maybe he could not be stopped.

"Okay, Paz, we're gonna have to come in. I'm gonna knock in the door. You're covered front and back, so don't try anything. Shlep is in front and Bolo's in the back. Last chance."

"No deal, Rudy." His voice was firm, low-keyed. It occurred to Hart that it was a moment that Paz had been waiting for for many years, perhaps for most of his life.

There was a crashing noise. Dukes was using a fireman's ax against the door. They saw part of the paneling splinter. Tony backed away, moved an easy chair into position as a barricade, and stood behind it, the gun leveled over the arch of the chair.

The ax smashed into the door again. Now they heard a whimpering, a growling noise. It was the bull mastiff. Its brain was upset, unnerved by the noise. At the third smash of the ax against the wood, the dog began to bark in savage reverberating rhythm.

A jagged chunk of wood splintered from the door. Hart and Paz saw Dukes' white hand reach inside and seek the bolt.

"You outa luck, Rudy," Tony. "You got to knock whole door down. I got Medeco, Kno-Pic, and Sergeant Keso on there. You got to come in yourself."

Dukes ripped at the paneling. The wood resisted him, tearing apart in narrow slivers.

"In, Angel, in," Dukes said. He was trying to encourage the dog to crawl into the room through the rent in the door.

Once more Dukes flailed at the upper part of the door with his ax, and this time it ripped apart with a harsh, protesting sound. The entire frame wavered on the old hinges and Dukes' face appeared in the wound.

"I warn you, Rudy," Tony said. From behind the chair he leveled the gun. In the bedroom, Hart could hear Lucy screaming for help. But no one came.

"Shlep!" Dukes shouted.

There was a weighted deathly pause, when Hart felt his chest heaving, his mouth full of dust, and heard Lucy's undulant wails from the bedroom. And then, in a blast that sounded like the unloosing of a giant's hailstorm, the room shivered and echoed with the noise of the shotgun. Shlep had aimed it against the stone pilaster between the two huge metal sheets covering the windows. But the weapon scattered its pellets, and the noise of them striking the rusted sheeting was unlike anything they had ever heard. It was the kind of brutal, resounding explosion that should have leveled the house. And yet no one was hit, the room still stood. Tony's fortress was scarred by a hundred bits of shot, but unharmed.

Nothing penetrated. In the aftermath of the deafening blast, as the room seemed to settle back, drowning in an endless echo, Dukes shoved the mastiff's clumsy haunches through the jagged hole in the door. The dog, barking, shaking its blunt black muzzle, loomed in the half light of the Paz hallway, baying, moaning, confused, uncertain what its master wanted.

Rising, Paz leveled his automatic at the beast. He knew how to shoot. You had to aim low. The piece jerked upward like a hunting rifle. As he had been taught once by an older boy in a lot outside Santurce, he squeezed the trigger gently, aiming a foot or so below Angel's slavering muzzle. Dukes saw the orange flash and hurled his body to one side. There was a clanging noise as the ax dropped from his hands.

"Good God, Tony, don't," Hart cried. "Not again."

A dark liquid flower bloomed on the dog's broad forehead. The yellow face turned maroon, the eyes flooded in blood, and the mastiff's thick forequarters fell, like a bag of potatoes, over the splintered half door.

"Crazy bastard," Dukes shouted. "I'll kill you for this." But he made no move to enter the apartment.

Outside, they could hear Shlep shouting. "Boss, boss. Let's beat it. There's people comin' out. Come on."

Dukes tugged furiously at the animal's inert form, mourning the four hundred dollars' worth of pedigree now reduced to a sack of guts.

When the shotgun blast struck the metal sheets, David leaped from his bed. It had come, he thought. Dukes had struck back, blowing them all to bits. Then, seconds later, came a second shot: shorter, fainter. The noise reverberated, echoed in the night. Carrie jerked her head up. In the moonlight, her eyes were terror-stricken, staring.

"Stay in bed," he said. "Don't move." Loomis walked to the window.

"Be careful," she whispered. "David, please."

He peered into the street. There was no smoke, no sign of destruction. The white car was standing by, its doors opened. Sharmak was at its side, calling, gesturing to someone in the house.

"Bastard, dirty spic, little punk." It was Dukes—choking in rage. Loomis leaned out. Dukes had appeared on the stoop. He seemed to be in a hurry, but he was impeded by something. Loomis saw him dragging a shapeless, shadowy form. It was the dog Angel, motionless.

"Like a dream," David said. "It's insane."

Shlep waddled to the steps and helped Dukes haul the dog's corpse to the street. Swiftly, they threw it into the opened trunk. People were looking from windows. Distantly a siren wailed. A flashing light painted weird patterns on the apartment house across the street.

"What happened?"

"Jesus, what a blast. What got hit?"

"Dios mío, que esta pasando?"

292

The Lincoln's engine roared and the car sped away. On the sidewalk below there was a dark trail of blood, gleaming under the harsh glare of the streetlight.

Carrie was sitting up in bed. "What was it? What happened, David?"

"A shoot-out. At Paz's place. I'd better go down."

"No. No. You've done enough."

In the street the sirens grew louder. The flashing red lights invaded their apartment. "Cops are here," Loomis said. "Tony . . . I wonder if he's hurt—"

"Please, please, David. Don't go."

But he was dressing already. "Look, Carrie. Paz is with us in this. We've been using him all along. He's got more guts than any of us. I can't let him down."

He was surprised that he was not afraid, not unsteady, as he walked down to the ground floor.

The police arrived, inspected the apartment, and did not stay long. Hart explained to them what had happened: the shotgun blast at the front of the house—no damage done except for some denting and scarring of the stone façade and the plates. And a dead dog.

Patrolman Dattolica made notes, rubbed his chin, interrogated David, and seemed uncertain as to what to do next.

"Go see Dukes," David said. "Ask him a few questions. He came here to terrorize these people. He broke the door down."

Dattolica paused. "I'll decide what to do, Jack."

"All right, but do something. These people aren't guilty of anything."

"An' I got permit for my gun, so lay off," Tony protested. "He send dog after me, I kill the dirty dog."

The patrolman said nothing. He was strangely hesitant, David felt.

As soon as he had left, Loomis went upstairs to reassure his wife and the Schlossmanns that nobody had been hurt. But

Schlossmann and his daughter had not emerged from their apartment. Violence in the night did not interest them. They would remain behind bolted doors until morning.

Paz was exultant. "I fix him. He laugh at my armor, but I show him. Damn birdshot bounce off like raindrops. Fix his lousy dog also."

Lucy, whimpering in the bedroom, refused to share his exhilarated mood. Nor could Hart. Dukes would be back. He would never forgive Tony. He lived by a code of violence, fear, intimidation. And even if he were fired, punished by the City, he would track Paz down, have his revenge. And it was Hart, with his high-blown notions of justice, who had brought Paz into this mess. Could they ever neutralize Dukes, end his tyranny over them?

A half hour later the police returned. This time a detective, a rotund, sweating man with lank blond hair, accompanied Patrolman Dattolica. Their faces loomed in the gouge in the wrecked door—noncommittal, disinterested faces. The detective let his flashlight play on the floor in the hallway, a yellow cone of light on the dark stains.

"Blood," he said—as if commenting on the weather.

"Dog," Tony said, his voice shivering. "Dukes' dog. I kill him."

"You admit you killed him?" the detective asked.

"You better believe. I am sorry I do not kill Dukes instead."

"Tony, please," Hart said. "Watch what you say."

Tony unlocked the door, undid the bolt chain. Lucy, in a wrapper, came in. "Officer, they started it. They shot first."

"You Paz?" the detective asked.

"I am Antonio Paz."

"Get your pants on. You're under arrest."

"What for? What I do?"

"Armed assault with intent to kill."

"Rudy do this, hah?"

"I don't know nothing about any Rudy," the detective said. "We got a complaint from three people. You fired shots here.

You killed a guy's dog. You'll be informed of your rights in the station house."

"Why you no arrest Dukes?" Tony asked.

"What'd he do?"

"He break that door down. He have his goons with guns front and back. How you think that door get busted? I got a right to protect my house, my wife and kid. I got a permit for my gun. Captain Gossett, he know me."

"Officer," Hart said, "Dukes' man Sharmak, the one they call Shlep. He fired the first shot. It was a shotgun, against the windows."

"Who the hell are you?"

"Dan Hart. I'm a community organizer with Father Hasslinger."

"Yeah? You live here?"

"I was helping the tenants in their fight with Dukes."

A hard smile bloomed on the detective's face. "What are you doin' here at two in the morning?"

"Getting the goods on Dukes. Tony will never be prosecuted for this, officer. I'm a witness. You're arresting the wrong man."

"Let us worry about that, huh, Hart?"

Tony, comforting a bawling Lucy, got dressed quickly.

"We'll take the piece also, Paz," the detective said.

"No. I tole you. I got permit."

"I don't a damn if you got a hundred permits. The gun is evidence. Let's have it."

Reluctantly, Tony fetched the gun from the seat of the armchair, where he had stowed it. He gave it to the detective.

"Lemme say goodbye to my wife."

"Go ahead. You'll be out on bail. You act like you're going away to Sing Sing."

"I am never in jail in my life," Tony said. "I am no crook, no killer. I just here to protect wife and kid and house. You understand?"

Hart put his arm around Lucy to stop her convulsive sobbing. She dabbed at her eyes. Hart released her and Tony kissed her discreetly, with no display of passion—not in front of a pair of cops—and whispered in Spanish. She sniffled, said she would get a lawyer tomorrow, and would see him in the morning.

"Let's go," the detective said.

Tony walked to him. His head was high again, and he strode in a dignified stilted manner. Deep in trouble, he was relishing it, playing the role to the limit.

"Do you have to handcuff him?" Hart asked.

"Regulations," the man said. He snapped the handcuffs on Tony's frail wrists. Paz studied them with pride.

"Okay, move off, Paz."

"What is your name?" Tony asked.

"What's it to you?"

"I want to know who arrest me. I want Danny to know, so when he go to Hasslinger and get lawyer, we know who do this."

"Fassnecker."

"Okay, Detective Fassnecker. How much Rudy pay you for this? When I work for Rudy he give three hundred to cop, four hundred to detective."

The man's square face betrayed nothing. He shoved Tony firmly in the back. "Move, Paz."

"But I think maybe you only worth three hundred. Tha's all you worth."

They walked into the hallway. Dattolica led the way with a flashlight. Tony, braceleted, followed walking in that odd upright stride.

"I tell you, Fassnecker," he said. "Today you arrest me for three hundred dollars, and tomorrow you sell your daughter for same. No different to a man like you."

Hart, watching them, prayed that they would not work Tony over in the car. He turned to Lucy.

"I'll call Father Hasslinger," Hart said. "We can get one of the Parish House lawyers, Mr. Feldman or Mr. Gascar. First thing in the morning."

She collapsed into the armchair, and was weeping softly,

with more shame than fear. "That crazy Tony," she cried. "He never stops. Know what he told me when he kissed me?"

Hart shook his head.

"If Rudy comes back . . . if he comes back—" She bawled again.

"Yes? What, Lucy?"

"There's another gun in the house. In back of the chifforobe —a repeating rifle." She howled her agony. "Jesus, I can't stand it any more."

Again Dukes and his lawyer were late for the hearing. Loomis and Hart, exhausted, sat at the table awaiting them. Oberlander had come in, nodded at his aide, Labato, and the two of them left. Somehow David had the notion they were going to meet with one of their superiors. Oberlander had taken the file on 502 West 84th Street with him.

"At least Tony didn't make the paper," David said relievedly. He showed Hart the *Times* report on the Housing Crimes Trial.

"It'll break Tony's heart," Danny said.

About fifteen tenants came to the microphone and leveled charges against various landlords. Complaints were voiced about a lack of hot water, broken locks, uncollected garbage, rats, and alleged acts of harassment.

But no one was mentioned by name. David imagined that Tony's wild outbursts were invitations to libel, and he was just as glad.

There was nothing on the shoot-out on West 84th Street either. Hart told him that the event had happened well past the morning newspaper's deadline. He had once worked in the Union Theological Seminary's public-relations office, and seemed to know a great deal about newspaper procedures. "It might make the *Post*," he said, "but I doubt it. No one killed.

Just a dog. There are always bullets flying around the West Side, and the papers don't pay too much attention to them."

A Parish House lawyer, a man named Gary Feldman, had been sent over to bail Tony out, and try to have the charges against him thrown out. Danny had given him a history of the case. Feldman was also a local reform political leader, and carried some weight with the police. Hart was hopeful.

After about fifteen minutes Dukes came in with his lawyer. Rudy was wearing the same sedate suit, but he had dark glasses on. He had had a hard night. O'Gara had been beaten up. Paz had killed his dog. And he had not gotten the tape from Hart. Behind the smoked glasses his eyes were baleful. The air of injured innocence was gone. He looked furious, full of spleen, ready to turn his fists on anyone who crossed him.

"You sprung Paz," Dukes said to them.

"We have lawyers also," Hart replied.

"You'll pay. All of yez. For killing my dog. That was a pure-bred mastiff. A blue-ribbon champion."

"I'm sorry for the dog. Don't you think you asked for it?" David said.

"We'll see who asks for what." He began to rub his fists. Tremark touched Dukes' arm. "Not now, Rudy. Let me do the talking."

Oberlander and Labato returned. They were ready to begin. Oberlander identified the hearing. Then he turned to Dukes.

"I've been over this file again, Mr. Dukes," he said. "I have a police report on what happened last night. I have reached the conclusion that there is concealment in your lease with Mr. Puttering."

"Concealment?" Dukes asked.

"I am convinced that your arrangement with Mr. Puttering was to empty the building."

Tremark was shaking his head vigorously. "No, no, no, Ray," he said. "There is no concealment here. Mr. Puttering wants a vacant building. But neither he nor my client have engaged in anything that can be called harassment. It is true the building will be demolished. It is true we—they—want it empty."

"Who is they?"

"Puttering. Haman, Lord & Fawcett. The syndicate who will build the apartment. But none of these people believe in violence. Perhaps some of Mr. Dukes' associates were overzealous. But they never harassed anyone."

"I am told Mrs. Gilligan has moved," Oberlander said.

"Yes, and under satisfactory circumstances. The men in apartment 3A, two notorious homosexuals, have also vacated. We stand prepared to make reasonable cash settlements with the remaining tenants, but for some reason they continue to hang on."

"If laws have been broken, something has to be done about it," Oberlander said. "The tenants have a right to follow up their claim."

The lawyer snorted. "One of the ringleaders of this affair, Antonio Paz, was jailed last night for killing my client's dog. Shot him dead in the hall. So you see the kind of people they are. What right has someone like that man Paz to come here and ask for justice?"

"If I may, Mr. Oberlander?" Hart asked.

"Go ahead."

"Tony killed the dog when Mr. Dukes tried to break his front door down. He was after the tape recording I have. Tony didn't fire first. Dukes' man Shlep let go a shotgun blast at the front of the house. It's all on file at the precinct."

Hart looked straight at Dukes. "It might interest Mr. Dukes that our attorney, Mr. Feldman, is filing a counterclaim, charging Mr. Dukes and his aides with armed assault, breaking and entering, and a few other things. You are going to be in court a great deal, Rudy."

Inhaling deeply, Dukes' chest expanded. The muscles stretched the white shirt, the gray jacket. Now Loomis feared him, he understood why others feared him. There were no restraints, no monitors in his makeup.

"See what I mean? See?" Tremark cried. "Threats again. Always threats. These people are playing a sharp game. They have dreams of twenty-thousand-dollar settlements. But they won't get them, and they won't blackguard my client."

"Mr. Hart, play the tape," Oberlander said.

Danny put Barri Dane's recorder on the table and pushed the playback button. A mashed noise was heard, and then, somewhat off speed, the super's voice.

"Dukes said he'd fix mah habit. Take care. Sonvabitch, he welshed. Ah'm gittin' half what he promised, less. Ah got a big habit—"

"Ah! Evidence from a user, a hopeless addict!" shouted the lawyer.

"Mr. Tremark, please," Oberlander said resignedly.

"He tole me screw the place up. We got to git the spics out of back room, heah? Then we bust the lock and let in the bums and the winos. Okay, we got to start a fire to git the spics out. Shlep brung me the gasoline in a jerrican, some rags and a coupla empty whiskey bottles. The idea was Bolo would toss one inta their john. But Bolo was chicken. Said he was afraid Escobar would git his relatives after him. Escobar got a big family and one guy carries a gun. So ah done hit. Shlep said Rudy would like me for that, gimme more bread for my horse. But he never did. . . ."

Oberlander had shut his eyes and was leaning back in his chair. His fingers tapped noiselessly at the table.

"Ah burnt the table in the queers' place, also. Hell, hit was easy. Had me keys to all the apartments. Dukes said, burn those faggots out. Not enough to set the whole place off, enough so's they git the message. . . ."

The cracked, voice droned on. At the end O'Gara identified himself and said he had made the confession under no pressure, and wanted to apologize if he had hurt anyone.

"I object to this," Tremark said. "I say it should be thrown out. I say that it should not go into the record. I wouldn't put

300

it past this bunch to have faked it. Who is O'Gara? Where is he? Why isn't he here in person?"

"Your client beat the tar out of him last night," David said. "He'll never appear now."

Dukes was smiling. What he did to O'Gara, he seemed to be saying, he would do to anyone who opposed him.

"I suppose you have one of your smart little affidavits, eh, Hart?" the lawyer mocked.

"I'm afraid not. After the beating your client gave the super, he vanished."

"An unreliable, half-witted addict. Who could believe him in person, let alone on a tape? A faked tape, I daresay."

Oberlander held his hand up. It was apparent he was about to make a pronouncement. "Gentlemen, I want to wind this case up," he said. "I don't think anything will be gained by interminable hearings, more affidavits, witnesses, and so on."

"Amen," said the lawyer.

"It is my feeling that the premises on West 84th Street are in the process of becoming a public nuisance. It is, according to Mr. Labato, deteriorating."

Hart fidgeted in his seat. David could see he did not like the way the hearing was going. "If it is, Mr. Oberlander, it's because of what Dukes did to it. Remember, it was the tenants who started to paint the hallways."

Ah yes, Schlossmann thought as he listened attentively. *My project. My great scheme to thwart the storm troopers. Failed, failed.*

"Let me finish, Mr. Hart," Oberlander said. "However this building was allowed to run down, it is past history. We have to look to the future."

"But crimes were committed in the past," David protested. "Wrongs were done. Doesn't your office permit any retroactive justice? Or haven't you any interest in these acts? What about last night?"

"I am going to try to give some satisfaction to all parties," the official said with marked impatience. "It won't be a perfect solution, but we rarely find them. Now, my understanding is that there are three tenants remaining in the building. Mr. Loomis, Mr. Paz, and Mr. Schlossmann. These people have leases. These people have a right to recompense and relocation. I am instructing Mr. Dukes to come to an immediate settlement with them, to arrive at a figure and conditions acceptable to all parties. . . ."

David looked at Hart. So, Dukes had won. Or had he? He would have to pay out cash. But that was not what any of them wanted. They would be glad to accept the money, just as Allister and Mary Gilligan had. But above all they had hoped to see wickedness punished.

"That sounds like something we can live with," Tremark said.

"That is not all. Inasmuch as the tenants may not immediately agree to the terms of Mr. Dukes' settlement, I am ordering that the rent paid by the three parties, Messrs. Paz, Loomis, and Schlossmann, be reduced to one dollar a month."

Neither Dukes nor his lawyer reacted. They did not care about the rentals. They never had. Their only goal was a vacant building by the end of May.

"We can live with that also," the attorney said. He could not conceal his pleasure.

"Of course," Hart said, "that will ensure that Dukes, or Puttering, will totally abandon the place and let it go to ruin."

"Let's be realistic," Oberlander said. "It's halfway there, with five empty apartments."

"You're helping him get what he wants," Loomis said.

"Mr. Loomis, sometimes events get ahead of us," the official said. "We'd like to do other things but we must face existing situations, even when they are unpleasant."

"And that means Dukes is going to get away with what he's done to people this last month?" Hart asked, his voice rising.

"I haven't finished," Oberlander said. "Mr. Dukes will reach a settlement with the three tenants. The rent will be reduced to one dollar a month, to give him added incentive to settle fairly. Finally, I am requesting of Mr. Dukes that he sign a consent injunction stating—"

"Hold it, hold it," the lawyer said. "That's out. I mean, Ray, that's out."

"Mr. Tremark, take it easy, will you? I am requesting of Mr. Dukes that he sign a consent injunction in which he will agree to halt certain acts which this office will specify, promising that he will never do these again. The injunction will be so worded so that Mr. Dukes need not acknowledge any wrongdoing, but will state that whatever it was he was doing, he will stop."

"I protest," the lawyer said. "That will be a black mark against my client."

"Would you prefer that we go to court?" Oberlander asked. "Would you prefer that we seek a permanent injunction?"

"No. No. Absolutely not."

Loomis now saw what Oberlander's scheme was: a little bit for everyone. He did not want to hold up the demolition of 502 West 84th Street. Obviously, landlords and builders and developers had rights also. The city had to move ahead. Tenants had to be reimbursed. But Dukes could not be allowed to go scot-free. He could not be permitted to win everything. Somehow, the City had to show in the records that they were aware of his tactics. And so Oberlander had settled on the consent injunction.

"I suggest you think carefully before you turn my offer down," the enforcement officer said.

"Why should I admit I done anything wrong?" Dukes asked plaintively.

"Mr. Dukes the file on you is too complete. Let me tell you something about tenants. They don't often band together and go to all this trouble unless they have legitimate complaints."

"That won't stand up in court," Tremark said. "That's an *ad hominem* judgment. You don't have a case against Mr. Dukes and you and everyone in the Housing and Development Au-

303

thority know it. Sorry on that one, Ray. He will not sign this consent injunction."

Oberlander leaned over to the silent Labato and whispered in his ear. "We will then have to subpoena Mr. Puttering and have him appear at this hearing," the official said.

Hart's mouth opened. "But . . . but . . . that's no solution at all."

"He's the landlord," Oblander said. "The owner of your building. We will ask him to sign the consent injunction also. And, under oath, require him to reach settlements with the remaining tenants."

Loomis looked at Hart with a miserable, defeated grimace. It was a joke, a dreadful joke. They had no more than a week to remain in the house. Puttering, the ghostly owner, had evaded service for *six years*. For Oberlander to say blithely that he would have him appear was as if he had just promised to produce Judge Crater. The victory for Dukes and Puttering was evident in the cynical turn of the blockbuster's lips, the air of detached boredom that Tremark affected. They had won.

Hart spoke with passion: "Mr. Oberlander, Puttering has given your process servers the runaround for six years. He was never caught on those harassment cases in the Bronx."

"We'll get him. I promise you."

Hart laughed. "You're like Owen Glendower in Shakespeare, Mr. Oberlander, a wizard who said he could summon spirits from the vast deep. And Hotspur said to him, yes you can summon them, but will they come?"

David stared in dumb admiration at the starved young man. It was surely the first time in the history of City hearings on harassment that Shakespeare (Henry IV, Part I, at that) had been cited. In his exhausted way, Oberlander looked impressed.

Tremark was not amused. "Hart, why don't you save that for those remedial-reading classes at the Parish House, huh?" He smacked the table. "Well, that's it. Can we go?"

The official shook his head. "Not yet. Mr. Hart has a point.

I am calling another hearing for 10 A.M. on Thursday. In that time we hope to serve a paper on Mr. Puttering and have him in this room to answer questions. But whether we do or not, you are to appear, Mr. Dukes. May I give you some advice?"

Dukes nodded. He was on guard, reserved. Something told Loomis that he was disturbed by the turn of events.

"Sign that injunction, Mr. Dukes, sign it," Oberlander said. "And I advise you to be on your good behavior."

"I think he will," Hart said raffishly. "I'm living in the building to make sure."

Tremark pointed a finger at him. "You know, I'm sick of your innuendos. I'm not happy with them."

"We aren't happy with the fires, the threats, the broken locks, the drunkards, and all the other things your client has done."

Tremark grunted. "We? *We?* Who are you, Hart? You aren't even a tenant. You're an interferer, an outsider, who stuck his two cents in. You're the cause of this whole thing, not Mr. Dukes."

"That's not true," Loomis said. "Who do you think signed those affidavits? Tenants. Who filled out the complaints? Tenants. Mr. Hart helped us get it cranked up. That's his job."

"His job," the attorney scoffed. "His *job*. We know all about him. He's never held a job in his life."

"That's enough," Oberlander yawned. "I want to end this. We will get in touch with Puttering. I advise you, Mr. Dukes, to agree to the consent injunction. The City wants it on paper. The Mayor is going to raise hell about harassment and re-location—"

"Ah, that's it," the lawyer cried. "Political. My client is the scapegoat."

"He is not. If you want my opinion, Mr. Dukes has gotten away with plenty." He pointed at the tape recorder. "We intend to follow up that evidence. The City does not look lightly on burning places down to chase tenants out."

"I never did no such thing," Dukes protested.

"We aren't sure," Oberlander said.

Tremark pursed his lips. "You threatening us with a trial, Ray?"

"It's possible."

The lawyer stared at the ceiling. "That's kind of rare in a case like this, isn't it? How many cases you been to court with last year? Two? Three?"

"We don't like to. But unless this injunction is signed—"

"Okay, Ray," the lawyer said. "We'll be back on Thursday."

"At which time," Hart said, "we shall produce new evidence to substantiate our charge that Rudy Dukes has consistently and deliberately abused and harassed tenants—"

Dukes leaped to his feet and with a sweep of his right arm struck the tape recorder and sent it flying off the table. Carrie screamed as it sped across the tabletop and sailed into an empty chair. Schlossmann watched, intrigued.

"I'll show you who's been harassed," Dukes shouted. "I been framed, that's what. I ain't through with you. I ain't signing anything."

"Now, see what you made him do?" Tremark asked, as Dukes, his face livid, flew from the room.

"Why can he get away with that?" Hart asked.

Oberlander closed his eyes. "The hearing was over anyway."

When the lawyer had left, Carrie and Schlossman moved to the table.

"Mr. Oberlander," Carrie asked, "will there be a finding of harassment against Mr. Puttering? Or will he and Dukes just sign the paper, and that's all?"

"Beg pardon?"

"A finding of harassment against Puttering," she repeated. "I don't know. I doubt it."

Hart patted Carrie's hand. "I saw it coming. It's a cheap way out for everyone." He looked at the official. "We don't want his money. We want to prove something. We want to make the city aware of people like Puttering and Dukes. If you let Puttering off the hook, there'll be other Rudy Dukeses terrorizing people tomorrow."

"The hearing's over," Oberlander said, with fatigued finality.

When the tenants had left, Labato pulled his chair to the table. "Whaddya think, boss? Will Dukes sign it?"

"He's nuts if he does. We don't have a thing on him. But I had to do something to stop the bum."

"We haven't stopped him yet."

The enforcement officer looked at the files on Dukes. No, the tenants were not lying. Dukes was a four-square, triple-ply rat, a sadist, a thug, everything they said. But how pin him down?

"Get that guy at Haman, Lord & Fawcett," he said to Labato. "The one working on the West 84th Street deal."

David went to his office after the hearing. He did not need Hart to explain to him what was in the wind. The City understood the urgent desires of potent people to clear the old building and proceed with a new apartment house. It meant jobs, money, income, taxes. But tenants could not be abused (or overabused, at any rate), and hoodlums like Dukes deserved some chastisement. The consent injunction seemed perfect—an agreement by Dukes to stop what he was doing, even if he admitted nothing. Then, a modest cash settlement, and departure. But Dukes and his lawyer refused to sign. They understood that with Dukes' record, the signing of an injunction would mark him permanently—a bad type, a troublemaker, a man who would have you at the Rent Administration as soon as he took over.

It occurred to David that there was a cruel irony in the affair of 502 West 84th Street. Dukes had been *used.* Bigger, richer, more powerful forces had convinced him that it was worth his while to pull their chestnuts from the fire. Now he was being scorched. And they would munch the sweet nuts. The injunction might finish him for good. Who would hire such a Jonah? First, the St. Charles Hotel murders.

Then the siege of West 84th Street. Puttering would be untouched. Oberlander was fairly certain that there'd be no finding against him, no "clout" on the property, as Hart had described the effect of a harassment judgment. So to what end had been their bitter struggle? To what end had he and Carrie hung on? And Schlossmann, that lost soul, that gentle heart, who had once seen hell, what had impelled him to fight, answering the obscene phone? Or Tony Paz, for that matter, that miniature man driven by disorderly courage? The high-rise would go up. Puttering would sell his land. Dukes would move on to other strong-arm jobs, instilling fear, bending people, breaking a few.

It was a relief to get to his drafting table and tackle the precise and soluble problems of a supermarket in Rockland County.

Schlossmann, more talkative than usual, took Carrie home on the subway. The old man launched into a detailed explanation of the origins of the Hanseatic League. He explained that voluntary associations of people, brought on by mutual needs, had always fascinated him. That is why he had joined in the activities of the committee. It had symbolized the kind of peaceful communal effort that he admired. And he was saddened that the committee no longer existed, that only he, the Loomises, and Tony were still active.

"But our spirit goes marching on, Mr. Schlossmann," Carrie said, as they approached the house.

"Oh, yes, Mrs. Loomis. Our spirits are still high. After all, the influence of the Hanseatic League was lasting. The League was founded in the thirteenth century, in Lubeck and Rostock, a union to safeguard commercial roads from bandits. And it grew to great importance. Its significance in terms of free trade, freedom of waterways, community usage of roads and facilities, is still valid. So perhaps, the tenants' committee of our doomed building will make some mark on the future of tenancy in this city. Do you think so?"

Carrie smiled at him. How could he maintain that calm scholarliness, that tolerant view of life, when he had been subjected to such brutalities? She knew about the wife and the sons consumed in the holocaust, the wanderings and starvation and endless pain and sorrow. And yet here was Schlossmann, reflective, ruminative, soft-voiced. She was ready to cry, ready to seize him and kiss his pale forehead.

"It's a possibility, Mr. Schlossmann. I don't think my husband would have stuck it out if he didn't feel we had an important point to make. David isn't a fighter."

"Nor am I, my dear. But when I saw Dukes, I saw Hess and Streicher. What could I do?"

The two young men who had moved into 1B a few days ago were seated on the basement steps. They were smoking. Carrie, who in her acting days had tried one or two marijuana cigarettes (they nauseated her), sniffed the air—pregnancy had sharpened her senses—and smelled nothing. The tall boy with the corona of frizzed orange hair was lolling on the top step. The stout dark youth—almost invisible behind a mass of matted black hair and beard—lounged below. They were in soiled T-shirts, and there was a weary air about them as if they had been working hard and were taking a break.

"Hi," Carrie said. "You boys still with us?"

"Yes, ma'am," the redhead said. "We're the new supers."

She remembered. O'Gara had been beaten during the night.

"Hope you don't need any plumbing fixed, or anything like that," the dark youth said. "We don't know too much. About repairs, and like that."

Carrie laughed. "We're used to no service. I guess you know something about this house. It's been warfare between Dukes and the tenants. There's only three of us left."

"Suits us fine, ma'am," the orange-haired boy said. "We're just sort of passing through."

"I see. Are you students?"

"Sort of," he replied.

"Columbia?"

"Well, ah. Yeah, students."

Obviously, he wanted to retain an air of mystery. Nothing surprised Carrie any longer. "But how did you end up here?" she asked.

The dark boy darted a look at the taller one, as if to co-ordinate a response. "We knew O'Gara from the joints around Columbia. He let us use the back room. When he got fired, that old dude Sharmak said we could be supers. No pay, but a place to sleep."

"Welcome to Dukes' castle," Carrie said. "I hope you know what you're letting yourself in for."

Orange-hair tossed his cigarette into the street. "Heck, we've lived worse than this."

Carrie pointed to the pitted marks on the façade, the in-dentations on the metal sheeting where Shlep's shots had im-pacted. "You saw those, I suppose?" she asked. "That was Mr. Dukes' handiwork. Not to mention two fires, dead dogs, and what-all. I don't mean to be a square, but I hope you two aren't under orders to chase the last of us into the street, are you?"

They stared at one another again, bland gazes, and Orange-hair began to snicker. "Heck, no, ma'am. We're just temporary. We won't be here more than a few days. School's almost over. Couple of finals and we split."

They did not sound like hoodlums, or addicts, or menaces of any kind. Both spoke well. They were polite, if enigmatic. A bit grimy, but the kind of boys Carrie could talk to.

Schlossmann had listened attentively while Carrie had en-gaged the young men in conversation. In the vestibule, he began to speculate. "Interesting young men," he said. "To be so foot-loose, so free of obligations. Perhaps I would have been better off in my youth had I cultivated a little of their soiled freedom. But Schlossmann went to schools, memorized his lessons, won prizes, rose the academic ladder. Am I suffering for it?"

"I doubt it, Mr. Schlossmann. Those youngsters aren't as joyous as they appear to be. I always find them a little morbid. They don't seem to be able to laugh."

310

"Perhaps there is nothing left to laugh about."

Halfway down the hall they heard shouts from the Paz apartment. "Daddy, Daddy, stop yelling at him!" they heard Lucy Paz wail. "Tony didn't do nothin'. It was that Dukes, that gangster!"

And then a harsh, loud voice: the fearsome Cavatelli, Lucy's father. "Yeah? What in hell was he jugged for? I know cops. Cops don't take no bribes from guys like Dukes. He got pinched and he deserved to get pinched. What a thing for us to live with! A son-in-law with a police record!"

It was the thundering voice of lower-middle-class righteousness and it brooked no opposition. They now heard—the sloppily patched door was partially open—Tony's response.

"He frame me. That Dukes frame me. He pay off the cops, he always do—"

"Crap. No cop would take money from a hood like that. You started in with him, dincha?"

"No. no, I swear. I tryin' to save my wife, your daughter. And my kid. Your grandson. Jesus, gimme a break. I defendin' my house from Dukes. He shoot first. Ask anyone."

Cavatelli's voice shouted him into silence. "I seen it coming. There is a certain element don't know its place. Sure, blame the landlord, blame the cops. Never yourself."

"Daddy, Tony is telling the truth. Dukes came here to steal something! Tony didn't shoot."

"Yeah, I never do. I ain't no killer."

"Yeah? Keepin' a arsenal inna house?" Cavatelli's voice alternated between sneer and threat. "You're a bum. A lousy bum, that's all you are." It was an embarrassment to listen to Tony quail. Their Tony Paz, all courage and defiance and style. What ravages the father-in-law must have been inflicting on his frail spirit! What did his *machismo* avail him now, before the insults of the retired garbage collector?

"A pity," Schlossmann whispered to Carrie, as he took her arm to help her climb the stairs.

"It's awful," she said. "He's such a brave man. To have to suffer like this. He kept us together, Mr. Schlossmann."

"Indeed. A hero of the streets."

But from the Paz apartment there now burst the angry voice of Lucy. She had endured enough of Daddy's abuse. "Where were *you* last night, huh? Where were you with all your big political friends in the Bronx when we needed you, huh?"

"I wouldn't ask them to help this element."

"*Element!* My Tony is twice the man they are! It was the minister, a Protestant minister, who came to get us out, with a Jewish lawyer! I hope you have to live with that disgrace in your heart for a long time, Daddy!"

There was silence in 1A. Lucy had struck a telling blow. They lived in a world of charge and countercharge, challenges to masculinity, propriety, loyalty. That Cavatelli had failed to bail his son-in-law out, leaving the job to auslanders, was an accusation he could not deny, and surely a cause for shame.

"Okay, okay, so I didn't come down—"

Schlossmann cocked his ear. Someone had slammed the door shut. He looked pleased. "Ah. The woman has triumphed. There is some good in the world. My dear, Mrs. Loomis, do not despair."

"I never have, Mr. Schlossmann."

At his apartment, he asked solicitously if she was strong enough to make it by herself to the top floor. She assured him she was. "*You* should take a rest this afternoon," Carrie said. "That hearing must have tired you."

"Tired? Goodness, no. I have new strength. I am going to resume painting the halls."

"Painting?"

"I regretted when we suspended the work after Mr. Dukes sabotaged it. I had enjoyed it immensely."

"Don't work too hard."

"Oh, no. Perhaps this afternoon I shall merely prepare. Clean my brushes. Stir my pots. I found it relaxing."

He tipped his ancient black hat, bowed again (the man

carried with him a memory of afternoon tea at the Adlon Hotel, poppyseed cakes, and apricot stollen), and excused himself.

In midafternoon, after Oberlander and his superiors had reviewed the Dukes case, a call was made to Haman, Lord & Fawcett. Discreetly, one of Oberlander's investigators, without giving his name, advised a lawyer that Dukes was in trouble, and that E. J. Puttering was being summoned to a hearing in the matter of 502 West 84th Street.

A few minutes later, young Cathcart, the junior executive to whom David Loomis and Danny Hart had spoken, was summoned to the lawyer's office.

"What's going on at this property of Puttering's?" the lawyer asked.

"Tenants complaining. Landlord getting a little rough. I gather the man is a hard-nose, and some of the tenants resented it."

The lawyer—he was an older man, white-haired, vested, softspoken, a man of dignity and probity—stared at a striking view of lower New York. "Cathcart," he asked softly, "how in heaven's name did this thing get this far?"

"How far, sir?"

"The City has asked Puttering's agent—this Dukes—to sign a consent injunction, stating he'll stop harassing tenants."

"That seems a decent way out for all concerned."

"If he refuses, they may go after a harassment finding against Puttering. They may go to the State Supreme Court."

"Oh, good God."

"You know what that could mean? With the bank rates going up? And the insurance companies frightened? Do you know anything about Dukes?"

"Two of the tenants came to see me about him. I said we had nothing to do with the management of the place, and they should talk to Puttering. I explained we were new at this thing in New York."

"It's ripe stuff, Cathcart. Some of those tenants aren't welfare cases or drunks."

"Fellow came to see me was an architect."

They both nodded as they acknowledged status. Like Conrad's narrator, they were agreeing that Lord Jim was *"one of us."*

"Wonder how *he* got involved in this mess," the lawyer said. "You know there was some shooting there. No one hurt. But one of the tenants, a Puerto Rican, was arrested."

"Oh, dear."

"We've got to resolve this. Cathcart, get in touch with Puttering and tell him something has to be done. I am told there are three tenants remaining in the building. They have to go, and quietly."

"He'll want our help if it means paying them off."

"We're under no such obligation. We are acting as brokers. Puttering cannot involve us in any way. He knows this."

"I might try talking to the architect. Is he one of the diehards? Fellow named Loomis."

"I'm not sure. We have to make it a point not to know who the tenants are, what their complaints are. Cathcart, this doesn't involve us, apart from seeing that the sale of the land is consummated."

"May I talk to Loomis—on my own—as a sort of private citizen?"

The lawyer pouted, an old man's suspicious pout. "I suppose so. But get to Puttering and warn him that we are not pleased at all with these hearings. If that man Dukes won't sign the injunction, we may see a finding of harassment. The thing will drag on, and the bottom will fall out of this whole package."

"I understand, sir." It seemed dreadfully unfair to young Cathcart that so much was riding on a strong-arm moron like Rudy Dukes, an invisible miser like Puttering, and a crew of rebellious tenants. Was there not any easier way to get things done in the greatest city in the world?

314

"Cathcart, remind Mr. Puttering of something I'm sure he'll comprehend."

"What is that, sir?"

"Thirty-million-dollar commitments do not grow on trees."

Dukes knew that Puttering would call him. They were down the stretch now, the jockeys going to their whips. Either the three tenants got out by May 31, or the deal fell apart. Of course there would be other deals, at later dates. A decrepit brownstone with three tenants in it could not stop progress. But it would be some time before the parcel could be assembled again. Puttering would have his million and a half dollar's worth of land. A new syndicate would be formed to build the high-rise. It was inevitable. But by then Rudy Dukes could be out of business.

He sat in his high-backed black-leather chair and listened as Shlep, in the outer office, regaled Martha and Bolo with his account of getting rid of Angel's corpse.

"So the ASPCA says we can't send no truck this hour of the night, and I says, it's a big dog and it's startin' to stink. . . ."

Shlep would have to go. With the new Dukes Corporation, the one he would establish after Puttering came across with a bonus, he would fire Shlep and get some decent help.

"The guy says, stick the dog in a box, and bring him here, and we'll burn it. So I get this old cardboard suitcase, and I stuff the mutt in, throw it in back of the Lincoln, and go uptown. Ninety-foist street. You wouldn' believe what happened. . . ."

Dukes did not appreciate Shlep's story. Angel had cost him four hundred dollars. More than the loss, it was the infuriating way he had died, a victim of that cockroach Paz. He would get Paz. He would get him and break his hands so he'd never want to hold a gun again, tear his tongue out, so he couldn't shout his curses. Tremark had told him they had a good case against Paz. They would get witnesses. They would press a criminal case against him. Didn't the cops arrest him? Didn't he have a record? It bothered Dukes that Paz had been sprung so soon. Hasslinger, and the smart lawyer, Feldman. Poverty program. Do-good Parish Houses. And that faggot Hart. They'd get theirs. . . .

"So I get out of the car," Shlep droned on, "and I'm dragging the valise to the ASPCA, when these two big spade kids, like maybe sixteen, seventeen, see me. I was parked on Foist Avenue, and it was a walk, maybe halfa block. So a kid says, mister, help you carry the bag? I says, get lost, kid, I don't need you. . . ."

And Mary. He had not heard from her since she had moved to her father's place in Jersey. But he had never wanted her so much. He had lost his taste for whores. They had never satisfied him. In prison he had refused to be drawn into the society of sodomites, the homosexual pecking order. They knew Rudy Dukes was too tough. He had broken a nose, bloodied a few mouths, and the queens had stayed away. They learned. A lot of people would learn. He had a sudden desire to punish Frank Gilligan, belt him a few times, drop him, warn him to get out of Mary's life. . . .

"Before I know what happens, these two coons grab the valise, rassle it outa my hands, and run away. 'Tough for you, whitey,' one kid hollers, 'next time give us the bag.' So it dawns on me. It's a heist! They think they got the crown jewels, so I holler back, 'Please, please, I'll give you a reward' . . ."

Martha Hallweg was limp with laughter. Bolo was tittering. They were light of heart, laughing at the dead dog. Scum. All of them. They'd all go, when he opened the new place. Westchester. A class operation. Why did people like Loomis and his wife have something that he didn't? What did they know?

". . . and they're gone, those two eightballs. I almost died laughing. Wait'll they get to their pad and open the suitcase and find all they got for their snatch is a dead mutt, fulla blood, and stinking like a dump. Serve the *schwarzers* right. . . ."

Shlep was a lump of lard, a smoked salmon on a delicatessen counter. He was insensate, unreachable. Nothing seemed to move him, enrage him, scare him. He plodded on, a hard-fisted, overweight old bum in his late sixties. He could still rough somebody up, could lie and cheat and threaten and bribe. But he had no class. He did not know how to dress. He sneered at Dukes' champagne and Dukes' fitted jackets and crocodile shoes. What did Shlep know about anything other than the filth of the West Side? For Shlep the world was a sleazy apartment, a spic mistress, his next meal, the racing consensus in the *Daily News*.

The buzzer on Rudy's desk sounded. In the outer office, the laughter at Sharmak's story dwindled. Martha spoke over the intercom: "It's Mr. Puttering. He says it's urgent."

Rudy picked up the phone. "Yeah?"

"Dukes, Dukes, what is happening? What are you doing to me?"

"Doing to you? I'm saving your skin."

"This is terrible," the landlord whispered. "Meet me at once. Same place as last time."

Dukes got up and put on his new olive jacket: vented sides, patch pockets, flared. What a pity that no one appreciated his elegance. He admired his trim, hard figure in the mirror. He was still needed; still the hard guy who held the key. Puttering understood that. The tougher the job got, the more the diehards resisted, the more did Puttering have to depend on him. He'd get his bonus. The money for Mary, the money to buy off the others. He would be on his way.

A black Buick with Jersey plates was double-parked south of the Chinese restaurant. The landlord was slumped deep in the seat. A withered hand covered his forehead, hiding his face.

"You sure you weren't followed?" he asked Rudy.

"I ain't sure of nothing. Maybe the whole FBI was on my tail. Maybe I'm working with the City, Puttering."

"Don't joke, Dukes, don't joke."

The landlord looked around. Things had gotten much worse. Puttering did not kid himself. That he had evaded service all these years was due only in part to his shifty tactics. There had to be some discreet fixing, a little *shmear* here, another there, a kind word to this man, a hint to that. But his attorneys had warned him that the Rent Administration was not fooling around now. The Dukes case, as it was now known, was a nightmare to them. Too many smelly corpses. Too many complaints. Too much going in and out of police stations. It had to end.

"Dukes, unless we resolve this, you are in trouble."

"Me? Me? I ain't got no million-and-half-dollar land deal going down the drain."

"I am afraid we will all suffer. I must make this clear to you. You are to do two things immediately."

"Yeah?" Dukes pulled away. The cologne was suffocating him.

"My lawyers say it is the only way out. You are to go to the Rent Administration and sign the consent injunction. They have had it issued by the State Supreme Court."

"What about you? Oberlander said they were gonna get you to sign one also."

Puttering's face drew itself into a pained frown. "They are willing to overlook me. That is the word my lawyers relay to me. The City will settle for a statement from you, which will satisfy these crazy tenants and keep them from taking us to court."

Rudy shut his eyes. The trap was closing. A deal had to be made. Haman, Lord & Fawcett would not tolerate any impediments. They would serve him up, plucked, cleaned, skewered, roasted, to the Rent Administration. He'd sign the injunction and he'd be marked bad. Puttering would slip through the net.

"You gonna testify against me?" Dukes asked.

"I will not appear at all. If you sign the injunction, all bets are off."

"They said they'd get you this time," Rudy mocked. "Oberlander says he's sure he can."

"It don't matter no more, my boy. The end of May is drawing near, and I don't care what happens once that building is emptied and our rights to it are not tied up in litigation. Let me explain something to you. If you refuse to sign this injunction, the City, having gone this far, has no choice but to seek a *permanent* injunction from the court."

"So?"

"Don't be naïve, Dukes. Once that happens we are all dead, enjoined from touching a brick in that building. The whole deal, all thirty million dollars, is held up. There was a case a few years ago where the landlord wanted to convert to commercial use and get four times the rents, where the entire package was stopped dead by injunction. There were lawsuits, trials, counterclaims, and millions and millions of dollars were involved. God forbid that should happen to us. I have obligations to Haman, Lord & Fawcett and other principals. Dukes, thirty-million-dollar commitments do not grow on trees."

"So I'm the patsy, huh?"

"I wish you wouldn't phrase it that way. I will look after you. You did some dreadful things to the people in that house. You went way beyond what I wanted."

"If you gave me enough dough to pay them off, I wouldn't of had to. Cheap bum, that's what you are, Puttering."

A prowl car tooled by. The patrolman noticed Rudy's Continental parked behind the Buick. He peered into Puttering's rented car. The landlord turned his head completely, so that all the officer saw was the wavy gray hair. Rudy waved to the cop. "Hi, Ed. It's okay."

"I can't be too careful," Puttering said.

"You want me to sign my name to this paper. What if I told you my lawyer says I don't have to? That they ain't got a thing on me? That the evidence is hearsay, their word against mine, no witnesses? What if I told you he says I'm nuts to sign it."

"Mr. Tremark is stupider than I thought. We are not arguing

the merits of the case. You may be innocent of everything. We are arguing whether I can sell my land to the interested parties. We are arguing millions of dollars, not a trivial matter of who signs what paper."

"You gotta do a few things for me," Rudy said.

"I have an open mind, my boy."

"You better. First, money."

"Naturally, naturally. I realize that our original deal was not the best in the world for you. The bonus for each eviction was maybe not sufficient to give you a margin of profit. But I did supply the additional amount for the couple in 4B. What was his name?"

"Allister."

Puttering reached inside his jacket. "Now here is the funds to finish the job." He gave Dukes a thick tan envelope. "There is six thousand dollars in there. That is the limit. Also three letters of release. Use it to pay off Schlossmann, Paz, and Loomis. How you see fit. Whoever needs the most. It averages two thousand each, but maybe the old German will go for less. You have three days."

"It ain't enough," Dukes said. "Look, Puttering, let's stop crapping around. You're in a hole. A worse hole than me. I got nothing to lose. You do. I want twelve grand in cash. Double this."

"You are out of your mind, Dukes."

"I paid Mary Gilligan five thousand to move. It damn near cleaned me out."

"Ah, that explains the lady's departure." Puttering managed a sour smile. "Dukes, never let personal affairs affect your business dealings. That was your money you spent. I agreed to the extra for Allister because we thought he was an impediment, the natural leader of the tenants. We were wrong, but we got him out. Now I am giving you six thousand to get the others out. That is all."

"A million and half bucks in land? Thirty million for a

320

building? And you give me a lousy six grand I can't even keep?"

"It's a start. I have plans for you."

"You're lying, Puttering. After this deal, every inspector in the city will be on the lookout for me. I won't be able to fix a cop or a caseworker or a fireman."

"Anyone can be fixed."

"Not when they're scared. I had a hell of time getting Paz pinched the other night. That minister and that Hebe lawyer showed up. They said they're going to the television, to the newspapers. The notorious Rudy Dukes. The Rudy Dukes case. How'd you like that?"

"I'll deny everything. I never told you to hurt people."

Rudy tapped the envelope against his knee. Oh, the beauty of it, the perfection. The more he thought of the impasse, the more he realized it had been Danny Hart, that jerk from the Parish House, who'd brought him to this state. Hart. Hart would get his. He had seen the glow in Hart's eyes at the hearings— staring at him, convinced that he and Dukes owed one another something, that they had to fight it out, test one another, go into the dirt.

What a match! Hart was a weakling, a man without the price of a meal or a suit. And he, Dukes, drove a Continental and had done time and had damn near killed a few people with his fists. How had Hart fenced him in like this, how had he aroused losers like Paz and Schlossmann?

Puttering would never understand. He would not even listen. There were no people in Puttering's world, except for his beloved family, those rich successful lawyers and physicians. There was only money, deals, mortgages, rentals, interest rates and insurance costs.

"Give me your word," Puttering said huskily. "Sign the consent injunction. On Thursday you will appear before Mr. Oberlander and sign it."

"What about you? You're supposed to be there also."

"They haven't got me yet."

"I want twelve grand."

"Sorry, Dukes. What you have in the envelope, that's it. My goodness, if you can prevail on those tenants to get out for less"—Puttering's head lowered and his voice was almost inaudible—"for nothing, in fact—who knows what can occur in such a decrepit building?—all to the better for you. But with discretion. Now that the City is alerted, it may be difficult. I leave it in your hands. Get them out. One way or the other. Personally, I would prefer to see them paid."

He was sweating, Dukes realized, still hinting that Dukes could burn them, smoke them, beat them, threaten them. So long as they were out and the City didn't act. Anything went.

Did it matter any longer? Dukes wondered. Did it matter whether the building was emptied, whether he got his stake, and was able to go into a legit business? He put the envelope in the inner pocket of his jacket. "Okay, Puttering. I got no choice. Except if I start to blab to the Rent Administration."

"That would be a bad move, Dukes. Who would believe you after all you have been accused of?"

Dukes bobbed his head, not in agreement, but as if reacting to the truth of the landlord's warning. But it could still work out. If nothing else, it had become a simple matter of mastery. Him or them. The tenants or Rudy Dukes. They'd all get what they asked for. Right down to the wire. And Hart would get something special.

As soon as he left Puttering he drove to his bank at the corner of Broadway and West 96th Street.

David did not like the way the Staten Island plans had been drawn up by the new draftsman. But he said nothing. The boy was black, young, earnest. But his training left much to be desired. In David's days of apprenticeship upstate, he would have been fired in short order for a set of drawings such as the youth had submitted to him. No matter. The kid deserved a break. At least he had a cheerful attitude and an interest in his work. Loomis had been too much scorched in the past six

weeks to want to hurt anyone. A little deception was sometimes useful.

"They look fairly good, Hank," he said to the eager tan
face. The black eyes were not hostile, thank God. "Let me run
over them and maybe we can get an early start tomorrow on
revisions. I have another of those hearings on Thursday."

The boy swallowed and returned to his table. No sooner had
David started studying the plans—*sloppy, sloppy!*—than the
receptionist summoned him. A Mr. Cathcart was waiting outside. He remembered Cathcart, the vested, proper fellow at
Haman, Lord & Fawcett. The one who had airily asserted
that they had no interest in Rudy Dukes, had never heard of him,
were not responsible for him.

Cathcart was waiting in the reception room. He seemed
anxious to talk somewhere else. David suggested the luncheonette in the lobby. Over coffee, Cathcart became expansive.

"We're concerned about your place," the young man said.

"Why?"

"Well, it's no secret we're brokering the building that's going
up there."

David paused. The man's gall made it difficult for him to
talk. When he and Hart had called on Cathcart, he had been
all evasion, ignorance. Now suddenly he was concerned.

"You'd like me to get out, I gather," David said. "You know,
people have been playing that tune in my ear for several weeks
now, and I barely hear it any longer."

Cathcart smiled: a toothy, handsome young man, by no
means stupid. "Mr. Loomis, why are you hanging on? My
information is that you've got this hoodlum Dukes on the ropes.
He's about to sign an injunction. I have a feeling you may be
offered an attractive settlement. What else do you want?"

"Justice."

"Beg pardon?" Cathcart looked as if someone had put am-
monia in his coffee.

"Justice, damn it. Mr. Cathcart, I am a man slow to anger.
It was my wife who finessed me into this attitude of martyrdom,

but now that I've gone this far I won't quit until the people responsible for what happened at 502 West 84th Street are punished."

"That's a big order. You mean you won't get out by the end of May?"

"Maybe. Maybe not. Remember there are two other tenants still hanging on. Maybe you should call on them."

The young man toyed with his cup. "I have a feeling they'll follow your lead. Mr. Loomis, I'm fascinated with this notion that you want justice."

"I'm old-fashioned."

"I admire you for it. Dukes *is* a gangster. I swear to you, no one at our firm knew the man existed until you and that poverty worker came to see me. We've investigated. You were right."

"Tell Puttering to fire him. Tell Puttering to sign the consent injunction. It's not satisfactory, but it will help set a precedent."

Cathcart paused before responding. "We don't have that kind of power."

"I'm not sure you don't."

"This isn't a black-and-white affair. Landlords and developers have rights. You must know that the City tries to keep landlords in business, even rotten ones. They knock the rent down, they try to get them to maintain services. But they don't like to punish them."

"Yes, I've learned a lot. Such as the rarity of harassment findings. I have a feeling we may hang one on Puttering and Dukes before we're through."

"That would be pretty chintzy for an educated man like yourself. It smells of vindictiveness. Is that necessary? Why not take the cash, move, forget the whole thing?"

"I hate to see people get away with too much. I went to that Housing Crimes Trial, and I admit a lot of those people were professional radicals, troublemakers, and maybe some of them lied—"

"They run one every month. Nothing."

"I'm not so sure. Those were human beings. People who might have some potential if they had a chance. Sure, there are deadbeats and drunks among them. But also some people who made a lot of sense. I wonder if the poor know some things you and I don't."

Cathcart looked out the window of the luncheonette into the late sunlight on lower Park Avenue. "I suppose they do. But that isn't why I came to see you."

"You'd like me to get out, and to tell Paz and Schlossmann to go also."

"Yes. For your own good."

"Is that a threat?"

"God, no, Mr. Loomis. Dukes is still on the job, and he's not a nice customer. Puttering told me that Dukes was going to finish the job for him in the next few days."

"So. It is a threat."

"Not from me. Mr. Loomis, don't pursue this thing. If you push it into court, if you keep bugging the Rent Administration, demand that a landlord be punished, you'll end up chewing on your own frustration. Why do you think Dukes has gotten away with so much? The law works in his favor. I know that's a miserable state of affairs, but it's the truth."

"And he's bribed people. Threatened. Beaten people up. Sorry, Cathcart. I'm going ahead with this. Somewhere this thing has to end." David felt suddenly confident. "Dukes had a man falsely jailed. Father Hasslinger, and his lawyer got into the act and put up bond for Paz. They're filing a counterclaim. This whole mess is going to Criminal Court and the newspapers."

"Really?" He seemed to have turned paler.

"I'm afraid we'll have to make mention of Haman, Lord & Fawcett and their part in this."

"We have nothing to hide. We've done nothing wrong."

"Then you shouldn't have to worry. About a trial or about that thirty-million-dollar commitment."

Cathcart reached for the check. "Can I have your home phone number? Can I call you tonight?"

Loomis nodded. But the young man never called.

Hilda Schlossmann, balancing two massive briefcases—she was taking home the examination papers from her advanced German course—came out of Hamilton Hall on the Columbia campus, and turned right. At Broadway, she would hail a downtown bus. It was a spring evening of mysterious beauty, but she did not react to it. She had learned to suppress emotion, to suffocate esthetic feeling. When the Metropolitan Museum had a retrospective of French Impressionists, she refused to go with her father.

"It would do you good, my dear," the old man said. "Do you know that Tolstoy wept when he heard the piano? That Mozart and Beethoven made the old fellow cry?"

"The worse for him. What is not intellectual in art is worthless."

But she did not tell him that she was afraid of reacting as Tolstoy did to the joys of music. She did not go to museums or listen to music for fear that she would weep. All that beauty, all that joy, all that harmonious color, sound, shape! And against it, the misery of the world. Having tasted the worst of life as a child, she feared and ran from the best. So even the soft loveliness of a May night—students tossing a ball on South Field, couples walking arm in arm, a record player scratching out a Bellini aria from a dormitory window—all these she shut from her mind.

Instead, she concentrated on the apartment she had looked at in the university's uptown housing development. It was small, cold, on a low floor. But it would do. It would have to do. They could no longer stay on West 84th Street. If she had been frightened before, the insane shoot-out had convinced her. The little man on the ground floor, the *lumpen* Paz, with whom her father was now good friends—he was clearly mad. And so was Dukes. Why should they be trapped in the middle?

As she emerged from the high iron gate on Broadway, she saw Rudy Dukes come toward her. She averted her eyes and started to cross the street.

"Hey. Hey. Miss Schlossmann."

She ignored him. But there was a red light, and Hilda was a dedicated obeyer of laws. Dukes came up to her and tried to relieve her of a briefcase. "Here. Lemme help you. I got the car across the street. I'll take you home."

"No. Please let go."

"Come on, be a sport, Miss Schlossmann. I been waitin' for you."

He yanked one of the bags loose, took her hard elbow, and steered her across Broadway to his car. "How did you know I came out here, and at this time?"

"I find things out."

At the car she hesitated. "I do not wish to ride with you, Mr. Dukes."

"Afraid of me?"

"Yes. I do not wish to put myself in your hands."

"For twenny blocks? What can I do? Miss Schlossmann, I wanna do you a big favor."

"I can take the bus, as is my custom."

"Nah, nah. I wanna give you some money. *Gelt.* A cash settlement. So you and your father can get out."

Hilda paused. She inhaled deeply, looked about her. Yes, it seemed safe enough. Students, those indifferent creatures with whom she did daily battle, moved about them. It was dusk, the sky lavender and rose, the air feathery, the noises of the city muted. For some reason, it reminded her of Berlin when she was a little girl. Or Zurich? Occasionally was able to summon up poignant images of places she had known before she had been taken to the camps. "Only to discuss this business between us."

"You'd think I was a rat or something." He held the door open for her. "Please."

The interior of the automobile was too rich for her. Too much luxury, indulgence, impertinence. Black leather and gleaming metal. A seat that seemed molded to her body. Instruments and dials and levers. A heavy armrest between them. Dukes sealed the windows. An air conditioner hummed. She looked sideways at his square, white face, the slanted eyes, the cleft chin. Inside his crocodile shoes, the cloven hoof.

Dukes was silent as they cruised south on Broadway. If she was dumbstruck by the car's opulence, he was momentarily sobered by her austere presence. She represented a whole other world. Students. Books. All kinds of words no one understood. Foreign languages. She must have earned fairly good dough. All that brains. And never been kissed. A virgin. A miserable lonely woman. Yet as Dukes glanced at her long face, the mousey hair bound in braids around her head, he realized that she was pretty. What a waste. Somehow, he was jealous of her impoverished, gray-sweater, flat-heeled world. She had something. He was not sure he wanted it, but it kept her going. What would keep him going?

Hilda could not overcome a shrinking fear of the man. He was a throwback, a brute without conscience or remorse, recognizing no rules. Her father (who had, against her wishes, immersed himself in the tenants' movement) had told her of Dukes' *modus operandi*, his talent for avoiding apprehension, skirting the law, neutralizing the police. He was an unextinguishable torch of evil.

"This is the best I can do," Dukes said. "I know you wanna move, and this'll help."

He gave her a white envelope. All her life Hilda had been taught to regard money as soiled, shameful, something refined people did not discuss. Schlossmann, drifting from job to job, from this threadbare publisher to that minor faculty, had never had the courage to inquire what his salary would be. Hilda felt that someday he would accept work for no wages at all. She was the same way. She was eternally grateful that Columbia let her teach, paid her, recognized her talents. Every morning when she entered the drab classroom in Hamilton Hall, she expected to find a uniformed functionary waiting for her. *"Miss Schlossmann, you are fired,"* he would say. *"No reason at all. Be grateful you are not being sent to jail."*

"Aincha gonna open it?" Dukes asked.

"I prefer not to."

"There's a thousand bucks in there. Best I could do. And a letter you and your father have to sign. I would appreciate you getting out by Monday. The dough'll help. You could go to one of them cheap hotels for a while. My office will help you relocate."

"Yes. I suppose you are right." She did not want to argue any more. There was something obscene about the transaction. But what? They deserved the cash settlement. Dukes had persecuted them. Was the money sufficient? Did others get more? She did not care any longer.

"I could cheat you," Dukes said. "It could be full of newspaper."

"I do not think you will. My father will count the money before he signs."

It was the prudent way out. A thousand dollars would not go far, but it was a help. She earned a respectable salary. She was in line for a promotion. They would be rid of the paint-smeared, paint-scented apartment forever, the threats, the uneasiness, the *Sturm und Drang* of 502 West 84th Street. In the new apartment, she would attempt to make some order out of her father's books and papers. Who knows? With a new, quiet place, he might finish his book.

"I guess you gotta know a lot to teach in a university," Dukes said.

"In your particular discipline, yes."

"Like, ah, you teach German?"

"Linguistics. The origin, nature, structure, and modifications of language."

"Boy, that's way outa my class." He looked at her solemn face, but she was staring ahead and would not return his smile. "I

329

gotta hand it to people with brains. Too bad it don't pay better."

He was, she realized, trying to be polite. But it was useless. They were light-years apart, separated by space voyages, an Eskimo and a Zulu trying to communicate, doomed to fail.

Schlossmann, rolling up his sleeves and donning his smock before resuming painting the corridor on the second floor, studied the blue number on his left arm. For some reason, he connected his adherence to the tenants' battle, and now his solitary resumption of the painting, with the fading cipher, the Third Reich's systematic record keeping. Unlike many camp alumni, Schlossmann had not had the numbers erased. He felt they were an important facet of his life, and he pondered them from time to time, wondering whether they should be made part of some obscure equation. An equals sign, perhaps, opposite the last number? With a corresponding series of letters, mystic x's and y's?

How restful it was in the hallway! He luxuriated in the chemical stink of the paint. Who was that artistic young man who had arranged the purchase of the paints? Lobello. An Italianate type, a Renaissance dandy. And his little roommate with the freckled, American face. Lost friends. He had enjoyed the brief history of the tenants' committee. Now most of them were gone, defeated by Dukes, bought off, expelled.

"The pleasures of simple work," Schlossmann said. He was amazed that the painting did not tire him. Tomorrow he would get on the ladder and start on the upper walls in the dull cream Lobello had selected. For the time being he was content to finish the lower wall in chocolaty brown. Sighing, he got on his knees, rump high, and carefully touched up the area where the wall met the sagging floor, using a smaller brush.

That he was working to no real purpose did not disturb him. He knew they would all soon leave. He knew that the iron

330

ball would level the house just as it had destroyed the old brownstones in back of them on West 83rd Street. But Schlossmann believed in the validity of symbolic gestures. He recalled the old Polish gentleman in the wheelchair, the retired machinist, who had bound himself to the chair and bound the chair to the radiator. There was a gesture! There was courage! In his modest way, Schlossmann decided, he would continue painting to the end, to the moment when the house was empty, ghost-ridden, creaking ready for the death blow. Thus he would reaffirm his determination to resist Dukes and his people, and the powers that created a Dukes.

"I could use a bit more light," Schlossmann said to himself. The droplights in their clever cages, which Lobello had provided, had vanished. Drifters and drunks wandered in and out of the building. Nothing was safe. The locks on the empty apartments were smashed. Several doors had been ripped from the hinges. Newspapers, empty bottles, rubbish of all sorts, littered the hallway and the empty rooms. O'Gara was gone, and there were now those two youngsters, polite enough, but with the lobotomized look of the narcotized young on their spoiled faces, inhabiting the basement.

"And the black gentleman and his wife," Schlossmann mused. "Excellent people. I wish I had spoken to them more. I am sorry they left so precipitously. Perhaps, perhaps . . ." He wondered if they would ever get together. Not likely. It was a shame. They were just getting to know one another.

He worked slowly, avoiding drippings, cleaning his brush, mopping up paint spots from the floor with a turpentine-soaked rag. The sharp odors invigorated him, and he thought of Ivan Denisovich and his fellow prisoners building the stockade. How better it would be if they were all at work—the charming ladies. Mrs. Loomis and Mrs. Paz, the homosexuals with their graceful manners, the attractive black couple. He set the brush down and picked up the roller.

"Papa, what in heaven's name are you doing?" Hilda cried.

"What do I seem to be doing? I am painting."

"Have you lost your senses? Painting this wreck of a house that will not be standing much longer?"

"A gesture, my dear. Schlossmann *redivivus*."

"Stop at once. It is too dark in here. You will exhaust yourself."

Hilda took his arm. Schlossmann was getting rather tired. He went with her to the apartment, took off his smock, and sat heavily in a sagging armchair. A look of vast contentment settled on his face.

"Papa, I have taken one thousand dollars from Mr. Dukes. I have agreed for us to get out. The university will find us a new apartment and we can make do in a hotel for a while. We will have to hurry, packing your books and papers, and so on. I would like for you to throw a lot of them out. Now please sign this paper, an agreement with Mr. Dukes. He is waiting below for it."

Schlossmann fiddled with his steel-rimmed eyeglasses—*take off your glasses, Professor, the man had told him, the Nazis will kill anyone who looks intellectual*—and read the paper. It was a promise not to prosecute Dukes or Puttering, or anyone else, to drop all claims.

"But this is Munich," Schlossmann protested. "My beloved daughter, you are asking me to sign a Munich agreement."

The photograph froze in his mind: Hitler, Mussolini, Chamberlain, Daladier, Czechoslovakia sacrificed by fearful, witless men.

"That is *narrishkeit*, Papa. We are talking about a piece of paper. An apartment. Not an entire nation."

"I have promised Mr. Loomis, and Mr. Paz," Schlossmann said weakly. "We are on the verge of forcing Dukes to capitulate. Mr. Hart—"

"Enough!" Hilda shouted. "I am sick of this vendetta! We are going!"

Schlossmann paced the room. Oh, all the books. If he could find some answer in one of them, in Kant, or Schopenhauer, or Buber, or Barth. What could he say to Hilda? He had walked to a corner, glanced at some old issues of the *Annals of the American Academy of Political and Social Science,* and turned, to find Hilda rooted to the frayed carpet in the middle of the room, her eyes popping, her mouth open yet silent, one arm pointing to the windows that looked out on the back yard.

Schlossmann turned. Like twin window cleaners, Shlep Sharmak and Bolo were standing on the sills, bracing themselves with one arm against the sides of the high portals.

"What . . . what . . . do you want?" Hilda gasped. "Get away. Get away, at once."

"Sign the paper, Schlossmann," Shlep barked. "Get smart, you old futz. Sign it."

"If I do not?" Schlossmann asked. "If I choose to stay?"

"You got no choice," Sharmak bellowed. "Sign. Take the money."

"Please, please, go away," Hilda wailed. "He will sign it. We are leaving."

Schlossmann walked toward the two men. Like caryatids upholding the building. Two ancient races, Sharmak, one of his own (sad to say), and the young man Bolo, a handsome admixture of Latin and Carib. What, Schlossmann wondered, had brought them to this estate? What made a man choose a career as a torturer?

"Ah, my dear gentlemen," Schlossmann said. "Will you beat me? Burn me? How will you force me to sign the paper?"

"Smarten up, grampa," Shlep said. "I got nothing against you. It isn't personal."

"I do not think it is. So much the worse."

"Let him have it, Bolo," Shlep ordered.

The two men unzipped their flies. As Hilda screamed and fled from the room, they urinated on the floor of Schlossmann's study.

For a few dazed moments, Schlossmann studied the steaming yellow streams, intrigued. He nodded his bald head vigorously. If only Hilda would stop her dreadful wailing! He had to think clearly, formulate some concept.

"Yes, yes," Schlossmann cried, as the puddles formed on the floor. "Yes, I have seen it. History repeating itself as farce."

Under their uninvolved eyes, the eyes of unfeeling functionaries, he grabbed the letter and scratched his signature at the bottom in a large flamboyant hand.

Shlep and Bolo, finished, stared at him with contempt. "Could have spared yourself all the trouble," Sharmak said. "Think we like doing this to people?"

After Hilda had delivered the paper to Dukes—she shivered, averted her gaze from Sharmak and Bolo, who now sat in the car—Schlossmann trudged upstairs to report his surrender to the Loomises.

"We understand, Mr. Schlossmann," Carrie said. "It's outrageous. We don't blame you."

"I could not hurt Hilda any longer. The poor child has seen enough suffering."

David felt abashed. It was as if Hilda Schlossmann's misery was of his doing, that he had been retroactively responsible for the sorrows of her life.

"Mr. Schlossmann, you're within your rights," he said. "Maybe you're smarter than we are, rid of Dukes once and for all."

"I am not so sure," the German said. "He is imprinted in my consciousness. I wish that my training had been in psychopathology, that I might study the phenomenon of a Dukes. His magical avoidance of rebuke. His invulnerability."

"I don't think he's that great," Carrie said. "He's a street brawler who was useful to some powerful people, that's all."

"More than that, more than that, Mrs. Loomis. I see him as part of the revenge of the cities. An agent of dark forces. Greed, brutality, a technology run wild. That man in the gleaming white car—he is perhaps more symbolic than we realize."

David now realized that Schlossmann, like so many of them —Paz, Sims, Allister, himself—had been captivated by Dukes, unable to function without thinking about him. In a terrible way, Dukes' corruption and brutality had been dividends of the long siege. He had been a ghost story told to frightened children around a campfire.

"Strange," Schlossmann said. "Such an ignominious surrender on my part. Have you ever seen a painting by Velazquez called *The Surrender of Breda?* In the Prado. Magnificent. A pantalooned Dutch functionary handing over the keys to the city to a Spanish grandee. Booted, ruffed, in slashed velvet. Perhaps Dukes and I should have done it that way, with a bit more elegance. But imagine! I capitulated to two pairs of kidneys!" Schlossmann was smiling.

"I'm glad you can laugh at it," Loomis said. "But I don't think it's funny. I intend to keep after Dukes until we get him. You wouldn't want me to quit, would you?"

"Not if it gives you satisfaction, Mr. Loomis. Ach, I am hardly one to give advice."

He bowed stiffly, a gentleman to the end. In the hallway, he turned and spoke again. "I had hoped to fulfill the poet's admonition—'something ere the end, some work of noble note may yet be done.' I have not behaved nobly."

"You have, Mr. Schlossmann, you have," Carrie said.

He made his usual European gesture—a lateral motion of his right hand—and left.

"The last of the Mohicans," Carrie sighed, as David took her in his arms. "Should we stick it out?"

"What else can we do?"

4

While it was true that the city had been trying to subpoena E. J. Puttering for six years, they had only tried hard for three of those years. This was during the period when Puttering's super Dzyzyc, was advising elderly residents of the Bronx apartments to "drop dead," "have a heart attack," "break a leg."

When the Bronx case dwindled away, as harassment cases tended to, the pressure to serve a paper on Puttering diminished. He had lain low, kept his nose clean, and until the Dukes case attempts to subpoena him had been desultory. But now Oberlander and his superiors in the Rent Administration vowed to hit Puttering, trap him, drag him in to a hearing. "Let's do it quick, Ray," the superior said. "Wind it up before the newspapers get it. They'll have a field day."

"Urgent, huh?"

"Let's not kid ourselves. Important people want that building to go up. I mean, realtors have rights also. Let's give everyone a little satisfaction, send everyone away happy. How many tenants left in that place?"

336

"Three."

"It could be a holdup. Can't they settle?"

"No holdup, boss. It's become a moral issue with them."

The superior frowned. "The worst kind. Do what you have to to get Puttering. Nothing'll satisfy them until you do."

The landlord's evasive tactics were based on a simple premise: never spend two nights in a row in the same place. Puttering's walled estate in Scarsdale was only one of several places where he bedded down. His son's mansion in Mount Kisco often was his place of rest, or his daughter's home in Long Beach, or his brother's apartment in the East Eighties. And of course there were hotels, motels, and frequent trips out of town. Puttering's wife spent a great deal of time in Palm Beach. She was older than he was, well into her seventies, but with the help of plastic surgeons, diets, and a massive will, she managed to look fifty. Neither could abide the other's company. However, his wife's residence in Florida gave him another sanctuary. In short, Puttering kept in motion. He was less a phantom than a wanderer on the face of the earth, and he rather enjoyed his life-style.

"He's got to come home sometime," Oberlander told Adriano Labato. "Keep a watch on his place in Scarsdale, and also his children's places. Surround the creep."

It was known to the Rent Administration that Puttering had a disturbing habit of leaving his place of rest at 4 or 5 A.M. He knew enforcement people. They enjoyed their sleep. Puttering many times had avoided the process server merely by departing before dawn. So, Labato, profiting from earlier frustrations, parked outside the Puttering estate in Scarsdale at three in the morning. There were three cars in the stake-out: Labato's across the street from the high locked iron gate guarded by two snarling Dobermans, a second vehicle at the rear entrance to the estate, and a third at the intersection of the street on which Puttering lived and a north-south artery where there was a stoplight. It was reasoned that Puttering would proceed to this corner, then turn south.

A local policeman tooled by, asked Labato for his credentials, and nodded. "He done something wrong?" the cop asked.

"Routine hearing," Labato said, secure under his short-brimmed hat. "The guy has beaten us out of it six years."

"Funny. I been on this beat *eight* years, I ain't seen him oncet."

There was a touch of admiration in their voices. Puttering was a pro, a man worthy of respect. Anyone who could beat the law for that long had to have something on the ball.

At 5:06 in the morning, when orange and yellow streaks appeared in the eastern sky, and Labato felt the need for some hot coffee, he heard the gate clanking, heard a bolt being moved, and saw the wrought-iron portal swing open. But no car came out. Instead, it was a stocky Negro in a white coat. He walked up to Labato. "You lookin' for someone?"

The inspector waited before answering. Smart dinge, he thought, wise eightball in a white coat. If he lied, what could he use as an excuse? Puttering would know in any case.

"Not really," Labato said. "We are taking a survey of car usage in the suburbs. What time they leave for the station and so on."

"Yes. Fellow in the back told me he was a insurance investigator. Seem like everyone out early."

The Negro walked back in. He would inform his boss. That would be it. Puttering would remain locked behind his castle. Labato wondered if he had done the right thing. They should have parked farther away.

But a half hour later, to his surprise, a maroon Cadillac, crunching on the gravel driveway, growled up to the opened gate.

Labato gunned his engine and turned his car into the path of the Cadillac. They were grille to grille. The investigator got on his walkie-talkie. "Red Caddy coming out. Looks like a rented car. Assume Puttering is driving. He's the only one in the car. Stand by. Over." His two aides acknowledged his call and started their motors.

The Cadillac could not move. Labato hopped out of his car, paper in hand, and walked up to the Puttering driveway. The white-coated Negro was lurking in the background. Distantly, Labato saw a looming Tudor mansion, lofty hemlocks and oaks. The wealth did not bother him as it bothered Rudy Dukes. Beneath his hat he was his own satisfied man: *four nice clean rooms inna Bronx, know what I mean?*

The window of the maroon car was wheeled down. A slender, good-looking man with dark brown hair was at the wheel. Labato saw at once it was not Puttering.

"Is Mr. Puttering there? Or at home?" he asked.

"I am Mr. Puttering."

"No you ain't. He's twice as old as you."

"I am Mr. Carlton Puttering, the son of E. J. Puttering."

"Ah. I see. Well, when do you expect him at home?"

"I don't have to tell you. I happen to be an attorney. I know my constitutional rights."

Labato took out his ID card and showed Puttering the subpoena. The young man studied both gravely. An old, old story. Talk about harassment!

"I am not interested, sir," the son said. "Now, if you please."

Labato pulled his car out of the way. The Cadillac sped off.

The investigator got on the walkie-talkie. "It was the old guy's son. Follow him anyway. I'll be behind."

The car at the intersection, a dusty black Ford, took after the Cadillac. Young Puttering appeared to be in no hurry. Since it was an hour of empty streets, a time when no self-respecting resident of Scarsdale would be up and about, the driver, Gunderman, had to linger behind with the Ford. To tail the Caddy would have been too obvious. In his rear window, he now saw Labato's car, also proceeding at a normal pace.

"Labato here," the walkie-talkie crackled. "We got to play the percentages. I'm sending Fanning to the tollgate on the Hutchinson River Parkway. We figure the guy is headed to Long Island. That was what he done last few times. Maybe pick the old man up at a motel."

"Just follow him?"

"Yeah," Labato said. "Don't get too close. When you get to the toll booth, remember the signal. One honk, two, three, left to right as they face you. Give Fanning a chance."

Gunderman nodded. He was another old-timer like Labato, secretive, silent, containered in dark suits and short answers. Puttering Junior appeared unconcerned. It was now almost daylight. There was no need for headlights. They proceeded for several miles, on to Weaver Street, which, Gunderman knew, led to the Hutchinson River Parkway. Labato's intelligence was good.

Puttering drove a bit more slowly. Then, to the tailing investigator's surprise, the Cadillac pulled into a two-lane access road leading to a public school. The school and the neighborhood were deserted.

Gunderman, to avoid suspicion, made a right turn, hiding the car behind a tree. He got out and, peeking from the edge of the corner house, witnessed an incredible occurrence. Young Puttering, looking about guardedly, walked to the rear of the car and opened the trunk. With tender embraces he helped his father out. There was no mistaking E. J. Puttering—gray hair, lush sideburns, tanned face, natty jacket, spiffy shoes. The landlord bent slightly, put a hand on his hip.

"Holy Jesus," Gunderman said. "In the goddamn trunk, like a kidnap victim."

He ran back to the Ford, spun it around, and called Labato on the radio. "The old guy was in the trunk," he said excitedly. "He's sittin' in front now with his son. I swear, I never seen nothin' like it in my life."

Labato clucked. "Yeah. He pulled that once before. We seen him climb out, but couldn't catch him. Remember what I told you about signaling at the booth."

The Cadillac sped on to the Hutchinson River Parkway, entering at Weaver Street. The morning was cool, bright. In the meadows and lawns of Westchester County, birds chirped their morning song. Gunderman kept a fair distance between his car and the Putterings' vehicle. Behind him, he saw Labato. By now Fanning would be approaching the tollgate.

The vehicles sped on—Larchmont, New Rochelle, Eastchester, Pelham. Soon they were approaching the Bronx. Gunderman knew the approach—there was a ball field on the right. There was also an exit. He prayed that Puttering would not sniff something and head off the parkway. Many people, not wishing to pay the twenty-five-cent toll, did, and then re-entered the parkway in the Bronx. But they were lucky. The Caddy slowed down, did not take the exit, but sped toward the center toll booth, the second from the left. It was a change booth marked by an "M," which was also good. He lined his own car up with the Cadillac, honked twice, long, loud bursts, and then pulled into the lane directly in back of the Puttering car. To his right, he saw Labato whiz by, rip through a tollgate, then stop and back up.

Gunderman saw the Cadillac's window roll down. An arm came out with a dollar bill.

"Hurry, willya?" young Puttering asked. Too late, the son saw Labato's car backing up. He could still, with a burst, wheel around him. Those heaps would never catch the Caddy on a straightaway. And then he noticed something odd about the red-faced man who had taken his dollar. He was wearing the olive-green cap of the toll taker, but he had on a gray business suit.

"My change please," Puttering's son said. The old man had covered his face, slumped deep in the seat.

From his inner coat pocket, the man in the toll taker's cap took a folded sheet. With a deft, professional move, like a boy sailing a paper airplane, he tossed it through the open window. Too late Carlton tried to close the window, jamming his finger into the push button. The paper landed in E. J. Puttering's lap.

"You are hereby served with a subpoena of the Rent Administration, Enforcement Division," Inspector Fanning said.

341

"Failure to comply will make you subject to fines, or imprisonment, or both."

A historic moment, Labato thought, watching it through his rear window. They should have recorded it on film. After six years, they had hooked the Phantom, hung one on E. J. Puttering.

"A fine thing, a fine thing," Carlton Puttering said. "To attack law-abiding citizens like this man, who has a heart condition."

Gunderman honked noisily. "Move on, Mac," he shouted. "Watcha waitin' for? Columbus Day?"

"You forgot your change," Fanning said. He held three quarters in his thumb and index finger. But the window was closed tight. The white paper rested in E. J. Puttering's lap.

"Go to hell," Carlton said. "I'll sue all of you before I'm finished with you. You'll find out what it is to invade a citizen's privacy."

Labato pulled over to the service area at the right of the toll booths. Gunderman and Fanning came over. They congratulated one another. Labato did not appear especially moved.

"Promotion, boss," Gunderman said. "You earned it."

"Yeah," added Fanning. "What a great idea. To stick me in the booth. We finally got him."

"After six years," Gunderman said admiringly.

They were all squat, immobile men, calloused, indifferent, tired of complaints, bad odors, long hikes up steep stairways.

"Yeah," Labato said, leaving to telephone Oberlander, "maybe we never tried too hard."

Mary Gilligan enjoyed it at the farm. She could take her parents only in small doses, especially her mother, cranky old lady Waslyk, but the relief from West 84th Street and the assaults by Dukes was welcome. Yet she was unsettled, uncertain. She was not a country girl. She could take only so much hayseed and manure. And the boys, oddly, ran wilder in Jersey than they did in New York. Both were good students and, for all their fooling around, did their homework, went to the library. Here, with nothing to do for a few days, perhaps a week, however long before Rudy found them a new place, they got into more trouble than she imagined possible. There was a small general store a few miles from the farm, and there, of all places, they were being offered marijuana. In New York grass was as natural as the air they breathed, and the boys had tried it once or twice and abandoned it. ("Bubblegum's better," Markie told her.) Here, under clear blue skies, surrounded by greenery, they would be tempted.

She had received no mail from 84th street. Lucy Paz had promised to send letters and to telephone collect if anything seemed important. But she had gotten nothing, and received no phone calls from Dukes. Tolerantly, she understood why. He was up to his neck in the hearings. The tenants' committee was after him. Dopes, to keep after him like that. Rudy was no angel. In fact he was a four-star son of a bitch. But why prolong the agony? He was ready to pay everyone off. He was willing to meet them halfway. Why try to hang him? She felt she had done the wisest thing. The five thousand dollars (she would have to keep a separate savings account, giving her parents' address) was a bonus she had never dreamed of.

But where would it lead? As soon as he was finished with the hearings he'd be after her again. Maybe he would change his mind. Frank was due home in a few months—if he chose to come home. She was suspended, dangling. She owed Frank something, owed the boys something. And if she ditched him, let him go to his Saigon girl friend, what was to guarantee that she and Dukes could make a go of it? She did not love him. But she was, she had to admit, drawn to him. The occasional beatings he had given her—how could she explain it to anyone?—had excited her. It was the unexpected in Rudy, she understood, the possibility of kindness, of terror, of love, of anger, that made him fascinating.

She would take things as they came. No commitment to Rudy. Not yet, anyway. She would settle into a new place,

get a new job, or if Mrs. Jaffe was willing to have her, go back
to the Butternut Bakery. The boys were the only important
factors in her life. Everything would be directed toward their
future.

Outside, she saw her mother, shapeless, stooped, weeding
the vegetable garden. She was indestructible, a hunk of sinew
and gristle, capable of a man's work, full of secret knowledge
about food, animals, plants. Mary took heart from the sight of
her mother's gray babushka, creased face, stumpy legs in cotton
stockings. "Can't get the best of us," she said, sipping her
morning coffee. "We're too tough, us Ukrainians."

The phone on the kitchen wall rang. Mary picked it up. It
was the local bank.

"Mrs. Gilligan? Mr. Bates at the Merchants and Farmers
Bank."

"Yes?"

"That bank check for five thousand dollars you just gave me?"

"Yes."

"I'm sorry we didn't catch this when you came here. But the
bank in New York has stopped payment on it. The man who
issued it, Mr. Dukes, put through a stop-payment order yesterday."

"I see. Is there . . . anything I can do?"

"I'm afraid not. He was within his rights. You should contact
him directly. Was any contract signed, any agreement made?"

"No." A wrenching sense of loss made her voice faint. At
the same time she began to feel an urge to laugh. "No. Nothing
in writing."

She realized that the news had brought her a sense of relief.
She was not in debt to Rudy Dukes any longer. Unencumbered,
she could tell him to drop dead. Unlike most of the people in
the building, she had never really feared him.

She would find her own place, her own job, raise her kids.
As she had so often done, and with a fair amount of success,
she would let the men make the next move. Dukes would be
no problem. He was finished, she sensed in her acute Slavic

344

way, a man going down, unable to stop the slide. And Frank —well, Frank would make his own mind up, and then she would decide. She had always been good at waiting.

"It seems a little ridiculous," Carrie said. "There's no one left to fight him." She and David walked into the dismal hearing room—for the last time, they hoped. Danny Hart was waiting at the door. His eyes had a feverish look.

"Good news," Hart said. "They slapped the paper on Puttering. He'll be here today."

"I can't believe it," David said.

"They did it. Oberlander organized it like a stake-out. E.J. had gotten cocky. Figured they'd never touch him. I couldn't believe my ears, but Oberlander swears he was hiding in the trunk of a car."

David did not smile. Ever since his involvement in the Dukes case, he had been afflicted by a dumb wonder at the lengths people would go to for money, the lunatic brutal things they would do, the total lack of rationality, decency, or decorum which greed could generate in men. He heard each new outrage, whether by Dukes, or by the landlord, or by the suave men of Haman, Lord & Fawcett, with a bemused ear, a stunned mind.

"I guess that's good for our side," Carrie said.

Tony and Lucy Paz walked in. The little man swaggered. He knew Puttering had been nailed. And now he was out of jail, on bond, ready to throw everything at Rudy Dukes. Carrie wondered about the baby. Perhaps they had negotiated a peace treaty with the Cavatellis. Lucy's mother may have agreed to watch Michael.

"Puttering'll force Dukes to sign the injunction," Hart said eagerly. "But frankly, I hope he doesn't."

"Why?" David asked.

"It's an easy way out. He'll get away with murder. The building's just about empty. Get ready for a cash settlement."

David sighed. He sat down next to Carrie in one of the

folding chairs in the space reserved for tenants. "I guess that's it," David said. "We've gained nothing."

"I'm not so sure," said Hart. "There's still a chance."

Carrie looked puzzled. "How?" With no sense of embarrassment, she found her hands supporting her engorged belly. She was weary of it.

Hart looked around craftily, a motion of his head and eyes that was not in accord with his guileless manner. "*Refuse*. Tony's agreed already. Refuse."

"Refuse to take his dough?"

"He's just going to offer you two thousand dollars, at the most twenty-five hundred. Old Schlossmann was so scared he settled for a thousand. He could have stuck it out. You and Paz can."

"What happens then?" David asked.

"Dukes will have to commit some outrageous thing and we'll trap him. I'm staying in the Pazes' place. Whatever he does, I'll get him red-handed."

David shook his head. He looked at Carrie. Was he right to endanger her any further? Did he have the stomach for any more of Hart's pursuit of the blockbuster? "Danny," he said "you stayed in Tony's place the other night, and all you succeeded in doing was getting Tony jailed. You can't beat Dukes at his own game."

"If we get some publicity for this—Father Hasslinger is working on the reporters—we may set a precedent. The City is impressed by precedents. They hardly ever punish a landlord. It's force of habit. Well, we may be able to change the rules."

"And get fried in bed," David said glumly. "Or have the walls and roof brought down on our heads." He looked solicitously at Carrie.

Oberlander and Labato walked in. If they were making little headway in the case, their files were surely growing fatter. Labato carried a huge blood-colored portfolio, Oberlander a thick manila folder. Whatever happened to Dukes, the City would have lots of data on him.

A few steps behind were Dukes, in his gray suit, and Tremark. At the sight of Rudy, Hart's face became luminous. "Oh, we'll get him," the young man said. "He's in a bind, don't you see? He's got to deliver for Puttering, but one way or the other, he's through."

Dukes did not act like a man in trouble. He walked in that short-stepping style, his hands held lightly at waist level, as if ready to block a punch or throw one.

"It's funny," Carrie said to her husband. "I'd feel better if Schlossmann were still with us."

"I miss him also. He gave us a kind of strength rooted in history. I always had the feeling he knew some things we didn't."

Tony Paz got up from his seat and walked over to them. "You talkin' about Schlossmann? I knew he never stay. Just us. You know why?"

David looked puzzled.

"We ain't afraid. David, you got a gun?"

"No."

"You better get one. Dukes never forgot anyone who cross him. You better get permit. I show you how."

"I don't like guns," Carrie said.

"Me neither," Lucy called from the seat. "Please, Mr. Loomis, tell him to get rid of it."

Paz patted his briefcase. "Never. Is my best lawyer."

Loomis had the dizzying sensation of plunging downward, of willfully threatening his life, his wife's safety, with some irrational adventure. It was one thing to respect Paz's pint-sized courage. It was another to risk your life, your family's, for some shimmering concept of ultimate retribution. Between Hart's demonic compulsion to bring Dukes down, and Tony's obsession with *machismo*, he might yet find himself or Carrie seriously injured.

He wanted to warn Tony about the gun inside the briefcase, to beg him to leave it somewhere—who was to say that the angry little man might not begin waving it, and who was to say that Dukes was not himself armed?—when the Putterings entered.

They were doppelgangers.

The two men were copies of one another, slender, elegant in sharply tailored clothes. Both were lushly tanned, their hair artfully barbered. But E.J.'s face was ravaged; young Puttering's smooth and firm. They moved with grace. David had difficulty believing that such men had countenanced and encouraged Dukes, or that the landlord had so determinedly played the role of Artful Dodger all those years. He seemed a respectable, affluent chap, a generous donator to charities, a kindly grandfather.

Oberlander and his aides came to the head of the table. The enforcement officer declared the hearings open.

At once, Carlton Puttering raised his hand and spoke. "Mr. Oberlander, I must go on the record as objecting to this procedure in its entirety."

"Later, will you, Mr. Puttering?" Oberlander asked.

"No. I want it in the record at once."

"Go ahead," Oberlander said, sighing.

"My client, who is also my father, is a sick man. He has a serious heart condition—"

"Made of stone," Tony Paz said.

"—and I object to the manner in which your agents pursued and intimidated him the other day. You indulged in invasions of his privacy, resorted to thug tactics, and I intend to file a protest with your superiors and with the American Civil Liberties Union."

"So noted," Oberlander said. He consulted his papers. "Mr. Labato, swear Mr. Puttering, Sr. I am going to interrogate him."

Carlton Puttering opened his mouth to protest, realized it would do no good, then nudged his father.

"Before you do, sir," the son said, "I understand this to be a hearing brought by the so-called tenants' committee of the building in question. Who are they? Where are they?"

348

"Right here," David said. "Myself and my wife. And Mr. and Mrs. Paz."

"Two tenants?"

"That's right," David said. "Your man Dukes saw to it that the others were frightened off."

"But not us, *cabrón!*" Tony shouted.

"I daresay," Carlton Puttering said, "that is not much of a committee. Why can't you stop these hearings, and arrange for a settlement with these two tenants? Why drive this thing into the ground?"

"Swear the witness," the enforcement officer said. He yawned, making no effort to cover his mouth. "Come on, Mr. Puttering. You have been subpoenaed and you will testify."

The landlord was sworn. Behind enormous dark glasses, he remained mysterious, elusive. Carrie was fascinated by him. How could such a sweet-looking, well-dressed old gent tolerate such monstrosities? Did he derive pleasure from them?

"Mr. Puttering," Oberlander said slowly, "on what basis did you hire Rudy Dukes?"

"Hire?" the landlord asked in a spectral voice. "Hire? He wasn't hired. He is a net lessee."

"On what basis, then, did you agree to lease the properties at 500 and 502 West 84th Street to him?"

"He came to me. He was recommended."

"By whom?"

"I don't recall. Other landlords."

"Did you know of Mr. Dukes' involvement in the matter of the St. Charles Hotel? And of his conviction?"

"Yes. I felt the man deserved a break."

"Is that the only reason you chose him?"

"Ah, he seemed competent."

"Did you not select him, sir, because you knew that he specialized in blockbusting, in forcing tenants to move out, and that that is exactly what he did in the St. Charles Hotel and other buildings?"

"I object to that," Tremark intervened. "Those are assumptions on your part. There has never been a single finding of that nature against Mr. Dukes."

Oberlander ignored him. "Does Mr. Dukes manage any other properties for you?"

"No," E. J. Puttering said. "Not at the moment."

"Will he, eventually?"

"He may, he may."

"If he successfully empties 502 West 84th Street?"

"Mr. Oberlander, why should we fool each other? I want a vacated building. Mr. Dukes was put in as manager to get the place emptied, in a reasonable, orderly way, so nobody got hurt. Sure, we didn't want any new tenants."

"The tenants' committee alleges a variety of acts of harassment by Mr. Dukes. I am submitting copies of these affidavits to you and your counsel. They include threats, fake letters, arson, wrecking of apartments, boiler breakdowns, the spreading of filth, the breaking of locks so derelicts can roam the premises, the polluting of the premises with a dead dog, and other acts. Are you aware of these alleged acts?"

"It ain't alleged," Tony Paz cried. "He done them."

Carlton Puttering rapped the table. "Mr. Oberlander, can you please keep this hearing from becoming a circus? That man is out on bond, after an incident involving the police. He is a dangerous man, with a record. Must he be here at all?"

"Mr. Paz, be quiet during testimony," the official said. "Now, Mr. Puttering, were you aware of these acts by Mr. Dukes and did you make any attempt to stop him, or did you condone them?"

Danny Hart looked at the floor. He was disgusted. Oberlander was giving the landlord the out he needed. Of course he had no knowledge of them. Of course he would say he never condoned them.

"Absolutely not," the landlord said.

His son leaned back. "May I remind you, Mr. Oberlander, that to pin harassment on a landlord, you must *prove* a direct link between the landlord and his agent. Now that is impossible.

350

To begin with, Mr. Dukes was not a mere manager in the accepted sense. He paid my father a sum for the rental of the properties. Once he did that, he was on his own. All that interested us was the rentals. There is no link between my father and Mr. Dukes. We have no knowledge of anything Mr. Dukes is alleged to have done to tenants. None at all. If by chance he has been overzealous, we certainly would not approve. But all that is academic, because E. J. Puttering was out of the picture."

"But he owned the buildings and the land," the official said.

"Of course," Carlton Puttering said.

"And desired the buildings to be vacated."

"We have never denied that," young Puttering said.

"Did you, sir, ever tell Mr. Dukes, 'I don't care how you do it, just empty the building'?"

The landlord slumped in his chair. It was impossible to read anything from his sallow, secretive face. Nor did his son respond. David had the suspicion that E.J.'s phones had been tapped. It was perhaps an unfair way to get evidence—he was not certain of the legal niceties—but it showed that the City had been on the job.

"I have said a lot of things to Mr. Dukes," Puttering answered, "but not those exact words."

"Mr. Puttering, there are sworn statements of fires, beatings, threats, sabotage of kitchens, wrecking of a man's study and his books and papers, boiler breakdowns, the smearing of excrement in hallways, the depositing of a dead dog in an airshaft, waking people in the middle of the night, the stuffing of keyholes, and other acts. I am not prepared to believe that all the tenants in your building are liars. Nor can I believe that these things took place without your knowledge."

"I never condoned them," Puttering whispered. "I never told Dukes to do them. He was on his own."

"As a lessee?"

"He was in charge. He paid me a flat figure, low because we knew the building was doomed, and he kept what he got over."

"Got what?" Oberlander asked. "A bonus for each tenant evicted?"

"No, just the extra on the rent."

"Nothing else?"

"No."

Puttering had just committed perjury. Hart's knee nudged David's under the table. Oberlander must have realized it, but he could not pursue the charge. An old hand, he knew the way these things worked. There would be nothing in writing.

Loomis leaned back in his chair, stunned by the brazen duplicity.

"You have paid, or will pay, Mr. Dukes nothing, for getting rid of people?" the official asked.

"I resent the way that is phrased," young Puttering said.

"So do I," added Tremark. "There is an assumption of wrong-doing."

"You have a point," Oberlander conceded. "I'll amend that. You did not pay Mr. Dukes a sum for each apartment vacated?"

"I did not. It was just his return on the rents he got."

Oberlander looked queryingly at Puttering, then drew a sheaf of white papers from an envelope. "Gentlemen, this is a consent injunction from the State Supreme Court. The Rent Administration has come to the conclusion that certain acts, possibly constituting harassment and certainly constituting violations, have occurred at the premises at 502 West 84th Street. It is therefore asking Mr. Rudy Dukes to sign the injunction, promising that these acts will cease. There is no specification as to the nature of the acts. Will you sign it, Mr. Dukes?"

"No," Dukes said. "On advice of counsel."

"Then we shall have no choice but to take this a step further," Oberlander said, "and ask the court for a temporary injunction."

"What will that mean?" David asked.

"Mr. Puttering will be restrained from disposing of the property in any way until this case is settled."

Puttering's face turned clay-colored under the tropic tan.

Danny Hart scrawled something on a pad. He shoved it toward David: HOPE DUKES REFUSES. WILL KILL E.J.

But David wondered: how long could they go on? And to what purpose? He thought of the thirty-million-dollar commitment, the money that "did not grow on trees," the families made miserable in the past two months by Dukes.

"Mr. Oberlander," Carlton Puttering said, "I request a recess. I want to confer with Mr. Tremark."

The official granted it. He whispered something in Labato's ear. There was a hint of bureaucratic satisfaction in their huddled heads.

When their adversaries walked out, David could not help noticing, the attorneys and the landlord were a step or two ahead of Dukes, leaving him in a leper's isolation.

"Why don't you want him to sign?" David asked Hart.

"They're off the hook. You and Paz will have to settle. The City will say they've punished Dukes and Puttering. The natural course of events. Cases have to be wound up."

"So nobody gains anything?"

"*They* do. Puttering gets his deal. Dukes, I don't know. He may be in a little trouble. But it's not a harassment finding. He won't get fined or even reprimanded. He just promises to be a good boy from now on. Puttering gets away with everything."

Tony Paz had walked over to the table. His enormous eyes were outraged. "Like I warn you people. Rudy is not human. Cannot get him. He come out of this bigger. Next owner who wants to scare people, he hire Rudy."

David was astonished at the short time the lawyers and their clients conferred. Yet there was nothing to be surprised about, he reflected. Not with thirty million dollars hanging fire.

"Mr. Oberlander," Tremark said, "my client, Mr. Dukes, agrees to sign this paper, but with great reluctance. He wants it on the record that he is the victim of a malicious campaign

353

by certain tenants and professional agitators, and that he will seek recompense in the courts via suits for libel and slander."

The effrontery of this made Carrie Loomis whoop—a loud shocked noise. David turned and smiled at her. The affair had reached a point of wicked absurdity! Dukes as victim.

"Sign here, Mr. Dukes," Oberlander said. He pushed the paper at Rudy.

Dukes scratched his bold signature at the bottom of the injunction.

"And now," Hart said, "I take it Mr. Dukes is particularly constrained not to harass the remaining tenants—the Paz or the Loomis families."

The four men across the table looked at him with varieties of hatred.

Oberlander turned to Hart. "That is correct, Mr. Hart. This paper has a binding legal effect. If it is violated, if Mr. Dukes goes back on his word, we will get a tougher injunction."

"And a finding of harassment?"

"I cannot say. That would depend on the evidence."

"What if Mr. Dukes or Mr. Puttering resists your attempts to enjoin them?"

"The City might take them to trial," Oberlander said. "You know the steps, Mr. Hart."

"I want to make sure Mr. Puttering and Mr. Dukes know them."

The sickly boy, the dreamer who was thrown out of the seminary, was a brawler, David saw. His eyes seemed to be fixed on Dukes' throat.

"Would it be within the rights of a tenant to go to court himself if he felt this injunction had been violated?" Hart pursued.

"Of course. We are all familiar with tenant-landlord court," Oberlander replied.

"I didn't mean that."

"What did you mean?" Tremark mocked. "If you're such a legal hotshot, Hart, what did you mean?"

354

"Criminal court."

"Dammit, I've heard enough, Ray," the lawyer shouted. "Can we be dismissed? Can we be dismissed, now that the City has exacted its pound of flesh from my client?"

The house rested silently, awaiting its death. Only the Paz apartment on the ground floor, blinded by Tony's metal sheeting, and the Loomis apartment on the fourth floor were occupied. The shaggy students came and went quietly from the basement. Occasionally Carrie or Lucy Paz would see them lounging on the steps, smoking, chatting softly, once with a frail girl in tattered jeans.

The front windows on the second and third floors, formerly the apartments of the departed Sims, and the two young men, had been smashed. No one knew who had done it. Kids maybe, Paz told David, more likely Bolo.

Within the house, the doors to the empty apartments had been removed by Shlep and Bolo. Rubbish littered the floors. A ripe, corrupt odor saturated the corridors. Rats hustled and scratched in the rooms. Tony Paz set traps and poison for them but it did no good. They were shrewd, tough city rats. "Like Rudy," he told Loomis. "Mean, smart."

"I guess it's time for us to go," David said to him.

"Well, when we force to. Danny says stay a few more days. At least we get paid off."

"I suppose so. But this weekend is it. We're finished after that."

Paz scowled. A surrender to Dukes was more than he could tolerate. The tiny man looked at the ugly façade of the brownstone. He had not helped, of course, with the metal protection. But now the windows on the second and third floors were gone also. He was tired of sweeping the stoop, the sidewalk, the halls. That morning he had cleaned up Schlossmann's paint brushes.

"I save them," he said to David. "Maybe I help fix up my father-in-law's place. Lucy and I gonna move in when we go."

Apparently some good had come of the battle of West

84th Street: Tony Paz was about to be welcomed into the bosom of his in-laws.

Dukes returned to the house in late afternoon. He had picked a good time. Paz would be at the fruit store, Loomis at his office. With luck, the two women might be shopping. Only Hart, that fink, that spy, would be lurking around. "You won't do anything without my knowing about it, Rudy," the queer had threatened.

Bolo and Shlep came with Rudy. They carried long boards and a tool box. They were going to nail up the windows on the second and third floors. Who could call that a violation? If some spic kids had busted the windows, it was for the tenants' own good that they be boarded up. Then he would nail up the sign: PROPERTY OF HAMAN, LORD & FAWCETT. It wasn't yet, but the deal was all but finished. Puttering would make a personal effort to pay off the remaining tenants; if he failed, they would be in deep trouble.

"Go on, nail 'em up," he ordered Shlep.

Sharmak and Bolo lugged the boards from the trunk of the Lincoln—it stank of the dog's blood—and started up the stairs. Dukes stared at the house. So damned much trouble, he thought. He never believed they would have had the guts to fight him. Most people were cowards. They feared a fist, a threat, a kick in the groin. They turned yellow. They ran. But this bunch had gotten their backs up. There were three of them who had done him dirt. Paz, because he had to prove something, Hart, because he was full of that holy crap. And Loomis. But why Loomis? Dukes felt unfairly injured by the architect's opposition. The man should have taken his money and gotten out, the way Allister had.

He needed something. One final act, one big push. Something they could never pin on him, something that would end the battle once and for all. Resting on the wrought-iron fence— he could hear Shlep and Bolo slamming boards above—he stared at the basement door. Who were those dirty kids he had seen? Some of the human garbage O'Gara knew from the West Side. He did not know their names. One of them had told Shlep that O'Gara had let them use a rear room. When O'Gara left, they had asked Shlep if they could live in the basement. They had tolerated winos, junkies, all sorts of bums in the house; two mangy students would not matter.

Dukes began to wonder about them. His mind curious, he walked down the chipped basement steps and tried the door. It was locked, but he had his own keys. He opened the door and entered the darkened room. Neither of the young men were in. Students, probably, Dukes reasoned, creepy kids.

There was a mélange of foul odors in the room—dirty clothes, urine, rotting food. Dukes' nose sniffed the soiled air. How these animals could live the way they did! And they were kids getting an education, kids from good families, he was sure. Sucker parents paying for it. He'd get rid of them. They were a complication.

Amid the stew of stenches, Dukes sniffed something else—a faint chemical odor. He toured the room, ripping apart the filthy cots, throwing the sleeping bags on the floor. Beneath a cot he saw the edge of a metal foot locker. It was painted olive drab and looked like army surplus. Dukes studied it a moment, then dragged it out. It was an old dented case, the paint flaking, one hasp held in place by a cheap lock.

Why would these two tramps bother to lock anything? What could they possibly own of value?

Dukes looked around the room. His eyes had grown accustomed to the dark, and he let the curtains remain closed. Nor did he bother to turn on the naked bulb over the kitchen table. In a corner of the room he saw some of the tools that McIsaac had left. From the pile, he took a small crowbar. Kneeling, he wedged the bar between the small lock and the hasp. With steady pressure, he broke the twisted hinge. It was an effort, and he was breathing hard.

Above, he could hear Shlep and Bolo hammering. The boards were going up. The house was dead, dead, dead. Loomis and

Paz must know they were finished. They would never get back at him.

Dukes pulled back the lid of the foot locker. A layer of thick plastic material confronted him, some kind of soft packing, a rubber substitute. He peeled it back. Smaller chunks of it had been wedged in and around the items in the locker. Whatever was in the case was fragile.

The first thing Dukes saw was a length of plumber's pipe. It was three inches in diameter, with a dull coppery sheen, standard stuff. There were six of them, all about nine inches long. Dukes set them aside. Alongside them was a roll of aluminum banding, and in a paper bag some metal clamps. He took these out also.

Now he was intrigued. The little pukes were up to something! But he was not quite sure what it was. He dug his hand into the locker. Pulling away another hunk of the foam rubber, he suddenly found himself staring at a small cheap clock.

"Son of a bitch," Dukes whispered. "If it's what I think it is."

He studied the face of the clock. It had only one hand. The minute hand had been yanked off. The clock was unwound, not ticking, and the protective glass face was gone. The hour hand was at three. Next to the nine a metal thumb tack had been pushed into the clock's face. He dug deeper into the trunk and found two more cheap clocks—unwound, glass gone, minute hand gone, a tack jammed next to the nine.

"I'll be damned," Dukes said. "Those lousy kids." But he said it with awe, a cynical admiration. Dukes knew what else to expect in the locker. Carefully he began to empty it. There were coffee tins with malodorous chemicals in them. Dukes did not know what they were—white and yellowish powders. But he did recognize the big can of smokeless black powder. He lingered over each item, marveling at the nerve of the youngsters, intrigued with his discovery.

Dukes knew a little about blasting. So far, he felt, the cache had an amateurish look about it. It was the kind of stuff that could knock down plate-glass windows, wreck an office. Oh, it could kill, also. But from what he had read of these brats, they went in for dumb sabotage. He could guess why. None of them had the courage to put someone away.

His probing hands told him he'd located something more wicked than the materials for a crude pipe bomb. Deep in the locker, bound with adhesive tape, he located three dozen sticks of dynamite. In a paper sack were a dozen dry-cell batteries, in another, a roll of wire, and finally, in a cigar box, a dozen blasting caps.

"They got it all," Dukes said, with a sense of identification. His slanted eyes studied the haul, and he breathed deeply: pipe, aluminum strips, clamps, powders, dynamite, wire, batteries, blasting caps and the one-handed clocks. The latter fascinated him. A cheap dime-store clock, time crippled.

"I get it," he said. "One wire on the body of the clock. Another on the tack. When the hour hand comes around and hits the tack, the circuit is closed. *Va-voom.*"

Upstairs he could hear Shlep and Bolo banging the windows shut. No need for that any longer. He had found his final, surefire, foolproof way of cleaning the house out. It would be an appropriate end to the miseries that the dump had caused him. Handling the materials as if they were gems, Dukes rewrapped them in the plastic stuff and returned them to the locker.

"I got lucky," he said.

But he would have to find the formula. He would want to involve the two creeps in the basement. Hang it on them. Send them up with it. Perfect. It had fallen in his lap, so beautiful that he could not, for a while, believe his good luck. It was about time. After the troubles with Paz and Loomis and the others, and most of all Hart . . .

Hart. Hart was like those two hairy kids. What if he were in with them? All those longhairs on upper Broadway seemed to know one another. Wouldn't it be better if he could throw Hart up with the others? Send them all into the sky in bloody bits? He recalled the house on West 11th Street—a big bang, a stew of bones and blood and muscle, a gang of those ratty kids getting what they deserved.

It required planning. It required a little thought. Maybe he could not do everything he wanted to do, but at minimum, he could wreck the basement, the boiler room, the lower floor. The explosion could probably be contained, so that if Paz and his family were home, they'd just get bounced around a little. Like most spics, they'd been on the floor before. They'd get over it.

He lingered in the dark room. Too good, too good. Gently, he shoved the metal box back under the cot. He ransacked the room, looking for other evidences of the young men's hobby. In the rattling old refrigerator—it had been on the blink since McIsaac's departure—he found two gallon wine jugs, containing yellowish liquids. He sniffed one: *gasoline*. The other was almost odorless, viscous, and he could guess: *sulfuric acid*.

Once more he studied the room, the inner door leading to the boiler room, measuring distances, wondering where the charge might best be placed. This good fortune having dropped in his lap, he was going to make certain that he utilized it properly.

He closed the door, paused for a moment to wonder if he should involve the students or do the job himself, and was interrupted by Shlep's phlegmy voice.

"Hey, Bolo, we're havin' our picture took," Sharmak shouted. "Smile, Bolo, you'll be in the papers. Hold up the hammer, shmuck. All your relatives can see you."

Damn Shlep! He was a lump of dirt feeding on his own brutality, his own indifference. But as Dukes ascended the steps he saw that Shlep had not been joking. Danny Hart was standing in the gutter, a 35-millimeter camera to his eye, snapping photographs of the men as they boarded up the windows. They were on the second floor, inside the old Sims' place.

"Smile, Bolo, yer on Candid Camera," Shlep taunted. "Hart, why don't you get a square meal instead of bothering us, hah?"

Bolo giggled. It was no skin off his nose.

Dukes stopped on the sidewalk and stared at Hart. "What in hell you doin'?" he asked.

"Evidence. I told you I'd be around here to the end."

As Dukes took a step toward him, he clicked off two photographs, moving backward so that he was able to frame both the manager and the men behind him.

"Won't quit huh, Hart?"

"No. I see you won't either."

Dukes chuckled. "You and me, Hart? What'd you say we was on? What'd you tell Paz?"

"Collision course."

"Gonna take them photographs to Oberlander? Show him I already violated the injunction they made me sign?"

"That's the idea, Rudy. I'll be there tomorrow morning with them. You're through, Rudy. Boarding up is a violation, a form of harassment when there are still tenants in the building."

"That a fact?"

"You must be aware of it. You were warned to leave the people alone. Now, as soon as you sign the injunction, you're breaking your word."

"So?" Dukes walked into the gutter.

"The Rent Administration will have no choice. There'll be a temporary injunction out tomorrow and that means the property is frozen. Nobody can be evicted, no sale, no boarding up, no demolition. And there goes that thirty-million-dollar deal."

Dukes yanked at his turtleneck collar, as if freeing his neck, loosening his muscles. "I shoulda paid you off."

"You couldn't afford me, Rudy. Why didn't you understand that? I'm no cop, or caseworker, or inspector."

"What the hell are you?"

"I'm not sure." Hart raised the camera and took another photograph. Shlep, infuriating Dukes, stretched his arms out and posed. "Look at me, Ma, I'm a carpenter!" the old man cried.

"Yeah, what are you, Hart?" Dukes asked again, almost plaintively.

"I'm your enemy, Rudy. We were sort of created to meet one another and have it out. I am sorry, in a way, that I have to do this."

Dukes advanced toward Hart, and the community organizer clicked off a picture of the enraged white face. Then he felt Dukes' hands grab the leather strap at the sides of the camera, pull the camera back, and smash it into his nose.

Hart shrieked. The move was so swift, so brutal, so expert that he barely knew what had happened, until he found he was breathing though his mouth. It was as if a pound of wet cement had spurted into his nostrils. Clogged, flooded with tissue and bone and blood, his nose was destroyed. It did not hurt terribly, but its dulled inutility was frightening.

"It won't help, Rudy," Hart groaned. He was sinking to the gutter, going down under short, hard blows to the neck, the side of his face, his forehead. Like a drowning man, he clutched at Dukes' chopping arms. Hart, in his weakness, frightened Dukes. People were supposed to swing back, cry, plead, show their terror. But all he heard from the youth was a bloody snorting.

"Won't help, Rudy," Hart mumbled. "Won't help."

"Should have done this long ago," Rudy said quietly.

Hart, like a dazed lover, was embracing Dukes' knees, his head bowed. Dukes removed the camera from his neck, smashed it to the sidewalk, stomped it once with his foot. Then, noticing a few people watcing—an elderly lady, a pretty girl in slacks, two small Puerto Rican boys, a white-haired gentleman in a beret—he grabbed Hart's arm and dragged him into the house.

A trail of blood followed Hart's unresisting form. His nose would not stop spurting. The blood stained his pale-blue shirt, dotted his faded jeans.

The Puerto Rican kids looked at one another, and without a word, ran to the discarded camera, picked it up, and raced toward Broadway.

It was cool and dim in the corridor. Dukes propped Hart against the freshly painted wall. "Why don't you hit back, you creep?" Rudy pleaded.

362

"Don't have to," Hart gasped. "You're through, Rudy, ruined."

"I'll show you who's ruined."

With his left hand he pushed Hart's neck against the wall, holding him upright. With his right fist, he drove punches into Hart's abdomen. With each blow, blood spurted from the young man's nose. Some of it landed on Dukes' turtleneck shirt. He studied the stains, and the sight of them infuriated him.

"Teach you, you bastard. If you'd of stayed out, I'd been finished here, on my way."

"Rudy, we had to have this."

"Yeah. See how you like it."

He dropped his left hand. Unpropped, Hart began to slither to the floor. Rudy hit him with fast, neat combinations as he went down—left hook, right cross, alternating between the young man's body and his bloodied head.

"Cry, you bastard," Dukes shouted. "Show me you're yellow."

Hart had fallen at his feet. His face was buried on the urinous linoleum of the hallway.

Shlep and Bolo stood on the stairway, and watched indifferently. Methodically, their boss was kicking Hart around the floor, hard blows with his forty-dollar shoes. Hart would grunt with each kick, shift his position slightly, bury his head in his arms.

"Cry, you puke," Dukes was muttering. "Cry, cry."

"Boss is *loco*," Bolo said. "Shlep. Maybe you better stop."

"The bum asked for it."

"He kill that guy."

"Not Rudy. He knows how to do it right."

Hart's form seemed to have been reduced to a bundle of bloodied, dusty rags. He could no longer protect himself. Dukes, panting, hissing, poised over the inert form, raised his foot, then stopped.

Sharmak and Bolo came down from the stairway. "Boss, we better get outa here," Shlep said. "Come on." He took Dukes' arm. Dukes threw him off.

"Boss, let's come on. The house is empty. One of them tenants could show up."

"The creep wouldn't fight back," Rudy said. Shlep looked into Rudy's white face—jaw working, mouth open. There were tears in Dukes' eyes. "Bastard wouldn't fight back. I should kill him."

"No, no, Rudy. Let's get out. Anybody could of beat him up. Let's get out."

For a moment Dukes appeared to lose the power to stand erect. His spine went soft and he rested against the wall. From the floor they heard Hart breathing in choking spasms.

"Gimme a hand, Bolo," Shlep ordered.

They helped Dukes to stand and took him outside to the car.

Carrie discovered Hart when she came home from shopping. She had seen the boards on the second-floor window, and she thought that perhaps a settlement had been reached. Well and good, she thought, we will go. It could not last. To hang on only to see Dukes punished now appeared pointless. Had it not been for Hart, she and David would have left. She still felt a rooting interest in the battle, a desire to see things done properly, some precedent set so that people like Dukes would be more careful in the future. But she realized they had come to the end of the line.

The house looked desolate, it was ready for the iron ball. On the first floor, the metal sheets, pitted by Shlep's gun, on the second, the boards, on the third, the smashed windows of Dane and Lobello's elegant place, and finally, their own, still intact, discreetly shaded.

"Time to go," Carrie said. She lugged her shopping cart up the steps. Moving backward into the hallway, her moccasins touched something soft. She turned, heard the choking noises, and saw Danny Hart.

"Oh, good God." With great effort, she struggled to one knee and turned the young man over. Hart was unconscious. The blood had caked on his nose, his mouth, and had matted his lank blond hair. Beneath his eyes were great blue-black bulges. One eye was shut.

"Oh, Danny, Danny," she moaned. "What did they do to you?"

But she did not scream. She had come this far in the siege of West 84th Street, and, like Hart, she often imagined some kind of apocalyptic finale. She thought of calling the police. But the Paz apartment was locked. No one was at home. Then she realized that Hart's survival was the priority. She walked out and moving as quickly as she could, made it to West End Avenue, where she hailed a taxicab.

She sighed with relief when one stopped. The driver was an elderly Puerto Rican with a thick mustache and pleasant manners. He nodded. He understood all about people getting beaten up, and the likelihood of blood in the cab. In a few minutes he had helped Carrie bear Hart into the taxi, and they sped uptown to St. Luke's Hospital.

"His nose is fractured," the intern said. "And there's a hairline break on the left cheekbone. But no sign of concussion. Come on in."

Carrie felt dizzy for a moment, then steadied herself. "He isn't seriously hurt, no internal injuries?"

"I don't think so. Oh, a busted nose is no picnic. Or a broken cheekbone. But they'll heal. You his wife?"

"No. A friend. He works with Father Hasslinger. He was helping us with a tenants' committee."

The doctor made a wry face. He was a stocky Levantine-looking man with a cultivated air of toughness. "Rough job," he said. "Whoever worked him over did it good. Bruises all over his body. Know who it was?"

"I have an idea."

Carrie had telephoned David at the office. He was on his way uptown. She had tried to get Father Hasslinger, but with no success. The black woman, Miss Liggins, who answered the call, was not certain where she could reach the minister—he was at City Hall, haranguing politicians. She herself was sorry that Hart had been beaten, but was not able to come to St. Luke's. What about Mr. Feldman? Carrie had asked. She remembered the name—the lawyer who had freed Tony Paz. She wasn't certain, Miss Liggins said reluctantly, but she would try to find him.

The call had nagged at Carrie. Even within the altruistic confines of the poverty program, there were jealousies, backbiting, personal rivalries. Clearly Miss Liggins was no admirer of Danny Hart, and while she regretted his getting drubbed, she was not eager to come to his assistance.

Danny was sitting up in bed. There was a thick tape across his nose, and another on his left cheek. Beneath his eyes—the left one was swollen shut, purplish-black—the blue bruises had spread like inkblots. His denim shirt was a mass of maroon stains, dried into sticky, runny patterns.

"Oh, Danny," Carrie moaned. "Are you in pain?"

"It isn't too bad. Full of Demerol." He had trouble speaking, forcing the words through misshapen lips.

"Was it Dukes?"

"Caught me taking photographs. They were boarding up the house. Violated the injunction."

Carrie groaned. "Was it worth it?"

Hart nodded, too vigorously for a man who had just sustained a murderous beating. "This is better. Got a criminal case now."

They were in a ward. On an adjacent bed, two elderly black men watched them with discreet pleasure. They were in faded-gray bathrobes, one bent double, the other morbidly fat. "Someone lay into him good," the doubled-up Negro said. "Yeah, someone know how to hit," the fat man agreed. They stared admiringly at Hart.

"Well . . . well what do you do now?" Carrie asked.

"We've got to get Feldman and Hasslinger. They know how to do this. They'll get us publicity. It's what I wanted."

"You're crazy, Danny. To get beaten within an inch of your life?"

366

"It isn't too bad. I sort of have a bad headache all over." He winced.

"All this to trap Dukes?"

"It was the only way. All that housing business, the Rent Administration, injunction, affidavits. Dukes could beat us at that any day of the week." He began to cough and Carrie cautioned him to stop speaking. Hart pointed at a glass of water. She brought it to his sore lips, but he could not sip it. Carrie found a bent glass tube for him. Refreshed, he started to talk again.

"We had to trap him into a criminal act, a provable criminal act. And here it is. Here I am."

"You sound happy."

"Not exactly happy. Fulfilled. It's the first time I've ever really done anything completely successful in my life."

Carrie looked at him in silence, dumbstruck. They may have flunked him out of the Union Theological Seminary, but did they know what a mystic, what a martyr, they had lost? Hart had seen the affair in biblical terms. A Miltonic encounter on the plains of heaven. And he had gotten precisely what he sought—a form of immolation, a surrogate dying god. Of course Satan was yet to be "hurled headlong flaming."

"I feel guilty," she said. "We all should. We never should have let it go this far. David and Tony and Mr. Schlossmann. We should have caved in and made a deal with Dukes."

"No, no, not at all."

"You could have been killed."

"I still may be."

Carrie rested her head in her hand. "Danny, stop. I don't think Father Hasslinger would approve of your theatricality. And I certainly don't. It's overproduction."

Hart was looking at the distant end of the ward. A nurse had entered. With her was a thick-set man in a rumpled brown suit. She pointed at Hart. The man thanked her and came toward them.

When the man got closer. Hart recognized him. It was Fassnecker, the detective who had arrested Tony Paz.

"Hart?" he asked. He had a high-pitched voice, odd in such a lumpish man.

"Yes."

"Sergeant Fassnecker." He held out a folded sheaf of white papers. "I have a criminal complaint against you. You got to come to the station house."

"Crim—?" Carrie's mouth opened in mid-word.

"You're under arrest."

Hart tried to smile. The adhesive on his face resulted in a pained grimace. "You must be joking."

"No joke." The detective looked around him. So outrageous, so unbelievable was his mission, that he seemed fearful that he might be stoned, lynched. The two black men on the adjoining bed watched with the professional interest of old losers.

"He get busted," said one.

"Yeah, but look at his face. Think what he do to the other guy."

Carrie found her voice and her indignation. "Officer, this is a mistake. Look at Danny. He's been beaten to a pulp. His nose is broken. How can you arrest *him*? Rudy Dukes did it. Dukes attacked him."

Fassnecker was studying her with an annoyed resentful air. He did not like her clean, neat face, the calm voice. Such small, intelligent women were to be avoided. Peace marchers and civil rights workers, full of legal answers and long petitions. What relationship she had to the bum with the ponytail and the busted nose, he did not know. But he could guess.

"Who you, lady?" he asked.

"I'm a friend of his."

"Yeah?"

"That's right. My husband was chairman of the tenants' committee. You have no right to do this."

Fassnecker was turning a ring on his pinky. "Lady, I got my orders. I got a complaint sworn from Mr. Dukes alleging aggravated assault by one Daniel Hart. Is this man the alleged perpetrator Daniel Hart?"

Hart worked himself to a sitting position. He had no idea he could hurt in so many places. Yet he rather enjoyed the scattered, variegated pains. Each had a tone, a quality of its own. The only one that really bothered him was the headache—an iron ring pressing against his forehead and his temples, joining in a steel knot at the occiput.

He laughed. "I could have guessed it. Carrie, did you reach Hasslinger?"

"They're looking for him."

Hart was on his feet, swaying. "Tell him to meet me at the precinct—"

"Wait a minute!" Carrie cried. "You can't do this! There has to be *some* justice in this damned city! You're arresting the wrong man!"

"It's okay," Hart said. "This may be what we want."

"But Danny, he'll get away with it again. God almighty, isn't there any way of getting the best of that rat?"

Fassnecker was looking the other way. It was curious. Whenever Dukes' name was mentioned he appeared distracted. An eye blinked, the flaccid mouth twitched. Hart moved his feet into his scuffed loafers and got up. A new ache bloomed in his groin. His nose seemed to have been impacted with topsoil.

"Let's go, Hart. I got a car."

Carrie took the community organizer's arm and led him through the ward. The cold disinterested faces of the sickly poor followed their passage.

"They git him," the doubled-over black man said to his friend. "When they got that long hair, the cops git them."

"Wife expectin' also. Bad time to git busted."

As the three of them—Hart, Fassnecker, and Carrie—left the hospital on Amsterdam Avenue, David came out of a cab. He saw Hart's bandaged, bloodied head, the tape weaving a grotesque mask on his face, and he turned, gasped. He had had no idea from Carrie's brief call that Dukes had beaten him so thoroughly.

"What? What in hell?" David cried.

"He's under arrest!" Carrie cried. "Dukes had him arrested! Look at him! Look what Dukes did to him!"

"Wait a minute, wait a minute," David protested. But it was a lost protest. Fassnecker, averting his eyes, acting as if he were making the arrest under the influence of drugs, or orders he knew were incorrect, or forged, or incomplete, was helping Hart into a Plymouth sedan.

"See if you can get Feldman," Danny called from the window of the detective's car. "Try the Parish House again."

The Loomises went back to the hospital. From a toll booth, they reached the Parish House. Hasslinger was on his way back. Luckily, Gary Feldman had come in to talk to a tenants' group. The attorney proved to be a taciturn, unemotional man.

"Hart? Arrested?"

Carrie gave him the address of the station house. Feldman knew it well.

"Same deal as with Paz," the lawyer said. "I'll be there."

An elderly nurse smiled at Carrie as she and David left the hospital to rehire the cab David had just left. The smile was natural: a friendly nod to the young mother-to-be.

"You should be in their maternity ward," Loomis said, as the taxi executed a wild U-turn on Amsterdam Avenue. "Not running to police stations. Do you really have to go along with me?"

"To the bitter end, love." Her eyes were wide: the chase was on. "Danny says we've finally trapped Dukes."

They lined up in front of the desk sergeant. On one side stood Dukes, hiding behind his outsized dark glasses, and his mod lawyer, the irritable Tremark. The attorney looked sour, disoriented. For once, David noted, his brash, ebullient air seemed absent. Now and then he would whisper in Dukes' ear; Rudy seemed not to hear. Loomis could guess. Surely he must have warned Dukes to avoid anything that would involve the police, lay him open to prosecution.

At the other side of the high desk were arrayed Hart, leaning on Father Hasslinger's arm (the prelate seemed bored, his eyes searching the corners of the room), and Gary Feldman, the lawyer. David was surprised to find a stooped, olive-skinned man, bald, diffident, with sorrowing eyes. From what he had heard about Feldman, he had expected a young firebrand.

"It's lunacy, lunacy," David whispered to Carrie. "They're arresting Danny, charging him with assault. Look at him. And look at Dukes."

"I guess Dukes got here first."

"Paz claims he's paid off cops. How else can you explain it? This is the third time he's had one of us busted. Isn't there any way of stopping him?"

The desk sergeant was asking Hart where he lived, whether he had any family. By now, Hart was so weakened that Father Hasslinger was answering for him. It seemed to bother the policeman, but he knew the minister, knew the political leverage he had, and he registered his disapproval only with a faint jerking of his head as he made the entries.

"Mr. Hart is my employee," Hasslinger said wearily. He was sweating inordinately, fiddling with his tight collar. "He has no relatives nearby."

"The complainant alleges that the perpetrator was illegally residing at the premises of 502 West 84th Street, which is under his management," the sergeant droned. "Squatting. Where does he live?"

"At the Parish House," the minister said.

The sergeant shook his head. His disgust with do-gooders was evident.

"This man Hart has been illegally and repeatedly sleeping in varying rooms at the premises in question," Tremark said. "He attacked my client when Mr. Dukes tried to evict him. A manager has a right to keep derelicts, bums, and squatters off his property. That's what this is all about."

371

"Okay, okay, one at a time," the sergeant said.

Under the harsh lights, closed in by dirty gray walls, old warped paneling, tired chairs, and scarred desks, David felt giddy. So it had come down to this: their knight-errant Hart, beaten to a pulp and *arrested*, on Dukes' complaint. The world was not only bereft of justice and decency, it was an insane, malicious world.

"I've come to a horrible conclusion," he whispered to Carrie. "We have to get out?"

"Well, yes. Dukes has won. There's no beating him. No getting the best of him. There's only one way left."

"Hmmm?"

"Somebody's got to kill the son of a bitch. I mean it. The law doesn't mean a damn to him. He's got us boxed in."

They looked at Dukes' insolent chalky face, the harsh angles, the cleft chin, the unreachable eyes behind the smoked glasses. He was unmarked, unhurt, unmoved. He had forged some occult contract with the world of brutality, the agents of pain and fear, and the tenants could not break it, or break him.

"Mr. Hart, you have been booked, and you are to appear in court at 6 P.M. and as of this moment you are under arrest. You are represented by counsel and you have been informed of your rights, is that correct?"

Hart nodded. Hasslinger whispered in his ear.

"All right. Case will be remanded to night court. Mr. Hart is under arrest on complaint of Mr. Dukes."

Feldman took a step toward the bench. He was wearing, David noted, a rumpled ill-fitting suit, and his tie had trouble finding his shirt collar. There was an air of cheap cigars and bad digestion about him.

"Sergeant, I'm Mr. Feldman, Mr. Hart's attorney. We would like to swear out a countercomplaint against Mr. Dukes."

"Your privilege. Clerk."

The business of typing the form proceeded. Dukes was huddling with his lawyer.

"My client alleges," Feldman said softly, "unprovoked attack, assault and battery with intent to injure, by Rudy Dukes. Look at my client, and look at Dukes. Who got hit? Whose nose is broken?"

Tremark shouted: "The case isn't being tried here, Sergeant! Tell Mr. Feldman to state his case. He'd better hurry up because we have witnesses who saw Hart attack Mr. Dukes!"

In the rear of the room, like two underground trolls, spirits from some nether world of monsters, stood Shlep and Bolo. Bolo looked ill at ease. He studied his pointed shoes. He was not used to peaceful appearances in police stations. On Shlep's face was that perpetual obscene grin.

"Them again," David said to his wife. "It goes for all three. They should be eliminated. I never thought I'd end up in that bag, but I can't help it. Carrie, we can't lick them. They know too much."

"Have your man raise his right hand," the sergeant said. "This means a complaint and a countercomplaint. You can discuss it in night court."

In the rear of the station, Patrolman Dattolica was man-handling two Puerto Rican boys, trying to keep them from advancing toward the bench.

"Keep them kids quiet, huh?" the sergeant asked. "Who do they belong to?"

Father Hasslinger excused himself and walked to the back of the room. David and Carrie followed him with their eyes. They saw now that Danny Hart's friend, the angry Mrs. Hall, was shepherding the youngsters.

"Here they are, Father," she boomed. "They come in on their own. They got it."

Hasslinger took a boy in each hand. They were not more than ten, spindly, handsome street brats. So Tony Paz must have looked, Carrie thought, when he roamed Columbus Avenue twenty years ago.

"Okay, okay? All set?" the sergeant asked.

"Sergeant, we have witnesses also," Feldman said.

Hasslinger brought the two boys to the edge of the desk. Dukes and his lawyer looked at them hostilely.

"These kids were on the street when Dukes attacked my client," Feldman said. "Boys, show the sergeant who hit who."

The bigger of the boys, a curly-haired cherub with immense eyes, pointed at Rudy. "This guy here, this guy with the dark glasses," he said. "He was kickin' the crap out of this guy here." He pointed at Hart.

"Man," the other said, "he really kick the crap out of him."

"How?" asked the sergeant. "With his fists? A stick? You saw it?"

"Nah, no fists," the curly-haired boy said. "With this." He opened a paper sack and took out a 35-millimeter camera. The lense was smashed, the body bent. "He sock him in the nose with this a coupla times, take it off, stomp on it. Then he drag the guy into the house."

"That your camera, Hart?" asked the sergeant.

"It's Father Hasslinger's. He lent it to me to take pictures at the house."

"You ever seen this before?" the cop asked Dukes.

Dukes was about to respond when his lawyer put an arm in front of him.

"My client is not required to answer any more questions here. He is aware of his rights under the Fifth Amendment."

"All right," the sergeant said. "They're *both* under arrest. In two hours you can go down to night court and let the judge hear it all."

Dukes was stroking his left cheek, as if touching an old wound, pondering some bruise that ached from time to time. He stared over the sergeant's head, refusing to acknowledge the presence of his enemies and victims.

"May I have a moment with Mr. Feldman?" Tremark asked.

The sergeant nodded. "Yeah, but wind it up. I got people backed up outside."

Dukes' lawyer and Feldman retired to a corner. "Gary, what the hell?" he asked. "Why push this thing? So they had a fight. So Dukes hit him a few times. Your man swung first. So there's two complaints, okay. Who knows who is wrong? Why do we have to push this thing to the end? Tell you what—"

But the mournful Feldman was already shaking his head negatively.

"—I'll make a deal. Call off your guy, I'll call off mine. Off the record, I'll get Dukes to pay for a limited amount of medical bills. He isn't that bad a guy. This thing runs a lot deeper than a fistfight. You know, there's a history of those tenants and Hart persecuting Dukes, trying to blackmail the landlord into big settlements. You knew about that, didn't you?"

Feldman pursed his lips. "Sure I do. That's why we're going ahead with this. With that beat-up camera and those two kids, we've got you by the shorts. We're taking you into night court, and if we don't get satisfaction there we're going to the D.A. Someone's got to stop that sadistic bastard, and it might as well be us."

Dukes' lawyer frowned. "Have it your way. I happen to think if it comes to trials, we can outlast you and outspend you. All the way to the top."

"We'll sure find out," Feldman said. "So far I think we got better witnesses. Those two hoods of Dukes won't get far with most judges I know."

Patrolman Dattolica, on the sergeant's orders, was clearing the room. As the participants approached the door, they were thrust upon one another—the two bargaining lawyers, Shlep and Bolo, Mrs. Hall holding each boy's arm firmly, and finally Dukes himself, his face like sun-bleached clay, his chest puffed out. At the barrier he came abreast of Carrie and David.

"I'll get you both," he said quietly.

"Go to hell," Carrie said. "Tony Paz was wise to you from the start. You're a dirty yellowbelly."

There was a large anteroom outside the chamber where the booking had taken place. As the people came into this room, a blinding, invasive white light imprisoned them. There were shouts, curses, a crackling in the air.

David knew what was happening. Father Hasslinger, or the resourceful Feldman, had summoned the television news reporters. Through the smoky shafts of eye-searing light, David saw two cameras mounted on tripods. Officious young men hustled microphones toward the group.

"Which one is Hart?" a reporter shouted.

"Which one is Dukes?" yelled another.

"Hey, Father Hasslinger," a third bellowed. "Line your people up, okay? We wanna make the night news. Tell those kids to get out of the way."

"Speed? You up to speed?" A cameraman was shouting at a sound technician. Another was focusing a long lens.

"Charlie, start rolling. Get some of the flavor of those people. Tenants on one side, Dukes and his lawyer on the other."

It was incredible to Loomis the way real people, participants in actual events, were immediately fitted into roles. There was no fakery, no scheming, no deception. It was simply that everyone behaved as if he had been anticipating the cameras and microphones and lights all his life.

"These is the boys," Mrs. Hall announced loudly. "Carlos and Ramon. They in my youth group."

"Hey, hey, Dukes!" a reporter shouted. "We wanna interview you!"

But Tremark, cursing, his face splotched with crimson, was steering Rudy away, asking a policeman where they could wait until night court.

"The guy with the bandages," another reporter yelled. "With the nose job. Is he your man, Father?"

Hasslinger, mopping his head, sweating gallons under the lights, took Danny Hart's arm and moved him toward the microphones.

"Not too long, fellows," Hasslinger said. He had been through this so often. It was all a question of when and how with the press. "Hart's lost a lot of blood. How about if he sits down?"

"I feel pretty good," Danny said.

There was a new outburst of activity. Danny was ringed by cameras, microphones. The lights burned on his bandaged, discolored face. He grinned crookedly. "Ready?" he asked.

"Hold it, hold it," one of the reporters said. He was a fierce young black journalist, mysterious behind huge eyeglasses. Looking about angrily, he said to a colleague: "Go get the dude who belted him, the guy in the blue turtleneck." He pointed at Dukes, who was trying to leave through a side door.

A sound man, recorder slung over a shoulder, bustled through the churning bodies and went after Rudy.

"Hey, hey, what's your name? Dukes? Hold it."

The man—he was an elderly union type, beneficiary of overtime, a tough contract, and an expense account—grabbed Dukes' right arm.

Rudy swung his arm out in a swift, brutal move. It caught the sound man in his stomach. He doubled over, unbelieving. As he did, Patrolman Dattolica, who deep in his primordial brain must have sensed that the winds were changing, jammed his nightstick against Rudy's back, shoving him out of the room.

The Loomises watched incredulously. It was the first time they had seen Dukes disciplined, subjected to a show of official force.

"I think something's beginning to happen," David said. "I can't be sure, but I'm optimistic."

"I'll believe it when it happens," Carrie said.

"The man who beat me up," Hart was telling his interviewers, as the cameras hummed, "is named Rudy Dukes, and he's the manager of a building on West 84th Street. He's been terrorizing tenants there for three weeks, and this is the culmination of his campaign. . . ."

Everyone in the anteroom was silent. Hart, his malformed

lips finding it difficult to articulate properly, talked on, answering questions, delighting in his role. Martyrdom was what he had sought. He had it now. Behind him, Father Hasslinger stared at the ceiling, mopped his head, loosened his collar. Perhaps he had guessed wrong on Hart. Maybe the young man would work out. Or was it possible that the Dukes case had been made in heaven for him? Had Rudy Dukes been the inevitable villain, a preordained Lucifer? Were they destined to be "in dubious battle on the plains of heaven?"

Cathcart and his wife, in their hilltop home in Darien, Connecticut, were reading in bed when the phone rang shortly after ten o'clock. They were serious young marrieds who did not watch much television and restricted their children's viewing.

It was Cathcart's superior at Haman, Lord & Fawcett. "Are you watching the ten o'clock news on channel five?" the man asked. "Put it on at once. We're in trouble."

Cathcart leaped from bed, turned the set on, and heard a reporter's voice saying:

". . . located at 502 West 84th Street, where tenants claim that a campaign of abuse, terror, threats, and harassment has made their lives a nightmare for the past three weeks. The climax occurred today in the alleged beating of Daniel Hart—"

The image emerged from the flickering black and white streaks: an exterior of the brownstone, unmistakable with Paz's metal shields, and the boards on the second floor.

"—attacked by Rudy Dukes, the manager of the premises, while Hart was taking photographs of the latest illegal act, the boarding up of windows. . . ."

The TV screen showed a milling crowd in the police station —Hasslinger, Loomis, Hart, his head covered with a bandage, his nose taped. A stout black woman appeared on camera with two undersized Puerto Rican boys.

378

"They in my youth group," she was saying. "They found the camera Dukes use to beat up this man. Here it is."

There was now a shot of a stocky man in a turtleneck shirt and dark double-breasted jacket, hurrying through a corridor, ducking away from lights and cameras, holding his arm up to hide his face.

"—Dukes, who has a police record, refused to be interviewed and swung at a channel five technician. . . . His attorney, Alvin Tremark, denied any wrongdoing, and claimed that his client had been framed by a tenants' committee seeking to blackmail the landlord—"

A lushly sideburned young man appeared on camera, shaking a fist, speaking swiftly.

"This whole thing was cleverly arranged by Hart and his associates, professional agitators, to discredit my client, and no such attack took place; it was Hart who was the aggressor, and this affair is nothing but a shakedown."

As if in editorial comment, the camera now came back to Hart's ravaged face, as if to say: *This is an aggressor?*

"Are you watching this, Cathcart?" the senior partner of Haman, Lord & Fawcett asked.

"Yes sir."

"Can you get in touch with Puttering?"

"I can try. It's impossible to reach him at his home, but he has an answering service."

"Get to him. Send him an urgent telegram if necessary."

"Yes sir. What shall I say?"

"Tell him to fire Dukes immediately. He is to handle that building himself."

"Are we empowered to give him orders like that, sir?"

"We are now."

There was a pause as both men watched the TV set. Hart, his voice distorted, was concluding his interview.

"My getting beaten up," he was saying, "is the least of this. I wasn't a tenant, I was just trying to help. It's the people who lived in that house who suffered the most—fires, threats to their children, obscene calls, the works. And for what?"

"What? What, Mr. Hart?" the black reporter asked.

"Greed. Insensitivity. Stupidity. Whatever it is that's ruining our city."

The camera moved away from Hart's broken face to Hasslinger. The minister looked impatient. They began peppering him with questions. He responded that he did not know the details of the Dukes case, but that it was of a piece with others he had handled.

"Why? Why does this persist?" the reporter asked him.

"A lot of people who should know better let it persist."

The executive's voice came through to Cathcart again. "You hear that, Cathcart?" he asked. "Get Puttering. This thing is getting too close to the bone."

"Yes sir."

"And Cathcart . . ."

"Sir?"

"Why didn't you tell me about that man Loomis who came to see you? And this fellow Hart?"

"I felt it wasn't our business. We hadn't hired Dukes. We had no responsibility for him."

"Hmmm. Yes, I suppose so."

The executive hung up. Thankfully, the report on the battle of 502 West 84th Street, the beating of the organizer, had ended. Cathcart's wife, studying him with grave green eyes, walked to the set and turned it off.

"Is it bad, dear?" she asked.

"Very bad."

"How bad?"

"Thirty million dollars' worth."

He was thumbing through an address book trying to locate Puttering's answering service when the phone rang again. It was a man from the *Daily News* asking if Haman, Lord & Fawcett had anything to say about the Dukes case. A man named Loomis, one of the two remaining tenants in the build-

380

ing, had accused the firm of indifference, and had given the newspaper Cathcart's name.

"No, we have no comment," Cathcart said, "none at all. We aren't familiar with the details of the case, and none of us had ever set eyes on Dukes, until we saw him on TV tonight."

The judge's name was Martinez. A good omen, Gary Feldman thought. They had awaited night court with some trepidation. Feldman knew how these things usually went—judges hurried the cases along, asked complainants to settle with a handshake and a promise, a fine, a reprimand, a short sentence. They wanted more than that. They wanted Dukes nailed.

"Look at my client, your honor, and look at Mr. Dukes," the Parish House lawyer said. He spoke gently, without emotion. Feldman was an old hand. A political leader as well as an attorney, he had learned that little is gained by badgering and insulting people in authority. "The evidence is in their faces. May I read from the attending physician's report at St. Luke's Hospital?"

"Not necessary," Judge Martinez said. "I have read it." He was a stout man with graying, waved hair and a pencil-line mustache. "I am puzzled by many aspects of this case."

"Your Honor," Tremark said. "A simple case of assault. Hart attacked Mr. Dukes. He was persecuting him for weeks, trying to frame him, spying on him, inciting the tenants to resist, to strike back, to vilify Mr. Dukes. There were two witnesses who saw the attack. . . ."

He gestured to the rear of the room. Shlep and Bolo again.

"Mr. Hart has witnesses also," Judge Martinez said wearily. "The boys who got the camera. Does your client deny that he struck Mr. Hart with the camera?"

Tremark looked at Dukes. Rudy seemed to have turned whiter. The angles on his hard forehead, cheeks, and jaw appeared sharper, more shadowed.

"I never hit him with no camera," Dukes said.

"With your fists?" asked the judge.

"In defense. After he jumped me."

"You deny this, Mr. Hart?" the judge asked.

"Your Honor," Danny said. "I've never hit anyone in my life. I can't fight a lick. I was taking pictures of those men boarding up the second floor. Dukes came at me and smashed my nose with the Pentax."

Martinez sighed. In back of the room he saw the usual night array of prostitutes, pushers, hustlers, the violent, the dispossessed, the rootless, the maimed and scarred detritus of the wounded city. He had come up through the West Side slums himself. He knew.

"Your Honor," Tremark said, "my client has no desire to pursue a vendetta with Mr. Hart or anyone else. He is a businessman and his business is managing buildings. I have advised him to settle this amicably and to let this incident pass. Perhaps he lost his temper after Mr. Hart attacked him without provocation, but he regrets it. He is willing to withdraw his complaint if Mr. Hart withdraws his, and will shake hands with him like a gentleman, and call it quits."

David Loomis, standing in the rear of the room saw Hart bend his battered head and whisper something to Feldman.

"No," Judge Martinez said, "no, I don't think so. Mr. Feldman has given me some information about this case, and so have you, Mr. Tremark, maybe more than you should have. I am not going to make a decision. I am going to release you both in your own recognizance, without bail, but I am sending the file on this case on to the district attorney, requesting that he examine it, and recommending that he hand down an information."

"*What?*" Tremark yelled. "Your Honor, you can't mean it! You're going to ask the D.A. to go to look into this? A simple little street brawl, two men smacking each other around?"

"I'm afraid this case is a little more complicated than a street brawl," the judge said. "You gentlemen know Mr. Oberlander? In the enforcement division of the Rent Administration?"

The lawyers nodded. On Feldman's saturnine face there was the trace of a smile. Tremark was trying to protest, unable to formulate a sentence. His lips fluttered but no words issued.

"I got a call from Mr. Oberlander about an hour ago," Martinez said. "He got word of this incident and I am acting on his advice. He is forwarding his files on this matter to the district attorney—"

"I protest!" Tremark shouted. "Those files are full of lies, innuendo, slander, invented testimony, junk put together by an alleged tenants' committee that had no legal status and that doesn't exist any more!"

"Counselor, why don't we let the district attorney's office determine that?" the judge asked. "No one's being indicted. I am merely asking for an information, for an impartial investigation. If your client, Mr. Dukes, is innocent, surely the district attorney will determine that. He, and Mr. Hart, and any other involved parties, are merely going to be asked to answer some questions. What could be fairer?"

"I still protest," Dukes' lawyer said. But his voice was fainter. "Your Honor is turning a trivial street fight into a case for Criminal Court."

"Ah, Counselor," Martinez sighed. "We have both been around. This case has overtones of something more important than two men fighting in the street. And you know it. Mr. Feldman, is this procedure acceptable?"

"It is, Your Honor," the Parish House lawyer said. "We're satisfied. I don't know what Mr. Tremark is agitated about. He is representing the man who went to the police first. Obviously he feels his man has been wronged, that an injustice was done to him by Mr. Hart. If that's the case, he should welcome the investigation. Our clients enter it on an equal footing."

"I don't need counsel to tell me what I welcome and what I don't welcome!" Tremark shouted.

"Both Mr. Dukes and Mr. Hart should benefit from the exposure," the judge said. "Let's find out what actually happened. Not just on the street but for the past few weeks."

Hart turned around and nodded at Loomis. He held his right thumb up.

Tony Paz came running up breathlessly as the people in the Dukes case came out of night court. David stopped him and told him what had happened.

"To the D.A. huh?" Tony cried. "And Oberlander send him all the files? Oberlander call the judge?"

"Apparently that's what did it," David said. "I'd have never believed it, after the way Dukes ducked everything."

Tony grabbed David's lapel and drew him near. "Me. I do."

"Do what?"

"I tell Feldman to call Oberlander. I figure by now the City want to get rid of Dukes. Sure, Feldman call Oberlander. Oberlander call the judge."

Paz was exultant, high on his own strength. There was an edge of hysteria in his voice, a sense of a victory that he himself did not quite believe. Hart and Loomis looked at each other uneasily.

They saw Dukes as he moved toward them, remote behind his dark glasses, the swagger less evident, the square head lowered.

"Don't start anything," David warned Tony.

"I don' start," Paz shouted. "I just want to say . . . you dead, Rudy Dukes! You through! We got you, you lousy blockbuster! I never afraid of you, I not afraid of you now!"

Dukes paused opposite the three men. His face was almost serene. The craggy features turned toward them, and then he walked away, voicing no threats, accepting Tony's shouted abuse and curses.

"With dignity," Hart said to Loomis. "What does it mean?"

"Be damned if I know," David said. "But he's still the main act, center stage."

Dukes was still in command. He had dominated their lives for so long, enforced his will upon them, threatened them with pain and vile language, wicked schemes, that it was impossible to look at him without a twinge of fear. Presumably defanged, tamed, brought to book, a man on the way down, he still flaunted that capacity to terrify.

Carrie was awake when David got home. She was excited, happy to learn that, at long last, the justice they had sought was about to be administered.

"Feldman said we were lucky getting Martinez as judge," he said. "Most night-court cases are handled swiftly, with minimum pain to anyone concerned. A street fight in the West Eighties? No judge wants to push it."

"Are you glad we hung in, David?"

"I suppose so." Loomis yawned. He was drained. He wondered how he would make it to his office tomorrow. In the deserted rooms and hallways, fearsome noises violated the night —rats scratched and scuttered, old fixtures creaked. The house was protesting, moaning, voicing its fears. It knew it was going to die, Carrie claimed.

"How did Dukes take it?" she asked.

"Silence. The stony stare. No threats, no fists. He seemed sobered by the whole thing."

"He deserved it."

David climbed into bed, turned off the lamp, and held her lightly. More and more, he was wary of the demanding, kicking life inside her. His rival, issue, heir, gift. "Probably not much. Assault and battery. A stiff fine maybe. But at least it'll kill him in this business for a long time. Hart thinks so."

"I hope it improves his character, at least."

David stared at the moon-painted ceiling, shifted his position, cushioned his wife's head under one arm. "I doubt it. Dukes is a world unto himself. I'm glad we shot him down. But—"

"I know what you're thinking. We didn't get to the heart of the matter."

"That's right. Puttering, and the speculators, and the red tape, and those thousands of vacant apartments I keep hearing about."

"Sweetie, we were just one small tenants' committee. I think we did beautifully."

"I'm not kicking." Loomis sat up in bed, lit a cigarette, and gazed out the window, at the smudged Manhattan night, the lights shining in numberless apartments, the high buildings full of love and hate and fear and, rather less frequently, joy.

"I have the feeling maybe it was a sucker's game," he said meditatively. "Dukes is out, we hope. But Puttering—not a mark on him. Haman, Lord & Fawcett—richer than ever. Something's out of whack. I don't think we put a dent in them. Maybe just worried them a little."

"But that thirty-million-dollar building—"

"Honey, that doesn't matter either. They'll get it. They'll get rid of Dukes and work it out some way. Oh, we'll manage, too. But the Escobars and the Fuenteses and the Pazes, and my friend Mrs. Hall, they'll be fighting this battle every day. We were just in this by accident."

"Go to sleep. Let's settle for a partial victory. Your last crusade."

"It's not my bag. Never was. I'll leave it to people like Hart and Hasslinger from now on."

Loomis was unable to sleep. For hours he stared at the walls, the ceiling, vaguely apprehensive in the ruinous house, the house emptied by Rudy Dukes, the house coveted by Puttering and the other lords of the city, the obstacle to progress that had to be brought down. In his brief career as reformer, he had come to realize that the shadows of injustice and greed and stupidity were not that hard to confront, and on occasion, could be overcome. But their *substance* was something else again, and he wondered about the difference for a long time.

Tony Paz was manic, drunk with joy, exulting in his triumph. In the morning, he went out and bought ten dollars' worth of toys for the baby and a spring coat for Lucy. He treated himself to yellow shoes and a tan snap-brimmed hat. Then he telephoned his father-in-law in the Bronx for a boastful report on the imminent triumph over Rudy Dukes.

"I show that guy," Tony shouted, making sure that the brooding Cavatelli would get the message. "I show that son of a bitch somethin'. He don' fool with Antonio Paz no more. I know my rights, I know my laws. Feldman gonna hit him with everything. The D.A. comin' to talk to me personally about the fight with Hart. I am gonna be star witness when we go to Criminal Court."

"When you movin'?" Cavatelli asked.

"Soon as Puttering come across. I am gettin' ten thousand dollars to get out."

Cavatelli did not believe him. "Ten grand? You're nuts."

"We see how nuts I am. They got to get us out now, me and Loomis. They pay through the nose."

Cavatelli loved his daughter and his grandchild dearly. The son-in-law he could take or leave. "Listen, Tony, Lucy and the baby better stay with us. Send her up for good, instead of just weekends." As an afterthought, he said, "You can come if you want."

"Yeah, if I want. No, I stay. I am gonna hang on till Puttering pay through his nose."

Cavatelli took small pleasure from the call. Not for a minute did he believe that Paz would ever see ten thousand. But he did not pursue the argument. Let him dream.

"How'd it go with them?" Mrs. Cavatelli asked, after Paz had hung up.

"They think they got a criminal case against Dukes. He beat up the goofy kid from the minister."

"Was anyone hurt?"

"Nah. Just the kid. The only reason they're gone to trial is there was a spic judge. They stick together."

Hasslinger was morbidly fascinated with Danny Hart's bruised face. His workers rarely suffered violence. They stood apart. People like Sarah Liggins, with her Eastern Seaboard accent and aloof brown features, never got hit. The poor were dimly afraid of them. Even bulky Mrs. Hall knew her way around. No one ever laid a hand on her.

Inevitable, the minister decided. Hart had to be the one to get drubbed, damn near killed. The doctor had told him that had Dukes kept kicking Danny any longer he would have ruptured internal organs. He was lucky to have sustained only a broken nose and a small fracture of the cheekbone.

"It was what you wanted, right, Dan?" the clergyman asked.

"I suppose so."

"Enjoying the stigmata?"

"It's not that bad. Of course, the saints never had Demerol. I'm pleasantly buzzed all the time."

Hasslinger had opened the office that morning to find Hart waiting at the door, a bandaged, discolored wraith. He had spent the night in the Paz apartment. Only Tony had been there; Lucy and the child had moved out.

"I don't know, Dan," the minister said. "I've never been high on martyrdom as a way of life. Not even for community organizers."

"It was the only way to get Dukes."

"To have him maim or murder you?"

"I didn't plan it that way. It had an inexorability about it. From the first time I saw Dukes, I knew we had to clash."

"Oh, brother," Hasslinger sighed. "You innocent. You dreamer."

Hart laughed. The motion of his face muscles hurt the bridge of his nose. He would ache for a long time.

"I was right. He had to beat me up."

"Some achievement. Dukes makes his living doing that. As do a lot of people around here. If not physical beatings, economic beatings. You ran into him, that's all. Don't endow it with any mythic aura."

"It wrecked him. That's one less blockbuster for us to worry about."

Hasslinger sipped at his coffee, grimacing at the cardboard taste of the soggy container. "Don't be too sure. If he makes a comeback, do me a favor. Stay out of his way. We'll go to the police. Feldman has the goods on him now, and he won't be able to go far."

Hart touched his aggrieved nose gently. He said nothing. He wanted no praise from Hasslinger, no rewards. The prize was the bandage on his bloodied head. For once in his life he had started something and finished it. The trial, which Feldman assured them they had to win, was a long way off, but it didn't matter. It was an anticlimax. When he had rolled in the dirt of the hallway at 502 West 84th Street, choking on his own blood, feeling his nose crack, absorbing the punishment of Dukes' fists and shoes, he had reached his apogee, his zenith. In pain and in humiliation, he had been redeemed, but he did not dare tell this to Hasslinger or to anyone else.

Dukes got the news from Puttering late in the morning.

"Sorry about this, my boy," he whispered, "but you are fired. You are through."

"We got a lease. I got a lease."

"Canceled. You didn't read it all. The owner has the right to cancel at any time if the lessee fails to properly maintain services in the premises. You have the worst record of maintenance of any building manager in the city."

"You old bastard. I wrecked the joint for *you.*"

"Sorry, Dukes. I have more important worries than your lease. By the way, you will return to me at once that additional six thousand dollars I gave you."

"It's five. I gave Schlossmann a grand."

"Return the five."

"Drop dead. Look out I don't catch you on the street. What I did to Hart is nothing. I can work you over so every bone hurts. I'll fix your cough, Puttering. You'll spit up your lungs and your heart next time."

"You don't frighten me, Dukes."

Puttering was calling from his son's twenty-room house. Carlton Puttering listened, watching the rhythmic rolling of the tape recorder. They would keep a record of all contacts with Dukes.

"Try and get your five grand."

"Dukes, be reasonable," the landlord said. "You are in grave trouble. You will go on trial in a few weeks. The district attorney intends to throw the book at you. It's an election year, and after that exposure on the television, the newspapers, you won't stand a chance. You are the notorious Rudy Dukes now. You ruined everything. I asked you to help me get a building empty, and you ended up beating and torturing people."

"Tough, tough."

"Give me my five thousand."

"It might help me keep quiet when the D.A. talks to me. And if you want me to shut up, not to involve you, you'll send me another five."

"You are a stubborn man, Dukes."

"Puttering, you still don't have an empty place. You got two tenants there, with leases, lawyers, publicity. You're worse off than me. I ain't got doodly to lose. I'm in trouble up to my armpits. But you, you old faker. You got that thirty-million-dollar deal to worry about."

"So let me worry about it. The Rent Administration is planning to take us to tenant-landlord court. The judge will order the tenants to accept a fair sum to vacate."

"Don't bet on it. Paz is nuts. Loomis is a crusader. They'll steal you blind. They got that smart Jew lawyer. You won't get off for twenty grand."

Puttering, in his son's elaborate den, looked at the framed diplomas from Michigan and NYU Law School, the citations and awards won by Carlton. How nice to be part of Carlton's dignified, refined world! How wonderful that his son did not have to deal with the filth, the slime, the scum, that he was required to confront! He appealed to his son for an unspoken word of advice.

The lawyer offered an indifferent shrug, as if to say: what is there to lose?

390

"Dukes? Dukes?"

"I'm here."

"You are fired, that is final. I gave my word to the interested parties. You are not only fired, but you are released from our agreement in toto. Moreover, we are going to advise the district attorney, the Rent Administration, and the newspapers—"

"Yeah, yeah. Screw Rudy. Lose him."

"On the other hand—"

Carlton Puttering turned off the tape recorder. No need to pursue these things endlessly.

"—if on a freelance basis, you wish to do as you indicated, without harming anyone, with no injuries or damages, then we can come to terms. I am not a hardhearted man, as those tenants think. I understand people's problems. You can keep the money I gave you, if the building is vacated in two days, what you don't have to spend."

Dukes grinned. They were back where they had started. Piecework. Nickel-and-diming tenants to death.

"It's a deal. I want your help when I come to trial. I ain't through with Hart yet. Or any of them."

"You will get our silent support, Dukes. But no more formal association of any kind. Now leave the premises. You are fired. And don't beat anyone up."

The conversation concluded, father appealed to son with exhausted eyes. Who had believed they would have to go this far? What had gone wrong?

"Did we do the right thing?" the landlord asked.

"Sure. He's finished. He can't do anything to us. We have to go to Haman, Lord & Fawcett. They don't want to lose out any more than we do."

"Money is tight, my boy."

"Maybe they can cook something up with their banking friends on the Coast. Those tenants simply have to get out. Worse comes to worst, we'll ask Haman, Lord & Fawcett to help pay for relocation."

"And the libel suit?"

"We'll go ahead with it. I intend to sue them all. Loomis, Paz, Hart, the minister, and any television and radio station that carried those lies about us."

"Is it worth it?"

"Why not? It will make it harder for the next gang of holdup artists. They'll watch their step before running to the microphones and the reporters."

It was late afternoon of the most lovely day of the year when Dukes got to the building. Genteel oldsters hobbled by, rejuvenated by the spring sun. He saw a dozen baby carriages and strollers, but not Lucy Paz and her child. He hoped they had gone to the Bronx for good. Paz himself, Rudy knew, was still around the neighborhood.

When Rudy had driven by in the Lincoln, he saw Paz scurrying along Broadway, his eyes wide, greeting shopkeepers, stopping to talk to a policeman, playing the wheel, the local tough guy. It pained Dukes. The shrimp would spend the rest of his life telling the world that he, and he alone, had gotten Dukes in trouble.

"For you, Rudy," Paz said.

Tony had spied the white car, and as Dukes slowed down and grinned icily at him, gave him the gesture: a fist and a crooked arm, a hand slapping at the bend.

"Not through yet, Tony."

"You dead, Dukes. You dead and you don' know it. Puttering send notices. He gettin' rid of you so fast you ain' got time to blow your nose. You better sell that heap. You gonna need money for the trial. No lawyer touch you, Rudy."

Paz hurried past him. A fruit peddler, a nighttime garage man, a weekend delivery boy, hustling flowers and steamer baskets. Dukes found it hard to swallow the truth. Except for Loomis, a man with some class, he had been cold-cocked by losers, misfits, rejects. It was a pity that Paz would not be at home for the surprise he had in store for them.

Yet he could not push things too far. If he got the place

empty, Puttering would give him a break. Not that the vulture loved him so dearly. It was the threat that had moved him: the threat that Dukes would talk and talk and talk to the D.A. All the lies they had told at the Rent Administration hearings, all the perjured testimony, all the evasions! Dukes, with one burst of angry truth, could ruin Puttering for a long time. It would be a pleasure.

Rudy Dukes, he assured himself, was still in business. As he studied the front of the old house, blinded, boarded, he realized that it was immaterial whether Puttering had agreed to let him make a last stab at the dump. He would have gone ahead. It was a challenge to his artistry. Was he not Rudy Dukes, block-buster, a feared figure, envied by writers, afraid of no one, a terror to pushers and junkies and winos, as hard a man as ever walked Broadway?

The house had resisted him. Not just the tenants, those doomed fools, not realizing they were on the way out, but the house as house. The high windows, the solid cornices, the long pilasters, the balustrade, the entire assemblage of stout blocks of brown limestone, had been his enemy. He hated it because it had survived so long, defying him, refusing to submit itself to the iron ball. It taunted him with its permanence. It would have to go, whether tenants fought him or not, whether Puttering paid him off or not. And to hell with the trial, to hell with Hart and his smart lawyer. That case was not over by any means. Tremark had a few tricks left. Once they'd settled that, who was to say that Rudy Dukes might not be on his feet again? There were plenty of places in New York where muscle was needed. The money boys would find him.

"Goodbye, house," Dukes said.

He looked up at the façade. He hoped that the Loomis broad, that smart blonde, was not at home. No matter. He'd control the thing. No one would get hurt. But nobody could live in the dump again; not for five minutes. The queers, the spade couple, Schlossmann, the spics, all of them did not know how lucky they were getting out when they did. Someday

393

those people would thank him. Someday the truth would be known.

"Not a thing to lose," Dukes said quietly.

Across the street, in front of the old high-rise, four boys were playing stoop ball. A woman super, broom in hand, was posted in front of a four-story brownstone, chatting with an old geezer in a Homburg. Both sides of the street were lined with parked cars. Dukes had left the Lincoln east of the house, double-parked, the doors unlocked. He would make a fast getaway. It was foolproof. Those two kids in the basement had been sent to him by a kindly angel. Dukes had long believed in himself, convinced that anyone with his courage, his hardness, his capacity to understand the power of fear, had to be a winner. It was being proven right now.

The basement door was locked. Dukes cursed and rapped sharply.

"Hey, hey, fellas," he said cheerfully. "It's Mr. Dukes. Your landlord."

There was a sound of shifting objects, motion. "Screw off," a dim voice responded.

"Look, kid, I don't want no trouble. Open up. You know the building's being vacated. I got some things to discuss."

"Ah, screw, Dukes."

"Listen. I got a key. I can let myself in. Why'ncha be sensible? Look, I'm letting you live here rent free."

"Okay, hold it a minute."

There was additional noise from within. The locker being shoved under the cot? The door of the old refrigerator opening and closing?

The door opened. The boy with the frizzy orange hair greeted him.

Dukes stepped in and shut the door behind him. His eye scanned the room. The top of the kitchen table showed only a carton of milk, a half loaf of sliced white bread. But the dirty coverlet on the cot was yanked up, caught between the spring

394

and the metal locker. The box itself was protruding several inches from beneath the narrow bed.

"What do you want, huh?" the boy asked.

"A favor. Siddown."

"Look, man, so okay, you let us live here. O'Gara said we could. He didn't say nothin' about you busting in like this on us."

"Shut up, squirt."

"Don't rank me, man. You got business to contract, tell me. You want us to move, say so."

Dukes sat down on a kitchen chair. He moved it noisily, bracing it between the youth and the door. "Where's your buddy? The kid with the black hair?"

"Out."

"Out? When will he be back?"

"Don't know. Come on, stop bugging me. I got studying to do."

"I bet you do. I bet I know where your buddy is."

"You're out of your tree, Dukes." He sat on the edge of the cot and began to rub his pale hands together. His eyes were a dismal green, and they looked frightened. The boy could not fathom Dukes, could not peg him, relate to him. This was no fudging professor at the university, no obvious, diagramed enemy, like a policeman.

"Out of my tree, huh?" Rudy asked. "I know where your friend is. He's out planting bombs, right?"

"Sure, sure." His voice shivered.

"Or looking for locations, hey?"

"Yeah. Now get out."

"Very tough. Oh, you hang very tough. I read about that blast at the building at Columbia. And the bank on Broadway. Knocked a lot of glass out. What'd you use—pipe?"

The boy said nothing. Dukes made no sense to him. Dimly, he had heard comments about the blockbuster from O'Gara, from some of the tenants and neighbors. They had spoken of him with a horrid awe, a bad man, a tough man. The difficulty was that the young man's ethical system and political program had no concept of a Rudy Dukes. The enemies were teachers, cops, corporate executives, the military, all classifiable and understandable: foes of the revolution. But what was Dukes? Where did he fit? How react to him?

"Kid, it's no use," Rudy said. "I seen what's in that box under the bed. I know something about explosives. Maybe more than you do. Ever hear of the UDT in the Navy?"

"No. I'm a premedical student."

"You'll crap too, if you eat regular. UDT is Underwater Demolition Teams. We used better stuff than you got. But it isn't bad, not bad at all."

The youth's eyes darted about—the barred windows, the locked door, the passage to the basement. He understood that Dukes was too quick for him, too smart. There was a chance that his friend Ward might walk in. Two of them might have a chance against Dukes.

"What do you want, Dukes? I'll rap with you."

"Good, good." He laughed, crossed his legs.

"You wanna rap with me, rap, you wanna hustle, hustle. Okay, you saw what's in the box. What if I told you it's for a course my friend is taking? Civil engineering."

They were not only poor hoods, they were poor liars. For a long time he had been reading about these children with their mad notions. Hundreds of them walked by him on Broadway—beards, filthy clothes, sandals, in robes, leather coats, a grim, determined group, mysterious to him, full of secrets he did not understand, overeducated, comfortably unemployed, eating and drinking on Papa's money. They confused him and aroused his hatred, but there was one thing about them he believed: *they were yellow.*

For all their bragging about their hardness, their bloody desire to overturn society, to bomb and burn, they were gutless. The hardhats had proved that a few years ago. A few belts in the gut, a double bank, a flat of the palm on the nose—and they whimpered and ran. They were wonders at scaring the pants off professors (just as yellow, that crowd), but they had no idea what it was to take a shot in the kidneys, and they surely did not know how to deliver one.

"Son, don't try to con me," Dukes said. "Get that box out and let's see what you can do for me."

"Go to hell, Dukes."

Rudy sighed and got up. He walked to the cot. The boy recoiled. He shrunk from the landlord, drawing his narrow legs up, lowering his head. Rudy feinted once with his left, directing a blow at the covered midriff, and when the youth tried to protect himself, Dukes crashed the side of his stiffened right hand against the slender neck. The boy screamed. Dukes grabbed his shirt and yanked him to his feet.

"Lay off, Dukes," he gasped. "We'll get you."

"Yeah? Who? Freaks, junkies, bombers? They're gonna hang one on Rudy Dukes?"

He began to slap the boy's face, methodically, right to left, left to right, and great scarlet splotches appeared on the pale skin. The boy began to cry. "Cut it out, Dukes."

"Bomber, huh? Revolutionary? Okay, Che Guevara, take out the locker. We got business here."

"No. I won't."

Dukes smashed his fist into the young man's right kidney. The boy screamed. Dukes hit him there again and he doubled over.

"Want a few more?" Rudy cried. "Where they really hurt? Know what it's like to get in the House of David? Ever get worked over by a New York cop? Who sends you the allowance? Papa in Great Neck?"

"Lay off," the boy sobbed. "I haven't done anything to you. I'm working for people like you."

Dukes grabbed the collar of his shirt and shook him. "Yeah? You gonna buy me a new Continental? A big apartment? Broads and booze?"

He threw the boy against the wall. Watching the door with one eye, he went to the cot and pulled out the locker.

"It's loaded," the youth said. His voice quavered. "It's full of hot stuff."

"I know it is, crud. Put it on the table."

The youth slunk toward the bed. He was whipped, terrified. With a groaning effort, he wrestled the metal box to the chair, and from the chair to the table.

"You're gonna make one for me," Dukes said.

"Why? Why should I?"

"If you don't, sonny, we're walking right into the police station. They love little finks like you."

"Where are you going to use it?"

"Right here."

"This house? This room?"

"The boiler room."

The youth's pinched face tried to digest Dukes' demand. It confused him. Dukes confused him.

"Dukes, we don't believe in wasting this stuff. It's a bad scene. We only use it on the power structure. We can't endanger ourselves by pointless acts. We could be busted on a dumb job like this."

Dukes raised his right palm, as if to crash it against the boy's cheek. The youth flinched back. "Jesus, you're a madman. You're out of your mind, Dukes, spaced out."

"I'll space you, you filthy animal. Let's see what you can rig in five minutes."

The boy lifted the lid of the locker. Evidently he had been at the materials when Dukes had walked in. The lengths of pipe were uncovered. A few batteries peeked from beneath the packing.

"Why should I do this?" the young man asked.

"I'll lean on you if you don't," Dukes said simply. "Can't you kids understand there's tougher people than you in the world? What makes you think you got any clout?"

"I'll take the beating."

"You'll take a lot more. You'll take twenty years in stir. You and your pals. I need some vigorish with the cops. They'll thank me. Want to take a walk right now? Captain Gossett is

398

one of them smart spades with short hair. He hates dirty little white bombers."

Eyes swiveling, the boy broke and ran for the door. Dukes moved swiftly around the table, caught his left wrist and twisted the arm behind the boy's back. He yanked it up, as hard as he could, and the youth screamed.

"Let go, Dukes," the youth wailed. "Let go. Goddammit, you'll pay for this. We'll waste you, you lousy hood."

Dukes jammed his knee into the youth's back, nailing him against the wall. "Go fix me a small one. Enough to knock out the boiler and bring down the first floor. Show me how much you learned in college."

He released the youth and shoved him to the table.

"Okay," the young man said. "The pipe is rigged already. Everything but the timer."

Dukes grinned. "For a bank? Recruiting office?"

"Drop dead."

Rudy looked at the three-foot length of coppery tubing. The ends had been covered with metal lids. Wiring led from a battery to the blasting cap. The loose ends of the wire would complete the connection to one of the drugstore clocks.

"Set it for a half hour from now," Dukes said.

"That's all?"

"Yup. Plenty time for you and me to get out and watch it from a few blocks away."

"Then what?"

"You're on your own. Dukes never welshes on a deal."

"What guarantee do I have? Maybe you'll turn me over to the pigs soon as this dump goes."

"Maybe I will. You got no real guarantee. And no choice. Come on, rig it."

The youth picked up the pipe. Gently, he fastened the cheap clock to it with a roll of electrician's tape. When it was securely anchored against the metal, he worked with the wire leads. One he fastened directly to the metal loop at the top of the clock.

The second one he wound carefully around the thumbtack opposite the nine. He made sure that the lone hand was as far away as possible from the tack.

"Don't touch me, Dukes, or fool around. No more of your kicks or punches. I have to move the hand."

"Not yet," Rudy said. "We're going to place it."

The boy picked up the pipe and the attached clock. He hesitated a moment.

"Move, kid. I got nothing to lose."

"I could kill us both."

"You won't. You're dog crap, kid. You can't fight and you can't hit back and you cry a lot. Move."

Holding the bomb close to his frail chest, the boy walked stiffly, ducking beneath the irregularly plastered ceiling, into the boiler room.

"Put it on top," Dukes said. "Next to the gauge. Right on it."

"It isn't set yet."

"Set it."

The boy wound the clock. The ticking was disturbingly loud, an insistent beat. Dukes was surprised. He had forgotten how loud a cheap clock could be.

"Listen, Dukes," the youth whimpered. "Half hour is dangerous. It puts the hand too close to the tack. Gimme at least two hours, so there's some space. Like if it's jostled or anything, it could move by accident and close the circuit. Let me put it at seven. It's safer."

"Who in hell cares about safety? Move the hand. What's the matter, kid? You afraid of a little pipe bomb?"

The boy held the mechanism close to him. He bent over it, his flaming hair like a huge flower, a weird orange dahlia or chrysanthemum. "Okay. Okay. There it is. I made it, like, forty-five minutes. It's still too close."

"Then handle it carefully, creep. Next to the gauge."

Utterly without fear, enjoying his mastery of the boy, reinforced in his belief that most people were scared stiff and reacted only to a fist or a gun, he watched with glinting eyes as

400

the youth set the pipe atop the boiler. This would end it. This would wind up the business at 502 West 84th Street. The cache would be found. The students blamed. One tattered corpse—if they ever located enough pieces to identify it.

"What's your handle, kid?"

"None of your business. I did what you wanted. Let's go."

"Not for a while. You and me are married until that thing pops."

"Dukes, you don't fool around with these. Please, please, let's go."

"Yellow little fink. What's your name?"

"Miller. Now let's get out."

Dukes was enjoying it in the basement. Whatever they had said about him at the hearings, whatever the D.A. would call him, there was one thing no one could call Rudy Dukes. *Yellow.* There was no ki-yi in him, there never had been.

"What's your pal's name, in case I need him?"

"Who?"

"The fat kid with no face and the black hair."

"Ward."

"Where can I find yez, if I need yez?"

"Jesus, no place," Miller bawled. "Dukes, can't we get out?"

"In about twenny minutes. I wanna make sure no one comes nosing in here. We'll wait in my car so's we can keep an eye on it."

The boy rubbed his forehead. "Dukes, you're in trouble enough. O'Gara told us. They're all after you. If anyone gets killed here, it's a murder rap. We don't kill people, we just shake them up."

"No one gets killed. The dump is empty."

Miller glanced at the ticking contraption. It was distressingly loud, a penetrating noise, and the boy—he lived in terror of the deathly objects he handled—was convinced someone would hear it. The solitary hand of the clock was shiveringly close to the tack. How could Dukes, that cheap gangster, be so calm?

"Go in your room, kid. We'll wait there."

"No. I want to get out. You better go too."

"Nah, nah. We'll play it close to the vest."

"No."

Something cautioned Miller. Suddenly he realized. Dukes would shove him into the basement apartment, slam the door, bolt it outside—perhaps knock him unconscious—and let him go up with the bomb. It would be perfect; a perfect way out for him.

"I said go, you puke," Rudy snarled. He grabbed the boy's flaccid arm and dug his fingers into the biceps.

"I know what you're going to do. Stick me in there—"

Dukes smashed his knuckles against the boy's mouth. Blood trickled from the torn lip.

A shaft of light, the sound of steps in the room, brought them both to attention. In the presence of the ticking destructive force, they were alert, uneasy. Dukes knew what a pipe bomb could do. It was simply that he could control himself. All his life he had valued an aura of grace, coolness, indifference. It boiled down to who was scared and who did the scaring.

"Ward!" Miller screamed. "Ward! Get out! Dukes made me set one!"

The squat youth with the matted black hair shouted back: "What? What? Where is he?"

"Keep the door open!" shrieked Miller. "Help me get out!"

Ward's shaggy head appeared in the doorway. Dukes spun around. "Get in here, you mutt. Get in here and get next to your friend."

But the young man was tougher than Miller. He had wrestled as a freshman at college. Blocky and muscular, Dukes saw, no coward.

"Dukes, this is nuts," Ward said. He saw the copper-colored pipe, the face of the noisy mutilated clock. "You wanna blow this joint, let us do it right. But we gotta get our stuff out. We gotta get out ourselves—"

Rudy was maneuvering his figure to the right, walking slowly.

402

He wanted to get between the boys and the door. There was a length of two-by-four resting against the entrance. That was all he would need to straighten them out. The police would find a pair of them—bits and pieces. Two kids blown to hell by their own experiments.

"Watch it, Dukes," Ward said. He backed away.

As Rudy's back was turned, Miller, drowning in terror, grabbed the pipe from the top of the boiler. From the corner of his eye, Dukes saw him move, feared that he was going to either break for the door or attack him, and he spun about again, sprinting the few steps across the basement floor for Miller.

"No, no, Dukes, let me disconnect it," wailed the redhead.

"Put it back," Rudy shouted. All his life he had been single-minded, a man who got a fix on things and followed through. That was why people like Puttering valued him.

"Get away, Dukes, get away!"

Ward fled through the door and into the basement room, tripped on the threshold, and raced up the steps.

Miller's frenzied fingers trembled as he tried to flick the hour hand, disconnect the wire leads.

But Dukes was already on him. They wrestled for the clock, and the sleeve of Rudy's tailored jacket brushed the hour hand. It moved toward the nine and the thumbtack.

For a second they froze, staring at one another. Miller's eyes flooded with childish tears. He may have called for his mother. Dukes was not certain.

Before eternity ate them, before their ears were shattered, their eyes erased, their bodies broken a thousand times, Miller thought he saw Dukes grinning at him.

The house was not empty.

Carrie Loomis was sitting in the bedroom, reading. The doors were bolted, but she was not afraid. In the afternoon, it was wonderfully peaceful. David had told her that they could not stay any longer. They had made their point. Dukes had been exposed. He would be brought to trial, and in all likelihood, convicted of assault on Danny Hart. Whatever the sentence, his career would be finished. And Puttering, under orders from the City, would have to settle with the remaining tenants, the Pazes and themselves.

"Hang on," Danny Hart said. "If we get Dukes, Puttering is next. If Dukes gets it in a criminal case, they'll have no choice but to find harassment. Puttering will get fined, and maybe he'll learn something. Maybe the others who do what he does will get the same."

Carrie didn't care any longer. They'd made their stand. They'd fought back. How much it had helped other tenants, other residents of the cruel city who would have to contend with some future Rudy Dukes, some other E. J. Puttering, she was not certain.

In a way she felt a bit guilty. The Puerto Ricans who had first felt Dukes' hand—those long-forgotten families who had wept their misery on the sidewalk—had had no resources. Nor, it developed, had the Simses, or the Schlossmanns, or even the interior decorator and the actor. She and David possessed that ineffable, mysterious power of the WASP. It had caused Dukes to hold back, to watch his step with them. It was not just their education, and their manner, or their blond, upright appearance; it was some occult strength. The blockbuster had known it all along.

Of course, Carrie reasoned, it made their obligations all the greater, and perhaps that was the lesson to be learned. She felt the baby kick at her. He was due in about a week according to Dr. Hershkowitz, and the child would probably find its first home a hotel. David was already thinking about a garden apartment in Queens—a dull, clean, stolid place. But the alleged "excitement" of New York was not proving the boon they had imagined it to be. Something sinister and out of balance was in the air, a sense of old grudges, old hatreds, of greed un-

404

controlled. It did not have to be that way. But their experiences had upset them, not merely in terms of the evident terrors of Dukes and his goons, but in terms of the structures and circumstances that had created the blockbuster.

She closed her book, rested her head against the back of the armchair—a gift from her mother's old house in Witherbee—and let the soft May breeze ruffle her thin hair. A small-town girl, she valued moments alone, privacy, a sense of isolation when she could collect her thoughts and analyze her life.

Now she was screaming noiselessly, rising, as if lifted by a giant's hand from the chair. Her ears were clogged. A deafening, devouring blast, unlike anything she had ever heard, had shaken the house, worrying its hardy stones, shivering walls and floors.

As the shock waves restored her body to the chair—it seemed to handle her almost gently!—she tried to stop screaming, understanding that no one could hear her. The unearthly detonation echoed and re-echoed in huge shuddering sighs, and then all was silent. Uncannily, the walls began to creak, to protest. She smelled a piercing chemical stench. Black smoke was drowning the room, and she got to her feet, running to the front. It was flooded with choking smoke. Below, she heard shouts and cries, and she knew that the explosion was in her own house.

"Steady, steady," Carrie said. "Not after all I've been through."

The telephone was working. Calmly, she dialed 911, the police emergency number, and in a shaking but clear voice, reported that something had blown up at 502 West 84th Street.

Then she walked toward the door, wondering if she should try to take anything with her. But they owned very little—no jewels, no furs, no bonds, no antiques. She stopped at David's drafting table, collected his set of Keuffel & Esser instruments, took a light coat from the closet, her purse, and again went to the door.

In the street sirens screamed. The room was becoming darker, obscured by smoke, and she began to cough. As she did, she

405

felt the twin stabs of pain in her lower back. The pain came again, and again, and again—a rhythmic cruel jabbing over her kidneys. She walked back to the telephone and dialed Dr. Hershkowitz.

5

No clear explanation of the explosion ever appeared in the press or, for that matter, in official files. There was a collective sigh of relief at the local police station when Rudy Dukes, a.k.a. Ratislav Duzich, was blown to bits. "Wasn't enough of him left to fill a pail," Patrolman Dattolica said wonderingly to Sergeant Cudlipp. What was retrieved was eventually shipped to Elizabeth, Pennsylvania, to a cousin, for burial.

The truth was that many people were delighted to be rid of Dukes, and the police were among the most pleased. "Thank God that fellow is dead," Captain Gossett said, with a wry West Indian smile. "Someone would get him sooner or later and this way it's a lot cleaner."

The police and Fire Department reports stated that an explosion caused by a pipe bomb, part of a cache of illegal materials, had destroyed the basement and ground floor of the premises. Two men died in the blast, Dukes, and a former Swarthmore College student named Andrew Dale Miller, twenty-one, no permanent address.

To add to the mystery, a naked man was seen stumbling along West 84th Street toward West End Avenue seconds after the deafening explosion occurred. He was a squat long-haired person, according to some boys playing stoop ball. His skin was blackened, his clothes burned away, and he was staggering as if blinded, bouncing from ashcan to parked car, making scary hissing noises. And then he disappeared. Vanished. How a burned naked man, barely able to see, could be eaten up in the city, puzzled the police. They reasoned that he had made his way to a sympathizer's pad and found refuge.

It was reasoned by the police that the blast was accidental. Dukes had probably come upon the two young men, discovered their store of explosives, and in his brutal way, had ordered them out. In the course of moving, something had been dropped or otherwise set off. Dukes knew his way around dynamite, the cops said. He had been in the construction business and understood what the stuff could do. It had to be accidental. And the case was closed. There was no one around to plead for an investigation into the deaths. Dukes' relatives in Pennsylvania were stolid, law-abiding farmers. Young Miller's family—his father was a wealthy dentist—likewise had no stomach for pursuing the painful affair.

But it was not only the police and the Fire Department who viewed the atomization of Rudy Dukes as a boon. In the offices on lower Broadway, where the badgered men of the Rent Administration had tried to discipline the blockbuster, there were the noises of deliverance.

"We got lucky," Ray Oberlander confided to Labato. "Sometimes you get lucky."

"Dukes had to go that way," Labato said. "Guys like that don't last."

"He lasted too long to suit me. The thing that got me was he enjoyed what he did. Other guys do it, but it's a rotten job. Dukes liked it."

It meant that the Dukes case dribbled away into nothingness. There would be no trial. No district attorney would question

Dukes and Hart, to determine the rights and wrongs of the matter. For the Rent Administration, it meant that the file on 502 West 84th Street could be closed, the papers, receipts, affidavits, allegations of violations, responses, inspectors' reports, routing slips, newspaper clippings, all neatly pierced with two holes at the top, joined with clever fasteners, and laid to rest inside manila folders, locked inside metal cabinets.

The house was finally unlivable. The boiler had been blown into fragments. The two lower floors of the building were unsafe. Tony Paz's living room sagged dangerously, and the walls were covered with dark soot. A great yawning gap had been torn in the exterior wall. Moving swiftly, Oberlander, with backing from his superiors, told Puttering to settle with the remaining tenants at once. There was some argument. Carlton Puttering was threatening lawsuits against anyone who had ever been remotely involved in the Dukes case. But E.J. had what he wanted—an empty building. The papers were being drawn up. The million-and-a-half-dollar sale of the golden land was underway.

Puttering, after a great deal of haggling with Tony Paz, paid each tenant three thousand dollars. The landlord felt it only fair. He would never recover the five thousand dollars of his money that Dukes had kept. A man could go only so far. Tony Paz was enraged. "Damn it, I know Dukes pay that Gilligan woman, his *puta*, I know he pay her five grand. And I know he pay Mr. Allister five grand. Why I am worth less?" Oberlander had no answer.

From his new home in the East Bronx, a basement apartment one block away from the Cavatellis, Tony bombarded the City with angry letters. There was never a finding of harassment against Puttering, and this particularly infuriated him. The case was closed after the three thousand dollars was paid to him and to David Loomis. End, closed, shut down.

In a miraculous way, Tony now began to identify with Rudy Dukes. In his heart he had found bloody Latin admiration for the way Dukes had gone out—*poof!* Whatever you could say about Dukes, he had *cojones,* he had *corazón, machismo.* Tony bragged about how close he had been to Dukes, what a formidable enemy he had been. He intimated that it was he, Antonio Paz, who was in some way responsible for the violent death of the blockbuster. Once, a man from the district attorney's office visited him at the fruit store (he still had his three jobs, and commuting from the Bronx exhausted him) and questioned him about the explosion.

For a few minutes Tony kept dropping dark hints. "I knew he go this way. I know plenty." Finally the man warned him—either tell what you know or shut up. If there were mysterious circumstances, there would have to be investigations, charges brought. Did Tony want to get involved? No, no, Paz cried. He thought guiltily of Lucy, busy in the kitchen, giving Michael his bottle. "Nobody got Rudy," Tony said. "Nobody was tough enough. I was the only one in that house with the guts to look him in the eye. I never afraid of him. I am just as tough a guy as Dukes, any day. But it had to be an accident."

He would live with that exhilarating knowledge all his life—*as good a man as Rudy Dukes.* The image of Dukes hovered over him, coloring his thoughts, influencing his conversation, forcing him to reminisce, to dramatize the past, to enlarge his role. And more and more, he found that he was identifying with Dukes. One day Lucy saw him wearing a pale-blue knitted turtleneck shirt, instead of his white permanent press, but she said nothing.

This belief in himself was reinforced one day while he was selecting Jaffa oranges for a customer. A prowl car rolled by. When it stopped for the light, Paz noticed something familiar about the cop at the wheel. He was a fat, wide-faced man, with pale skin and straight blond hair. It was Fassnecker, the detective who had arrested him after the shoot-out, and had later arrested Danny Hart. Yes, it was the same Fassnecker, to whom Tony had once said, "You will sell your daughter for three hundred dollars." He had not sunk that low, Paz reflected, but he was on the way down. Excitedly, Tony phoned a friend at the precinct and got the story. Captain Gossett had busted Fassnecker, about a month after Dukes' death.

The taunts were forming on Tony's lips as he stared at the green-and-white car and helped his customer load her shopping cart. "How you like it, Fassnecker?" he wanted to say. "How you like what Rudy Dukes' money do for you?" But he must have been maturing, for he said nothing. *La hara,* the cops, they had a rotten job. Fassnecker had been punished. Why make it worse?

On a winter's night that same year, the year of the siege, Tony had another strange experience, a haunting reminder of the Dukes case. Driving the garage truck down West 104th Street to help someone start a stalled car, he suddenly saw Rudy's white Lincoln again. After Dukes had died, the car had disappeared. Shlep had probably claimed it. Or had he? For now, ghostly and filthy under a streetlight, Paz saw again the Continental. Its massive tires were gone. The hood was open and savagely bent. The guts had been ripped out. The front doors had been torn from their hinges. Dead, dead, like Rudy. It made Tony sad, and for a moment he wondered if it was not another Lincoln, a double of the blockbuster's. Then he saw the twisted, dirt-smeared plate: RD 147.

"*Carai,*" Paz said, awed by the dimension of Dukes' defeat. "Rudy go, car got to go also."

By the time the wreckers had moved in on 502 West 84th Street, the protracted agonies of the siege were all but forgotten. There was a flurry of interest in the case when a group of tenants in the East Nineties, subjected to harassment—of a more refined nature—took a page from the Dukes affair and organized a committee, summoning reporters.

A young man from one of the TV stations that had helped bring Dukes down decided to investigate. He was interested in how the City was following up the accusations of the tenants' group. With the Dukes affair now setting precedent, they were surely better prepared to defend people from such outrages. There was silence at first. But the young journalist was persistent. More important, he had political connections. An uncle was close to the Mayor. So it was agreed to let him look at the files on the Dukes case, provided he did not use them, quote from them, or copy them.

After repeated delays, excuses, unexplained impediments, the files were released. Oberlander himself carried the fat manila folders into the outer office, where the young reporter waited. "Remember, kid, you gave me your word," the enforcement officer said. "No notes, no copying, nothing in print. It's for your guidance, and besides, Dukes is dead, so what the hell? But there's always a chance of one of those crazy lawsuits. Puttering is still threatening to sue everyone who was involved, from Hasslinger down. This character Paz has been after Feldman to see if he's got a case against the City. So give us a break and lay off."

It took the reporter a half hour to realize that something was drastically wrong with the files. What he found was a collection of documents relating to Rudy Dukes' labors at the St. Charles Hotel. There were complaints, letters, sworn statements, inspectors' reports—all involving the welfare hotel and its miserable occupants. But as far as 502 West 84th Street was concerned, he drew a blank. There was nothing. Not a note. Not a letter.

"How about it, Mr. Oberlander?" the journalist asked.

"It can't be. It's got to be there. It was only a few months ago."

The official had Labato check the files, then another man. Then they went back to the Housing and Development Authority's central files and combed them. It was useless. Mysteriously, the file on Rudy Dukes and the battle of West 84th Street had vanished. Some phone calls were made. Some paper pushers were bawled out. A memo was written. But the files never appeared. They had been lifted in the dead of night, spirited out of the building, and had either been destroyed or were being held somewhere. But to what purpose? No one knew.

Some suspected Puttering's hand. But no one could prove it. And the landlord reverted to his incorporeal state, a wraith, a man who lived in rented cars. His signs were still visible around the city, the name E. J. Puttering, the number of the answering service. Unscathed, he had survived the Dukes case, gotten his money, sold his land, persevered. "No matter what that bum Dukes did to you, Pop," his son said one morning, as they lingered over breakfast in the lawyer's home, "you got to admit he did the job."

"Yes, he did the job. Poor Dukes. I used to feel for him. Almost like another son."

"I'm insulted."

"Not like you, Carlie. Like a bad boy, a kid who gets in trouble. Frankly, until he turned against me, I had an affection for him. So tough. You couldn't scare him."

Dukes lingered in Puttering's sour mind. He had color and flair and was not afraid of the raw edges of life, the sight of blood, the use of pain and the acceptance of it. All these were attributes that Puttering, who feared his visits to the dentist, could admire.

In the middle-class placidity of his garden apartment in Queens, Loomis wondered about Dukes. Had the bitter conflict proven anything? He had talked to Oberlander a few times, to Father Hasslinger, to Danny Hart. They all felt that procedures for prosecuting such cases would be tightened. The City would move faster. Inspectors would be sent out at once. The penalties would be made stiffer. Oberlander assured him there could never be another Dukes case.

"Of course that doesn't mean there won't be any more harassment," the official said. "But at least some guys will think twice."

Father Hasslinger and Danny Hart, admitting that the Dukes case would alert tenants and officials alike, were less sanguine.

"They'll tighten the rules," the minister said, with his usual air of quiet cynicism, "but the poor people getting booted out won't have a prayer. None of this would matter too much if they had someplace to go. You people were lucky. You could find places. My people can't."

One day in late June, Danny Hart called David at his office. He was leaving New York. He was mildly annoyed that nothing had happened to Puttering, and he seemed to regret that Dukes had come to such a violent inexplicable end.

"You sound sorry he's dead," David said. "Everyone—Captain Gossett, Oberlander, Tony, those people at Haman, Lord & Fawcett—was applauding when he got his."

"I am sorry. I have to tell you this, David. I never hated Rudy Dukes. I wasn't afraid of him, either, not at his worst."

"Intrigued with him?"

"I guess so. He laid it on the line. It was all there to see. He was like—like—a lightning rod. He caught it all. He was almost beautiful in his nastiness."

"You're unbelievable, Danny," Loomis said. "You miss him."

"I do. He was a challenge. You could put your finger on Dukes, locate him, work on ways to fight him. You can't most of the time in my line of work."

David asked him what he was doing now. Hart sounded vague. He hinted that Hasslinger would be happy if he moved on to some other organization. A few weeks later the Loomises got a post card from Hart. He was in Tucson, Arizona, engaged in educational work with the Pima and Papago Indians. "The air is cleaner here," Hart had written, "but for a thick-headed moralist like me, the failures and the corruptions are every bit as distressing as those of New York."

There was no return address on the card, and David was unable to respond. He wanted to, if only to ask Hart if he thought that the resistance to Dukes had been worth it—the stratagems, the meetings, the hearings, the involvement of so many people, the risks they had run.

But if Loomis had lingering doubts, his wife had none. Carrie had always been more of an optimist than her husband. Hope, joy, involvement—all of these came naturally to her. When the house was destroyed (she had been helped out through a back

414

window by two gentle firemen) she had gone immediately to St. Luke's Hospital, and that night had been delivered of a howling, red-faced seven-pound girl. From the maternity ward, they moved into an enormous furnished suite in the Concourse Plaza Hotel in the Bronx, near Yankee Stadium. After a month of hotel life—it proved to be fun—David located a modest, clean, dull garden apartment in Flushing, Queens.

Busy with the infant, Carrie nonetheless found time to immerse herself in several volunteer groups dedicated to the housing problem. She subscribed to their angry newsletters, went to their meetings, became a quasi-expert on the housing problem.

"It's basic, David," she would say, "the roof over the head. Study ancient history. There had to be shelter before there could be anything else. And they'd better build homes and apartments for people, or there'll never be any progress. It'll just get worse."

"Am I supposed to feel guilty over the sixty-thousand-dollar homes I'm designing?" he asked.

"No, but we have to have the cheaper ones also. You can reduce the student-teacher ratio forever, and give everyone a job, but if a man can't have a clean, decent house, forget it."

Loomis knew she was right, and he was glad she had become a gentle activist. The truth was, she was more courageous than he, more adventurous. Things had come too hard to him for him to take chances, make stands, break with tradition. A reluctant leader, he sometimes marveled that he had ever gone through as much as he had with Hart, and Tony Paz, and the Schlossmanns and the others.

He and Carrie often thought about their allies in the committee, and they talked of seeing them, holding a reunion at their apartment, but they knew they never would. The essence of the city was its transitory, fictional quality. It was hard to maintain old associations, nurture the friendships of accident and convenience. They often saw Liz Allister's icy face in magazine advertisements, but she and her husband had never truly been members of the embattled band. And once, Carrie, at Columbia for a lecture, saw Hilda Schlossmann striding with that distracted purposefulness across the campus. Hilda walked by with a frozen stare and Carrie realized she had no desire to converse.

Some months later the Loomises read of Schlossmann's death. He was in his early seventies, the short obituary in the *Times* said, identifying him as a historian and economist, author of twelve books (all in German) who had recently worked as an editor and translator. The news saddened them. There seemed no bottom to the unhappiness in the man's life, and they understood why the committee had meant so much to him, and why he had been so enthusiastic about painting the corridors.

Loomis reached no sharply defined conclusions about the reign of Rudy Dukes, their resistance to it, the outcome. In general he felt they had done the right thing, and he valued the brief friendships they had made during the fearful weeks on West 84th Street. But he was a cautious, conservative man, and he developed no encompassing concepts.

In early summer he received a badly scrawled letter. It read:

Dear Mister Lomis:
Please forgiv not sending you this sooner, but it take time to get it. We thank you for your help to Youth Group. The children had had a very nice picnic Memoril Day. Because you were kind enough to lend us the money. Father Hasslinger thank you too. He is a good man. We do not see yr. frend Mr. Hart no more here they say he gone to work with Indians. Thank you again.

Mary May Hall

Inside the envelope was a check for the thirty-nine dollars he had lent Mrs. Hall the day they had attended the Housing Crimes Trial. It was signed by the woman and countersigned by Hasslinger. Loomis had forgotten about the loan, and was resigned to never seeing the money—as Tony Paz had mocked —but here it was, gracefully acknowledged, with more sincerity than he encountered in his daily routine.

416

He showed it to Carrie, and she began to cry, for reasons that eluded her. "No tears, honey," he said. "Hasslinger doesn't believe in them." He kept the letter. It had nothing to do with the events on West 84th Street, but it reached his heart and it told him that he and his wife had done the proper thing in battling Dukes and the forces that created and encouraged him.

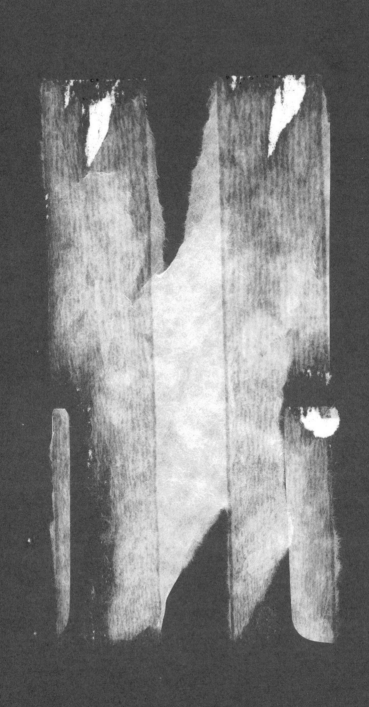